Jessica,
My Daughter

Jessica,
My Daughter

A NOVEL BY
ARI IBN-ZAHAV

Translated by Julian Meltzer

CROWN PUBLISHERS   NEW YORK

c. 2

Bl

Jessica,
My Daughter

A re-telling of the story of "The Merchant of Venice," based on old Venetian records, which explores the tragedy of Shylock, deserted by his daughter Jessica, a member of a persecuted race, and defeated at the very moment of his personal revenge. Translated by Julian Melzer, this novel has been dramatized in New York as "Shylock's Daughter," and will be promoted to special Jewish and drama groups.

Chapter One

"IS IT NOT IN TRUTH A WONDROUS SPECTACLE?" MARVELED DON Samuel Morro to himself as the gondola carried him to the north of Venice, on his way to the ghetto. Splendid palaces rose, almost straight out of the water, on both sides of the broad canal. Their balustrades were heavy with tracery tinted in a rainbow profusion of hues, the gates were ornate with gold or bronze inlay, and before them stood the *pali,* the mooring-poles striped with the livery colors of the nobles who owned these mansions. The window-sills were tumbling with gay masses of flowers, and over the roof-tops flew great banners embroidered with the crest of Venice, Queen of the Adriatic — the winged lion. Across the bridges that spanned island to island swarmed the people of Venice, almost all clad in their holiday finery — handsome men, beautiful women. Here and there rose a voice lilting in song, or the thrumming of a mandolin imitated the gurgling of the waters. The brilliant blue sky, so peaceful, the pleasant turquoise waters, the proud towers, the white marble with delicate veining of yellow, blue, deep red and violet — all these blended with exquisite harmony. "Paradise indeed!"

The fabulous quality of the scene faded, the prospect grew drab as the gondola turned right into the Rio di Noale, and then left into the Rio della Misericordia, and drifted through a narrow canal with gray and dirty water. From afar Don Samuel could see the small and isolated island on which the tall gray houses seemed merged as one huddling mass — the ghetto. It was as though he had passed through a sparkling dream and suddenly been awakened to find the familiar realities pressing round and choking him. For these were the dwellings of the Jews in that Venice famed for its freedom and its suzerainty of the Adriatic.

The gondola halted in the middle of the Rio di San Girolamo. He alighted and, crossing the narrow dilapidated bridge, saw before him the iron gate of the ghetto leading into a cavernous gloomy street thronged with people. "What an abyss!" he thought. A despondent mood came on him and he stood there for a moment with darkly troubled heart.

"Why are you hesitating, Jew? A dog's kennel is good enough for the likes of you!" jeered the constable at the gate, and his companion gave a loud guffaw.

That was the reception given to Don Samuel Morro at the ghetto gate. "How much better," he thought, "that I have come here only as a guest; how good will it be if I get away quickly to Turkey." But when he entered through the gate the mood lifted — he was among his brethren. A young man of tattered dress took his box and bundles and asked, "Where can I lead you, Messer?"

"To the house of the money-changer Shylock."

"Oh, oh," rejoined the porter hastening to add, "the Almighty has blessed him with everything. He is as wealthy as the Doge. His only daughter is the fairest in all Venice and his wife died a year ago."

"And what is the blessing in his wife's death?" smiled Don Samuel.

"Upon my life, all women are accursed, Messer. My first wife gave me twins, and my second wife wants me to provide her with dishes fit for a king. 'Joseph, give, give!' is her endless refrain. Upon my life, she is as demanding as if I had married her out of the house of a money-changer. Upon God's life, even a young virgin would follow Signor Shylock, old as he is — and his wife a miserable, sickly harridan. The Almighty blessed him when He took away that old hag. He's free now — ho, yes, Signor Shylock is a great man. The Christians fear him."

Don Samuel looked eagerly from side to side as he walked with the porter. The houses were all alike — high and shabby-gray; the shops too were identical, small and dingy, and their goods were almost the same, heaps of old clothing. Yet the faces of the passers-by showed courage, and even the eyes of the pale-faced women fingering and choosing the rags on the thresholds of the dim shops — even the eyes of these wretched women shone with a rare pride. Slanting rays, reminders of the sun, lit the squalid street only here and there at the corners of the alleyways, yet how lovely the children were, playing and romping in the deep shadows of the buildings. Most of them were red-cheeked, with merry eyes. When, a few minutes earlier, he had stood at the gate and peered into the narrow thoroughfare crowded with the flitting shadows of men, he had felt as if he were being pushed into a prison, but now the sight of his brothers and sisters of the ghetto lifted his heart above all that had been weighing so heavily and so painfully. "No, no, they shall never defeat us," he thought, and a smile wreathed his lips as he remembered the ancient solace from the days of the first tyrant of all: "As they oppress him so shall he increase and multiply."

The porter went on prattling all the way to the house of Shylock, and Don Samuel learned from the man's chatter many things about Shylock's household. Shylock, he gathered, was the treasurer of the community, and had contact with all the world. He was a man of quick temper, and was not afraid even of the Signioria, the Doge's Council — far less so of the rabbinical elders of the ghetto. Once a *sbirro,* a policeman, had come to Shylock's house to look for Hebrew books, and had angered Lancelot, his servant, who had thrashed him thoroughly. It was said that Shylock paid a fine of three hundred ducats — but what was that to such a rich man? "And the gambling with dice and cards! The rabbis forbade gaming on pain of excommunication, but did that matter to Shylock? They do say, though, that he has now given up gambling." So Signor Shylock was a self-willed man, like all the rich folk.

The porter rattled on, and when they reached Shylock's house, he murmured, "Do you know, Signor, what a wise man once said? I joined a quorum in a house of mourning and a wise man was there. Oh, he knew a lot of things. He said there's justice in Venice — Shylock wanted to give thousands of ducats to the Signioria so that he need not wear the Jewish hat, but the Doge would not listen. It's just as hard for a rich man to redeem himself from death as it is from wearing the Jews' hat. So the wise man said. Upon God's life, Shylock didn't go to the Rialto a whole year so that he shouldn't have to wear the hat of shame

—he's a hard and obstinate man is old Shylock, Signor, may God smite all the wicked!"

Don Samuel had come into a large square formed by the frontages of handsome dwellings. It was the part of the ghetto in which the rich members of the community lived. Shylock's house was at the center of one side, opposite the Ashkenazic temple. As Don Samuel went up the stairs he was met by Lancelot, Shylock's manservant, a Christian about forty-five years of age.

"Are you Signor Morro? My master awaited you yesterday," he said, after greeting the guest. Stefano, the other servant, who was about twenty-five years of age, took the baggage from the porter and carried it inside. "My master is downstairs, in his business shop."

Lancelot motioned to Stefano to take the visitor to the banking-shop. Several people were there. A man of about sixty-five, lean and of furrowed countenance, his long full beard pushed impatiently aside as though a sudden storm had shaken it, stood behind one of the tables. His red-rimmed eyes darted about hotly. He exploded with anger as he spoke to a Christian clad in an embroidered gown.

"I gave you hard cold cash," shouted Shylock, "and you're offering me some oil-spotted canvas as payment. I want my money!"

"In the Virgin's name, these are the two best paintings by Francesco Bissolo. Now that he's dead each one of them is worth five hundred ducats, and I am offering the two of them to you for two hundred."

"I don't want your bargains. First you're glad that we take paintings and furniture for the money you owe us, and then you howl that the Jews swindle and rob you. Sell your precious paintings to a Christian, and give me back the two hundred ducats I lent you."

"For shame! I've never said anything but good about the Jews."

"There's no such Christian under the skies of Venice! Anyhow, I've more than enough paintings of your saints here. They

4

are packed up inside that cupboard and are of no use to me. If you wish, you can sell mine and earn a commission."

Lorenzo, the Christian inspector appointed by the authorities to supervise the Jew's banking business, interposed at this juncture.

"Bissolo's paintings adorn the Doge's palace. Let me see them, Signor Shylock, and I will tell you if it is worth your while to take them for the two hundred ducats."

"I don't want paintings. They are not worth money," rumbled Shylock. His outburst of wrath seemed to have subsided. Lorenzo, the young Venetian noble, had power to cause him harm, and Shylock yielded whenever he intervened in a transaction. "All right then, Signor, sell your paintings here. You can complete the matter with Signor Lorenzo."

Before another client could approach Shylock, Don Samuel accosted him, put out his hand and said, "My name is Don Samuel Morro."

"May the Almighty bless you, Don Samuel! You have grown into a fine man," Shylock declared. The first time he had met the youth had been at Ancona — a child of three years then, dandled on his father's knee. "I was becoming worried about you. But, there, of course I was not really worried — I have so many other troubles. You saw for yourself no doubt."

Lorenzo sent a hostile glance at the handsome young Jew to whom Shylock had given so affectionate a welcome, and looked away and down to the ledger open before him.

Don Samuel's first words were, "How glad I am to be able to meet you face to face and to thank you for the kindness shown to me a year ago when I fled from Pesaro."

"One forgets old troubles with the new," Shylock interjected.

"I know that you paid a goodly sum to ransom me from the captain who took me out of Pesaro, Signor. I know too that —."

Shylock shot a swift look at Lorenzo, and signed to the other to say no more. "You are probably tired after your long journey. Let us go up to my house and take a glass of wine."

As they left the place Shylock warned, "That elegant young gentleman you saw inside is just as wicked as the rest of them.

5

The Signioria put him there to supervise my business — it's the law on all money-lending concerns — and you have to be careful what you say in front of him."

"But you spoke bitterly in his presence to the Christian who owed you two hundred ducats."

"That wasn't good, my son, it wasn't good, I know. But what can I do? They never want to pay their debts to the Jews, and matters have become seven times worse in the past four years, since that evil tyrant of the house of Carafa, that Paul IV, mounted the Papal throne in Rome. He ordered all borrowers who owe money to the Jews to pay in their debts to the Camera Apostolica. Thank Heaven that Venice is not under Rome, but even here a Christian believes he need not repay his debt to a Jew, and they use all manner of devices to wriggle out of paying back the good hard cash they borrow."

They entered Shylock's house and the old man ordered Lancelot to bring two glasses. He then took a bottle of wine out of a closet, and filled the glasses. Lancelot brought them fruit and cakes.

"Do you wonder then that I get angry?" Shylock went on, when the man had left the room. "The weaklings and tender-hearted cannot become money-changers. Timid bankers soon lose their money. I am not afraid of Lorenzo. He came in as an inspector, but he has become my agent. He is a noble of the Calergi family and has many friends among the upper classes. He brings me good customers and gets a percentage. It makes quite a good income for him. And, indeed, what Christian would fill the pockets of that good-for-nothing as I do? His father, may his bones decay, lost fifteen thousand gold ducats at dice, and they sold all his furniture to pay up. The son needed the money — he is just as extravagant as his father — and when a Christian needs money, a Jew is good enough for him to come to. And he's a shrewd fellow, shrewd enough."

"You are smart enough to have bound his hands with golden fetters."

"Nonetheless you must take care, Don Samuel, not to speak ill of the Christians to his face. That young Esau is as wily as a serpent, and he bribes the guards at the ghetto gates to come in and talk business with me of an evening."

"Now that I'm here, Signor Shylock," Don Samuel went on, "I want to thank you again with all my heart for having saved me from the hands of those wicked people at Pesaro. Had it not been for a Jew of Venice that captain would have sold all sixty of us refugees as galley-slaves."

"I am glad you were among those saved and brought to Istria. Your father, may he rest in peace, was a respected money-changer, and it is really a great pity that Donna Grazia Mendessa could not have rescued him."

"She did all she could. At her request the Sultan wrote to that Haman and urged him to release Jacob Morro, agent of Donna Grazia, but it was too late. My dear father was then in prison at Ancona but in another cell. Thirty of us escaped through the window after bribing Haman's guards, but as my father was an old man, he fell off the ladder and was killed on the spot."

"I know all that, Don Samuel," Shylock murmured sympathetically.

"And last year, when Guido Ubaldo, the Duke of Urbino, expelled us from the city of Pesaro, I landed again in the same trouble as at Ancona. It was during Passover, when I was on the ship and in sore distress that I read the passage from Jeremiah, 'For they have digged a pit to take me.' But now, a few days before Passover, when I am safe in your house, I can truly say with the Psalmist, 'They have digged a pit before me, into the midst whereof they have fallen themselves.'"

"Very well said, Don Samuel. They have not fallen into it yet but, rest assured, the Psalm will be fulfilled — they will do so. I can see their fall coming, and it strengthens me. Sixty years ago Venice was the mistress of the seas, the only place through which the trade flowed from East to West and West to East. But since the voyages have begun around the Cape of Good Hope the bridge of Venice for the commerce of East and West has been breached; and the great Turkish Empire is beginning to threaten Venice and the whole of Italy.

"Yes, indeed. Venice was once sole sovereign of all the traffic

7

in wheat, timber, ivory and gold from North Africa; of the oils and spices and embroidered silks and the gold from the East — but now she is no longer the only one, thank Heaven! The bones of the saints can work as many wonders as they will, but here in Venice they have no longer any monopoly over the goods which pass between merchants, the good honest merchandise. They still sell salt, timber, precious fabrics, glassware, and weapons to many countries. Yes, they sell arms and weapons to Suleiman the Great too, and he will destroy Venice with those weapons. My only regret is that I am too old to see that happen! Even the wicked Popes protest against the slave-trade; yet the vaults of Venice are overflowing with the gold earned in the buying and selling of miserable creatures.

"The wealth of Venice is turning its head—whoring and feasting and merrymaking. It is with these Venice satisfies its lust — and it is already showing the symptoms of one who has filled his belly to bursting. We the Jews are an ancient people, and we have suffered greatly. But we know that the Omniscient does not let the tree decay. The best of them are wicked, and that was a fine Psalm you quoted, my son: 'They have digged a pit . . . into the midst whereof they have fallen themselves.' That old Haman in Rome is now working his wickedness even among his own friends. He has thrown his own favorites, his Cardinals and Princes of the Church, into the dungeons. That is the beginning of the end — thus was the beginning of every end."

"Bravo, Signor Shylock!" Don Samuel applauded him at the end of this discourse. "Those are comforting words to me, a refugee who has suffered the hardships of Ancona and Pesaro."

"Time is the healer of all hurts, my son. You will forget. You come of the house of a great money-changer. They tell me that you were your father's right-hand man."

"I was chief clerk in my late father's business-house, and I worked the whole of last year for a money-changer at Capo d'Istria."

"And I heard from my friend Tubal that you are well-versed in the Scriptures and other learning."

"I do not know how wide or profound my learning is, but my

father hired good teachers and spared no expense to teach me the Law and knowledge and also music and dancing. My teacher in the Law when I was young was Rabbi Benjamin Nehemiah, may he live to a ripe old age. Then he was called from Ancona to a position of honor at Civitanova. After that I was taught the Law and Latin and astronomy by Rabbi Shlomo Yehya, may he rest in peace."

"You can continue to study astronomy here — *they* cannot block the heavens to our eyes!"

"Rabbi Shlomo Yehya," Don Samuel proceeded, "was one of the most noble of the martyrs at Ancona. As he approached the place where he was to perish, he —"

"Forget Ancona, my son. I need a wise and honest young man upon whom I can rely. You shall work at my side in the banking house and weigh out the money. And if it suits you, you shall teach Hebrew to my daughter Jessica. She is of an understanding mind, and is quick at her studies."

As he spoke he glanced at his daughter's portrait on the wall at the back of Don Samuel.

"How shall I ever thank you, Signor?" the young man murmured.

Shylock regarded him gravely for a moment and answered, "By being a good teacher to my daughter. She knows some Hebrew, but I would like her to read our books as a man, as one of ourselves. She is proficient in Italian and I very much want her to know the language of our fathers too."

He told Don Samuel that Jessica had learned to write letters from Samuel Archevolti's *Ein Gannim,* and went over to a desk to bring the young man the volume printed in Venice six years earlier. He turned the pages to show his guest a passage which struck him as of peculiar significance: "Woe to those sons who have been banished from the table of their fathers to a place of bitter waters."

"Bitter waters are those in Venice indeed!" he cried.

Shylock composed himself, and returned to the subject of his daughter's education. "Do not, I beg you, compel her to 'eat of the unripe grapes in the vineyard' of Manoello."

9

The other was taken aback at the remark and, although he had no wish to offend his host, he returned, "But he is a great poet. He is one of the intimates of Dante."

"I have heard that they call Dante great, but I cannot see why. I have tried to read his writings — but, well! *The Song of Songs* is poetry, Ibn Gabirol's *Royal Diadem* is poetry, but not the *Commedia*. Gabirol quotes that passage from Job, 'Though He slay me, yet will I trust in Him.' And what does Manoello do with this passage? He weaves it into lecherous verses — that is really a little too much! Manoello is nothing but a Jewish Aretino."

Shylock meant Pietro Aretino. But what he knew of poetry was based upon hearsay; so to avoid an argument upon a matter alien to his knowledge, he pointed to the portrait hanging on the wall behind Don Samuel and said, "That's Jessica, my only daughter."

"He is perhaps not a Jewish Aretino, but it was well said," Don Samuel replied to his host's previous remark before turning round to look at the painting. It showed a vivacious brunette, a mixture of the Jewish and Italian races, smiling gently. Had he not been shy, he would have admitted that he had never before seen a creature so lovely.

"What a face!" he thought. Aloud he said, "Who painted it?"

"Some Venetian fellow called Paolo Caliari Veronese, a young man of about thirty." While Don Samuel examined the work, Shylock went on, "He shows a lot of promise and will rise to fame and riches. I still remember Robusti, or Tintoretto as he is called, from the time he helped his father to paint our house for the Passover when I was a child. But now that he has become celebrated, he turns his nose up at a Jew. And the old one of that school? All know him: Titian, who mixed his oils at Aretino's side, so that the brush might glide smoothly over the canvas. Titian had Aretino to eat at his table, and in return Aretino fed Titian — with flattery and praise. These artists and sculptors do a better business than banking and shipping. They create their images of their Savior, because they're greedy for profit, the artful rascals!"

Deep in contemplation of Jessica's sweet countenance, Don Samuel paid no great heed as Shylock rambled on.

"The artist is a young man, you say? He has golden hands," he said at last, keeping his eyes on the portrait.

"What's the advantage to an artist in having golden hands? They put all their energy into painting Christ and Mary and the Apostles and miracles — what benefit is there in all that? They turn the heads of the gullible and get their money. His hands blessed? Why, any painter would have little difficulty in doing my Jessica in oils. She is a painting in herself."

"Still, it is a remarkable portrait!" Don Samuel insisted. And then, realizing he had raised his voice rapturously out of enchantment with Jessica's great beauty, he turned from his fixed regard of the painting and changed the subject. "Have you baked your unleavened bread for the Passover yet, Signor Shylock?"

"Naturally. The festival is only a few days off."

"It will be my festival of freedom after three years of bondage and wandering."

"Your real festival of freedom will come when I succeed, with the Almighty's help, in getting you aboard a ship going east to Constantinople."

"The festival of freedom for all of us will dawn when we can all set sail for the land of Israel."

"Well said, my son," exclaimed Shylock. He mused for a moment, stroking his beard, before resuming. "They keep careful watch over young people, and I must warn you not to fall into the hands of the coast guards. It will take a month, two months, perhaps a year. I shall not put you in any danger. For you are a Marrano, the son of Marranos."

"I was only two years of age when my father had me baptized."

"Nevertheless, my son, although it is possible to become a convert back to Judaism in Venice, one will be persecuted by the clergy. Of course recantation is permissible, and the arm of the law is strong here in Venice, but those emissaries of the tyrant at Rome work underground to accomplish their mission here in the Republic. So take care, my son, lest my servant or Lorenzo learn that you are a Marrano who has returned to our faith."

At this point Shylock began to rage against the gentiles. The young man was alarmed. "The servant-folk will hear," he objected.

"Never fear. Lancelot has been in my household for twenty-eight years. He knows that I have concealed a Talmud in the house. He is as faithful as a house-dog. The other one, Stefano, is witless, and follows Lancelot about like a cat."

Mention of the Talmud reminded Shylock of the burning of the other Hebrew books five years previously. He broke out into violent cursing of Pope Julius III, who had then decreed the destruction of the holy writings.

"The Jews dubbed him the Prince of Mercy and, no doubt, in comparison with Paul IV, he was an angel. But even so, he then and always yielded to Paul, the hateful man who was at that time the head of the Inquisition. And then Venice, which has always boasted of its independence of the Papacy, adopted the same edict. Thus are the Venetians lovers of liberty and the rights of man, except when it affects the Jews."

Their conversation over, they went out to attend the afternoon service in the synagogue across the square. Before they left, Shylock asked Lancelot if Jessica had returned from the city and without waiting for a reply, rapped out furiously, "When she goes into the city, she forgets to return; and when I go I must hasten to settle my business at the Rialto and hurry back to the ghetto — I cannot endure seeing their faces."

As they walked across the square, Shylock told the young man he had found a room for him in the house of his friend Tubal, who would be glad to accommodate him. It was best, to ward off idle gossip, that he should not live under the same roof as Shylock and Jessica.

"The mockery of the multitude is like a sharp sword. Sometimes I play at cards with Christian clients. The evil is always against me in that evil game, and why should I lose my money? I do it for the sake of business; and the chatterboxes said of me that I had been lured on by the evil gods of chance and spent my days in the Rialto playing at dice and cards. The rabbi forbade it upon pain of excommunication, so what did I do? I paid a wise rabbi a handsome sum of money and he printed me a fine strong motto with a lead pen, making the rabbis powerless to carry out their threat. What do these rabbis know of the needs of a Jewish merchant, whether he lends money or deals in precious stones, when he has business with the gentiles at the Rialto? And so I won."

Shylock went down to his banking house for a few moments, and Don Samuel waited outside. He thought of the cordial welcome the old money-changer had given him, and his spirits rose. He recalled all he had heard that afternoon, and the painted image of Jessica fired his imagination. Shylock had said she was a painting in real flesh and blood. He could hardly believe it possible. The father was of wrathful visage, his features coarse, and his eyes colorless. How could such a fragile lovely being have sprung from his loins? His face was turned to the door at the head of the stairs down which they had come.

Chapter Two

IT WAS ON THE FIRST PASSOVER EVE THAT DON SAMUEL FINALLY SAW Jessica. She was a tall girl, slender and dark, and her face showed her to be of great resoluteness. Her dark-brown hair, parted in the middle, was coiled at the nape of her neck, and her eyes were large and deep-set. But above all else, Don Samuel's emotions were aroused at her voice, which lilted with golden cadence.

"No doubt you sing," he remarked.

"How did you know that?" she parried with a smile.

"She knows how to sing," Shylock interposed. "Lancelot sang to her while she was still a child and later she was taught. Lancelot had — and still has, for the matter of that — the voice of a broken bassoon, but she has the tone of a violin."

"How you exaggerate, father!" Jessica laughed.

"No, to be sure, I have never lavished praise, not even on my own daughter."

"A seemly confession, father."

"The Jew of our day is a man of wrath, and no angry heart is likely to be wonderstruck, or to dole out excessive praise."

"Yet if you were to sing the praises of our guest, that might mean a good deal."

"True, true! Don Samuel has only been a day in the banking house, and yet he has a grasp of the business as though he had been with me a month or more."

"How glad I am to hear you say so," asserted Don Samuel, looking at Shylock. A strong impulse seemed to be forcing him to turn his head toward Jessica, but he fought the impulse with all his will. "I am glad to know that you can sing, Signora. I shall teach you Hebrew songs."

"But Hebrew songs are very sad," pouted Jessica.

"And why, pray, should we Jews have songs of rejoicing?" her father exploded. "Because of the burning of the Talmud? Because of the Marranos burned at the stake? Because of that wretched thing?" He pointed at the red, conical Jews' hat perched on the window-ledge. "This big house, which I built with my own money, is not mine but belongs to the gentile who owns the land. That old tyrant at Rome sets his cardinals at the Jews like dogs. Even Venice pulls out of her closets ancient laws which have grown musty and hoary with age, and not a day passes but some new law is revived. Why should we sing merry songs? Even the sea chanteys, the rowing songs, turn into dirges in our throats, may the Almighty pity us."

"Tonight is the festival of freedom, and we must demonstrate our joy," Don Samuel reminded him. Yet deep within his heart lay a gnawing melancholy. He remembered his father's house, which had been razed to the ground: the spread table, the many candles, the tasty viands, and particularly the *scacchi,* the pieces of unleavened bread cooked with the meat-soup which his mother knew so well how to make. "You are an orphan of father and mother, seated at the table of strangers," said a voice within him, stirring his sorrow; and only the presence of the lovely maiden helped him overcome his despondency.

"In another three days they will be observing their Easter," declared Shylock. "It's an evil time, and no Jew dare leave the gates of the ghetto. It is the law that windows overlooking their streets be curtained, so that we shall not see their procession with the banners. But what have we to do with their saints? Their priests incite against the Jews, saying that we killed their Christ and Messiah, as though it were in the power of man to kill a Messiah. . . ."

"Oh, please stop, father," Jessica broke in with upraised hand. "It is because of that hatred that all the evil has come."

"Even they do not claim it thus. On the contrary, it is because of the evil that our hatred has grown," rumbled Shylock. "They are all a flock of evil people."

"And does not the blood-libel prove it, Signorina?" said Don Samuel. "Is there a more debased libel? The cardinals and the Pope in all his glory believed in its truth."

"The nobles are caught fast in the hands of the mob!"

"No, that is not so. The mob is caught in their grasp, in the grasp of the nobility," Shylock interrupted his daughter. "The clergy tell the people of the crucifixion of Christ. They hear it in their youth, and they see the crucifixion vividly in their imagination — is it a wonder that the Christian lad grows up to hate and despise the Jew? In the first year of my marriage, I saw with my own eyes a Jew of Hungary being stoned to death near the Rialto. Why? He saw a lost Christian child crying and took him up in his arms to hand him over to the police. Someone cried 'There's a Jew going to murder a Christian child,' and the mob began pelting him with stones."

"And the blood-libel in Rome four years ago," Don Samuel supplemented. "If it were not for the sagacity of the physician, and the miraculous disclosure that the crucified youth was killed by a Christian, then the very worst would have befallen the Jews of Rome."

Jessica remained silent. To Don Samuel there was something disturbing in her silence, but he gathered that she feared her father's diatribes might be reported to the authorities, and he refrained from adding fuel to the blaze of rancor in the old banker's heart. To allay her uneasiness, he said, "It was not the Christians, but the convert Hananael of Foligno, who launched the foul slander against his former brethren of Rome."

But Don Samuel's words kindled Shylock's rage all the more; he heaped abuse and curses upon all proselytes. He was especially bitter about two converts, Vittorio Eliano and Giovanni Battista, who, he said, had shamed the pious memory of their grandfather, the sage Elias Levita. It was they who told Pope Julius III that the Talmud was corrupt and it was their treachery which caused it to be proscribed on the Index and burned.

"Elias Levita complained that he was suspected of changing his faith because of his friendship with Cardinal Viterbo and Bishop Grimani of Venice. We followed his bier to the cemetery ten years ago, and yet he was punished after his death for having lived ten years in the palace of a cardinal, and for having taught him the lore of our religion." Shylock laughed cynically. "Yes, contact with the Christians is a calamity. The fathers have dealings with them, and the children are spoiled and contaminated."

Jessica rose before her father had finished speaking, and went out into the kitchen. She left the room to prevent her father and the young man from noticing her embarrassment. From her childhood she had become accustomed to seeing Christians in the house; and, like the grandchildren of the sage Elias Levita, upon whom her father had vented his scorn, she felt no deep gulf between the Christian and the Jew. Christianity ruled supreme, and the Christian world abounded in art, beauty, freedom — was it so sinful for a person to wish to live other than as an outcast dog? Generation after generation awaited the Messiah who never came; yet it might be that the Messiah had really arrived in the guise of the Christian faith.

And what of love? If a Christian and a Jewish maid loved each other and cherished the dream of giving happiness to each other, could they find it in the ghetto? Could she say to her Christian suitor, "Embrace Judaism and become one of the despised, the gibed, the mocked! Wear the red hat and forsake the beautiful, gay world"?

After grace, Jessica sang the traditional chants from the Passover *Haggada — The Omnipotent Will Build His Mansion, Who Knows One,* and *One Lamb,* beloved of the children — but she sang almost mechanically, without thinking of the words. She remained blind, too, to the presence of the handsome gentle youth who sat opposite; her thoughts were focused upon another, who dwelt outside the ghetto walls, and who had come up to her two days earlier when her father was in synagogue and whispered with all the charm of a Venetian noble, "I want you to be happy, Jessica. What a shame that such a lily should droop in the filth of the ghetto." And yesterday, too, when her father was in the synagogue, that other had come up again from the banking house to see her, but she had warned Lancelot to say she was not at home.

Yet why had she grieved all night at refusing to receive him? As she sang the *Haggada* melodies, she closed her eyes and saw the vision of the adored, glittering, fascinating Venice, Queen of the Adriatic and the world; its purling waters murmured their benign caresses, laving her spirit; the sunshine bathed her; and the great ornate palaces, which had always seemed thousands of miles away though she passed close to them, were open to her.

"You have a wonderful voice," said Don Samuel, breaking into her ruminations as she ended *One Lamb.* She smiled faintly, but made no reply. A few moments later Jessica, with the excuse that she was tired, said "Peace unto you" to the two men and went to her bed-chamber.

Shylock and Don Samuel went on reciting the *Song of Songs.* The older one directed the words to the House of Israel and the Holy Spirit, but Don Samuel for the first time in his life comprehended the fervent love lyrics in their full clarity, devoid of all mystic content:

O my dove, that art in the clefts of the rock, in the secret places of the stairs, let me see thy countenance, let me hear thy voice; for sweet is thy voice, and thy countenance comely . . . thy temples are like a piece of pomegranate within thy locks. . . . Behold thou art fair, my love; behold, thou art fair;

17

thou hast doves' eyes within thy locks. . . . Thy teeth are like
a flock of sheep. . . .

How beautiful are thy feet with shoes, O prince's daughter. . . .

Was it not a paean of exalted love? Did not the same feelings
rise from the depths of his heart, and cloak themselves in these
inspired passages? The letters of the printed book danced before his eyes; they seemed to move across the parchment and
shape themselves into words, into couplets, into paragraphs breathing love. . . . Never had he recited the *Song of Solomon* in such
an ecstasy of emotion; it appalled him to feel that the longing for
a maiden might be greater than the yearning of Israel for the
Divine spirit.

The moon rode with Don Samuel as, saddened and out of sorts,
seized by a vague unrest, he went home alone through the ghetto
alley-ways to his lodging at Tubal's house. He walked with slow
and measured pace, thinking deeply and sorrowfully. It seemed
to him that he only now fully appreciated the great tragedy over-
shadowing his life since the fall of his father's house. If his
father, the respected money-changer, were still alive, Shylock
would have deemed it an honor to ally himself in marriage
with the house of Jacob Morro of Ancona, agent of Donna Grazia.
But now Don Samuel was a poor youth dependent upon the
charity of his patron Shylock, whom he could never ask for his
daughter's hand.

As he lay upon his couch, the night passed without sleep. Vision
after vision crowded his mind: Jessica loved him and eloped with
him to Istria; he was in Constantinople, Donna Grazia remembered her esteem for his father and appointed him her agent;
Shylock wrote to him, "I am sending you my daughter for wife."
And when his vain reflections fatigued him, he resigned himself to
his fate, and was glad to remain Jessica's teacher. He would be
with her daily, feast his eyes upon her, refresh his ears with her
golden voice — that at least was magic consolation for one who
but yesterday had been a refugee convert in Istria.

When he opened his eyes early the next morning, his first
thought was of Jessica. He saw her in the sunbeams capering on

the wall, and for her sake he donned his Sabbath garments, imagining it was in her honor that the festival spirit flowed through the ghetto streets; he heard the song of last night's *Haggada* in the chanting of the reverent Passover morning prayers by the cantor and his chorister. In another hour, a few more moments, the service would end, and he would once again be near her, watch her beloved face; her lips and eyes would smile at him, and her delightful hands would place the food before him. An unwonted gladness filled his young heart, and when Shylock at the end of the prayers beckoned him over, Don Samuel felt that he was being summoned to savor the greatest experience of his life.

Jessica gave the young man a courteous welcome, and during the meal conversed freely with him, plying him with questions about life at Capo d'Istria. He answered her composedly and with eloquence. Later Shylock went to his couch, and Don Samuel remained longer in Jessica's company.

He felt more heartened as he left Shylock's house this time and, arriving at his lodging in Tubal's house, went straight to his room and threw himself upon the pallet. He was not tired, but he wished to be alone. He recalled every word that Jessica had spoken, her gestures, the lilt of each word; he thought of a sentence and lost himself in a maze of cogitation over hidden meanings. When he dismissed them, another sentence would come to mind and he would try to divine her real intention. Each movement, her trilling laughter, had a motive for his meditation. But when the grim reality of his position as a poor refugee forced itself back to thought, the hidden meanings and imagined motives vanished like gossamer day-dreams, and he was again downcast. He felt himself in a prison; the walls of the ghetto drew in and suffocated him; the afternoon noises in the narrow ghetto streets became an unbearable din; and in his longing for Jessica, he smoldered with suppressed wrath against the Christians, whose wickedness had caused the downfall of his father's house and condemned him to exile.

Then Don Samuel remembered that upon the first evening of his encounter with Shylock, he had said that he would see to it that he reached Constantinople, but it might take a month, two months, or a year. "I am in no hurry, Signor," Don Samuel whispered to himself. "I am in no hurry. Let it take a year, two years, any number of years." Constantinople, of which he had dreamed since the day of his flight from Pesaro — which only yesterday he had felt to be an earthly paradise — he now saw as a land of exile.

Chapter Three

ON THE FOLLOWING MONDAY, IN THE WEEK AFTER PASSOVER, DON Samuel gave Jessica her first lesson. Shylock had not exaggerated: his daughter had a fairly extensive knowledge of Hebrew. Don Samuel had brought a portfolio of letters — all correspondence between Jews in Italy in the fifteenth and sixteenth centuries was in Hebrew and, with the names erased, served in portfolio form as hand-books for the study of Hebrew. They had been written from Siena a few years earlier, during the time of the revolt against the Spaniards.

"You shall read this letter," said Don Samuel, "and I will translate the more difficult words, point out any mistakes, and analyze the grammar."

Jessica read the first letter easily. Explaining the historical import of the times described, Don Samuel told her that even the Jews had taken part in that holy war with enthusiasm. The children of Israel loathed no people more than the Spaniards, who had ravaged the vineyard of Israel with such malevolent fury. Nor was there a more loyal people than the Jews, if treated with a mite of affection and compassion. He read the words of Rabbi Samuel Usque on Turkey: "As though she were an old mother, the beloved mother Jerusalem."

"There is no more forgiving people in any part of the world than ourselves," he proceeded. "Just imagine for a moment that the eyes of the blind are opened and the Signioria, repenting of its oppression of the Jews, tears down the walls of the ghetto, or removes the edict imposing the hat of shame — even your father, who is so bitter of heart, would forget the evil and embrace every Christian he met in the streets."

Jessica laughed. "You are right, Signor: my father would forget all. But he would never embrace anyone. I do not remember his ever having caressed me or even my mother."

Joining her laughter, Don Samuel said, "There are those who embrace with their eyes, Signorina."

"Your remark, Signor, is worthy of a sonnet."

To cover his confusion, and to strengthen his assertion about Jewish loyalty to their benefactors, Don Samuel read another of the letters in the portfolio:

"I was filled with pride to hear that you have all taken up the sword of battle this day to fight the holy war, to hurl the spear and take the lance against the Spaniards who mock the Almighty. . . . May the Lord bless you. . . . And now, my son, return unto the Lord and his behests, and the walls of the enemy will collapse in the same way and manner that Joshua shattered the walls of Jericho. There is great virtue in a war for the Almighty."

Upon concluding the reading, Don Samuel added, "These are private letters written in Hebrew, and were not intended for public knowledge."

"I was not at the battle of Jericho, and I cannot say whether indeed Joshua felled the walls in the holy war." Jessica smiled. "But it is our calamity that we don't see what is happening around us. Can the study of the Torah in fact break down walls and defeat the enemy?"

"One must not doubt the truth of the narrative given in Joshua," he replied. "Nor is there any doubt that the Torah is the only weapon which can help us. And with its help, we can exist in spite of the evil decrees in every generation."

Jessica gazed at him and asked, half-mockingly, half in earnest, "Do you really believe that the Torah is a weapon?"

Don Samuel was somewhat taken aback. All that Jessica had said was pleasing to him, and he had no desire to criticize. But he felt that his concealed affection for Jessica must give way to the profound faith which had not deserted him even in the dungeons of Ancona.

"Yes," he answered sincerely. "The Torah is a bastion against which no weapon can succeed. And so it is with our people — Israel and the Torah are one."

Jessica refrained from argument, but from the expression on her face he knew that he had failed to convince her. He quoted her episodes from history to show that attempts to destroy the Torah had been in vain, but she remained unresponsive. Finally he said, "The Christians, who have canonized our holy fathers, and to whom our Scriptures are holy, believe in our law and Torah unknowingly, and preserve us as a people unknowingly and without conscious desire. Their hand is stretched out to destroy us, but their hearts perpetuate us."

"That is excellently said," she rejoined.

Don Samuel felt easier, and he continued to instruct her in some of the rules of grammar which she had forgotten or never learned.

When he left the house, he meditated upon the sundry matters which Jessica had raised, and a feeling of foreboding weighed on him. It was not the essence of belief which concerned him; Jessica, he felt, was undoubtedly a believer, and even the sages and rabbis had entertained far greater doubts than those she had expressed. Yet it seemed to him that when she asked whether he truly believed the Torah was a weapon, she was mocking him, and must have regarded him as a simpleton. It irked him deeply.

Entering the counting-house, Lorenzo asked him, "Did the lesson you gave his daughter have to take so long?"

"Why, of course," he answered in surprise. "She is an intelligent girl, and anyone who knows as much as she does wants to know more."

Lorenzo lowered his eyes, and pretended to immerse himself in the ledger. But he was brooding, the figures seemed blurred, and a tempest seethed inside him. He had long been weaving a net beneath Jessica's feet, gradually and with great care, so that even she was unaware of it. But now this young Jew had appeared, and he was compelled to hasten. Yet one false step might lead to his losing both his post and Jessica. If he but tried to speak ill of Don Samuel to Shylock, the wily old man would immediately understand that he had designs upon Jessica; and before thinking of the consequences, he might even raise one of the great weights from the scales and kill him on the spot — for he was a proud and wrathful Jew. Even if he escaped Shylock, the old Jew would guard Jessica and keep her under lock and key.

Jessica herself treated him with kindness, but she displayed no sign of love for him. Because of this Don Samuel, he had gone up to her two days before the festival and told her that he wanted her happiness. As she had not spurned him at once, it was a sign that she was not indifferent to his feelings, but she had refused to receive him again on the morrow. Lancelot had told him secretly that Jessica was in the house but had asked him to tell all comers that she had gone to the city. He had seen her once in the past week, but all that she had replied to his protestations was, "My father will come soon. Go to your work."

What did it mean? He had asked himself the same question time and again since then, weighed up the issue continually, and it was not clear whether she was avoiding him, or had a regard for him but was apprehensive of her father. Yet if she wished to be rid of him, she would no doubt tell her father; and if she was drawn to him, she would say, "Let us meet in the city, in the Square of San Marco, and have converse," or something similar. What did it mean? The more he thought, the greater was he gripped by love of Jessica. O misery! What evil chance had brought this accursed young Jew here? To his undoing, the Jew was handsome, of pleasant address, and of her own faith. At that moment, his whole world revolving around Jessica, he became jealous of Don Samuel, jealous almost that he was a Jew. No woman in Venice meant as much to Lorenzo as Jessica; with a wife like her, life would be worth living — even in the ghetto, nay, even in a hovel on the sands of the seashore. He knew it was best not to go up to her apartment and grovel before her; a woman respected a proud man and despised one who crawled. And if every woman were the same as far as that went, how much more so a Jewess who would have to give up her father's home to accompany him. It was the law of nature in the relations of man and maid, he thought. But he waited impatiently for the moment that Shylock would return from the Rialto and go to synagogue.

The minutes crept by like hours, until he could no longer control himself and went outside. To Hades with it! Why were the streets of the ghetto so crooked? If he went upstairs to Jessica now, her father might dart out of some corner, and he was a man of quick temper. Lorenzo whistled once, twice, three times. The dormer window on the upper floor opened, and Stefano stuck out his tousled head. Lorenzo winked at him and said, "Send me Lancelot."

The elder servant came down at once. The young noble slipped a coin into his ready hand and whispered, "Dear Lancelot, I must go upstairs to her for a moment."

"She is out."

"I can see in your face that you are lying."

"She is not at home."

"That is unfair, Lancelot. You are a Christian, and if I bring her into the true faith you will gain spiritual credit."

"One must think of this world when in this world."

Lorenzo placed a gold ducat in the man's grasp. "Stand at the corner and run to call me down when the Jew comes."

"That's dangerous, Signor," Lancelot protested as he put the ducat in his vest-pocket.

"I must speak to her for a moment."

Lancelot finally nodded, and Lorenzo leapt up the stairs. As he entered, he slipped a coin into Stefano's hand, and Stefano said, "Thank you, Signor," and showed him into the dining-room.

Jessica came in almost immediately.

"Why have you done this, Lorenzo?" Her voice trembled. She glanced fearfully at the door. "How did you know that there's no one with me in the house?"

Lorenzo smiled. When he had composed himself, he said, "Lancelot watches downstairs. I could not help coming to see

24

you, Jessica." He began at once pouring out his heart to her, accompanying his words with verses of love. Jessica stood as motionless as a palm-tree before him, yet her eyes lit up with a strange fire. But when Lorenzo tried to approach and take her in his arms, she drew back and faltered, "You are a noble of the house of Calergi, Lorenzo. It is not right to assault a woman."

"Forgive me, Jessica," murmured Lorenzo. "But you must know that my very soul is in your keeping. I become desperate when I think that a young man spends hour after hour in your company."

Jessica wrinkled her placid brow in an effort to divine his meaning. "Samuel Morro has given me the impression . . ." he added. "It's impossible that he should. . . ."

She smiled. "But that's impossible!" she repeated. She looked at him closely. "He's my teacher. He is an honest man."

Lorenzo tried to turn her against Don Samuel, but she interrupted him, "My father is a discerning man, and if he is full of Don Samuel's praise, there must be something in what he says."

"Jessica, you know that your father has a tendency to exaggerate, whether for bad or for good."

"You too are given to exaggeration," she retorted, and added quickly, "But what of it? I have no feeling for him. And you — what have you in common with a Jewess?" A teasing note came into her voice as she surveyed the Christian nobleman kneeling before her.

"Love has brought me to you, Jessica. Life in the ghetto is an inferno. I cannot see you sinking in this mire."

"Does it really seem to you that I am sinking in mire?"

"But, Jessica, the world is so beautiful. It is so free outside. A rose like you needs the sun and space, eyes that will revel in our beauty, lips that will speak of your classic features, hands that will paint you. Once you are one of us, the artists will compete with each other to put you on canvas as often as they painted Queen Caterina Cornaro of Cyprus."

"Which Caterina do you mean — the one by Bellini or the Titian?" she bantered. Bellini had painted the famous beauty, the daughter of the Republic, when she had aged and little of her loveliness remained. But Lorenzo paid no heed to Jessica's raillery. In poetic terms, copied from Aretino, he depicted the fair city of Venice: the carnivals, the Doge's colorful processions, the music and song and laughter; and his words echoed in her heart. It was as if he gave expression to her innermost desires.

Her mother had given birth to Jessica in a gondola; Lancelot had strummed the guitar and sung to her in childhood the tunes of Venice, and her heart had soared gaily — as gaily as the Venetians in their happy-go-lucky unrestraint, their freedom from care — to the lands beyond the seas, the splendor of palaces. And here before her, seeking her favor, was a young man who had the power to give in full measure all that for which she had ever craved. What reason was there to withhold her assent? As she drank in Lorenzo's vivid phrases, she thought of how when her mother was alive she would have scorned the idea of running away to follow a Christian; she had loved her mother deeply, and was as her shadow. But a barrier had always separated her from her father. Would he grieve if she left him? He was always embittered, a man of quixotic rage. He spoke of the Christians as murderers and robbers; but Lorenzo was no murderer, and there were many like to him, many — and in their hands lay the gifts of freedom, of happiness, which they were ready to share with all, if only — if only one accepted their religion.

Her last thought startled her. How could one assume a religion in which one had no belief? Don Samuel's father had taken their religion; Don Samuel himself was baptized in his childhood; but when they had fled Portugal, they had returned to their own faith, and the father had died for it.

The door suddenly opened, and Lancelot thrust in his head Lorenzo understood the signal and halted his impassioned pleading in mid-sentence. He put out his hand to Jessica and whispered hurriedly, "I shall await you at four o'clock tomorrow in the Square of San Marco."

He waited and then when she smiled dreamily, he left feeling confident of her assent.

"He asked me to inform him when Messer Shylock returned, little Signorina," said Lancelot, returning to the room.

"It was well that you did so, good Lancelot. My father would have lifted his hand against Lorenzo and we should both have been ruined."

"It is for fear of that that I came upstairs," went on Lancelot. "The truth is that your father has not yet returned from the city."

"You are wise, Lancelot," she smiled.

"How can I be other than wise, and I your servant these nineteen years since your birth?" Jessica did not answer. She was again deep in reverie. Lorenzo's words sang in her ears like the echo of a distant melody. "Had I waited until master Shylock appeared, Lorenzo would not have had time to get downstairs without being caught."

"Take care, Lancelot, lest you betray a word of all this to my father."

"I have warned Stefano too, Signorina. Signor Lorenzo is a good man, and of great wealth." Jessica smiled again. She knew that Lorenzo was possessed of no great riches, but Lancelot deemed every nobleman to be wealthy. Then she assumed a severe expression, threw a stern look at Lancelot, and rebuked him. "You ought to have told me that Lorenzo wanted to come up to me."

"Confound him, he carries a dagger!" Lancelot expostulated. "He called me to come down, and ordered me to remain on guard — what could I have done? I am a poor servant." But when he saw that Jessica gave no sign of unbending, he added, "If he tries to come up again, I'll crack him over the skull."

"Don't you dare touch him, Lancelot," Jessica admonished. A half-smile curled her lips and Lancelot was reassured.

"He asked you to meet him in the San Marco, but if you meet a merchant who knows you, he will bring word to Messer Shylock. Don't say that I didn't warn you, little Signorina Jessica."

"Thank you, good Lancelot," she murmured. She approached

the gilded Venetian mirror and examined herself. Lancelot stepped aside and went out.

Jessica remained a long while before her mirrored reflection, thinking of Lorenzo's visit. He had not been able to overpower his feelings, and had come upstairs to see her; he was jealous of Don Samuel, whom she only pitied — was it not proof of his true love for her? Thus Jessica, as she smiled at the mirror. How good to be a beautiful woman. Don Samuel would be overjoyed if she consented to be his; the sons of the community elders were dying for her, and even Christians, to whom Jews were as dogs, cast amorous glances at her. Beauty was the greatest gift with which the Almighty had endowed Eve. The gentiles reviled and despised the Jews, and Lorenzo was no different from the rest — was it not divine vengeance that he should kneel before her? She played pleasantly with the thought.

She stretched luxuriously upon the couch reveling in her pride. The agreeable feelings that only a beautiful woman may know, spread and blossomed within her. She sang beatifically to herself the love stanzas of Gaspara Stampa, the gentle poet who had expired of her own ardors, and the bewitching couplets caressed her spirits like the hand of a lover — no man's hand had yet fondled her face, but thus did she imagine in the coolness of the night the hand of the unknown who would suddenly appear from nowhere and captivate her heart. The twilight brought sadness to her, not the sadness of grief but the aching melancholy of a formless yearning, a divine restlessness, and she longed at such a time to be the only lovely woman in the world — toward whom all men aspired.

Her pensive mood disappeared quickly when her father returned from synagogue. He entered as was his wont, ill-humored and sullen, reviling the Christians. There had been an auction sale that day in the Rialto, of goods which Christian debtors had forfeited in pledge of loans from Jewish money-lenders, both individual and the community coffers. Most of the pledges which he, Shylock, had offered for sale yielded less than his capital — a plot to cheat him, which he attributed to a cabal of gentile merchants. And what insults he had to undergo! One called him "dog" and another "leech"; a third had spat aside; a fourth jeered at him, "Soon you will put on a ducal crown." He always had to suffer contumely on the day of a sale, and would have sent a Christian in his stead had he not feared that the man would conspire with the purchasers to defraud him of half the value of his goods. This time he had dallied in the Rialto, and it was dusk when he reached the ghetto gates. He had to bribe the guards to admit him and thus escape the heavy fine for remaining in the city of Venice after the gates were closed.

When Jessica tried to soothe his ruffled temper, Shylock snarled, "Your complacency annoys me as much as the loss of the money! Do you believe, too, that I have gold mines?"

"No money is worth that much anger, Father," she said. She saw that the top button of his coat was missing. When he grew high with fury and had to contain himself, he always wrenched off his buttons; and Jessica had become accustomed to his coming home with the buttons off. To please him, she threaded a needle and searched for a suitable button in her work-basket. Shylock drew it from his pocket.

She approached him with needle in hand and murmured the conventional fetish phrase, "Excuse me, Signor, I am sewing on a donkey," bred of the superstition to ward off the evil influence which may harm anyone whose garments are being mended with needle and thread upon his person. She repeated that no money deserved such ire, but he cut her short: "You lose money and swallow insults, and she tells you quietly that it's all naught!"

"That is not what I said, father," she answered gently.

" 'That is not what I said, father,' " he mimicked her. "Then what did you say?"

"I meant that your anger will bring disaster upon us."

Shylock's tempestuous mood made him restless, and he goaded Jessica to be quick with her mending.

"If I haven't had heart-failure yet of the anger I've had to endure after the many years of dealing with these wretches, you have no call to worry about disaster."

He was silent during supper. His ears still resounded with the gibes in the Rialto; he mentally calculated the losses upon the pledges and now and then he swayed and breathed heavily. Jessica read his thoughts from his lined and deeply wrinkled countenance. She wanted to pacify him, but was afraid to speak. At the end of the meal she went to her room.

It was good to be alone in her own chamber, away from her brooding father. It was rarely that she saw a smile upon his face. His snarling bitterness cast a heavy pall upon the house, and it became a prison, a ghetto within a ghetto. No, it was not her father she loved. He had never spoken to her softly, as befits a parent to his only daughter, the sole remaining child of four children. She could leave him with no sense of filial disloyalty. How often had she been courted, and fine matches offered to her! But she had not wanted them; and now she marveled at herself for not having jumped at the opportunity. She would gladly have gone with an old clothes' seller, a charcoal vendor, a porter, if only to get out of the house of her irascible father.

As she lay upon her bed she thought at length of the day's events. Don Samuel had given her the first lesson; Lorenzo had knelt to her; Lorenzo wanted her to go with him. Why shouldn't she? He was a genteel youth, of noble family, and if she became his, the wide, free world would open to her. The whole time that Don Samuel had been in Venice, she had not thought of love for him; it had not occurred to her that he was the man she could love. Yet from the moment that Lorenzo had tried to depreciate him, out of jealousy, she had begun to think of the young Jewish refugee not as a teacher but as an eligible suitor. Thinking of Lorenzo, she thought of him too — and sometimes Lorenzo was a barrier between herself and Don Samuel, and sometimes Don Samuel was the barrier. In the evening, when her father returned disgruntled and enraged, it was easy for her to think of escape with Lorenzo, but her thoughts of Don Samuel prevented her from considering giving up her people and her faith. She faltered at the thought of following a Christian and embracing his religion.

On the morrow Lorenzo left Shylock's counting-house at midday and stationed himself in San Marco Square promptly at four of the clock. He waited long for Jessica, but she did not come.

Chapter Four

ONE DAY IN THE FOLLOWING WEEK, WHEN DON SAMUEL HAD concluded his lesson, she told him that they would have to put off the lesson of the next day, since she had to go to the city.

"But you will not be there all day," he said. "Let us have the lesson a little earlier or later."

"We shall see tomorrow," she rejoined.

Don Samuel left the house grieving. His daily meetings with Jessica had somewhat allayed his feeling that this daughter of princes would never become his wife. It were better for him to sit opposite her each day, to watch her ruby lips, than to be sunk in dejected contemplation of his future. But the fear that one day he might not see her brought back the original despair which he had felt on the nights of Passover. Those evenings seemed now so far away, a separate period of time in itself, like a lone barque drifting on the ocean of the days.

Tubal and Shylock met twice weekly in the evenings to study Talmud; and Don Samuel now joined them. There were no Hebrew tomes in Tubal's house except the *Zohar* and other Cabalistic literature which were not on the Index; so they foregathered at Shylock's house to immerse themselves in the Talmud.

Don Samuel did not see Jessica when he came that evening to Shylock's home. She was in her room, reading a new Italian book, a novel of Antonio Grazzini. Don Samuel bent over the Talmud with the two old men, but his heart was with Jessica the whole time. Why did she not come in for even a fleeting moment? His ears were alert for the least noise at the door. It seemed to him that she was whispering with someone. Was it possible that a stranger could enter Shylock's house at night and spend the evening with her? He knew it must be merely his imagination, but even this uncertainty tortured his spirit.

It was the third time that Don Samuel had attended these

31

nocturnal studies and, as on the former occasions, both old men praised the younger one to whom the abstruse paths of the Talmud were so clear. Shylock, in his customary way, vilified those who had condemned the holy writings to be burned.

"Do you remember, Tubal, those terrible days of the book hunt? How they fell upon our houses like wild beasts of prey, threw our precious volumes into sacks, and dragged them like so much rubbish to the San Marco Square, where they made a bonfire of them? Night after night, for ten days, the flames could be seen from the square as far as the ghetto. The barbarians of Venice danced around the blazing books like imps of hell . . . Yes, Don Samuel, you had Ancona, ours was San Marco."

"Yet you have all the volumes of the Talmud," Don Samuel pointed out.

"The edict did not touch books in the hands of Christian scholars," Shylock replied. "I secretly paid a goodly sum for these to a Christian prelate."

"For our many sins the Talmud has once again become the oral Law and is being forgotten," sighed Tubal. "There are still sages who teach the youth, but for fear of being given away they give them only oral instruction; and what will transpire unless the ban is removed in the next few years?"

"The tyrant at Rome is already eighty-four years old," Don Samuel said, with a meaningful look.

"There is no hope to be had from the Christians," cried Shylock. "We prayed for the death of the evil Marcellio and our prayers were speedily answered; but after him came the most wicked Paul, and he has been on the Throne for over four years. A little Pharaoh went, and a big Pharaoh succeeded him! My father said that the day the Jews were exiled God made them greedy for bribes. But the worst part of it is that this Pharaoh won't be bribed; the Jews of Rome wanted to count forty thousand *scudi* into his hand to avert the hat of shame but he refused."

"Had it not been for the stream of gold which the Jews of Portugal poured into the ample pouches of the cardinals," mused Don Samuel, "not one of them would have escaped alive.

My father, may he rest in peace, had many a tale to tell of the persecutions. You are right, Signor, their greed is our saving."

"And the Venetians are worse than any other gentiles," Shylock cried. "Their whole life is a carnival; they wear a fine mask. They have grown accustomed to that way of life for generations. But I know them well. There is wickedness and rapacity and immorality and licentiousness beneath that mask. There is the love of everything in the world except the one love of thy neighbor, every lust in the world. And the greatest of them is the hatred of Israel, confound them!" He recalled the large sum of money which he had offered to the Doge's treasury to avoid wearing the Jews' hat and cried "Yes, and when it comes to the badge of shame, they all go demented, like a bull shown a red rag. May they all be stricken blind, so that they cannot distinguish between the black of the ducal beretta and the red hat they force us to wear!"

Tubal tried to subdue his rancorous mood. He said that the Venetians were totally unlike the Romans, in proof of which was their tolerant attitude to the Jews before Paul IV ascended the Papal throne. The Venetians were bearable then.

"Not to me!" exclaimed Shylock. Tubal continued to calm him.

"The sole consolation is that the tyrant of Rome harms his fellow-Christians too. They've burned forbidden books in all the towns of Italy, and ten thousand of their volumes were put to the bonfire here in Venice."

"Anything that pertains to the teachings of Luther sends that old man in Rome out of his mind," observed Don Samuel. "The Almighty Protector sets the one at the other's throat. Paul wanted to swallow the world, but it stuck in his throat as a bone."

"And yet the Venetians, who detest him, give lip-service to his desires in religion," added Shylock. "The more especially his anti-Jewish decrees."

"Heavens above, they don't copy him in everything," Tubal protested. "You exaggerate so much, my friend."

"They have the Adriatic, but we have the broad sea of our

Talmud," said Don Samuel proudly. "Our sea is stronger than theirs and will protect us."

"Well said, Don Samuel." Tubal delightedly patted the young man upon his shoulder.

"I thought the same when I was young," said Shylock. And after a thoughtful pause, he went on. "The Almighty created mankind wisely: by the time one generation ages the next comes, young and ardent with hope, to ensure that eternal Israel shall not perish. Yet what wonder is it that the poor in faith turn from the Almighty and go over to them?"

Don Samuel in a trembling voice told the two others the desecration caused in Pesaro before the execution of the Marrano fugitives from Ancona. The Duke's brother with a few of his bullies took the Scroll of the Law out of the ark, tore the parchment to shreds, and then, clothing a swine with the scroll cover, sent the beast grunting into the synagogue.

Tubal wept in sympathy. Shylock, irate, said, "I pray for one thing, for revenge! The defeat of Paul in his recent war, that was revenge. The famine in Rome, that too was revenge. The floods, the great decline in the trade of Venice, Suleiman's threats against this haughty peddler of goods that is Venice — all these avenge us. They are as the breath of life to me, and my heart glows at the prospect of their once being as tortured and as miserable as we."

"The Messiah will bring an end to all oppressors," interjected Tubal piously, standing up as he mentioned the Messiah.

"The divine acts of vengeance are the echo of the Messiah's footsteps, and when confusion reigns supreme and one Christian shall raise his hand to smite his fellow-Christian, father against father and brother against brother, then will I say — The Messiah has come!" Shylock pounded the table in his excitement.

Jessica heard snatches of the talk from behind the closed door of her room. She knew of old what upset her father, and although she had no patience with the degree of her father's acrimony, she opened the door and glanced into the room.

How beautiful she was, with her deep eyes dilated with fear at her father's vehemence! Samuel smiled at her reassuringly.

"Your father has just said something which ought to be carved in letters of gold," he told her. She remained standing on the threshold for a moment but then, without saying a word, closed the door and returned to her room.

Shylock smiled briefly for a moment at Don Samuel's remark and putting out his hand to take leave of Tubal, said, "Remain for a moment, Don Samuel. I have something to discuss with you."

The few moments which it took Tubal to leave the house seemed like hours to Don Samuel. "Something to discuss with you," his master Shylock had said. Perhaps his dream was to be realized at last, that dream he had had on the night of Passover. Would Shylock say to him "Be my son . . ." ? And Jessica embrace him and whisper, "I felt that I was yours, that I loved you with all my heart from the first moment, but my pride, the pride of a daughter of princes, made me conceal it from you until the moment came"?

Yet, no, no! He must not be deluded. Jessica regarded him as a teacher, a mere teacher; and Shylock as an intelligent youth for whom he would be glad to arrange a marriage with a good wife, but not with his daughter. Yet in his mind's eye, he saw Jessica in a wedding dress and he, Samuel, standing beneath the tasselled canopy awaiting her. And the whole ghetto was merry, and the eyes of the young men surveyed him darkly with envy — him, the poor lad, who had won the hand of the fairest of all the ghetto maidens, of all the world.

Shylock came round the table and sat down at Don Samuel's side.

"I want to ask you, my son, to teach her not only Hebrew, but the rules of conduct and life," he began. Then he unburdened his heart.

Jessica was his youngest child, the only one of four. Leah, her mother, peace upon her ashes, had spoiled the child; he, too, loved her deeply, and she was all that remained to him of his past. Although the strain of his life hindered him from showing her signs of affection, he did love her and placed all his hopes in her, his sole heiress, who would perpetuate his family to the

next generations. The Almighty had given her grace and intellect, and if she sometimes complained that he spoke too
harshly of the Christians, it was only out of her love for him —
her wretched father whose soul was so tormented. She was a
girl and feared for his well-being, lest he be done harm — as
though there was any harm which the Venetians could do him
which they had not already attempted.

She was not the only one of the younger generation in the
ghetto who yearned toward Venice. There was in that cursed
city a magic spell that snared the heart — and it was not good.
They would soon begin their carousing and revelry at Easter,
and it would last for weeks; and before they ended one festival,
another began — they junketed the whole year round, and what
extravagance did they spare? Jessica loved their festivities, their
trivial games. She had from her early youth been attracted by their
gondolas, their brilliant gardens, their squares adorned with
marble statues which were forbidden by the Torah. She was
not the only one, he repeated; there were many among the
the youth like her. They had imported many of the revels into
the ghetto; at first the rabbis had forbidden the masquerades
and music of the Christians, but they had soon realized that because of the ban the younger folk flocked to the city of Venice
and had even been led into embracing Christianity. So they had
lifted the ban.

Yet Jessica, like the daughters of other rich men, loathed the
merry-making in the ghetto — what had it in common with the
gay frolics in Venice itself? It grieved him deeply — but not
because he feared any untoward consequence. She was a learned
girl, Jewess in every vein of her, but he, the father, hated the
Venetian oppressors so much that her very wish to behold their
spectacles sorrowed him. He had always objected to her going to
witness their carnivals, but her mother was tender-hearted and,
rather than let the girl pine, had concealed from him the fact that
she went into Venice. He had often quarreled with his departed
wife over it, but in vain. As a greater precaution he never allowed
her out alone, the faithful Lancelot accompanied her, and upon
his return he told of all that she had done.

What *had* she done? She had watched and been happy. Last year, one of mourning for her mother, she had not taken part in these amusements — she loved her mother deeply — but shortly afterwards she had returned to the practice. He had forbidden all her girl friends to come to the house, so that she might not be misled — but even that had not helped. Jessica had no other fault, she was charitable and generous, but this fault gnawed at his vitals and he would know no peace until he had eradicated it. Thus Shylock at length.

Finally he said, "They have some sort of a feast tomorrow — I think they call it the Hunting Festival — but when don't they have a merry-making and a carousel, out upon them! You must prevail upon her to stay at home."

"She did indeed tell me," Don Samuel murmured, "that she would not take the lesson tomorrow, as she had to be in the city."

"I knew it! But you are wise, you can turn her from it."

"She told me not to come tomorrow."

"Don't heed her, Samuel. The festivity is in the afternoon. Come beforehand, and find some expedient of keeping her home."

"I will do so, Signor Shylock, but you must inform her in the morning that on no account must she forego the lesson."

"Very well, my son. I shall tell you tomorrow in the counting-house at what time the lesson will be given. She will not disobey if I order her."

"And why not order her not to go to Venice?"

"Because she would not heed. She says that we old people do not understand the character of these vanities. You are a young man, and if you can, with your eloquent speech, persuade her that these frivolities are worthless, that they are the folly of the enemies of our race, she will pay attention."

"I hope so," muttered Don Samuel.

"But of course she will!" exclaimed Shylock. "And in any event, she must not go so often to the city. In forty years of ghetto life I have grown used to everything, but whenever I see Jessica going out with that veil on, my blood boils within me. What a vile invention it is! At the time of the Destruction four hundred boys and girls were taken captive into shame and preferred drowning; in Germany the daughters held their necks out for their fathers' hatchets so that they might escape being disgraced; and the sisters of these, the daughters of Israel, are mocked at: 'See, they wear the veil of ignominy, of the bawdy-house!' And still I am accused of overdoing my hatred of them!"

Don Samuel defended Jessica. She had been born in the ghetto, and saw no dishonor in wearing the veil — "On the contrary, the veil that covers the virtuous daughters of Israel defeats the purpose of shaming, and loses all suggestions of ignominy."

Shylock smiled wryly at this reasoning . . . .

Going home, Samuel was saddened and distrait. The visions he had conjured up before Shylock began to speak had almost assumed a garb of reality, but now they had evaporated. Jessica had worn a wedding dress, he had stood under the canopy awaiting her, but she had not come . . . A cold sweat broke out over his body as he saw in his imagination the capering crowds around the marriage-canopy. But now the people turned their backs at him and the urchins jeered, "You coveted a place in the house of the rich man, O beggar!"

On arriving at Tubal's house he went straight to his room and flung himself down upon his pallet. He was encouraged to feel that Shylock had placed his trust in him. He would succeed in arousing her aversion to the festivals of Christian Venice. Shylock would be grateful and then — then he would say, "She is yours, my son." He meditated upon what he would converse with Jessica upon the morrow. The thoughts tumbled through his mind, but his troubled soul feared that he might not succeed in the task which Shylock had given him and thus end the faint hope that Jessica might become his wife. Yes, it must be a vain hope, since Shylock's manner was only one of pity to a fugitive belonging to the former banking family in Ancona. All that night Don Samuel tossed sleeplessly upon his couch. He rehearsed to himself what he would tell her, heard her replies, for a fleeting instant saw Jessica triumphant, then saw himself in triumph. When he awoke in the morning his head was in a whirl. There was a heavy load upon his mind, and during the early prayers in the synagogue his eyes were fixed upon the holy ark, his lips murmured the customary liturgy, but his heart — his heart was full with the traveler's prayer — "O Lord, make my journey successful this time!"

Hardly had he entered the banking shop than Shylock said, "Come at two o'clock for the lesson."

"Did she object to my coming?"

"It is of no importance. She agreed."

Lorenzo, who, always on the watch over Don Samuel, overheard the short exchange, discerned the satisfaction on Don Samuel's face, and trembled slightly. He had fixed a meeting with her at four o'clock in San Marco Square — had the old man suspected something, and was he foiling his plans? It would go ill if the wrathful old Jew learned of what was afoot between his daughter and Lorenzo. Yet, why the young one's question and the old one's answer? Perhaps Jessica had objected to something and the old man had made her obey him.

The hours passed with leaden feet, both for Lorenzo and for Don Samuel. They were both silent that morning, each deep in his own musings, each awaiting the hour of two in the afternoon. Neither stopped working at noon. Lorenzo said that he was going to the city at three o'clock to take part in the Hunting Festival, and it was not worth breaking off earlier; Don Samuel's excuse was that with his stomach disordered he could not taste food. At two o'clock Samuel went upstairs, and Lorenzo sat on below as though petrified.

But he speedily recovered, and a great anger swept him. He gripped the hilt of his rapier violently. One thought filled him: to kill the young Jew of Capo d'Istria! But the image of Jessica came before him as she stood above the open grave and cried aloud, "Foul murderer!" His anger subsided, he grew listless and vacant-minded. He stood upon the threshold of the shop as though dawdling, ostensibly scanning the passers-by idly, but in reality keeping a sharp watch over the staircase of Shylock's house. Then, after a long while, he saw Stefano coming down. His face lit up, and he ran after the man, thrusting a coin into his hand and whispering urgently, "Please, Stefano, go inside and call Lancelot out to me."

"Don't worry, Signor," the man replied. "Lancelot will leave with her for the San Marco at four of the clock."

"How do you know it?" Lorenzo questioned him.

"There are no secrets between Lancelot and myself. He cannot hide anything from me."

"But nonetheless go and bring me Lancelot."

"As you say, Messer." Stefano retraced his steps, and Lancelot soon came down.

"I shall be there with her at four of the clock. Await us, Signor Lorenzo, at the Rialto landing-place." Lorenzo wanted to bombard him with questions, but he disappeared almost at once, fearing that his master might perceive him talking with Lorenzo.

Don Samuel was in the meantime with Jessica on the roof of the house, where she had awaited him at two o'clock. She watched the gondolas taking the residents of the surburb islands to its heart, to the San Marco, to attend the festival. From afar she could see people disguised as various animals, and around them the frolicking youths and maidens in the gondolas floating down the Grand Canal. She had received Don Samuel coldly, and he was at pains to appease her.

"I said nothing ill of you to your father, Jessica. But the conversation drifted by chance to you and today's lesson, and I could not lie to him."

Jessica made no response. Her silence irked Don Samuel.

"Let us hurry with the lesson, I must go to the city," she then vouchsafed.

"We shall have a conversation today," he said.

"I am tired," she murmured. Don Samuel believed her. Had she been his sister, he would have placed her head upon his chest to rest her, he would have stroked her head to soothe her.

"I shall speak Hebrew, Jessica, and you will speak Italian. I want you to relax." His low pleading voice dissipated her anger and she made no refusal.

Don Samuel spoke of various matters and, as he generally did, went on to describe his days at Ancona, that time which was etched upon his heart as though with a steel engraving-tool. He told of the imprisonment of the Marranos, the crypto-Jews, the eighty men and some of their wives; of those who had escaped with the Papal emissary who had been bribed; of the twelve first martyrs at the stake; of his father who had fallen from the ladder when he too had tried to flee; and of his teacher Rabbi Shlomo Yehya, who was among the twelve last martyrs.

"Rabbi Shlomo Yehya, may he rest in peace," said Don Samuel in a voice charged with emotion, "was a great man of polished manner and tongue. He spoke Latin and Italian with as much ease as a cardinal. When he was brought with the others, fettered hand and foot to the place of burning, the priests besought him to abandon the Law of Moses and avoid this frightful death. They tried to persuade him, knowing that if a man of his caliber yielded, the others would follow suit. But he cried out in a loud voice:

" 'Though many princes and potentates may send me to the stake, it is not for my sins that I have been condemned to this death, nor because of any wrong which I have committed against God and man. It is because I have clung to the faith of my fathers and worshipped the God of Israel. For God is supreme in the heavens above, and there is none like unto Him here below, and I give myself to death in the sanctity of His name, and Him do I beseech to gather my soul into the Bundle of Eternal Life. And the blood of His servants will be avenged of those who seek to do it evil. His wrath shall overwhelm them, and his fury strike them down.'

"And as he ceased speaking," went on Don Samuel, "Rabbi Shlomo ascended to the stake, an innocent sacrifice, and intoned the blessing, thanking Him for all mercies and sanctifying the Name, and threw himself into the flames in rejoicing and gladness. Thereupon the other martyrs were tied to the stakes prepared for them, and they too were burned with the Name upon their lips."

Jessica made to check him, but when she saw his exaltation, she refrained and, sitting upon the bench set on the roof, surveyed gondolas bearing the masqueraders to San Marco. Her seeming indifference vexed Don Samuel, and he had almost risen from his place to chide her for being heartless when she cut short his intention by asking, "And whence have you knowledge of all that your teacher said?"

"I heard his words with my own ears, Jessica. We were twenty-seven sentenced to life servitude in the galleys. We saw the whole shocking spectacle and heard the seductive words of the priests, may they be evermore effaced, and the words of Rabbi Shlomo Yehya, may his memory remain blessed in eternity." Samuel's annoyance had passed, and he went on to tell of himself, how he had been saved. "We were then coaxed to change our religion, and the oldest among us said, 'Why should you go to a living death? Repent and live.' A great fear overcame us and we agreed to forswear the Law of Moses to save our bodies, but in our hearts we remained as firmly devoted to Him as before.

"Then each of us was clad in a four-cornered garment of leek-green coloring, with a red device in front and a square patch at the back, so that all beholders might recognize us, and we were sent under guard through the kingdom of Naples to the galleys. But at one of the resting-places I said to the others, (they were all young), 'What is life in the galleys, at the oars? Let us overcome the guards and flee, and return to the true faith!' So when our guards slept, and only two were sentinel, we fell upon them all together, took away their arms, beat them until they lay motionless, and fled. Many of us managed to reach Turkey, and I and others came to Ferrara and Pesaro, and there we came back to the true faith."

Don Samuel gazed into Jessica's countenance. He saw no expression of admiration at his courage and gallantry. She comprehended his surprise and remarked, "You do not impress one as a man of courage." There was a somewhat disparaging note in her voice. He was despondent for a moment, but said, "There are some people, Jessica, who of their nature are volcanoes. The strength within them is curbed and held in for the great moment, and there is no greater moment than danger — it makes every man brave and courageous."

The girl gave him a glance as though she had not heard what

he said. He grew annoyed again, but reflected that if he left her now, he would never see her more. He controlled his rising temper and said, "Let us go down, Jessica. I cannot see them at their revels."

"But it is all so gay!" she cried, starting out of her abstraction. "See that long line of gilded gondolas; and the singing and music seem to carpet the canals with golden sound — have you no ear for the delicious music?"

"You know, Jessica, that I love song and music, but this festival atmosphere reminds me of Ancona, and conjures up the whole terrible scene. I shall never forget the tortured face of the old woman Majora, the last in the row of twelve first martyrs who went to the stake — yet how proud she was in her torment! And the martyrs were followed by a great mob, women and children among them, and the earth shook to their stamping and howling and the beating of the drums."

"Your memories of Ancona always frighten me, Don Samuel."

"And I am frightened by that wild merriment," he retorted. "You may call it freedom, but I — the license of fools."

Jessica had not heard him. From afar came the song of the revelers, and she hummed the melody under her breath. Don Samuel could check himself no longer and asked her in vexation, "Jessica, how can you sing their songs when your ears echo with the agonized cry of the martyrs at Ancona?"

"You are here only a short time," she answered evasively. "You do not know Venice and her people — look at the shimmering water, as though the sun had shed all the light of its orb into the canals; and the people attired in so many colors, as if they had come from another world, a world of mirth and laughter."

"No, Jessica," he interrupted. "The waters of Venice are very turbid and gray. Who built the first ghetto, if not the Venetians? Who forbade the Jews to consort with the Christians or to build synagogues? It was Pope Eugene IV, a native son of Venice. And Paul II, who was also a native of Venice, brought racing to Rome, and first had donkeys galloping round the arena and then horses, and all the crowds applauded and cheered. And the profligate game continues to this day."

"Please do not compare Rome with Venice — this Venice is a city of children."

"Children? Ask your father, and he will tell you otherwise."

"My father! He does not appreciate their spirit, and he makes himself hateful to them."

Don Samuel smiled grimly. "Has he then to try so hard to arouse their hatred? So long as they bring up the Christian children with prejudices as they do now, there will be hatred of everything that is called Jew — See, the broad horizons, the mansions on both sides of the Grand Canal?"

"Isn't it all so splendid!" Jessica cried with animation. "The tiny waves kiss the steps of the palaces night and day, caressing their feet."

"And all that is closed to the Jews," he sighed. "Yet it ought not to worry us, Jessica. The ghetto encloses us so that our sons and daughters may not be snared and brought to apostasy. No, they will never exterminate us! A light is rising in the East. The sword of Suleiman the Great is brandished afar, the day is not distant."

"Beware of what you say, Don Samuel," Jessica warned, touching his hand. At that moment Samuel forgave her all giddy foolishness.

"We have no call to be afraid here, Jessica," he whispered. "They have shut us up within walls to deprive us of our liberty, but they do not realize that they have given it to us. We can speak here what is in our hearts, to pray for their overthrow." Seeing that Jessica was amazed at his speech, he added: "You are astonished. A tiny mosquito killed their forefather Titus the Great. A hundred, two hundred, a thousand years hence — the day will dawn. A Jew, their Messiah, destroyed the pagan world, and there will come the time when this — their world too in which they live today — will be demolished, either from within or outside. Today you hear the echo of the approaching tread of the Angel of Death on the other side of doom; tomorrow the trumpets will ring out here in the country."

She listened for a moment and then, averting her gaze — "You too are blind. I thought you to be more moderate, and yet you are as full of ire as my father. Only the clergy, the legates of the Pope, incite the people, but the people themselves know how to love, they wait for love. Venice itself was built for lovers."

"They shut up the Jews on this muddy island out of love, is that what you mean, Jessica? Their trade in slaves is for love — the love of gold. When I fled a year ago with the other fugitives from Pesaro, the captain was about to sell us all into slavery and would have done so had the Jews of Venice not ransomed us all for gold and brought us to Istria."

"Seafarers are renowned as men of evil."

"And he who sits upon the Holy Chair?" he asked heavily. Drawing breath, he proceeded: "Their great artists, whom both you and I admire, who depict the Crucifixion in a thousand ways and vie with each other to portray the Agony, they accustom the Christian mind from immaturity to see blood streaming from the limbs of the human body, and they are responsible for the spirit of cruelty among the Christians no less than the Popes and the cardinals and the bishops who in the name of Mercy and Compassion preach animosity and brutality. And what is the outcome of it all? That hatred which is ingrained in their very souls becomes of its nature inured to such 'small' things as persecuting Jews and wiping out communities — it lusts after 'salvation' upon the grand scale; battles, battles, it seeks more battles — and so each man shall eat the flesh of his brother, and they shall all be consumed. This thing they call love has shown that they deserve nothing less than extinction!"

"Stop, stop, Don Samuel," begged Jessica, her face seeming to him to have become as gentle as of yore.

"I must not say sinful things, for I have found shelter in your father's house," he said ruefully.

Jessica seemed glad at his admission. For some reason, she wished to see him tranquil and untroubled, and the pause gave her an opportunity to change the subject.

"You have no doubt learned that my father is a stern man, yet he is full of praise of you. He says that you are a scholar and learned man, and you have a counsel of perfection even in

45

matters of finance." She smiled disarmingly. "It would be good that he learned from you, and not the other way, my teacher."

Her words astounded the young man. He was certain that she had spoken the compliment willingly. How his arms ached to embrace that fragile body! But the fear that she would cast him, the teacher, a look of displeasure, froze his arms at his side. He dared not touch her, even with his little finger. He could not, however, fully restrain his speech.

"From the day I crossed the threshold of this house I have breathed freely. It is a privilege to be your teacher, to look into your face, Jessica. The purling voice that echoes the music which fills your soul falls pleasantly upon the ear of man."

She did not protest in so many words, but took him up on the question — "If the music which fills my heart is so strange to you, what do you find in the tenor of my voice?" Don Samuel sought for a polished metaphor, but she continued, "Listen, Don Samuel, to this ditty. It is one that good Lancelot sang for me, when I was a child, whenever I did not wish to eat, or could not sleep. And so it is that I have known the Venetian love-songs from my childhood." She began humming the tune to herself, but as she proceeded it rose full-throated. A shiver shook Don Samuel as an ague and he could not help saying, interrupting her, "Yet when I hear it or any song like to it, the tragic song of the victims of Ancona bursts from my throat."

Jessica made no remark but said, as if to herself, "This song bears me upon wings into space, into the space of the seas and the skies, into the spacelessness of the heart." She went on humming the song. Don Samuel shot her a glance, and recited quietly the first stanza of the dirge of the martyrs of Ancona:

> The heavens stood aghast, they no longer shone,
> Upon the woe of My people they mourned,
> From the month of splendor all glory had gone.
> The humble were summoned before the king,
> Sacrificed to kingship, to their doom they trod.
> All wept at the fate of the chosen scorned —
> The raging fires consumed the Being called God.

Jessica halted him. Her head fell forward upon her breast. Don Samuel, who was singing, gave her a sidelong glance. How beautiful she was in her sadness! Like a living statue of Rachel the Mother after the weary refugees had stumbled before her. . . . He began the second stanza, meaning to continue until the song would melt her heart and she dissolve into tears.

But she stood up, and he broke off. For a moment she gazed at the gondolas drifting up the sparkling Grand Canal, unwinding its coils like some gigantic serpent. She composed herself and said, "It is late, Don Samuel, I must go."

"There is but one request I have to make of you, Jessica," said Don Samuel as they descended the stairs from the roof.

"I am not accustomed to granting the requests of young men," she answered banteringly.

"I believe you intend going to the Hunting Festival. . . ."

"That is true."

"Then don't, Jessica. The sisters of the Ancona martyrs may not take part in their heathen celebrations; and our holy books were burned in that square."

"But the Hunting Festival is an innocent and merry fete."

"Yet in that square they desecrated all that you hold sacred. From its paving-stones cry out the ten thousand thousands of the letters of our writings which clamor for vengeance."

She meditated for a moment.

"On the contrary, Don Samuel, their eyes pop out when they see the fair daughters of Israel who come out of the ghetto. Perhaps with my dull face I can disturb the rest of a few of them — it is but a small revenge that a daughter of Eve, such as myself, can wreak upon them."

Her ardent wish to attend the festival had brought the words to her lips. The earnest Don Samuel heard them with a beating heart and pressed her hand warmly for the vigorous expression of the sensibilities of a proud daughter of Israel. With soft pleading he tried to dissuade her from going to San Marco Square.

"I know little enough joy in my father's house, Don Samuel. Let them plant their gardens, and we shall enjoy them, don't you think?" She made a graceful gesture with her hand in parting and went into the house.

The young man stood for some minutes longer, deep in thought over her final words. What difference in the revenge over which father and daughter pondered. Yet both did meditate upon revenge, he reasoned, and the daughter's was to be preferred: it was no vain quest, a thing of the future, but a real revenge that savored its consummation day by day. Whoever knew the great fascination exercised by a lovely woman could comprehend how powerful was this secret revenge. It was the first time that Jessica had been so charming, so sweet; mayhap it was the beginning of that feeling for which every scrap of his being prayed with such fervent hope — Jessica's love. Once again he saw in imagination the same visions as of the night before: he was standing with her beneath the canopy, and she so bewitching in her white gown, the skies so azure, the path they trod suddenly strewn with flowers which had sprung up at that very instant.

He was jerked out of his day-dream when he stood at the threshold of the counting-house, and met Shylock's inquiring eyes.

"She — she — she is going," he stammered.

"I knew that you wouldn't succeed," Shylock grated with suppressed anger. "You are not strong enough."

"She is a very wise girl, Signor. You have naught to fear."

"I knew that without your saying," snapped the old man, and fell silent. Don Samuel found no courage to go on speaking to his employer, and his heart pounded sorrowfully. It was the first time that Shylock had displayed any censure of him, and it hurt him. At that instant the brutal, threatening figure of the captain who had wanted to sell him into servitude during his flight from Pesaro sprang into memory, and he shuddered. He spent the afternoon disconsolately, every ounce of energy drained from him, and felt that something boded ill.

Leaving his work at dusk, when the ghetto gates were closed, he saw Jessica entering the door at the top of the stairs, followed by Lancelot. He caught a glimpse of her face for only a fleeting instant, but it seemed to him that she espied him and hurried inside to avoid a meeting.

Jessica went to San Marco Square, accompanied by Lancelot, and Lorenzo awaited them at the Rialto bridge. No sooner had she stepped out of the gondola than Lorenzo tendered her a bouquet of roses, and other revelers showered her with flowers, as was the custom during the Spring fetes — a custom copied by Venice from the carnivals at Rome, which were of the type of harvest festival.

As they approached the San Marco Square, center of the merry-making, the drabness of the gray ghetto was banished from Jessica's mind. Laughter and flowers, flowers and laughter. The young "hunters" used flowers to "shoot" with, instead of arrows, and the garlanded girls seemed like walking arbors in full bloom, pink and saffron and mauve, and the violet of forget-me-nots and the deep green of laurel. The great square was a multi-colored garden swaying in the breeze.

"What a glorious sight!" she breathed.

"How lovely you are in all this loveliness," whispered Lorenzo at her side, drawing her closer to himself for a swift moment.

Soon Jessica was covered with flowers, and her radiant, proud face drew the gaze of the passers-by. She threw nuts or pellets made of sweetmeats at passing handsome youths, and by the time they had come up to thank her, there was a score of other people congregated about her.

"I'm not walking, I'm being swept along," she cried in tinkling laughter. There were tens of thousands packing the great San Marco Square.

Beside the many masked "animals," there were hundreds and thousands of other costumes: Turks with fezzes, Chinese with pigtails, as Marco Polo had described them, swarthy Berbers from Africa, monks walking arm-in-arm with flouncing girls, pirates and corsairs, beggars cloaked in sheets, a medley and motley of types. Here stood one clad as a lawyer from Padua, and hundreds flocked around him — he was loudly demanding the punishment of a monk who had fled the monastery at night and gone in pouring rain to the house of a young widow to hear her confession. There in woman's garb stood a man on an upturned barrel, and declaimed from Aretino's *Dialogues;* modest women edged away from him. Although the policemen took no heed of bawdiness during a festival, they motioned to the orator to desist. A quarrel began between the crowds and the *sbirro,* and the former won, as someone else jumped on the barrel and shouted, "Here are the shoes which Aretino made for me!" and the man went off into a vociferous ode, with the excited crowd applauding, forgetting that the celestial Aretino, who had taken that appellation himself, was the son of a cobbler who had climbed to fame and the love of vestals.

Once the jostling crowds separated Lorenzo from Jessica. "Have I done wrong to agree to go with him?" she thought for a flash. The impulse seized her to leave the place and return to the ghetto. But she felt Lorenzo's hand back in hers — and was happy once more.

"I have paid for a place on yonder balcony. Shall we go up to it?" asked Lorenzo.

Jessica pouted. "I am not pleased that you spend your silver for me."

The San Marco Square was not at that moment any spot for converse. Just then a comic trio passed, causing universal merriment and guffaws. Each had two faces and two bellies, yet they only had one pair of hands and legs apiece. How had six people devised a costume which made them seem three? Many of the onlookers puzzled while the three two-faced creatures performed all manner of strange antics which convulsed those nearest to them, and the laughter spread quickly, from group to group, until it seemed that the whole vast square with its teeming thousands was dissolved into a gigantic laugh, and the pigeons perched in the embrasures of the towers and in the spires of the cathedral, though long accustomed to the din of a multitude, whirred their wings, fluttered uneasily, and flew off in alarm, as though an earthquake had rocked the edifice.

As the gales of laughter swept through the merry throng, Jessica's glance fell upon a band of grotesque beggars, each of whom bore a small earthenware pitcher upon which was written;

"For pity's sake, a morsel of love." In a flash, the recollection darted into her mind of what Don Samuel had said the week before, that no more devoted people existed than the Jews, if they were shown a scrap of love. Involuntarily she thought that in all that great assemblage there was not one particle of love for her people and race, and her face blanched. The sad visage of Don Samuel came before her, and it was as if his reproachful eyes seared her soul for having succumbed to the whim of attending a Christian festival.

"Why are you so wistful, Jessica?" Lorenzo's voice broke the train of her thoughts. "Don't think of that island from which you have come."

"And to which I shall return!" she exclaimed. She feared at that moment that Lorenzo was scheming to detain her.

They were now standing before a marionette booth. She went inside with Lorenzo, and the puppets at their pranks brought them to tears of laughter. From there they sauntered on until they came to a fortune-teller, who foretold that the whole world would bow and kneel before her, and that she would marry a young nobleman. The old crone gave Lorenzo's description as Jessica's future husband.

"You probably coached her in advance," Jessica said as they left.

Lorenzo was taken aback for a moment, and they broke out into a gay laugh. "Only a Jew could be so cunning."

She took offense at the remark, and he hastened to apologize, saying that he regarded her as the daughter of a Jew and not a real Jewess herself.

"But I am a real Jewess," she retorted with a charmingly mischievous expression. Lorenzo hugged her closely, for the first time, and she cried, "Don't! You'll crush the flowers. There is no compassion in your heart." Both went off in laughter.

Jessica was by this time fatigued and they went up to the balcony which Lorenzo had hired for the day. What an enchanting vista it provided! A sea of heads, an ocean of flowers, hundreds of "beasts" capering to the tapping measures played by the musicians, and the people and maskers and the many raised voices blending into harmony of sight and sound. How wonderful! Jessica felt that she must have sprouted wings — she felt so carefree and feather-light.

Her glance fell on the towers of St. Mark, the thousands of pigeons nestling within the orifices, flying from spire to spire and steeple. Why did the birds seem so sad? She again remembered Don Samuel's words that the letters in the holy books rose up from San Marco Square and cried out for their vengeance. She knew that it was only a figure of speech but, lifting her eyes, it seemed as if she heard a cascade of cursing descending upon the moving heads of the holiday throng. Some strong impulse compelled her to leave, and she suddenly felt herself an alien among the merry people around. The gaiety became discordant.

"It is late. I must go," she said, and left the balcony. Lorenzo coaxed her to remain a while longer, but she refused. "I have no wish to vex my father."

Lancelot, who saw that she really wished to go home, added, "It's impossible, Messer. I promised the master that I would return with Signorina Jessica before the gates were closed." Lorenzo trod on his foot, but Lancelot ignored the hint. "I cannot risk my place," he said.

Jessica turned her back upon the square, and went left to the Rialto. "Leave me now, Lorenzo. I fear that my father will be there."

"At this time no Jew dares remain in the Rialto," he answered and, walking at her side, stroked her hand and poured out his protestations of love. "When can we meet again outside the ghetto, dear Jessica?"

"Lancelot will inform you."

"Tomorrow? The day after?"

"We must not meet too often. It will arouse suspicion."

"And why should you care, my Jessica? I desire your happiness. Your dear company is more precious to me than anything in the world."

She only smiled and made no protest when he pressed her to him, but her eyes roamed from one side to another in fear lest she be recognized. Then, in the distance, she saw someone wearing the red hat and she drew herself out of Lorenzo's clasp. It was a poor peddler carrying old clothes on his back. When they had passed the Jew, Lorenzo again took her hand.

"When shall we meet again, Jessica?" he tremblingly repeated.

"Lancelot will tell you," she reiterated.

She was glad when they came near the gondola mooring-station. Lorenzo wished to accompany her, but she was adamant.

"I must think of my livelihood. I would starve here in the city," said Lancelot, beckoning to a gondolier to approach.

"What a pity we left the square, Jessica my love," whispered Lorenzo. "The real fun begins after sunset."

"You may return there then," she said as they parted.

"Without you, the square is like a forest with wild beasts."

Lorenzo waved at the gondola until it had disappeared from view up the canal. Indeed, Jessica ruminated, it is a forest of wild beasts; and it was better to have left the San Marco and the palaces lining the canal. The gondola swerved right, into a narrow passage, and they left the wine-red waters of the Grand Canal. The graying mantle of late twilight descended around her, and her thoughts became as gray. She was now sorry that she had gone to the Hunting Festival, and upon landing at the gates and hurrying into the ghetto, it seemed that she had been miraculously snatched from the fangs of the wild animals. Yet as she hastened through the narrow alley-ways of the ghetto, she felt a nameless uncertainty, as though high buildings on either side were about to topple over her. She almost leapt up the stairs into her house.

During supper Shylock did not glance at his daughter, and they exchanged no word. She knew full well what his silence portended. She was accustomed to it, but this time her mind was troubled. As soon as the meal ended, she went to her bed.

Jessica remained long awake. Don Samuel was a fine youth of whom her father was fond — if she told her father that she loved him, he would cry out in pleasure, "That is what I prayed for!" Yet what a lover Lorenzo was — how carefree! Her father was old and was near to death and she had only just opened her eyes to see the light of life — should she sacrifice the whole of

her life for him? Is that what God demanded of her? He had
put her on this earth as free as the other maidens of Venice —
was it His will that she spend the gift of youth in the ghetto-
prison? And what had it harmed those who changed their
faith not out of love, but to seek honor, position, power? Was
she not sinning against Don Samuel when she chattered about
the gondolas and the masquerade while he spoke with such emotion of what he had suffered at Ancona? Don Samuel was an
intellectual man . . . . Lorenzo breathed the essence of Life . . . .
How cultured were Don Samuel's hands, how deep his eyes . . . .
What gay laughter Lorenzo had . . . . Don Samuel . . . Lorenzo
. . . Lorenzo . . . Don Samuel . . .

Her heart and mind swayed to and fro in unison with her
thoughts, and she was cradled to sleep.

Chapter Five

THE NEXT FEW DAYS WERE HARD FOR JESSICA, VERY HARD. UNTIL
now she had dreamt of the unknown lover who would come
out of the nowhere and carry her off with him, just as every
girl who had reached the brink of womanhood. Several times
her father had tried to talk her into a match, but she had refused to hear of an unromantic marriage. She wanted love, a
great love, the sort of love of which she had read in the Song
of Solomon, the Iliad, Boccaccio, Dante's poetry, Francesco
Petrarca, and the later poets. Now the love which had lain dor-
mant within her for years and bided its time had flowered into
fragrant blossom under the caresses of Lorenzo and Don Samuel's
melting voice as he said "Jessica" — the ardent looks of both.
One day she would wait impatiently for the hour of the lesson so
that she might see Don Samuel; another day she would languish
for Lorenzo, the handsome nobleman who held in his grasp
the key to the great, free, beautiful world. At times despair
would succeed high hope, and she felt lost and lonely. It was
only with a supreme effort that she managed to conceal her distress from both Don Samuel and Lorenzo.

Don Samuel thought of Jessica with humility. He waited until she would say to him, "I love you, my heart's chosen," yet he knew that such a day would never come — the proud Jessica would never reveal her heart to a man, even though she loved him deeply. Why should she love him? She was a rich man's daughter and of unsurpassed beauty, and he was the orphaned son of a once-rich father, a refugee who had found transient shelter in her father's household. And her father — certainly he would never give away his daughter to such as Samuel Morro. Often he told Don Samuel that he had never forgotten his wish to proceed to Constantinople, and Don Samuel had gathered that the old man wished him gone.

But Lorenzo schemed toward his ambition with courage and resoluteness, the way of the free man beneath whom the ground is firm. His love had sharpened his powers of observation from the very first moment, and although Jessica had assured him that there was nothing between her and Don Samuel, he realized that "the Jew from Capo d'Istria" was an obstacle to his plans. As Shylock's agent, he brought him clients of the upper classes. In the past, he had generally settled these affairs during business hours in the banking-shop. But now he arranged these meetings for the evening, so that he might see Jessica upstairs. He often found Tubal and Don Samuel in the house (whenever the Christians entered, the students hid the Talmud) and his choler rose at seeing Don Samuel sitting at Shylock's table as a member of the household. But he always concealed his temper, knowing that one incautious glare or move would arouse Shylock's suspicions. Usually Jessica did not come into the chamber in which he sat with the clients; he knew that she was in an adjoining room, and even raised his voice when speaking, so that she might know he was near. Her studied absence pierced him like a lance, and the pain added to his consuming desire to win Jessica.

A fortnight passed from the time of his meeting with Jessica in downtown Venice. During the two weeks he had several opportunities to have a few words with her. Going upstairs when Shylock went off to the Rialto, he pleaded with her to meet him once, just once, in the evening — but she declined. At last he overcame her scruples through Lancelot.

"You have never seen, little Jessica, the city of Venice at night. I will take you there," said the servant.

"How can I go out? My father would know it."

"I have arranged that. When your father retires to bed, I shall go out with you quietly, dress you in a man's cloak, and come to the ghetto gate."

He added that Lorenzo would be waiting in a gondola at the bridge outside the gate, and would arrange with the guard to allow her to steal out and return.

"Ah, Jessica! Venice is like a fantasy of dreams," said Lorenzo on the morrow when Lancelot told him of his talk with her. To see Venice at night! To glide in a gondola when no other Jew dared show his face on the Grand Canal! She struggled with her conscience, and a profound fear gripped her heart that Lorenzo might not let her return; but she trusted in the good Lancelot, who promised her faithfully that he would bring her back. Ah! Venice after nightfall, the Grand Canal in the glowing night! The serpentine canal would carry her as seductively as the serpent of old had wooed the Woman of Genesis, and she longed to taste of the Tree of Knowledge of night life in fabled Venice. . . .

At ten o'clock that night, when the sound of Shylock's snoring reached Jessica's room, she left the house stealthily with Lancelot. When they had reached the ghetto gate a sudden fright seized her, and she wanted to return.

"It's impossible," Lancelot whispered. "Calm yourself. I shan't take my eyes off you."

"Watch me and watch him too." She trembled, pressing Lancelot's hand thankfully.

A few minutes later she reclined in the gondola. Lancelot sat beside the oarsmen and she with Lorenzo on the soft couch beneath the awning. Lorenzo pressed her to his heart, thanked her fervently for having agreed to the excursion with him, and she was reassured. The gentle murmuring of the water beneath the oar whispered the secrets of romantic dreams, and Lorenzo's words of impassioned love answered them; the colored lanterns above the quays and bridges twinkled at her like great stars, and their reflections in her imagination became shining flags glistening upon the waters of the purling canal as in some remote world far, far from reality. . . . Was she indeed seeing all this with her own eyes? She often pictured similar scenes in her dreams — could she be dreaming now?

"Just say the word and all this is yours, every evening and every night," her mind told her. "No, Jessica, do not covet a world that is not yours," replied stern conscience.

"Are you happy, fair Jessica?" Lorenzo murmured. She smiled dreamily. "Why are you silent?"

"I see all this for the first time — I am absorbing it all."

"You are a bad girl, Jessica. I have often asked you to come out with me. This ought not to be the first time."

The arrogance which is part of the character of every beautiful woman brought an answer to her lips: "This is the first time and perhaps the last."

"No, no, Jessica. Venice awaits you. It is the first time that I see it in all its wonder — your beauty has cast this spell of loveliness upon it." He drew her closer.

As they came near the Rialto, a glad song burst from Lorenzo's throat. His fine Italian tenor rose melodiously in a golden spiral of notes. Her happiness glowed in her eyes, and an auriole of light shone about her dark hair. She rubbed her finger against his thumb — no, it was no dream! She was awake, she saw, she heard, she felt all this. . . .

When they alighted at the bridge of the Rialto, Lorenzo led her along the narrow pavement on the quayside and Lancelot followed them. They walked left into a dark square, and then to Dandolo Square, where they entered a glittering casino, the habitués of which belonged to the noble families. Lancelot remained in the corridor.

They passed a number of small rooms into which Jessica peeped. The women were attired in wide silk dresses with full, bunched sleeves adorned with finely embroidered gold and silver thread. The men wore short black mantles or long cloaks, rapiers at their sides. The precious stones upon the women's hands and the chased, jewelled hilts of the rapiers sparkled in the candle-light. Laughter and song mingled about them, and above the medley of sound rose the shouts of the gamesters at cards and dice. Embracing couples, whispering together, were the sole occupants of some of the rooms.

Lorenzo escorted Jessica into a small chamber with purple hangings and only two velvet-upholstered chairs.

"I want to be in the room where they are playing," she said.

"I shall order the musicians here, Jessica."

"I don't want to be alone in a room with no other people," she declared, and stepped back. Lorenzo followed her.

"Are you afraid to be alone with me?"

"I am not afraid at all. No one can do me harm. But I came here to be among people."

They entered a hall in which a number of couples were seated. Jessica took a chair at one of the tables and Lorenzo sat at her left. He called for wine.

"And I want some of that warm Chinese drink," Jessica said. The tea had that year been brought to Europe by the Portuguese, and the wealthy Venetians had been the first to introduce it into their households.

"How do you know of the beverage?" Lorenzo asked.

"A Holland merchant brought some for my father. It's an excellent drink."

"Don't you ever take wine?"

"Outside the house I drink but little. Tonight I prefer not to have it at all."

"The Jewess is far too clever!" Lorenzo thought to himself crossly, but he ordered tea.

They sat there for a long while. Lorenzo could not keep his eyes from Jessica, but her eyes wandered restlessly. Everything appeared so fresh, so beautiful, and the feeling oppressed her that she would soon have to go back to the ghetto. Must she? The ghetto seemed to her so distant, as though on the other side of the Adriatic, somewhere on a barren, lonely island — did she have to return to it? She regretted having yielded to Lorenzo and come to the city. Venice was no longer an enchanted dream-city, it was a place of tangible realities — from now on she would long for it as for some magnificent castle in which she had lived and from which she had been banished.

"Drink a little wine," Lorenzo cajoled her. She sipped a drop from his glass. Two old musicians, wearing discarded gentleman's attire, came up and played tender love-songs. Lorenzo tried to embrace her, but she eluded his grasp.

"It is not done, Jessica," he remonstrated. "When the musicians play for a couple, it is customary that they embrace."

"Have you no shame?" she flared up. Lorenzo laughed. "An embrace that comes of habit isn't true love," she cried.

The musicians played their violins with closed eyes, opened them for an instant and, when they saw that the young gentleman and his damsel were not in each other's arms, modulated their voices more softly to muted strings. Finally Lorenzo threw them a coin and they scraped their way to a neighboring table, at which sat an elderly noble in a gold-brocaded doublet with a young lady at his side.

"That is one of the members of the Signioria," Lorenzo told Jessica aside.

"Has he no wife?" she asked artlessly.

"What ought he to do?" chuckled Lorenzo. "She is an old woman, and the sap of life is rising in his veins."

Jessica watched the wrinkled-visaged old man fondle the girl at his side, while his sagging lips mouthed passionate whispers. The sight aroused her disgust. She allowed Lorenzo to hold her arm, stroke her fingers, imprint kisses upon her hand, but when he tried to embrace her she drew back. Lorenzo played with her fingers and, seeing the two rings she wore, remarked, "I haven't seen two such large diamonds on the hand of any young girl before."

"My father had them from a merchant of Frankfurt. They cost two thousand ducats. My late mother left them to me."

"Your eyes shine more brightly," Lorenzo vowed in a low voice. To himself he thought: "Confound it, that beastly old Jew has the riches of Croesus!"

Jessica gazed at the diamonds and the image of her mother formed itself in their glinting depths. At some distance from them sat a lean old matron festooned with jewelry, at her side a much younger man. The old woman bore a slight resemblance to Jessica's mother, and she felt indeed as though she were in the same room with her mother, and that she would soon glance at her. The diamonds in her rings glittered at her angrily: "Hurry, Jessica, flee for your life! Do not disturb the lasting rest of your dear mother! She defended you from Father, who never let you leave the ghetto, and he was right. . . . Do you know whose hand is caressing you? Perhaps it was his hand which flung the holy books into the bonfire . . . or pelted the stumbling old Jewish peddler with stones. See that old man sitting opposite you; he has left his old wife at home and is expiring of love for the young courtesan. 'What ought he to do?' asked your companion — such is their love, my child, my child! . . ."

"I must go, Lorenzo," said Jessica abruptly, starting out of her reverie.

"But it is only midnight, dear Jessica."

"You agreed to the condition that if I wanted to return, you would not hinder me."

"Just a little longer, sweet Jessica —" He kissed her palm.

Two players dressed in the masks of man and woman entered the hall. They presented Boccaccio's tale of the monk who disguised himself as an angel and tried to persuade Lisa the beautiful that he was the Archangel Gabriel who had come to earth out of his overpowering love for her — and Lisa believed him. . . . A gale of laughter shook the gathering, and Jessica too laughed herself to tears.

"It was very funny," she told Lorenzo when the actors had finished and were about to portray another scene.

"And you, naughty one, wanted to go!" he rebuked her.

His words reminded her that the hour was late, and she rose. Lorenzo begged her to stay for another half an hour, quarter of an hour, but she turned a deaf ear to his blandishments. They passed room after room, Lorenzo at her side. Here she saw a drunken couple lolling on a carpet amid the laughter of those standing on the threshold; there someone was retching and sick. A quarrel had broken out among some intoxicated gamesters over their cards. She hurried through the rooms until, coming into the corridor, she saw Lancelot curled up asleep. Jessica touched him upon the shoulder and he awoke. He jumped up as the lackeys around him tittered at his discomfiture. "He drank some of the dregs out of the gentlemen's glasses," one said. "He's a little overcome."

"It's not decent of you to be drunk, Lancelot," she expostulated.

"I am not drunk," he replied, rubbing his eyes.

"Never mind, Lancelot, so long as you don't shout in your cups where silence would be more seemly," Jessica smiled.

"Don't worry, little Signorina Jessica. I know my position."

They left the casino. The streets were dark and empty. Here and there a lantern flickered, tired voices in song came from somewhere — or it seemed to Jessica that they were tired — and soon they were at the gondola. She wanted to take leave of Lorenzo, but he insisted that he would not permit her to travel home in the dark night with a half-tipsy servant.

"I can be depended upon far better when drunk than he sober. I know you, the nobility," Lancelot thought, but he kept quiet.

They sat once more in the cabin, the servant alongside the gondolier and Lorenzo sprawled at Jessica's side, their backs to Lancelot and their faces to Venice. The air was cool and he wanted to protect her with his body but she shrugged him off.

"You are very stubborn, Jessica," he remarked.

"As every woman," she dimpled.

"As a daughter of the Jews?" he smiled.

"Possibly."

He sat silently for a while. He waited for her to speak, to lean against him — but the moment did not come. When his stratagem failed, he again stroked her hand and murmured softly into her ears with all the eloquence of the Venetians.

"Why are you so silent, my Jessica?"

"I am afraid my father will awake and find me gone," she

answered. But it was not the real reason. Her father slept soundly at night and if he awoke it would never enter his mind to see if she were in her bed. A mysterious sorrow had seized her: perhaps because they were floating away from Venice, or perhaps the memory of her mother troubled her heart.

"Lovers are sad," Lorenzo whispered.

"And why are you not sad, Signor?"

"I am very sad, Jessica, and only the wine I drank gives me courage. It was such a wonderful evening, sad and beautiful. When can we meet?"

She evaded the question and said, "I have but one request to make, Lorenzo. Promise me you will fulfill it."

"Nothing would be too difficult for you. Command me to swim the Adriatic!"

"It's much less that I'm asking. Please, don't come upstairs when my father is away."

"That is far more difficult than swimming the Adriatic, Jessica."

"You will be found with me and it will be too late to draw back."

"But how can I keep away?" He brooded. "All right, I agree, provided you promise to come out with me again one evening soon." Jessica hesitated. "Why are you silent? Another Jewess would be delighted if a Christian took her out freely into the nights of Venice."

"I am not the foolish Lisa. I know where all this is leading."

"Have I behaved improperly? It is best I should know it while there is time."

"Remember you are a Christian and I am a Jewess!" The cry almost burst from her throat, but for some reason she could not utter it.

"It is best I should know it while there is time." His voice shook.

"I did not say you had behaved improperly, but you must understand my position too. This step means leaving my father and cutting off from the whole of my past."

"I will be your father. I will be your past and your future, Jessica." His lips were near her forehead.

"If I loved you not the least little bit, Lorenzo, I would not steal out with you secretly at night. But if you really love me, you must understand my position and have patience."

"There is no man in Venice who will love a woman as Lorenzo his Jessica!"

"Either I shall never be yours, Lorenzo, or I will be yours with all my heart and soul, like the daughters of my people."

"Your people are too morose, and love is not for the morose." It was in Jessica's mind to say that every oppressed people must go its way morosely, but she could not tolerate such an argument, and merely smiled. "Yet the people of my race know how to love. The first great love of which we know was that of Jacob for Rachel, the second of Yehuda for Tamar his bride, and the third of David for Bathsheba."

"Yes, they were indeed great loves. I had never thought of it before."

"I want to have a love as pure as Jacob's and Rachel's."

"But you will not have me wait fourteen years," he jested.

"If I remained single another fourteen years, you would not wish to look at me then," she laughed.

Lorenzo chided her for entertaining such suspicions of him. She thought of Don Samuel. He had come into her mind when she had said she wanted a love as pure as that between Jacob and Rachel. She could expect such a love if she accepted him. But the darkness in the narrow canal dispelled all thought of the young scholar. Venice was glowing with light, Venice floated on gay evenings, and Lorenzo was Venice. . . .

The gondola halted at the bridge outside the ghetto gate. They alighted.

"And so, Jessica, when do we meet again?"

"Lancelot will inform you."

"Tell me but the day, and I shall hope for it as for the stars."

"The unexpected is more delightful." She put out her hand in parting. He moved to take her into his arms, but she recoiled.

"Do not anticipate!" she warned. She withdrew her hand and went through the gate, which had swung open.

Lorenzo jumped into the gondola and returned toward Venice. Out of the stillness his voice in song came back faintly to her ears, and the fading notes caught her in a net of silver mesh. The dark alleys irked her, and she held on to Lancelot tightly. A night watchman came toward them. "Don't be afraid," Lancelot whispered, and as the man drew close, the servant said in a loud voice, "What say you, Camillo? There is nothing like the Tuscan wine in all the world"—and the watchman passed by without accosting them.

A few minutes later Jessica was safe in bed. Pangs of remorse hammered in her heart: she had told Lorenzo too much and now her soul was no longer free. Men playing at cards, women with bare bosoms—the Venice of imagination was far more delightful than the one in reality, and she had destroyed the Venice of her dreams forever. Had she not accepted Lorenzo's invitation this time, she might have planned her life more carefully. What would her mother have said if she were still alive?

She conjured up the vision of Venice shimmering under multi-colored lights as she floated down the Grand Canal that evening, the flaming torches of the people strolling to the casino, the strains of music, the madcap gaiety and, above all, Lorenzo's courtship of her: his eyes brimful of love, his caressing hands of love, his lips redolent with the fragrance and speech of love—the love of a free man, a nobleman, to whom all the world was open. Love, love . . . And yet her heart smote her, and she suffered the agonies of remorse.

"Shall I confess all to Don Samuel and tell him, I love you, pure Don Samuel, hasten and take me with you?" she pondered. "Hasten and take me with you!" she murmured several times aloud, but in her heart of hearts she felt like loathing him for his gentleness, the innocence of him in spite of all his learning, and for not being as masterful as Lorenzo and, at the same time, even more so. Strength, will power, that was what a woman expected of a man. . . . She lay languidly and watched the gloom of night filtering through the window-panes. She goaded herself not to sleep as though she feared that if she closed her eyes, they might not open ever again.

Chapter Six

Two days before Ascension Day, the second of May, the new Capitano Grande, the chief of police, honored the ghetto with his visit. The small square in front of the synagogue had been swept clean from the early morning, and in the center a divan had been placed for the noble guest. The members of the small committee, including Shylock the communal treasurer, welcomed him at the gate and escorted him to the temple square. The Capitano Grande was clad in a black velvet doublet with balloon sleeves. Attending him was his assistant, a young man, wearing a bright sleeveless doublet. Both men were clean-shaven, and their large eyes reflected the tranquillity of carefree men.

The guest sat upon the divan and his assistant stood at his left side. Opposite him stood the bearded elders in their Sabbath headgear. The two groups symbolized the great gulf between the city of Venice and the ghetto: on the one hand, the ruddy-cheeked, self-assured Venetians at peace with the world; on the other, the Jews, their faces lined and their eyes, which had seen so much wanton wickedness, deep in their sockets. Shylock was the only one of the elders who stood with raised head, and in his hand he held a small pouch. The Capitano Grande made a brief speech, promising the Jewish "residents" his full protection. Then Shylock approached, bowed his head, and tendered the pouch which contained sixty ducats. The visitor rose and returned to the principal gate, to which the elders accompanied him.

That had been the custom from the day the ghetto was founded. Since he had served as treasurer, Shylock had given four such pouches to successive chiefs of police; and, as always, he was brimming with indignation.

"The promise which the Capitano Grande gave was a false

one," he declared to the rabbi and Tubal, who walked at his side. "And those ducats he got out of us were real gold." He paused. "Sixty ducats! How many clothes we could have bought with that money for the poor children, and how many sugared cakes we could have had baked for the poor at Pentecost — so that we need not go on continually raising money from the few well-to-do men."

"But the outlay was worthwhile," Tubal ventured, "if only to see with our own eyes how the Capitano Grande of noble family demeans himself to take a present of sixty ducats."

"You are wrong, my friend," cried Shylock. "We are as dogs in their eyes, and if a silver purse hangs around a dog's neck, I too would take it without feeling disgraced. If they only hated us! They are contemptuous of us, and we are like so much offal to them."

"For our many sins," groaned the old rabbi, "for our many sins."

Platitudes like these always roused Shylock's ire. "Are our sins greater than theirs?" he demanded. "Our own wicked are as the righteous compared with the most upright of the righteous among them!"

"Do not say such things against heaven," the rabbi reprimanded him. "We were given the Law from Sinai, and it is bounden upon us to fulfill all the six hundred and thirteen precepts, which we do not, for our sins."

The rabbi's reply by no means mollified Shylock.

"The Almighty endowed us with charity funds," exclaimed Shylock querulously, and began counting them upon his fingers. "The Free Loan Fund one, the Ransom of Captives two, the Poor Brides' Dowry three, the Good Samaritan four, the Wayfarers' Aid five, the Loving Soul six. . . ."

"Stop it, Shylock," Tubal protested. "Don't you know the saying: He who gives not to Jacob gives to Esau?"

"For our sins we have charity funds on every finger, on every joint of the finger," Shylock grumbled on. "And they have crawling, creeping creatures with funds dangling from them back and front: they trade in slaves, their palaces are full of

66

bawds, their hands are bloodstained — what is the use of speaking about our many sins?"

The rabbi walked on with downcast head and, out of indignation against Shylock, remained speechless. To mollify him Shylock went on, "Yes, give to a charity fund, I say, but not to the Capitano Grande." But again his vexation overcame him, and he added, "To give them ducats of gold? I'd give them the golden ducats of the Haggada: Wrath one, fury two, anger three, distress four."

"Be careful of tell-tales," Tubal warned him in a low voice.

"I do not conceal stolen goods and I have no fear of them," Shylock cried. "And whoever does it and helps the Christians at their pillage and desecrates the Name, may just as well tell on me. Not a *scudo* will he get out of the Prisoners' Aid Fund."

This was a covert allusion to an incident of a few months earlier when the small committee approved twenty ducats for one accused of concealing stolen cloths, and this might have led to the resignation of Shylock as the treasurer, and the rabbi as the head of the community — the two leading offices — the first because of his wealth, and the second because he occupied the unpaid post of head of the largest community in the ghetto, as was the custom among the rabbis of Venice.

Someone remarked upon Shylock's allusion, and again there was almost an explosion of the wrath which had been subdued with so much effort. The rabbi commented,"Why revive first sins, Shylock? Let each man go about his business."

Shylock went up to his house to partake of the midday meal. Jessica divined only too well her father's mood after the "visit" of the official delegate, and was careful to say nothing to upset him. He thundered invective against the Venetian scoundrels and, as he had previously ticked off on his fingers the number of communal funds, he counted in like manner the heavy taxes levied upon the community of twelve hundred individuals, mostly poor — the annual tax for the permit to dwell on Venetian soil, the marine police tax, the canal preservation tax, the war tax, and more withal. Jessica remained silent. He recalled the Church of San Jeremy tax — the island ghetto was in the same neighborhood as the church — and raved:

"And the dues to their blessed Church of San Jeremy? If Jeremiah were to arise from his tomb, he would sound a new lamentation over this unholy device of the Jews having to support their church — a nest of oppression and persecution against us!"

"You must not complain, Father. The lot of the Jews here is much better than in the Papal kingdoms. The law protects the Jews here, and you certainly have nothing to be vexed about." But if she thought to calm him, she was mistaken.

"What am I doing here?" he demanded. "Better bread with salt than the disdain and contempt and extortion we suffer! *Condotto* — a fine name they've chosen for extorting money for the permission to remain in their country — *condotto,* pah! They've made a contract with us, they say. They allow us to breathe the air of Venice, as though they created these islands and this water, and this foul air of the filthiest of the islands of Venice, they keep on asking for ducats and more ducats, to be heaped with gold! I'm sorry now that I did not go to Palestine in my youth. I thought it a bad example for the rich to leave the community a prey to the Venetians in order to save their skins. But it was a mistake, a donkey's mistake and now I am old, and have no one at home to understand my error."

Jessica made no pretense of understanding his spirit. She never understood him and least of all now. A door had been opened to her in the great world, and as her love grew for Lorenzo, the greater grew the barrier between Shylock and herself.

"I have no one in this house who can understand me," he proceeded. "And when I tell you to take a husband, so that I can have a son who can relieve me of the burden, you are afraid, as though you were still only thirteen."

"Please stop it, Father," she murmured.

" 'Stop it, Father! Stop it, Father!' " he mimicked her. Do you believe you'll always remain young and the men will squint at you and whisper, What beauty!"?

Jessica rose, offended, and hurried to her room. Shylock jumped up, pulled open the door of her room and, standing on the threshold, shouted, "Isn't it hell enough outside without your embittering the rest of my years in this house? I'm mocked outside and have a stubborn daughter at home."

"I get it from you!" Jessica stormed. He stood still for a moment, then broke out again.

"From me? Why haven't you got a sense of honor too? Their festivals attract you, their revels are more precious to you than your own father! You bring shame upon my head and I gnash my teeth with disgrace."

Jessica wanted to reply, but he slammed the door of her room and stalked out of the house.

Upon entering his banking-shop, Shylock's gaze fell upon Lorenzo, and he felt as if a sword had pierced his chest. Actually he was the best of the inspectors sent by the authorities to supervise the old banker's business and, the main thing, he was overfond of money, a welcome quality among inspectors. But at this moment, when he was seething with rage against the Christians who held merry-makings for which Jessica hankered, the presence of the Christians working for him was distasteful. "If they've already locked us up in the ghetto, why don't they leave us alone?" he thought. It was enough that the Christians jeered at him in the Rialto without his having to tolerate some of them, including this supervisor, in the house which he and his father had built with so much effort.

A short time later Shylock was summoned to come immediately to the rabbi's house opposite his own. He found there two constables of the Doge's own staff.

"The day after tomorrow, on Ascension Day, the Sensa festival begins," one constable opened. Shylock knew from past years what they were after, and interpolated, "Times are bad, taxes are heavy, the precious carpets pledged with us we had to sell at public auction legally."

One of the men cut him short. "We know that tune, Jew! Tomorrow at ten of the clock we shall send for twelve carpets, eight cubits long by eight cubits wide, and you will be paid their assessment."

"We are unable to afford so valuable a gift," Shylock insisted.

"The whole of Venice is pledged with you Jews. The banqueting hall of the Doge's palace must be ready by two of the clock tomorrow afternoon, and if the carpets are not ready you'll tread the Bridge of Sighs — to the dungeons."

"We'll try to obtain six," the rabbi tried to bargain, but the constables turned on their heels and left without further word or parting salutation.

"For our many sins, for our many sins," moaned the rabbi, rocking himself to and fro.

"'For our many sins,'" raged Shylock, "they'll grab everything, they'll impoverish even the few rich men in the community, and the rabbi will resign himself to it and beat his breast to the refrain 'For our many sins.'"

"Does the choice lie with you not to give?" the rabbi queried him.

"Perhaps that is the way. Let them put all of us in prison, every single one of us. I can't see them clapping the whole community in the dungeons."

"I see that you have a better opinion of them than I have," the rabbi smiled ruefully.

Shylock lowered his head and breathed heavily. "What will be the end of it all? We toil and they stuff themselves — they'll reduce us to the last crust of bread, we'll all become hewers of wood and drawers of water."

"The eternity of Israel will not betray us," said the rabbi piously. "We have been giving the authorities tens of thousands of ducats every year for scores of years, for generations, and they've not finished us."

Shylock stood up, heartened. "And they won't finish us either! We'll give them the carpets. We'll give them furniture fit to receive princes, all at their own evaluation, of course. They'll take our gold with their left hand and return us tenfold pains with their right. Let them now eat and drink. The morrow will come, and we Jews will still sprinkle earth over the grave of their Republic!"

"Amen, may it be His Will!" supplemented the rabbi devoutly, lifting his eyes to the ceiling. Shylock shook his hand in parting, saying: "It's their Ascension Day. May they all ascend to heaven."

The Sensa festival, which began two days later, went on for a fortnight. It was the celebration of the Republic's marriage with the Adriatic. On Ascension Day the Doge went out with his Council of Ten in the *Bucentauro,* the gorgeous state barge, to the sandy shore of the Lido. He threw a ring into the Adriatic, saying: "Lo, thou art sanctified to us, O sea, as a symbol of our dominance for ever and aye!" Thousands of gondolas swarmed after the *Bucentauro,* with the populace clad in gala finery and jewels. Practically every man, woman and child in Venice went out to the Lido sands to witness the magnificent spectacle which had been held annually for hundreds of years, and visitors came from neighboring countries to admire the greatest ritual in the world. Pavilions had been erected in all the squares, especially the Square of San Marco, in which merchandise from all parts of the land was exhibited. Ascension Day was not only the occasion for the hilarious jubilations of the Sensa, but also the great fair for merchants who came from far and wide, East and West. Treasures beheld in no other city or country were displayed in the pavilions of St. Mark's Square. The Sensa festival had lasted only eight days in preceding centuries, but in the last generation, in the sixteenth century, when the prestige and power of Venice began to decline with the opening of the Cape of Good Hope route and the rise of the Turkish Empire, the Sensa was celebrated for two full weeks with immense pomp and circumstance, so as the more vividly to demonstrate the power and wealth of Venice. In the days of the Doge Lorenzo, who had occupied the ducal seat until three years earlier, the Sensa had out-shone in brilliance any preceding observance. The Doge himself was of the family of

Pietro Orseolo, with whose memory the glittering celebration was associated, and his wife Zilia was a descendant of the Doge Enrico Dandolo the Great, conqueror of Constantinople, who was the moving spirit of the Fourth Crusade at the end of the twelfth century.

When the Doge had cast the ring into the waters of the Adriatic for the first time, he had said, "For all the days of my life the Sensa will grow in splendor as befits my fathers and the fathers of the Dogaressa." And that in fact was what happened. Each year the number of visitors increased, and this year delegations had come from all Christian lands, including the most remote; the rulers of the Stato del Mar — the Greek islands and adjacent shores which belonged to the Republic of Venice — and the Republic's ambassadors at foreign courts and at the Vatican also gathered; and the waters of Venice witnessed a vast array of gondolas and rowing-boats and canoes of all types, lavishly decorated with banners and carpets and other fabrics upon which their owners could lay hands, ready to cross to the Lido.

Lorenzo made certain a week before the Sensa of a place in a gondola for himself and Jessica. His good friend Antonio of the Barozzi, agent to the Doge's Court, promised him two seats in his gondola, which was one of the simplest of the nobles' gondolas. Antonio was a merchant, and it was not his habit to invest in property which brought no returns. Antonio and Portia, his wife, had been told by Lorenzo of his love for the Jewess, daughter of the richest banker in the ghetto.

"We'll go out in the gondola of a *primo nobile* to the Lido tomorrow. We'll be among the first thousand," Lorenzo informed Jessica upon the eve of the festival, when he found a moment to run upstairs to her.

"I cannot come, Lorenzo," she replied.

"My good friends who own the gondola await you. I cannot go without you."

She kept silent.

"Samuel Morro's hand is probably in this!" he blazed out.

"It's untrue!" she retorted.

"You told me ten days ago that you were looking forward to the Sensa."

"I am still looking forward to it, but I cannot go out on the first day. The Sensa will last fourteen days. We'll see later."

"You have to—"

Jessica drew herself up and rejoined, "I do not have to."

"To Hades with you then, Jewess!"—Lorenzo felt like saying to her and departing. But her proud mien transfixed him, her large and brilliant eyes stirred him, and he stood as a suppliant before a princess.

"Please, Jessica, don't send me away," he pleaded.

"I haven't sent you away, but I will not tolerate being bullied by a man."

"Forgive me, dear Jessica."

"I have forgiven you, Lorenzo—" Then, after a pause: "I shall come to the Sensa, but I cannot leave the house in the first days of the festival."

"I thank you with all my heart, dear Jessica—when will you come?"

"I'll let you know through Lancelot." She reflected. "Do not come and ask me. I beg of you not to come up to the house, and if request has no force, I forbid you!"

"As you wish, Jessica." He bowed and left.

How good she felt when he left, and how bad. She was proud of herself for having been so sharp with him, apprehensive lest she had exceeded the measure and injured his Venetian, Christian self-esteem to the point where he would not return. "Or perhaps now is the time for me to be rid of him?" she asked herself. Everything in her cried for life outside the ghetto, yet she was possessed of an obscure fear of that life in the city of Venice. Was it anxiety for her father which bred this fear? Did the memory of her mother stand as a barrier, as the ghetto walls themselves, between her and the gentile Lorenzo? Or was it the influence of Don Samuel which deterred her from taking part in the Christian celebrations? She could not say, she could not make her mind up. Her heart wavered between fear and love, resignation to her Jewish fate and mutiny against it — between the fiery love of Lorenzo and the mute love of Don Samuel — and it seemed as though both had seized her, were tugging at her, and that her body was being torn apart. . . .

On the morning of the Ascension Day, the Jewish shops were closed, as on all Christian holy days, and Shylock remained at home. Don Samuel this time gave Jessica her lesson in the forenoon. It was a talk, or rather a monologue, for he spoke and she kept silent. To hide her inward confusion, she put a question now and then, for form's sake, as to the meaning of some Hebrew phrase. It seemed that two hearts were beating within her. At one moment she regretted having rebuffed Lorenzo's invitation to accompany him to the Sensa; then she felt drawn to Don Samuel, wanting to take his delicate head within her arms, and wordlessly to place her future in his hands — forever and ever. She interrupted Don Samuel in the middle of his discourse.

"I have a headache, Don Samuel. Pray let us put off the lesson," she urged.

"Were you sleepless last night, Jessica?" he asked tenderly, like a father asking an adored child.

"Yes, I thought of my mother. She was alive a year ago, and now . . ." Tears filled her eyes. Don Samuel found nothing to say. He expressed his sympathy by stroking her hand. Jessica sighed deeply. She remembered Lorenzo's caresses: the passion tingling in his fingers as he stroked her hand; and Don Samuel touched her without responsive thrill. "The Lido sands will be gay with music and song today, and my mother lies buried there in the earth," she continued in a muffled voice.

"Her soul has gone to heaven, Jessica," he whispered. On rising to leave, he said, "I'll come back in the afternoon, and we'll sit on the roof and watch together the endless line of gondolas — will that please you?"

"Of course, Don Samuel." As he stood at the door she added, "You understand me better than my father does."

"He is troubled in soul, Jessica. You must understand him too," Samuel ventured.

After the lesson Shylock detained Don Samuel for a short while. He spoke to him of business matters and, as was his wont, abused the Christian debtors who were delinquent in repayment. Don Samuel looked at him and nodded his head in assent, but he only heard half-sentences. His ears echoed Jessica's silver accents: "You understand me better than my father does."

Walking home he seemed borne upon airy feet. He had stroked her graceful hand for the first time — and she had not objected. How gently she had told him that he understood her disposition. Jessica was a little girl, little yet sweet, and he had but the one desire to take her into his arms like a tiny child, to press her to his heart. But when he entered his room, a profound dejection overcame him. Had he vexed her by saying that she must also understand her father? Would she think that he was reproaching her with an unfair attitude toward Shylock? The two hours he had to wait before returning to Jessica passed liked days, like weeks — he craved to be near her again, to look into her face, and to be assured she was not displeased with him.

That morning the skies had been sparkling blue, May-time in Italy, and only a light breeze blew in-shore from the sea. At noon fleecy cloudlets, frail and gossamer, tumbled in regiments and legions across the sky as though they had come to behold the Sensa. The breeze grew, the cirrus joined into one great heavy cloud which canopied the sky. As Don Samuel walked back to Shylock's house toward two o'clock, a light shower fell. Gloomy autumnal thoughts oppressed his spirit: perhaps Jessica was angry, would remain closeted in her room, and refuse to come out to him; or perhaps she had changed her mind and gone out with Lancelot to the city of Venice.

He breathed more easily when he entered the house and found father and daughter at their meal.

"Will you eat with us?" Jessica invited him.

"No, thank you. I have already eaten," he replied. He judged from Jessica's tone that she harbored no resentment of him, and reproved himself for having wasted the long hours in idle conjectures. Shylock's glance fell upon Don Samuel's rain-wetted hat, and a joyous gleam lit his eyes as he exclaimed, "Rain! May it spoil their precious amusement!"

The skies had meanwhile grown more thunderous, and a heavy rainfall began — the like of which Venice had rarely before experienced at this time of year. The Doge's departure for the Lido was delayed an hour, two hours; but the rain did not desist. A gusty wind whipped the puddles, the streets were flooded, and people stayed indoors. The Doge nonetheless left in his stately *Bucentauro,* followed by several scores of gondolas with the aristocracy. But the other thousands of gondolas remained moored at the canal-sides, and the populace kept at home.

The storm rattled the window-panes, and Shylock rejoiced. "That is the music of the God of Vengeance! The voice of the Almighty upon the waters! They prepared for many weeks for the festival, they spent tens of thousands of ducats and stole carpets and furniture from us, but God above sports with them!"

Lancelot, who had gone out to the festival, came back drenched. He related that many hundreds of boats had overturned and been carried out to sea. The pavilions in San Marco Square were flooded. The gondolas had suspended all passenger traffic on the canals, and he had been compelled to run the roundabout route over the Rialto bridge and across the bridges spanning the narrow canals.

Stefano stood in the doorway and, surveying Lancelot, who was soaked from head to foot, burst out into hearty laughter. "I begged him, Signor, to let me go to the Sensa just once!"

"I thought you a wise man, Lancelot," Shylock chuckled. "The wisdom of princes and potentates cannot prevail against Him who is all-wise."

Lancelot went out cursing whoever had invented the Sensa, and when he saw Stefano grinning at his sorry appearance, he cuffed him soundly. Shylock walked about the room and spoke as though to himself, "This is the first time in my life that I'm really enjoying myself." Turning to Don Samuel, he said, "See, Don Samuel, Stefano was annoyed with Lancelot for not taking him along to the festival, and how exultant he was at Lancelot's misfortune; and we the Jews, who are harried from dawn to dusk, how should we not exult when the Almighty mocks at them and spoils their celebration? They spit in our faces, and He returns their spittle to them full measure in a flood."

Don Samuel returned a forced smile. Jessica sat with lowered head. When Shylock's gaze fell on her, sitting as if his words had meant nothing to her, he grew exasperated and shouted, "And she sits mourning, as though the Temple had been destroyed before her eyes! Please, Signorina, put on your holiday gown and your veil of honor, and go off to the splendid festival."

Jessica jumped up, stared at her father for a moment as if she meant to answer him, but thought better of it and walked rapidly to her room, closing the door behind her.

Don Samuel burned hotly at the affront. He was reluctant to excite his quick-tempered employer further, but could not contain himself entirely. "She had a headache. I cut short our lesson because of it."

"Nonsense!" Shylock snapped. "If it were not for the rain, she would not have stayed home."

Don Samuel forbore to say anything more. He too was sorry in his heart that the festival had been called off. He would have been with her alone on the roof-top; he would have gazed into her flashing laughing eyes, looked at her lovely limbs and body, patted her smooth hand. It was as though he had lived in anticipation for this festival occasion many years, from the early days of his youth, and now his festival had gone with the rain.

Chapter Seven

THREE DAYS LATER THE OVERCAST SKIES OF VENICE CLEARED AND THE Council of Ten announced publicly that in spite of his illness the Doge had acquiesced in the will of his people and would leave on the morrow, a Monday, once again at the head of the procession of celebrants to the shores of the Adriatic. The populace forgot the great damage done by the storm and in tens of thousands flocked the next day through the narrow streets

77

and into the squares, biding the time impatiently for the afternoon.

When Shylock left for a brief call at the rabbi's house, Lorenzo managed to summon Lancelot and asked him to inquire of Jessica if she would attend the Sensa with him that afternoon.

"Lancelot's eyes are in his head," the man said. "I have already asked her but she declines."

"Then go and persuade her to meet me this evening," Lorenzo urged. He took out a coin but Lancelot refused it.

"Camillo and Salarino, the guards at the gate, won't let us pass through at night," Lancelot stated.

"I'll give each of them two ducats," Lorenzo promised.

"They're risking their posts, and I'm not going to sneak out with my little mistress and mislead her."

The young nobleman went on coaxing him, but realized that Lancelot was plotting something with the guards and said, "I want to meet you in the city."

"I too am risking my livelihood," Lancelot complained. But he agreed to a meeting with Lorenzo at two o'clock at the Rialto bridge.

"You will travel with me in the gondola as my servant, Lancelot," said Lorenzo. The man was overjoyed at being privileged to go out to the Lido with the nobility. His eyes wandered about, lest some Jew of Shylock's acquaintance might see them together, and hastened to take leave of the other.

Returning to the house Lancelot told Stefano of his talk with Lorenzo. Stefano warned him not to be duped.

"Don't worry, my friend. He won't buy me for a mess of pottage," said Lancelot boastfully.

"How much will you ask for?"

"As I agreed with Camillo and Salarino — three thousand ducats gold, not a *scudo* less. I'll go on telling him lies about Don Samuel until he sees red."

Lorenzo left the ghetto and saw Camillo at the gate.

"Is it true that you won't let the Jewess pass the gate at night?" he demanded. "Lancelot told me." The constable muttered something inaudible but the nobleman pressed him.

"Salarino my comrade has gone out to buy some wine, Messer. He knows the matter better than I," he said.

Lorenzo waited until Salarino arrived, but the constable did not await a question and burst out, "If four people imperil their living, Messer, they must have some guarantee."

"Four? What four?"

"I and my comrade, Lancelot and Stefano."

Lorenzo turned on his heel, jumped into a gondola, and asked to be rowed to the Rialto. He sat and brooded. That gang have schemed something, he thought. He tried to guess what bribe they would demand, and it did not occur to him that thousands of ducats were at stake. He had no money of his own and spent all that he earned — he was, after all, one of the nobility — but never had he regretted more not having saved up something for such a contingency.

Lorenzo awaited Lancelot from one o'clock and the servant came half an hour early. They went by gondola to Antonio's residence; Lorenzo went in and then came out with eight men and women. The males wore embroidered mantles with rapiers at their sides, while the women had on their fingers sparkling stones which blinded Lancelot's eyes. "I always thought that only the Jews had gems," he thought, "but the jewelry of old Leah, Shylock's wife, were grains of sand compared to these."

The party entered a gondola decorated with carpets, and Lorenzo motioned to Lancelot to get aboard. Lancelot did not dare step on a carpet. He had never sat in such a splendid gondola, not even in his dreams.

A trumpet sounded. The gilded *Bucentauro* moved off, followed by the gondolas of the Council of Ten — the *magnificoes* — and several vessels with prelates bearing holy relics, statues, and other ritual ornaments from the Cathedral of St. Mark. After them came the gondolas and barges of the members of the Grand Council and the rest of the aristocracy. The hundreds of gondolas lined up outside Antonio's house moved off and a few minutes later their turn came. Thousands of banners bearing the heraldic device of the winged lion, the crest of Venice, fluttered in the breeze, and the strumming of mandolins mingled with the piping of flutes and beating of drums. The gems of the women sparkled on all sides, as though the stars had descended to take part in the Sensa, Lancelot thought fancifully.

Some time later Lorenzo came over to Lancelot, who was seated on the back bench.

"Now tell me what you want," he asked.

"I don't want anything," Lancelot rejoined after a brief pause.

"You are very artful," Lorenzo shook his head disapprovingly.

"Of course I'm clever if I've managed to get a ride to the Lido in a gondola fit for kings," the man chuckled. But his face resumed a serious expression.

"I've never troubled you for aught, Lancelot. I've always given you a ducat."

"Yes, thank you very much, Messer." Lancelot gazed at Portia, wife to Antonio. "Who is that lady?" he asked.

"You too have discernment, I see," Lorenzo smiled. "She is the wife of the owner of this gondola."

"Jessica is more beautiful than she," Lancelot remarked.

"You know that I love her, Lancelot. She grew up on your knees and trusts you. It's your duty as a Christian to help me."

After a moment's silence, Lancelot embarked on a long speech. He narrated how Don Samuel sat every evening in Jessica's company and never left for a moment on the Sabbath. Once he opened the door of her room suddenly and found them fast in each other's arms. Ostensibly he taught her but actually they had long talks together. They spoke in Hebrew but it was enough for a man to see their gestures to know of what they talked. Don Samuel was a cunning Jew. He had captivated the old man and would gradually win Jessica's heart, and he would win her, never fear. . . .

One prevarication bred another, and Lorenzo sat as though stunned and bewildered, drinking in the poisoned talk. The blue skies seemed to him to grow dark as they had been yesterday and the day before during the storm, and the gay music sounded in his ears like dirges. The happy laughter of his friends in the gondola irritated him; and had he not wished to hear every word Lancelot had to say, he would have put his fingers into his ears. No shadow of suspicion entered his mind that the man might be lying. For a moment he grew infuriated at Jessica: The Jewess is tricking me! But his love was deeper than his anger, and the more he believed Jessica was drifting away from him, the greater his ardor to capture her, no matter what.

"You are a good Christian. If you help me to convert her to the true faith, you'll be doing a pious deed." Lorenzo's voice shook.

"It's a very complicated affair, Messer, very complicated, and it can't be solved by a pious deed."

"Ask what you wish, Lancelot, so that I may achieve mine."

Lancelot wrinkled his brow and without looking at the nobleman said: "Stefano is in the house and I can't do a thing without him. There's two already. Then Camillo and Salarino at the gate take turns at the watch, one goes on duty one night and the other the next. There's another two. Their danger is much less than mine and Stefano's because their officer rarely comes along at night to see that all's well. But I and Stefano would have to quit the old Jew's household."

"What of it? You'll find work in a Christian house," Lorenzo soothed him.

"It's not as easy as all that. A servant clings to his job like a dog to his kennel. I've been serving in the Jew's house for twenty-eight years and two months."

"Then what do you want?" Lorenzo asked. But Lorenzo went on as if he had not heard. "The old Jew will find out, there's no doubting, and we must be ready to clear out. I told Stefano: 'I've great influence over little Jessica, I'll convince her that she must marry Lorenzo. We two will go South, buy a farm and become farmers.' I'm to get two-thirds to split with Stefano, and Salarino and Camillo will get a third — they've agreed."

"Tell me once for all how much you're thinking of!" Lorenzo cried impatiently.

"It's a big sum, Messer. The whole thing's not worth it, Signor Lorenzo." In his wiliness Lancelot began tantalizing the ardent suitor by urging him to give up Jessica. He pointed at the handsome ladies seated opposite them. "Venice is as full of beautiful women as the water in the canals — why should you demean yourself and chase after the Jews?" He did not look at Lorenzo, who smiled sadly and thought, "What does this base menial know of life?"

"What are you calculating upon?" he asked aloud.

"Not just largesse, Signor, but gold ducats."

"How much?"

"I'm afraid to say. Try to guess, Messer."

Lorenzo thought for a moment. "Six hundred."

The servant burst into a bellow of laughter. The occupants of the gondola turned their heads to inspect the convulsed man. Portia said something in an undertone to the others and they turned away again.

"Don't laugh so loudly," Lorenzo frowned at him. "You're among aristocrats here."

"How can I but laugh? Can I buy two farms in the South with two-thirds of six hundred ducats? I can only buy land in the desert for small money like that, Messer."

"Then tell me how much you want, and be done with it."

"Six hundred and a cipher alongside," Lancelot uttered, sketching a nought in the air with his finger.

"Have you gone out of your mind, slave of a Jew?" Lorenzo almost shouted.

"I told you beforehand that the whole affair wasn't worth your while," replied Lancelot composedly.

"You've learned from the Jew how to skin people!"

"But you want us to help you to get the Jew's soul away, to entice his only daughter away, Signor Lorenzo. What is that sum against the price of Jessica, who has no peer in all the world? Five years ago something similar happened and three thousand were paid to those who helped and their helpers' helpers, and she was as the garlic rind compared to Jessica."

"Have you ever seen a sum like that in all your life, you slave of a Jew?"

"My bread and water are certain and I have no need of money

but if I leave the Jew's house I'm not going to look for new masters."

Lorenzo fell silent and mused. He knew that he could not put off Lancelot and his fellow-conspirators with a paltry amount and wondered where he could raise the money. He might ask his friends for a loan — but would they give him thousands of ducats? But he was afraid that if he lost this opportunity it might not return, and he began to bargain with Lancelot. They reached the Lido without arriving at a compromise. Only on the voyage back to Venice did they come to an agreement. Lorenzo promised Lancelot three thousand ducats — he quoted the incident of five years ago which Lancelot had recalled — and the servant gave in as if unwillingly, shaking his head dubiously and saying that his friends would stone him when they knew how meager the amount to which he had agreed. They even agreed that Lorenzo would deposit the money with the sacristan in the Church of San Jeremy, to be paid over only after Jessica was anointed at the baptismal font.

"I'll handle this matter carefully," Lancelot promised, "but you mustn't upset it all by hurrying." He described Jessica's temperament and added, "She has an inclination toward you and she loves Venice, but one false step will overturn the whole basin."

"I rely on you, Lancelot."

"That's not enough. From now on you mustn't come upstairs into the Jew's house. I'll be your spokesman to her. I'll bring her out in the evenings to Venice, not against her will, heaven forbid! You can't outwit a girl as smart as our Signorina Jessica. I wouldn't mislead her for all the riches in the world, because I love her as my own daughter, or my sister. But when the proper time comes, perhaps in a month or a couple of months —"

"Two months?" Lorenzo protested.

"We haven't fixed a date, Messer. She weighs each move carefully — even her father doesn't know her as well as I do. You've given me a difficult task and you have only one task — patience."

Lancelot's chiding manner was not to Lorenzo's liking but he felt greatly relieved that Jessica's servant had given him his word to do everything to ensure that she become his. He had no cause to doubt Lancelot's genuine intentions for, after all, the man wanted to earn the large sum promised him.

When they alighted from the gondola at Venice, Lorenzo besought Lancelot to persuade his mistress to accompany him that evening to the casino. The servant refused and shook his head obstinately to the young man's pleas. "Put the money down first and then I'll begin the job."

Lancelot walked off to the nearest gondola-stage to return to the ghetto. Lorenzo gazed after him enviously — that coarse domestic would shortly be seeing the most gracious creature in all the world. . . .

But now that Lancelot had gone, the problem of finding the money overwhelmed him. Three thousand gold ducats and he hadn't even three hundred in his pocket! Antonio was the only one who could help him — would he lend him so large a sum? With trembling knees he mounted the stairs to Signor Antonio's residence as though entering a court of justice to hear sentence of life or death pronounced upon him.

Chapter Eight

BUT IT WAS NOT UNTIL TWO DAYS LATER, ON THURSDAY EVENING, that Lorenzo found the right opportunity to bare his heart to Antonio and Portia.

"After all, three thousand ducats is a huge sum," Antonio said. "You are putting our friendship through an ordeal."

"As soon as she will get away from the Jew, I will return you the money many times over," Lorenzo replied, and he smiled significantly.

"We will do it out of friendship alone," interrupted Portia, and Antonio agreed. "I never want to make profit out of a good deed," he said.

"I thought that . . ." Lorenzo stammered.

Antonio smiled at him forgivingly, and continued, "I have on me a larger sum of money than you want: four thousand and six hundred ducats. But I intended it to pay for the ship arriving from India which I bought from Filippo. He was on the verge of bankruptcy and I saved him with my purchase."

"But the ship has not arrived yet," Portia remarked. Lorenzo threw her a grateful look. Antonio thought awhile and answered, "That is so. The ship is due to arrive in about fourteen days, and no sooner does she lower her anchor than I have to pay the full sum. And if I don't, I must pay a thousand ducat fine and thus lose a purchase worth three times its price."

At this, Lorenzo interjected, "But two weeks is an eternity! After all, I have dealings with money-lenders. If you will agree, Antonio, I am sure I can easily obtain such a loan."

"Under no circumstances!" Antonio retorted. "I do my trading in cash only, praised be Holy Mary! I would ask you to wait two weeks but I know very well that even then I won't have any cash, because all my ships are out to sea. A loan? These days only the mighty, under whose tread the earth trembles, are ready to make loans. It is not dignified for me to knock on the doors of money-lenders."

Lorenzo was stunned. He knew he could not wait a week, not even a day. It occurred to him for a moment that he might be able to raise the loan from Shylock who was eagerly looking for trustworthy borrowers. But at the last words of Antonio, he held back from mentioning the matter, and he cried, "Two weeks! And do I hear this from Antonio, the agent of the Doge!"

"Antonio, the Doge's agent, acquired all he possesses only because of his caution," replied Antonio.

Once more Portia intervened, saying, "On one side of the scales of decision hangs the possibility that you will have to raise a loan, my dear, and on the other side, the great act of piety to lead a straying soul into the true faith."

"It is precisely what I am thinking, dearest," Antonio interrupted her. "It is clear that God is proving us, for it is vouchsafed to only one in millions to bring into our faith a member of that stiff-necked people. And, I ask you, what meaning has life without the joys of Paradise?"

"Only the rewards of Paradise are to be cherished, for this world is but a vanity of vanities," agreed Lorenzo. In his imagination he saw himself at night holding in his embrace the lovely form of Jessica who had become his wife, and his blood coursed hot within him.

"Make our friend happy, Antonio," urged Portia in her melodious voice. She raised her shining eyes to heaven and like a dove's wing she lowered her long slender hand on Antonio's shoulder.

"You are right, Portia," Antonio replied, caressing her hand. "This is a most important matter. Sometime today or tomorrow our friend Graziano is due back. He is the only prospect I have from whom I might be able to borrow such a large sum on a long term." And, turning to Lorenzo, he asked, "For how long do you need the loan?"

Lorenzo was overjoyed. And, after he had overwhelmed Antonio and Portia with his thanks, he replied, "Until she will leave his house, let us say two months —"

"To make sure, let us say three months," said Antonio. "And all I expect from the money she will bring you is what is coming to me, not a farthing more in order, Heaven forbid, not to lessen the merit of my pious act."

"How happy I am to see you so pure in your faith, my dear!" cried Portia, and drawing his face between her delicate hands she kissed him.

"The first kiss that Jessica gives me will be before your eyes, my noble friends!" Lorenzo cried in a voice choked with jubilation.

Portia threw him a charming smile and Antonio, as if he had just come to the end of a thought, said, "Graziano is just the right man for this."

"And what if he will not come in time, my dear husband?"

"He is coming in a day or two."

"And even if he will not come in time," continued Portia, "there is still the possibility of getting a loan."

"A merchant just like Antonio!" enthused Lorenzo. "I am the person who . . ."

Antonio interrupted him. "I do not like loans, except when I have no alternative."

As he spoke, Antonio opened an iron closet in the wall and took out two money bags, which he gave to Lorenzo. Lorenzo tried hard to conceal his excitement. He embraced Antonio, kissed the tips of Portia's fingers, and went away rejoicing. And Antonio and Portia sat for a long time on the sofa talking about what they had just done. They were happy that they had successfully passed through the test of friendship as well as of piety, for in reality it was they and not Lorenzo who had performed the great meritorious act.

Graziano did not come in two days. Not even in a week, and Antonio became uneasy. Portia tried to reassure him. And Lorenzo, who called on them every evening, told Antonio that he was prepared at all times to obtain the loan for him. But Antonio put him off from day to day.

On the ninth day, Graziano returned. He had been in England where he had purchased a large stock of garments. How overjoyed was Antonio when he beheld the magnificent gondola bearing his neighbor to his palace! That evening he went to pay his respects to Graziano, but he did not mention the matter of the loan to him because there were many visitors present. The following morning Antonio thought that it would be well to let him rest up from his journey. But on the next day he called on Graziano and told him what he wanted of him, but without mentioning the purpose of the loan.

The short-built Graziano with the elongated face cast an uneasy glance at his friend, and on his fleshy lips there spread a smile that extended even to the wrinkles in his face. He pulled Antonio onto the sofa beside him and replied, "I never carry with me such a large sum as you have mentioned for longer than two days, because money was created for the purpose of multiplying itself in trade."

Antonio pretended indifference in order not to lower his dignity. Graziano poured wine into two bowls and, laughing, continued, "I came pretty near being stranded on the journey because I had spent all my money on merchandise in England and France. I even bought some Spanish-dyed feathers — if Suleiman the Turk wants them he can have them!" He spoke in a loud voice, and rapidly, gesticulating with his hands like a dumb man. He recounted with enthusiasm the details of his business affairs.

That evening, when Lorenzo called on Antonio, the latter told him that he would have to raise the loan.

"Never mind! I will take care of that!" cried Lorenzo, but his heart pounded painfully. The only one he knew who could lend such a large sum was Shylock — but what if he should refuse?

"Shylock is the right man for this," he said.

"Shylock — ?" echoed Portia through finely chiseled lips, and looking at Lorenzo she began to smile. Antonio, regarding them both, began to feel light-hearted. Suddenly, Portia and Lorenzo burst into loud laughter; Antonio smiled.

On taking leave, Lorenzo embraced Antonio, and kissed Portia's hand, as she said to him in the firm voice of a man, "Love is the highest happiness. Soon you too, friend Lorenzo, will be happy."

That night Lorenzo could not fall asleep, fearful that Shylock would turn him down; but after he had drunk three bowls of potent wine he dozed off.

In the morning he arrived at the banking shop earlier than usual, and as soon as Shylock came down Lorenzo told him that he had an important client who wished to borrow from him three thousand ducats.

"Three thousand ducats?" Shylock repeated in amazement. It was the first time that Lorenzo had brought him so large an application.

"It's for Signor Antonio, agent to the Court."

"Three thousand! Well, just as I loathe the small loans of three ducats which the Signioria has forced upon us, I am averse to giving one man as large a sum as that."

"Signor Antonio is a nobleman of the Barozzi family."

"You come of a noble family too, and I wouldn't lend you three thousand."

"I respect you for being so frank, Signor Shylock. Though Signor Antonio has ships in all parts of the world, he is hard-pressed for ready money."

"Who is this Signor Antonio? I know all the merchants in the Rialto — is he short and thin?"

"No, he is tall and handsome."

"Hasn't he a long nose slightly crooked?"

"Yes, that's he. He's one of the most illustrious merchants, agent to the Court."

"And I always took him for a proselyte!" chuckled Shylock. He remembered that Antonio had jeered at him several times, but did not bring it up. After all, which of the Christian merchants had not taunted him, or spat in his face? "There's no doubt he's a safe borrower, but it's a lot of money."

"One of his ships is carrying a cargo worth tens of thousands, and he has four cargo vessels," Lorenzo said. He argued with Shylock in favor of the loan but when he saw that the banker was in no mind to hurry, he declared, "He's my friend. He doesn't need the money for business. He needs the three thousand because only two weeks ago he performed a worthy deed which required a large sum."

"A worthy deed? I was right then in saying that I suspected him of being of Jewish stock," Shylock laughed.

"No, he is a descendant of Marco Sanodo, who conquered the Cyclades in the days of Dandolo the Great."

"Well, the main thing is that it's a large sum."

Lorenzo went on lauding Antonio and, seeing that Shylock still hesitated, remarked, "He performed an act of charity and for my part I'm ready to waive the commission on the loan."

"Your being among Jews for a few months has had a good effect on you," snickered Shylock. He shaded his eyes with his hand and ruminated over whether or not to grant the loan. "Twelve per cent without the cost of the commission," he thought, "that's a slice not to be sneezed at." He rose. "I'll think about it," he said.

"I promised to bring your reply this morning."

"Why the panic? I'll think it over awhile and let you know." Shylock went out of the shop. He was going to consult his friend Tubal.

"I know that long-nosed knight," Tubal told Shylock. "He's very esteemed among the merchants. He's a fabulously rich man, confound him."

"And he's just as wicked as the rest," Shylock supplemented. "Why should I make it easy for him to get what he wants?"

"They're all as wicked as he is," contended Tubal. "Why should you give such a sum to three or four merchants when you can have business with one who's safe?"

"And Lorenzo is waiving his commission."

"What — ?" said Tubal with open mouth. "Then it's a good business."

"He's a friend of Antonio's house and actually he's quite a good fellow. But you're right, Tubal, it's a good business." As he was about to leave, he added, "It's generally not so bad when those proud gentiles need us."

Returning to his counting-house, Shylock told Lorenzo that he agreed to grant Antonio the loan, but he wanted it perfectly clear that Lorenzo was to give up his commission. Lorenzo nodded his head affirmatively and said nothing to hide from Shylock his great delight.

"How long does he need the money?" Shylock asked.

"Three months."

"It's not too long — very good, three months. On no accoun longer."

"Signor Antonio is now in the Rialto. Shall we go to him?" Lorenzo suggested.

"No!" declared Shylock. "He's a borrower like all other client Let him come here."

"I'll go and fetch him."

"Not now. It's a big affair and cannot be concluded in th open shop with people coming in and out. Let him come t me this evening. He is of the Barozzi. The guards will let hir come into the ghetto."

"But he's a *magnifico*, agent to the Court." Lorenzo tried to argue Shylock into going with him to Antonio.

"No! Let him seek his loan in the Doge's Court on the strength of being a scion of a great soldier of the time of the Doge Dandolo, if it pleases him. And, by the way, why cannot his *magnifico* friends like the Contarini, the Memmo or the Poloni lend him the money?"

"They have no open heart for a good thing," Lorenzo winked. "Even if you wrote on the promissory note that you guaranteed a pound of your own flesh if you didn't pay up on the date of maturity, they wouldn't lend the money to anyone who needed it."

"But if you offered them modestly twenty or thirty per cent, they'd give their loans willingly! That's worth more than a pound of flesh!"

"True, true. That's how they are," Lorenzo smiled ingratiatingly.

"At all events," Shylock declared, "whether he's a *magnifico* or a *primo nobile* or anything else, if he needs me he can come to my house, and at an hour that suits me."

"You're quite right," Lorenzo returned. He left the shop to tell Antonio that Shylock agreed to the loan. At the corner of the street he collided with Lancelot, from whom he inquired about Jessica.

"Very well indeed. She is happy and cheerful — but be careful, Messer, that she doesn't learn a word of all this, or everything is lost." This is what Lancelot always said whenever he met him.

Lorenzo turned his back on Lancelot and hurried on his way. "She is happy and cheerful —" He loved her, and yet why did these words of Lancelot grieve him? "An obstinate Jewess!" he thought to himself, and grave doubts began to trouble his mind again, but not for long.

Cheered now that Shylock had insisted on Antonio's coming to his house and that he, Lorenzo, would be able to see her and feast his eyes upon her loveliness, he sat in the gondola and looked up the palaces along both sides of the canal. In his imagination he saw himself living in one of them soon, perhaps in two weeks or possibly in two days. . . . He no longer doubted that Jessica would be his — he relied utterly on Lancelot, who obviously knew what lay before him.

Shortly after sunset Lorenzo brought Antonio to Shylock's house. Shylock was delayed at the synagogue, and Lancelot sent Stefano to bring him.

"Is Jessica at home?" Lorenzo asked Lancelot.

"No, she has gone to visit a friend."

"Perhaps she's in the company of that beastly Jew from Capo d'Istria?"

"Heaven forbid, what has she to do with him? She is having supper with a young lady friend of hers." Lancelot bowed and withdrew.

Antonio looked at Jessica's portrait.

"Is that she?" he marveled. "Why, that is the face of a Madonna!"

"You won't now say, my friend, that Lorenzo has left his senses!" the young nobleman cried proudly. "That painting is the work of Paolo Caliari Veronese."

"I believe that I saw a Madonna of his somewhere very much like this portrait," Antonio remarked. He tried to remember where it had been. "I know. Caliari Veronese gave this likeness to 'Venice' in that oil-painting of his called 'Ceres Bringing Her Gifts to Venice' — a remarkable artist! He is getting famous and is becoming a dangerous competitor to Tintoretto — but he is so peculiar in his behavior: he roams about like a hunter, as though men were beasts of the field."

"That is probably also by Caliari," said Antonio, pointing at the head of a young Jew done in oils hanging upon another wall.

"That's the master of this house in his youth," Lorenzo grinned

"Caliari hadn't been born then." He added, "Yet the pigments are as fresh as if they'd been put to canvas only yesterday. If I hadn't known that Tintoretto was only forty years old, I'd have sworn it was his work."

"Probably old Titian did it. The Jew's father was a wealthy man, a money-lender from the sole of his foot to the crown o his head, and he had no lack of money," said Antonio with brusque certitude.

But Shylock in his youth had been painted by the famous Jewish artist Rabbi Moses of Castelazzo, who had been permitted by the Signioria of Venice in his time to publish the Bible illustrated with his paintings. It was the same Rabbi Moses the painter who had thirty-five years ago brought David Hareubeni to his house in the ghetto and presented him to the community leaders.

"The Jew is late," Antonio grumbled.

"His servant has gone to fetch him," replied Lorenzo absently. His eyes were fastened on Jessica's portrait.

"How comes a Jew to have Christian servants? The Council has forbidden the Jews to employ Christians as servants."

"But they can hire Christian servants on the Sabbath to turn out the lights and stoke the fires in their synagogues, and they employ Christians in their houses under the pretext of their being synagogue sextons."

"These Jews know how to evade the law," remarked Antonio with asperity. "They can crawl through the eye of a needle." Lorenzo saw that his friend was on edge with impatience at the tardiness of the Jew and began to speak in praise of Portia.

"Your Portia is more beautiful than she," he said, indicating Jessica's portrait. Antonio's face lit up.

"She is also generous and intelligent," he boasted. "Was it not she who told me, 'You must do this for our Lorenzo'?"

"Portia is the cleverest of all the women of Italy and the kindest of all the women in the world."

"That is true. Wisdom and kindness rarely go together in one person —"

"It's seldom that a golden heart and the divine form of a goddess and the lovely face of a Madonna blend as with your Portia," Lorenzo vouched. "The Lord was in good spirit when he created her."

Antonio glanced up at Jessica's portrait again. "And He was in good spirit, too, when he created her," he smiled. "You are earning a fine woman and great piety with her, my friend."

"And you, my friend, are partner to this pious deed, you and your Portia."

"I am glad I helped you, Lorenzo—" Then, after a short pause: "I recollect that friend who gave me his assistance when I went to Belmont to win Portia's heart. It was shortly after Bassanio passed her by for Nerissa her servant maid. The nobles and princes came once more to try their luck at choosing the proper casket which would gain them Portia's heart, and I was one of them. And then a friend lent me a large sum of money so that I might come to her in a splendid ship surrounded with servants, as was fitting for one seeking the hand of the rich heiress of Belmont. Just imagine, she sold all her fine estates and came with me to Venice because I wanted to engage in trade—"

"I hear footsteps on the stairs," Lorenzo said.

"And now," Antonio added, "she loves Venice as deeply as she loves me; and me as she loves Venice."

"I hear two voices," said Lorenzo disquietedly. He feared lest Shylock was bringing Don Samuel whom he detested.

"We were delayed a little," Shylock said as he entered the room with Tubal. "Have you been waiting long?"

"Very long," Lorenzo replied. "This is Signor Antonio."

Shylock gazed with sharp eyes at Antonio, who seemed only upon the threshold of his prime and wisdom, and reflected for a moment with envy that this young man was one of the greatest merchants in Venice and agent of the Court.

"Signor Antonio!" he cried. "I know you from the Rialto. Three thousand ducats! A large sum, Signor Antonio." He turned to Tubal and asked him to come back in an hour.

"I told you that the matter brooked no delay," Tubal complained. "We had almost concluded our business."

Shylock opened the door to Jessica's room and said to Antonio and Lorenzo, "Please go inside a few moments. I shall be free almost at once." Lancelot lit an oil-lamp and, when both noble men had entered, Shylock closed the door. "Did you see th face of the agent of the Court when I told him to go into th second room and wait for me, Tubal? How often has he insulte me in the Rialto, damn his name! I take pleasure when I can humble a proud gentile."

"If the affair weren't urgent, I'd go. After all, he's an important aristocrat."

"Doesn't an aristocrat eat and drink, as you and I?" Shylock demanded. Then his face grew overcast. "You always come to take big donations of me, Tubal, as though I were the heir of Anselmo del Banco himself — always exaggerating, exaggerating. . . ."

"The Almighty has helped you, my friend. Most of the community are poor. It's forbidden to engage in trade or craft in Venice itself. The Jews live off each other in the ghetto and have a life of penury, and even the poorest of the poor gives half of his shekel to settle the Holy Land. If there are a few rich ones, it is proper that they should help to fulfill the greatest act of piety which the poor cannot afford — the redemption of the captives."

"In effect you're right, Tubal. But if I go on like this for ever, all I'll have left in my bank will be the worthless notes of Christian bankrupts, confound them." He sighed deeply and groaned, "Woe is me! Woe is me!"

" 'Every one that thirsteth, come ye to the waters,' " Tubal quoted the first verse of Isaiah, 55th chapter, in Hebrew — the customary response to the invocation of "Woe is me." "You said the same ten years ago, and the Almighty helped you, my friend. Just imagine that you were one of those about to be sold into slavery, and I was Shylock, and I didn't want to give the eight hundred ducats required of me — what would you say then?"

"It's no good, it's no good," muttered Shylock. "The pirates know that we'll ransom our brethren, and there's no captain who hasn't gone in for piracy."

"Of course it's no good, but it's worse not to help those unfortunates. We're getting near Pentecost, and it is the first time this year we're being asked to redeem captives. If I give four hundred, you ought to give four times as much."

"Exaggerating, always exaggerating," Shylock mumbled. Tubal

discerned that his friend would give the whole sum. "Well, then, I'll put you down for the contribution imposed on you."

"It's no good, it's no system," Shylock grated his teeth. "But if there's no alternative, I'll give what I'm asked to, but not in one amount."

"Does He too impose conditions when He confers His blessings on you? If we don't ransom them within a day or two, they'll all be sold as slaves — and how shall we be able to celebrate the Pentecost tomorrow night if they're to be in slavery on the day of the Lawgiving because of our hard-heartedness?" Shylock made no rejoinder. Tubal shook him by the hand and, on parting, said in a choked voice, "Thank you, my friend. You will be privileged to see the solace of Zion and Jerusalem!"

"If only, if only," Shylock mourned. "The waiting for the Messiah is hard for us to bear." Tubal repeated his blessing and left.

While Tubal was negotiating with Shylock, Antonio inside Jessica's room was fuming as though he had been brought to the Jew's house to be mocked at. Lorenzo pacified him. He was delighted to be waiting in her room. Here was her bed, there her shoes. He sat at a small table at which she sat every day. . . . He waited every minute for Jessica to come in, to be alarmed, and to say, "Fly from here. Do not bring disaster upon me!" Whereat he would laugh heartily and reply, "Your father brought me in here, Jessica, do not be afraid"; and a lovely smile would be his reward. "Isn't it wonderful, Jessica, God Himself arranged that I should sit upon your chair, opposite your bed, at your father's wish," he would say; and she would whisper gladly, "Such are the little ways of the great God of Love."

Breaking the silent communion of his imagined dialogue, the door opened and Shylock invited them to enter the dining-room.

"We have waited over-long," Lorenzo remarked as a sop to Antonio's esteem.

"I had a far more important affair, Signor Antonio," Shylock asserted. He motioned them to the sofa, and sat opposite on a chair. "And now, Signor, I promised Lorenzo I would give you the loan you have asked for three months. Three full months? You know it isn't my custom to give loans for the period they are usually solicited. Let us say then, ten weeks. Under no circumstances can it be more! But, of course, that is only a trifling detail. The important thing is that I am prepared to comply with your request since you need money because of the worthy deed you performed a short while ago, and also because Lorenzo is foregoing his commission. A rare thing indeed, both you and he will be sanctified — San Antonio!"

Antonio's face reddened. "You are mocking at us, Jew!" he snapped.

"If not I, then who will mock at you? Our poor who go round the streets buying old clothes and crying, 'Hep! Hep!' or our daughters and wives who grow blind over sewing and cleaning their tatters?"

"Your daughter seems healthy and sound enough," Antonio interjected with a smile, glancing up at the portrait.

"Thank God! How many girls in the ghetto have a well-to-do father? Shylock who can have himself a golden hat must wear this one, this crimson rag that some buffoon devised! And why? So that I may be recognized in the Rialto as one of those who can be gibed and spat at, to be pelted with stones and peeling!"

"It is not we who enact the law," Lorenzo tried to mollify Shylock. It was by no means pleasant that Signor Antonio had to listen to these rebukes from the Jew. Antonio at that moment reflected how just was the law excluding the Jews from the life of the citizenry — were it not for such discrimination, a Jew might reach the Doge's seat!

"But you're glad of it, every Christian in Venice is pleased with the fifteen edicts issued by the Vatican, although none of you will agree to have the Pope as the ruler of your Republic. The doctors you need you permit to live outside the ghetto and wear the black *beretta,* in spite of the Pope's ban. Don't you need us too, the bankers? Just imagine Venice without the Jewish money-lenders — desolate islands inhabited only by reptiles. You call us 'usurers' because we live off the lease of the money we lend, just as a landlord lives on his rents. If you need money and do business getting you fifty per cent, a hundred per cent, why do you revile us for asking ten per cent? You ought to give us twice as much without hesitation."

Antonio read a hint of large interest in Shylock's last words. "We performed an act of charity, and now I hope you won't demand an exorbitant interest rate."

"I hope that I am not helping, even indirectly, to build a church with my money," Shylock said.

"No, no! An act of friendship!" cried Lorenzo.

Jessica came in. She was astounded at seeing Lorenzo. He was confused and lowered his head so that he would not meet her father's searching eyes. Jessica sought something in a closet.

"Go out, Jessica!" her father ordered.

"In a moment," she replied.

"At once!" Shylock shouted, jumping up. Jessica hurried out.

"Why do you harass the girl, Jew?" Antonio asked. Lorenzo gritted his teeth but remained silent — had he not come to take the loan he would have heaped oaths upon Shylock.

"I cannot stand the inquisitiveness of women," Shylock answered. "Business affairs are for men, and not women."

"Your behavior is likely to give the impression that you are accustomed to shady dealings," Antonio sneered.

"Here is the inspector; he knows my affairs," Shylock returned. Antonio's sneer had cut him to the quick and as the opportunity was his, he decided to reciprocate. "Have you a house, Signor Antonio?" he asked.

"No," the other replied. "A shrewd merchant doesn't invest his money in houses, he does business with it — they repay manifold the rent that he gives."

"So that if you forbade us to acquire houses, it was only for our own good, and we never realized it," Shylock said bitterly.

"And his noble wife hasn't one precious jewel; gems are a dead treasure," Lorenzo supplemented his friend.

"Then all your wealth is at the mercy of the waves," Shylock laughed.

"I have a great trade and it is spread upon many waters."

"Job had sons and daughters, cattle and sheep and camels, and one day he lost everything. The Sabeans fell upon the oxen and took them away, the Chaldeans made off with the camels, the fire of God burned up the sheep, and a great wind from the wilderness smote the four corners of his house and it fell upon his sons and daughters — and he remained as naked as the day he left his mother's womb!" He spoke in high temper and his eyes flashed animosity. Antonio was boiling. Lorenzo tried to correct the bad impression made by Shylock.

"That was thousands of years ago, Shylock," Lorenzo smiled.

"Ships are made of timber and the anger of the seas is like the anger of Genesis!" Shylock retorted. Antonio remained silent. He found it undignified to enter into an argument with the Jew. Shylock was not satisfied, and added, "Job in his country and time was greater than the *magnificoes* of Venice."

Antonio could no longer control himself and said sternly, "Don't forget, Jew, that one of the Barozzi sits before you."

Afraid that the whole deal would fall through and would cause hardship to Antonio, Lorenzo rapidly interceded, "Shylock is a good man but he is a Jew of some temper."

Shylock was delighted at having provoked the proud noble out of his composure, and replied; "I am no man of wrath, but even if a noble of the house of Barozzi wishes to borrow money from me — and such a large amount! — it is my right to test his mettle. Signor Antonio, many a time in the Rialto you have rated me about my moneys and my usances; still have I borne it with a patient shrug, for sufferance is the badge of all our tribe. You come now to me, and you say, *Shylock, we would have moneys.* What should I say to you? Shall I bend low, and lend you three thousand gold ducats! Shall I do this, Signor Antonio?"

"If you will lend this money," declared Antonio, "lend it not as to your friend."

Lorenzo muttered some indistinct words of appeasement. Shylock realized that he had gone too far, and did not wish to lose this excellent transaction, particularly as the loan would cost him no commission payment. He changed his tone and said; "Look you, Signor Antonio, what there is between us. You spurned me many a time, and I was silent, because the Jews have only one alternative — to suffer and be silent or to rebel and die, and I seek life as you do. My blood is red like yours, my heart beats like yours — have I come out of a womb of flesh and you of a womb of gold? I believe in my God as you believe in yours — why then this mockery and contumely?"

Speaking thus, quietly and collectedly, other than his wont, Shylock felt that he must show some gesture of appeasement, and the idea struck him that he could show that a Jew had no greed for gain. The idea became a strong desire in a lightning flash. "Yet, in spite of all this, we are all sons of the Adriatic, and I would live with you in friendship and fraternity, and here is the proof — I waive the interest."

Antonio and Lorenzo opened their eyes wide and stared at their host in great astonishment. "Are you jesting with us?"

"No, no!" responded Shylock earnestly. "I waive the interest."

"I said that you were a good man, Shylock," cried Lorenzo and wrung his hand.

"Would you still say that a Jew is a usurer, an unfair man?"

"Most fair — a charitable man —"

"I have brought the bond with me," said Lorenzo.

"He is quick," Shylock smiled. "The truth is that I have only two thousand ducats, and I have promised eight hundred ducats to another."

"You can get the balance tomorrow from Tubal your friend and put the other off for a few days," Lorenzo urged Shylock.

"Tubal has no ready money at the moment, and I cannot defer my promise. It is my contribution to the ransom of the captives whom Christians are about to sell as slaves."

"Eight hundred ducats as a gift?" Antonio marveled.

"Yes, yes," Shylock answered proudly and with some spirit. "It's the finest investment — capital and interest in the World to Come."

Lorenzo sat perturbed. He feared that unless the transaction was completed at once, Shylock might go back on his word. Antonio took Shylock up on his last statement: "It's very generous of you, very generous."

"But on your part it is very bad," Shylock sighed. "I sacrifice my precious moneys so as to expiate the sins of the Christians.

But of what use is it to complain? So long as we have the money, we shall ransom them and they'll become human beings once more."

"And when will Signor Antonio get the three thousand?" Lorenzo broke in.

"In a few days, not later than the beginning of next week. It's a large sum! My friend Tubal will help me to raise the balance required."

Because in reality Antonio needed the money only three or four days later, he said nothing and arose to go. Then Lorenzo, who was displeased with the postponement, rose too.

"Thank you, Shylock," said Antonio. "I am impressed by your generosity in lending me this money without interest."

Shylock's resentment flared up again. These Christians had heard of his reference to the captives sold as slaves with as little concern as if he had told them that the Christians were bringing horses to auction.

"And I grieve," he told Antonio, "that you listen calmly when you are informed of human beings sold as slaves and bonds-women, as though it were a law of nature. You revere the memory of your ancients who were tortured by the idolators, and spend your money lavishly to purchase their bones, and yet there are thousands of us, tens of thousands of innocents, whom the descendants of those tortured by the pagans now put to the fire and sword for their faith, which is the cradle of your own faith — you send them to the stake, rack their limbs in the dungeons, tear their flesh with pincers —"

"Not I or Signor Antonio," muttered Lorenzo. They walked slowly to the door and Shylock followed them. He went on speaking in a low voice, as though ruminating aloud: "Yes, they rend the flesh with pincers — tear off flesh from the living body." He suddenly lifted his bent head and said, as one struck by a brain-wave, "Wait a moment please." A broad smile spread over his bearded face and after a pause he added: "Lorenzo told me this morning that the nobles would not lend money to their brethren even if they pledged their flesh. The very idea of pledging flesh smacks of a great humor, doesn't it?"

"True," said Lorenzo off-handedly. He wanted to get his elegant friend away from the clutches of the Jew who addressed him with such cutting irony.

"I adore jesting, Messer," Shylock went on. "And so, Signor Antonio, let us go to a notary and you shall seal me there your bond; and, in a merry sport, if you do not repay me on such a day, in such a place, such a sum or sums as are expressed in the condition, let the forfeit be nominated as an equal pound of your flesh, to be cut off from what part of your body it pleases me." Antonio became sullen. "If it pleases you not, then God be with you."

"Why all this? Is there anyone more safe than Signor Antonio?" Lorenzo questioned.

"I know that a pound of man's flesh, taken from a man, is not so estimable, profitable neither, as the flesh of muttons. But I said it in sport, and if it comes upon me to jest thus with a Christian, why should I not do it? I do not ask anything that is against the law — what is my power that I should seek that which is not lawful? Yet I desire, Signor Antonio, that you should have the feeling that a Jew can and is entitled to hack off part of your flesh. Then perhaps it will shock you the more when you hear of the flesh of Jews being hacked off, or when they are thrown living into the flames, or stoned to death — for that too has happened in Venice!"

"I am afraid of that condition, Signor Antonio," Lorenzo said hesitatingly.

Antonio had no fear. Quite apart from possessing many cargoes upon their voyagings, he knew that this was a jest. He only paused for a moment to reflect whether he should degrade himself and accept the Jew's condition. His glance fell on Jessica's portrait. "I must abase myself," he thought. "The Jew mocks at me while my friend takes away his daughter with my money."

"The choice is yours, Signor Antonio," Shylock goaded.

"I am afraid," Lorenzo said uneasily. He knew Shylock of old to be a severe and wrathful man and he felt that there was something serious underlying this apparent drollery.

"Have no fear, friend," Antonio ejaculated. "If a Christian

acts charitably toward his intimate, let him do it with a full heart. My first vessel will reach harbor in two months at the latest, and another two are to arrive at the same time." Turning to Shylock, he said; "Let it be so, Jew! I am ready to seal the bond as you wish — when shall we meet at the notary?"

"If I fail to obtain the money before tomorrow morning, let us put off the affair until the beginning of next week, because we celebrate our Pentecost tomorrow evening."

"And our own Pasqua di Rose begins on Sunday," Lorenzo said dejectedly. "Promise Signor Antonio that you will settle this transaction by tomorrow."

Shylock thought for a moment. "Well, let it be so. As I have the mind to go on with this jest, it is best to complete it for the holiday, don't you think, Signor Antonio? But one detail I forgot though Lorenzo knows of it: two and a half months by the Jewish calendar, two and a half months from today."

Antonio stared at him uncomprehendingly. "Let it be so, let it be so," cried Lorenzo. "It's only a difference of a few days, Signor Antonio — it's a trifle complicated."

The old Jewish banker counted the date upon his fingers, without referring to a calendar, and declared, "You will have to repay me the money on the seventh of August instead of the eleventh — well, tomorrow at ten of the clock promptly at the notary, ha! ha! And the condition which you accepted, ha! ha!"

"It is a devilish and blasphemous jest," Antonio interrupted him, "but as I cannot forego the money at this time I'll accept it." He turned his heel upon Shylock and went on, and the disconsolate Lorenzo dragged after him. When they were still on the stairs Lorenzo fell upon Antonio's neck and in a choked voice thanked his savior.

"Will the ships come in time?" he kept on repeating.

"Of course they will, my friend."

"Then that scoundrel Jew's day of mourning for his daughter will come much sooner than one of your boats!" Lorenzo exclaimed and froth rose to his lips. He now felt that Jessica was truly his and there were no bounds to his happiness.

Shylock walked to and fro in his room, his eyes sparkled with joy, and he mumbled to himself, "There's still a brain in your old pate, Shelah! 'A blasphemous jest,' said he — blasphemous jest be damned! That I compelled him to sign such a shaming bond is worth the loss of the eight hundred ducats which Tubal got out of me this evening."

Chapter Nine

LANCELOT SPUN HIS SINISTER WEB AROUND JESSICA WITH CONFIDENCE yet caution, and she did not suspect that his unflagging devotion had an ulterior motive. When she was alone in the house the servant would find some pretext to come into her room and start a conversation, indirectly leading the discourse round to Lorenzo. He praised him to the skies and was fulsome about his taste, and the words were balm to her distressed soul. The qualms she felt the first few times on going out secretly at night had now passed and she left the house after dark more frequently now. She knew that no harm could come to her in company of the careful and faithful Lancelot.

On the first two occasions Lorenzo took her to amusement houses, but from then on they spent the evenings alone or with friends at Antonio's house. At first she felt out of place amid all this splendor and gaiety which smacked somewhat of dissipation; but soon her heart began to clamor for it all, and the mean ghetto, particularly of an evening, began to irk her more and more. Portia always gave her a cordial and gracious welcome, and saw to it that her guests were respectful to the Jewess. She was shrewd enough to know how to win Jessica's heart, and in her cultured way encouraged the young girl who had fallen between two worlds and fostered the resolve in her to follow her heart. Each passing day the step she was intending to take seemed to become less difficult, more feasible.

Yet the weeks went by and she could not summon up the determination to cross the ghetto bridge and go to Venice once and for all. It felt better for some reason to defer the audacious step, and the more Lorenzo spoke to her the longer she put off the day of her flight. "Tell me three days in advance," Lorenzo begged her, "and I will show you how to carry it out." She promised him. At every assignation with her, he would ask "When?" and she would answer, "Soon I will let you know something, my Lorenzo."

Fresh doubts had come to assail her, but in the depth of her heart she knew there was no repenting. She could not return. She had savored the night life of Venice, she had spent many a merry evening in Antonio's house, and she could not for a moment imagine life without all these. In her sleepless moods, when the doubts got the upper hand, she pictured the beauty of Venice, the tender wooing of Lorenzo echoed in her ears — and she was reassured. Out of the gloom the image of Don Samuel would appear; he rebuked her, threatened her, predicted the worst, and she stroked the edge of the pillow, without knowing what she did, and sought refuge with Lorenzo — sought and found it.

Every time Lorenzo met her, he wanted to ask her to exploit her father, but he held back. Even his heart, the heart of a lover, was eaten by uncertainty; and so long as he was not sure of her, he feared that a suggestion to steal from her father would anger her and that she would no longer come to him. For that reason it was convenient for him too that Jessica had not set the date for her flight. Yet at every meeting, when Lancelot waited in the corridor of Antonio's house for his mistress, Lorenzo went out and upbraided him for not bringing the matter to a speedy conclusion. "Little Signorina Jessica takes her steps slowly but surely," Lancelot assured him. But at times Lorenzo vexed him so much that Lancelot would say, "I'm ready to forego all the effort I've put into this affair. Take your money back from the sacristan and let's call it off." The slave of a Jew is capable of anything, Lorenzo thought as he left the man.

Lancelot had his own troubles with Stefano, and especially the constables at the ghetto gate. They had naïvely believed that it was a matter for a week, and Lancelot explained vainly that he could not mislead Jessica, bring her to the city and then not take her back home. They could not understand such tenderness.

"And what if she is angered at you? The main thing is that you will get the reward," they said. When they threatened that they would refuse him entry one of these nights on returning from the city with Jessica, he was alarmed at the possibility. But he immediately thought of a way to frighten them. "You cannot play games with Signorina Jessica," he said. "She'll at once jump to the conclusion that Signor Lorenzo asked you to do this, and will get scared of him. And what will be the upshot? She'll wait outside all night, and come in the next morning, and won't want to hear the name of Lorenzo again. And you'll be left high and dry with empty pockets."

The answer found its mark with Camillo and Salarino, but still they gave him no rest — day after day they made his life a misery outside as did Stefano at home. Lancelot cursed the day, sometimes in all sincerity, that he had thrust his head into this wretched mess. But he knew there was no escaping now and that he must complete it; for if he gave up and the affair fell through, the ghetto constables would disclose his plot to his master Shylock, and he would have to quit the house without a *scudo* in his pocket, and wander the streets abandoned and starving like a leprous dog.

So, the hardest lot of all was Lancelot's share. Jessica suffered from changes of mood; Lorenzo, from impatience and pining for his lady-love; Stefano, because he had to stay awake on the watch until they returned, for fear that Shylock might awake; and he, Lancelot, suffered more than all of them: Lorenzo abused him as did the Jew, Camillo and Salarino of the gates threatened him with all manner of dire things, even murder, and most difficult of all were Jessica's moods.

He could not understand the meaning of all her agitation and irresoluteness if she indeed loved Lorenzo. "She isn't sorry for her father," he thought, "so what stops her?" His simple mind found no other explanation for her hesitation than that she also had a fancy for Don Samuel, and she was still trying to make up her mind whom to follow.

He concealed this suspicion from Lorenzo so that he might not exert more pressure upon himself. But he kept his eyes on Don

Samuel. He found excuses to come into the room when Don Samuel gave his lesson to Jessica; he never saw anything wrong, but nonetheless could not rid himself of the suspicion. Sometimes during the lesson he would command Stefano to bend and spy through the key-hole if Jessica and Don Samuel were not embracing and kissing. Stefano often ran back to Lancelot in panic and panted, "I saw something like that," but when Lancelot hurried to peep through the key-hole himself he never saw a thing. "You're probably seeing what you want to see," he finally upbraided Stefano. "One can't rely on you even for these little things." And from then on he himself remained stooped at the spy-hole and kept vigil upon every movement that Don Samuel made. He never saw a false move but still his mind was not at rest. "He looks at her, confound him," he told himself uneasily, and whispered an imprecation through the key-hole.

During the hot summer days Jessica only took three lessons a week. When Jessica told Don Samuel after the Pentecost that during the summer she would take the lessons only on alternate days, he was perturbed but, containing his distress, asked, "Do I tire you?"

"No, but the days are very warm," she replied.

"Our sages said, 'If you leave me a day, two days shall I leave you —' It were better that we shorten the time and take the lesson daily," he said.

"I want to be free every other day," she replied curtly.

Don Samuel had not the courage to insist. "She probably understands why I proposed the idea," he told himself, and a slight flush mounted his face. To conceal his embarrassment he said that he had a lot of work in the banking shop and left.

The first few days when he did not see Jessica were hard for him, and he grieved all the more when he came twice a week in the evening to study Talmud with Shylock and Tubal and Jessica never came into the room in which they sat. But he resigned himself to the position. In his heart he justified her: how could a refugee, dependent upon her father's charity, dare await her love? Nine years ago a decree had been issued for the banishment of the Marranos "the impostors and forsaken of God," and under the influence of the Inquisition, foul winds blowing from Rome were now abroad in Venice; if the aged Paul lived much longer, the Marranos were faced with persecution and forced labor and even with burning — so that even if Jessica did desire him, was he entitled to hide his fears from her? He would bring calamity upon her; and if she were dear to him, should he seek her love. . . . These thoughts troubled Don Samuel, and with them he drove away the sorrow at her changed attitude toward him, sharply censuring himself for having conceived vain aspirations toward the beautiful, irreproachable daughter of princes. Yet he always waited eagerly for their lesson, and when he left was always depressed that it was over.

Don Samuel taught Jessica the Scriptures, and especially the Hebrew language of that period from letters which he received. He used to read her the communications of Rabbi Benjamin Nehemiah, who wrote to him from Civitanova, because of the trenchant style, and even copied the letters he sent to his teacher and friends at Capo d'Istria to read out to her. His own letters were most eloquent and the thoughts he expressed upon Judaism were noble. But Jessica never praised them — which grieved him deeply. He determined each time not to read his letters to her, but when he sat of an evening in his room, writing a letter and copying it, he polished the style and rounded the phrases so that he might read them during the next lesson. He had not hoped that the letters would win her heart, but he very much desired to impress her as a wise and intellectual person, so that she might give him an occasional thought for a fleeting moment in the day-time or at night. It was the sole surviving flicker of the many flames which lit his heart in those first days, and the tiny flicker he could not, would not extinguish.

Upon the seventeenth day of *Tammuz*, after the fast, Shylock invited Don Samuel home to supper. They had been told that day in the synagogue by a visitor from Rome that the proselyte Andrea del Monte, whose slanders had caused the Ashkenazic synagogue in Rome to be closed down two years earlier, was once more stumping and inciting in the Roman provinces. Shylock fulminated throughout the meal, as was his custom, at the oppression and persecution, and Don Samuel referred scornfully to those Israelites of faint heart who fled the struggle and bartered their immortal souls for gross materialism. Jessica tried to change the conversation to a less painful topic, but Shylock continued with as great acerbity as if he had been saying all this for the first time.

The meal over, Tubal came, and a few minutes later Jessica retired. Shylock took out of a hiding-place the first volume of *The Strong Hand,* saying; "I bought this copy of *The Strong Hand* from a Christian too for a goodly sum; Don Samuel doesn't know that the order to destroy all books was given because of the printing of *The Strong Hand.*"

Don Samuel protested that every Jew in Italy knew of the matter in all its aspects but perforce had to listen as Shylock told the narrative again. Rabbi Meir of Padua had prepared the manuscript of *The Strong Hand* for publication and gave the printing rights to Bragadini who established a printing-shop for the purpose. Rabbi Meir had previously offered the book to Giustiniani, who had succeeded Bomberg in the printing trade at Venice, but they had not agreed over Giustiniani's terms, which were unacceptable. When Giustiniani learned that Bragadini was putting out *The Strong Hand,* he hurried off and printed another edition, which he marketed at a lower price. What could Rabbi Meir do? If he went to law, what would transpire? The matter would drag on, and meanwhile Jews would buy the cheaper edition of *The Strong Hand.* He approached Rabbi Moses Isserles of Cracow, whose word was respected throughout the Dispersion, and laid the matter before him. Rabbi Moses Isserles excommunicated Giustiniani's edition and the impostor was given a mortal blow. But Giustiniani did not take it lying down. He brought the slander to the Pope in Rome that *The Strong Hand* written by Rabbi Meir of Padua contained strictures and obloquy against the Christian religion. Bragadini went and told the same tale about Giustiniani's edition. Both found proselytes who read into *The Strong Hand* what they wanted to find. The end of the matter was that the dispute between the two printers led to the proscription of both editions and of all the Jews' books. "The Venetian pirates grab hold of Israel's praying-shawl, and Israel suffers the knocks," Shylock stormed.

"Shylock, Shylock, how long will you go on like this?" Tubal remonstrated. "Give thanks to the Creator that we are still alive in spite of all their rascalities, and that even *The Strong Hand* is in your house."

Don Samuel pondered what he had just heard from the old banker. "The anger over injustices keeps our hatred alive, and the hatred of this human wickedness is the barrier which keeps us from assimilating into them, God forbid."

"You have refreshed me, my son. You are a Jew in all your limbs and veins!" Shylock cried, pounding the young man on his back.

"And I wanted to speak to Don Samuel this evening of another matter, important and esteemed," smiled Tubal. He first dwelt at length upon the grave wrong of living alone without a wife, and went on: "Since the days of the Ancona interdicts you have been a wanderer, but now that you have come to rest in Venice, you must take a wife." Don Samuel tried to stop him but a faint hope rose in him that the other might suggest that Shylock give him his daughter, and he let him proceed. "There is among us one of the greatest rabbis in Poland, Rabbi Mordecai Jaffe. He's a prodigious scholar too, a man who has a deep knowledge of the system of the stars, as they call it in the Italiano 'astronomy' and not 'astrology.' . . ."

"I shall not build a house in Israel," Don Samuel vowed, "until I have truly settled."

"It's not a good match at all for Don Samuel," said Shylock. "Rabbi Mordecai Jaffe is indeed a great Jew, but his daughter is not good-looking and her father is a pauper — Samuel is worthy of another wife."

Don Samuel sent him a thankful glance. "There is time yet," he said politely to Tubal. "Let us meanwhile look into the book." Thus the embarrassing subject was skirted and they dipped into *The Strong Hand*. Half an hour later Shylock lifted his head and said, "I am tired. Let us continue some other time, and I still have business to talk over with Don Samuel."

Tubal rose, exchanged a few more words with the others, and left. Shylock asked Don Samuel quite out of the usual to mount to the roof with him. Samuel asked if he had not yet blessed the new moon, but Shylock made no answer. But when they sat on the bench beneath the parapet, Shylock began, "I have long wanted to speak to you, Samuel. If I know how to divine the heart of a Christian borrower, I certainly can divine the heart of a Jewish lad."

The pale moonlight which illumined the furrows of his wrinkled face imparted a profound gravity to Shylock, and Don Samuel interpreted this opening speech as the prelude to some accusation. Perhaps one of the clerks had slandered him? Or perhaps Shylock had seen how he had stroked Jessica's hand that day? Shylock sensed the young man's distress and continued in a fatherly tone.

"You have done nothing wrong, my son, since you are incapable of wrong. In the eyes of the Christians you are wicked, my son, because you assaulted those taking you to hard labor and fled for your life and returned to your own religion; but in my eyes that is the greatest act of all your life, you have glorified the name of Israel, and may you be blessed for that."

Don Samuel felt that a heavy stone had been rolled off his heart but he had not yet divined Shylock's full meaning. "I believe," the latter continued, "that you desire my Jessica —" Don Samuel blushed and an embarrassed smile rose to his lips. "Perhaps my eyes, the eyes of a father, deceive me, but there's no gainsaying that she's the fairest of all girls in the ghetto."

The young man's face lit up. The lonely watches of the night . . . the moon, the stars . . . Had he not heard all this before in a dream? As one who had dipped into astrology he had lifted his eyes to the constellation as one seeking his fortune among the stars.

"She is very beautiful and wise," he rejoined in a low voice.

"Have I not shown that I can read the heart of a Jewish lad!" cried Shylock triumphantly. He rose and opened the door leading off the roof, peered out to make certain that no one was eavesdropping, muttered a curse upon those "gentiles" of his who could not be trusted, and re-seated himself alongside Don Samuel. His face became gloomy. "Jessica is the apple of my eye. What have I in life? My wife is dead. I have mourned three children — what else have I from life than grief and mortification?"

"Do not transgress with your lips," Don Samuel murmured.

"I am telling you all this after careful thought. I have no desire for a rich banker's son as my son-in-law; I have the money. Nor am I anxious to have a learned scholar who cannot tell the difference between a ducat of gold and a ducat of silver — when I die, what will such a one as he do with my money? I have built up my banking-house with great effort, and there is a purpose left to my wealth even after my death."

"I have nothing to say," Don Samuel trembled. "The Almighty brought me to your house."

"But bear this in mind, Samuel. The Almighty brought you to my house not only to obtain a wife you deserve but also that you might do something for your downtrodden people. For years I have dreamed great things, I have wanted to federate all Jewish money-lenders into one association, agreed never to lend a penny to the Christians. Even then their ecclesiastical authority would not allow them to take interest — and what would be the outcome? The interest rates would soar skyward because a Christian would want to be amply recompensed for the feared torments of hell. The great merchants would be bankrupt, their poor craftsmen would die of hunger, and in all the chaos which would overwhelm the Christian lands, Suleiman the Great would fall upon them and ravage them as the locust."

"A marvelous idea!" exclaimed Don Samuel. He was thinking of Jessica but made an effort to listen to Shylock.

"I know that such an agreement on our part would provoke frightful persecutions, but what matter? It was a Jew who said 'My soul perish with the Philistines!' That thought has buoyed my spirit for many years but it has encountered the rock of bitter reality. You had Ancona, my son, and so did I. When you came to my house and told of what befell you at Ancona and Pesaro, I felt again all the pain of my great dream which had been shattered to pieces against the cliffs of Ancona and Pesaro."

Shylock fell silent for a moment. Don Samuel held his breath and gazed into the old banker's furrowed face as he resumed. "The fugitives to Pesaro from the sword of the wicked Haman, confound him, sent a delegate, one of the few survivors, as they recorded in their parchment, to the communities in Turkey to beseech their brethren not to send their ships and trade to the port of Ancona but to Pesaro. For several months not a ship from the East called at Ancona and the Christian merchants lost great wealth. They at once began quarrelling among themselves — for such is their way! The Salonika community agreed to continue the plan on condition that the communities of Constantinople, Adrianople and Broussa joined them, since the voyage to Pesaro was more expensive and the Salonika merchants feared the competition of their brethren in other communities. The Broussa community agreed half-heartedly but the other two great communities didn't agree at all. Why? Because the rabbi of Ancona, Rabbi Bassoula, at the instigation of several Jewish merchants among the leaders of the community there, who had been injured by the plan, sped messages to the heads of the communities in Turkey and warned them that if they continued the plan the Pope would spill his wrath upon the Jews. And so the plan was ended before it could get its claws into the living flesh of the tyrants of Ancona."

Don Samuel had known the whole matter thoroughly before, just as he had heard of *The Strong Hand* incident earlier, but he did not venture to interrupt the narrator.

"The blood of the martyred innocents cries out from the earth," Shylock groaned, after a pause, "and the port of Ancona welcomes ships carrying the cargoes of Jews! Are we not a disgusting people? Are we worthy of being esteemed as human beings if we have no self-esteem of our own?"

"You are right, Signor," Don Samuel sighed deeply. "We have nothing left but vengeance, and the generations of Samson and the Maccabees and Bar Kochba are long past."

"So long as there are Jews who go to the stake like your teacher

Rabbi Shlomo Yehya, the valor of Israel has not perished!" Shylock cried with upraised head. But once again his head fell upon his chest as though a heavy load had been placed upon it. "The occurrences at Ancona and Pesaro weighed me down to the earth and as a result I have aged and my hands are feeble. But you, Samuel, young and wise — and what I have heard from you several times is close to my heart — you are able, I am convinced, to realize my dream and in good time make of the money a weapon with which to smite our enemies."

"I shall never forget their iniquities — how can I thank you, master?"

Shylock raised his head and gazed into Don Samuel's face. "With deeds! To be a banker is not easy. He has the power, and so he serves as a target for their barbs, and his life is one of rage and insult. But it is all worth while for the one exalted aim — to fight these Christians! Money is our sole weapon, and it is as though we are heaven-blest to be greedy for more and more, to accumulate and accumulate — for the proper day and the proper purpose."

"How right you are, master," agreed Don Samuel. "Perhaps this great act will cause the good ones among them to open their eyes and throw off the yoke of the priesthood; or a new Christian will rise who will respect us and leave us in peace."

"And if no new Christian arises, may they go to oblivion! The perpetuity of Israel shall not die, and it is their own ways which will betray them, my son. The dissipations of the Venetians, the felonies of that bestial tyrant of Rome are the first signs of their disintegration!" He moved closer to Don Samuel, the cloud seemed to be wiped off his ravaged face, and he added, "And as regards Jessica, my son, I advise you to go gently and kindly with her — these qualities alien to myself are in you."

"I love her deeply," Don Samuel said, "and I hope that she will requite it."

"She is obstinate, my son, and no man has yet pleased her."

"It is from heaven. The Almighty preserved her for me."

"She would like a prince's physician because there are still physicians who are allowed to travel freely outside the ghetto.

I understand her, the accursed wall burdens us all — but the physicians are all married and elderly. I told her: 'Interdicts threaten the physicians of Venice too; the tyrant of the house of Carafa goes on prohibiting and proscribing, and not even the doctors of medicine will escape him — even the great Lusitano Amato was compelled to flee to Turkey.' So I told her. But she won't listen. I warn you, my son, to go softly and carefully with her, do not hasten matters, and win her heart with wisdom."

"The Faith will help me," Dan Samuel vowed. Shylock rose. His glance measured Don Samuel who had also risen, and his heart was glad; it seemed to him that he had grown by a cubit.

"I get cross with her, rebuke her — but what shall I do? It is hard for a Jew in this wicked generation not to be filled with rancor — but I love her with all my soul, and I have not the heart to compel her to take a man for whom she has no feeling. But you are the man, you will win her heart. I place her in your hands, and my blessing with it." He took Don Samuel's head between his two hands, and said in a choked voice, "Your name is Don Samuel, you possess the ways of Don Samuel of the house of Abarbanel, may he rest in peace. Be like him, the leader of the Jewry of Italy, and may my daughter become a second Donna Bienvenida Abrabanella!" He placed his lips upon Don Samuel's brow and kissed him. Don Samuel was so moved that he remained speechless.

Upon returning to his room and lying down on his couch, Don Samuel's faculties returned to him. His heart was happier, and his soul felt as though it was borne upon pinions. . . .

Chapter Ten

AT THE MIDDAY MEAL UPON THE MORROW — IT WAS A FRIDAY — Shylock lauded Don Samuel effusively to his daughter. He had pondered the whole morning whether to tell her of his conversation with Samuel but finally decided it was best to forbear. She was sceptical, the little innocent, of his real intentions, and he feared a contrary result if he confided in her. He also counseled

Don Samuel, before he went up for the lesson, not to reveal anything to her, whispering; "Do not tell her, do not pluck the fruit before it is ripe. She is in your hands — go slowly, one step after another, my son."

But for Jessica her father's hint sufficed. He was kinder to her than she ever remembered. He spoke all manner of things about Don Samuel and did not desist throughout the meal from airing his golden opinions of the youth. It did not occur to her that her father had spoken with Don Samuel, but it was clear that her father wished to marry her to him.

She was despondent all the afternoon. Whenever he had suggested the son of one of the rich men, she had found some blemish in him: this one was short, that one witless, and the third had inelegant manners. Yet if her father suggested Don Samuel and asked "And what fault have you found in him?" — what could she reply? It were best to discontinue the Hebrew lesson, but such a step would provoke her father into telling her openly what he had that day hedged over — and what could she say? "And really why shouldn't you become Don Samuel's?"

The question popped out of nowhere and refused to leave her. No one could better endow his wife with happiness than Don Samuel: he was kind-hearted, wise and sensible. . . . He would take over her father's business, and if her father no longer had any dealings with Christian customers his acrimony would depart and he would become another man in his declining years. . . . But no! Her father would not relinquish the helm until his last day, she would continue to live in this house of wrath — and it was all so revolting to her, strangled her. If she married she would have to leave this house and go far away, to live a life totally unlike her life today. This new life to which she aspired could not come at the hands of a Jew: Venice was the most tolerant of all the kingdoms and territories of Italy to the Jews, and if there were a ghetto and isolation here, what of the other places?

She reclined upon her sofa with closed eyes and images crowded her mind: Venice gay with life . . . she afloat that first evening with Lorenzo upon the Grand Canal — multi-colored lights, the shadows of the towers, the small gondolas in which couples sat, embraced, drifting out of nowhere into nowhere — to the shores of happiness . . . the illumined brilliance and laughter of the casino, at Ridotto . . . Portia's splendid mansion . . . the gates of the palaces wide open, the wide heaven, the wide waters. . . . She saw Lorenzo in her mind's eye as Atlas son of Jupiter — bearing the globe upon his shoulders and laying it at her feet. She felt better. It was as though someone had placed a large scale before her: on the one balance was a model of glorious Venice with all its canals and bridges, and over its towers were the proud *gonfalons* of San Marco; and on the other, the mean huddle of the ghetto island with its sordid drab-gray houses and flat roofs; on the one scale stood Lorenzo with a reflection of the whole of gay Venice shining from his eyes, and on the second stood Don Samuel, his eyes as gloomy as the narrow ghetto alleys. "Choose one of these!" — which should she take? She followed her eyes and heart, and without hesitation placed her hand upon the magic kingdom. . . . "Lorenzo my beloved! You are my father, my uncle, you are as all the world!" — She mused upon his caresses, his ardent speech, the silver tones of his voice in song, and her heart beat as though it sang inside her and she was joyous as never before. . . .

Don Samuel's entry into her room brought a pang of bitterness into her heart. He was soft and spoke quietly as was his manner, yet the inward happiness of his soul did not escape her. The suspicion rose that her father had spoken to Don Samuel about her. She now recollected that Lancelot told her that morning of her father going up on the roof with Don Samuel the previous night and spending a long time there.

"I will teach you a new song this time," he said happily.

"I have no heart for songs in which there is a 'Woe is me' and a lament in every stanza."

"I have brought with me the songs of Joseph Sarfatti. You saw from the song I taught you a fortnight ago that these are not laments."

"Yet if they haven't a 'Woe' in them, you insert one — that is the Jewish habit," she smiled. "Italian songs have breadth."

"Expansive songs that come from dark and narrow hearts!" Don Samuel cried. "Their poets are so numerous, yet none has found within himself one spark of humanity to voice a single protest against the endless tormenting of the Jewish tribe that lives in their midst — and these are called 'celestial songsters'!"

These words were now inimical to Jessica. Everything within her rebelled, but she made no rejoinder lest his suspicions be awakened. Don Samuel opened the book and said, "Before we take a new song, let us repeat the one I sang you a week ago." He sang it softly:

> The sweet grace of your eye-lid has power
> To snare all glory from the world,
> And the tender orbs deep in their bower
> Are like to a moon whose light is pearled;
> And it gently envelops your gaze
> As a diadem lambent with rays.

Jessica sang it with faltering voice. When she finished she gave a forced laugh. "You managed to steal one 'Woe' into it."

He did not respond but asked, "Why do you sing so falteringly, Jessica? Your voice is always so much better than mine, but now it lags."

"I have not been singing at all lately," she answered, not looking at him.

"True, I have noticed it. Whenever I came up the stairs, I was greeted by your golden voice, but not of late. Why is it, why, Jessica?" Her face grew clouded but she kept mute. "When you are not singing you seem so miserable, like a bird in its cage."

Jessica whispered as though to herself, "And it is the song-bird which is usually caged."

"That was nicely put, Jessica," smiled Don Samuel, stroking her hand. She did not dare remove it. "Perhaps I am to blame, Jessica, for pouring out my bitterness before you, for having talked and read to you too much of Ancona, of Pesaro, of torments and oppression. Here is a love-song by Sarfatti which has none of all this in it."

"You said that Sarfatti dwelt long in Venice. Some of its

spirit breathes in the song, and the melody is almost Italian — perhaps it is taken from an Italian song."

"Now I will read another ode by Sarfatti which is still more beautiful," he said, and recited:

> You slumber, I am sleepless and repair
> To linger beneath your abode, my fair;
> You slumber, yet I am beset with care
> Rising within me and clouding the moon;
> You slumber, and the allure of your charm
> Steals sleep from my eyes and ravels my calm;
> Each one of my longings rests in your palm,
> And as molten wax, in your fire I swoon.

"What a lovely song! It is as I said, he lived in Venice," Jessica remarked. Her eyes sparkled and, sensing her excitement, Don Samuel was enraptured. There are no stronger ties to bind the heart of a woman to you, he thought, than a beautiful love-song. He closed his eyes and sang the song with as great devoutness as a prayer.

"Why has he this time chosen love poems?" Jessica asked herself. It was now clear to her that Shylock must have spoken of her to him. The warmth of his voice pervaded the room, lapped around her, penetrated her being, and the drop of bitterness which had come into her heart with Don Samuel's entry into the room seemed to swell and grow until it filled every chamber of her soul, to its very innermost places.

Don Samuel repeated the song, more devoutly, more thrillingly. Jessica glanced at his face. It was not as flesh and blood, but as some ethereal spirit which had formed itself out of the notes of the song. A feeling of pity stirred inside her: poor Don Samuel, good Don Samuel, how could he know that she would never be his, never? He had done no wrong to her — it was better that she should warn him in time that the tapestry of love he was weaving around her and himself was a snare to his feet, a yawning abyss. . . . Yet what could she tell him? He would ask "Why have I not found favor in your eyes?" and how could she reply? The lineaments of his face all spoke of love of her, and her urgent pity squeezed her heart, brought tears to her eyes.

To hide her embarrassment she smilingly said that he had thrust another "Woe" into the song. He did not understand that this was an irony directed at himself, not deprecation of a Hebrew song, and said, "It is a fact that one of the most passionate love-songs in Italian which has been popular in the Roman provinces for generations was composed by a Jew, and a Hebrew poet at that." Without awaiting her query, he began:

> Love sang the Ave Maria ne'er,
> Love never kept to faith or the law,
> Love is a heart without fear and awe,
> And brooks no measure set on it e'er.
> Love is the dominion of the fair —

Don Samuel had forgotten how it continued. He remained standing for a moment, his arms wide and his eyes questing, as though seeking within the space of that room the broken thread of song; but when he could not remember, he lowered his eyes and said to Jessica, "What breadth, what depth! As broad and deep as love itself, and the composer was a Jew — Manoello."

"What powerful strength," Jessica supplemented, but without looking at Don Samuel. "'*Amor* never kept to faith or the law' — does not this truism by a Hebrew poet endow the authority to break with all tradition for the sake of the master of everything, whose dominion is limitless?" she pondered. Yet because of her thoughts she was reluctant to ask Don Samuel to repeat the words, and possibly remember the next stanzas. Had not the Master of All placed these verses on his lips to show her the path to pursue — without grief or remorse?

"And now let us sing Sarfatti's new song together," he said.

She sat with downcast head, avoided his gaze, and with a superhuman effort replied, "The melody is a little difficult. Please sing it again yourself."

Don Samuel sang it a third time. A note of joy crept into the wistful tune and from time to time he looked at Jessica, but she sat motionless, like a lovely marble statue. His lips voiced the words of the song and his heart dreamed and quested in the future. He saw in his mind's eye Jessica's proud head falling on his bosom, her sculptured arms embracing him — No! she was not obstinate, as her father had said last night, she was yielding and delicate, she was a little girl brimming with goodness and loving-kindness.

Jessica's heart could no longer endure the choking sensation which had overcome her. "Don Samuel is perfection itself — why are you alarmed of him?" a voice welled up from somewhere inside her; and would he be furious, admonish her? No, if she confessed to Don Samuel all her caprices with the Christian, their wanton revels, he would spurn her and flee. . . . He would ask in a stifled voice, "Has he kissed you?" She would be silent. "And you him?" She would keep silent. Her proud heart would not permit her to lie nor beseech his forgiveness, to forget the past.

"Let us now sing together," Don Samuel suggested. He sang in a loud voice, but her own voice caught in her throat and was weak. Manoello's words remained in her mind as though carved out of rock — she knew them perfectly after only one hearing — and they banished Sarfatti's fragile-airy verses. She felt that she would burst into tears if she went on singing, and stopped. Don Samuel stopped too.

"What is it, Jessica?" he asked.

"I cannot —"

"Why? It is the eve of the Sabbath. You probably have a great deal of work yet before you."

She mustered all her strength and said, "Please, Don Samuel, please leave me alone now."

"But why? Is there greater pleasure than watching a proud young maiden like yourself moved by feelings of love? Please go on singing, Jessica."

"Believe me, I cannot."

"It is my first request of you, Jessica," he pleaded.

"And my one request is please leave me! Please, please, do not distress me, dear Don Samuel!"

He rose. "Thank you for having called me 'dear' for the first time," he exclaimed. He pressed her hand in parting and added, "I shall not distress you, Jessica. It is my heart's desire to give you only happiness."

On leaving he did not enter the banking-shop but went home.

He wanted to be alone, alone with his image of Jessica. Every shade of the grief which had paled her countenance testified to the origin — love. And the same grief permeated his heart and sang him paeans of glory as from a remote world, a world whose skies and earth and creatures were love. . . . How much in harmony with his spirit now the passages from the *Song of Solomon* which he read every Sabbath Eve! When he reached the verse in the eighth chapter, "O that thou wert as my brother, that sucked the breasts of my mother!" he recalled the mystic interpretation which Manoello had given to this book. For a long while he forbore to continue reading the last chapter and thought of the conclusion which Manoello had set down upon this very passage: "For love is the great principle around which the whole Torah revolves." This exalted aphorism by the poet, the measures of that eternal Song of Love which he had been reciting, the last words which Jessica had gushed forth — they commingled into an unearthly diapason, now muted, now clear, and gave wings to his spirit.

Yet such was not Jessica's mood when left alone. Her ears echoed the words she had just spoken to Don Samuel: "Please do not distress me, dear Don Samuel!" *Dear* Don Samuel — the words had been blurted out without thinking. And he, the dear one, had left her alone because she asked it. How often Lorenzo irked her when he came upstairs in her father's absence in the city or the synagogue. He knew that it hurt her and he paid no attention, yet Don Samuel had not become obdurate, he had not pleaded with her — he stood up and left. Mingled sorrow and pity burdened her heart when she thought of how Don Samuel had wished to stay with her and she had caused him pain in sending him away. Did she not love him if she felt this pity and compassion for the man? Did she love Lorenzo with a full heart, as she had thought until now, if she felt compassion for another man who loved her? A deep blush suffused her cheeks as she thought of what had passed between Lorenzo and herself: he had embraced her times without number, had taken her to the house of his friends — she had vowed that she loved him, that she was his, only his. . . .

As she sat immersed in her sorrowful thoughts, Lancelot entered. "Little Signorina Jessica, why did you cut short the lesson today?" he asked. She did not reply, looked earnestly into his face and, stretching out her hand to him, said in a choking voice, "Good Lancelot, I know from my childhood that you think only well of me. You have done much for me to assuage my longing for liberty. You are better to me than my father and yet you have unknowingly caused me pain — why did you help me to grow fond of Lorenzo?"

"Why? Isn't he a fine chap — and good-hearted? And of a noble family, a pure Calergi!" Lancelot cried, but when he saw that her face did not change at his words he put on a mournful expression and whispered lugubriously, "We promised we would come to him this evening, but I am your slave, little Signorina Jessica. If you have no wish to go to him any more and want to remain shut up in the ghetto all your life, I won't force you."

"Too late —" She fell upon the couch, buried her face in a cushion, and burst into a paroxysm of weeping. Stefano peeped through the half-open door but Lancelot motioned to him to be gone. The last two words she had uttered, for which he had waited many weeks, filled him with elation. He patted her head and murmured in a fatherly tone, "Leave your tears here, little Signorina Jessica — it's a Jewish trait. Lovelies like you don't cry on the other side of the ghetto wall, and certainly not in the arms of one like Lorenzo —"

"Lo-ren-zo!" her muffled voice quavered behind the cushion, and Lancelot went out of the room well satisfied.

"Too late" — The words which had burst from her heart seemed suddenly to erect a barrier between herself and all to which she was accustomed: her father, Don Samuel, the religion of her forebears, all these were now behind her, and before her was Lorenzo. The spasm of tears seemed to have torn from her bosom the last fluttering remnants of the uncertainties afflicting her, and she determined to remain that night with Lorenzo, to return nevermore to her father's house. If she postponed her flight again, she thought, there would be new doubts, especially if she went on seeing Don Samuel — she must leave the house once for all that evening, that very evening, and never see Don Samuel again, never again. . . .

Shylock closed his banking-shop after the third trumpet-call proclaiming sunset. He hurriedly changed his clothes and went to the synagogue to welcome the Sabbath. Jessica lay on her bed before her father returned from prayers. She could not look him in the face, fearing the encounter might weaken her resolve. She asked Lancelot to tell her father that she had a headache and had gone to bed early.

Returning from the evening service, Shylock asked Lancelot about Jessica, and the servant answered as he was instructed. Shylock entered her room. She lay with her head to the wall and pretended to be asleep. He whispered her name several times but, when she failed to respond, went out quietly. She had never heard her father pronounce her name with such deep affection. Or was it her imagination? Yet she had heard his voice with her own ears, and it had been tender and loving. Could it be that she had seen him for the last time at midday and would never see him again? Her father's voice singing the Friday evening hymns reached her and a strong impulse seized her to get out of bed and see him for the last time.

But the impulse passed. No, she consoled herself, she would see him again, she would stand in the window of one of the houses at the Rialto and see him. . . . But Don Samuel she would never see again — he would leave Venice and go to far-off Constantinople, where he would find his happiness and forget her. At this thought the pincer-fingers of hesitation again squeezed her heart, and her thoughts of Lorenzo were mingled with sad musings on Don Samuel. "What do you care if he forgets you?" she chid herself, yet something weighed upon her. How good, she thought, that her father had not invited him to supper — had *he* been in the house, she could not have withheld coming out. She would have gone into the dining-room to see him for the last time! He would have gazed at her prolongedly and her father, who had already spoken to the young man about her, would have invited her to sit at the table. Now he would have spoken to her without inner restraint, and perhaps he would have sung — "You slumber" he would have sung with profound feeling, and she could no longer have summoned up the courage to leave the house and go to Lorenzo, to remain in his arms. Fate was on her side: she would see neither her father nor Samuel that evening — in another hour it would vanish as swiftly as a nightmare. . . .

The lights went out all over the house, and a short while later the door opened slowly and Lancelot entered, carrying over his arm a man's cloak and the ghetto hat in which she always disguised herself. She got out of bed. Her teeth chattered and she tremblingly sought a warm gown in the darkness.

"Are you cold?" Lancelot whispered.

"Please go outside, I want to dress," she replied. Lancelot placed the cloak and hat on the sofa and withdrew.

Jessica dressed hurriedly and went into the corridor where Lancelot was waiting. Suddenly she remembered her mother's two precious rings and returned to the room. She thought she heard footsteps in the adjoining room and began shivering. Should she jump into bed and cover herself to the head? She remained rooted to the spot without breathing and recovered only when Lancelot re-entered. With shaking hand she took the two rings out of a finely-chased casket and went out.

As they were passing out of the ghetto gate Jessica looked back. "Why are you looking so long at the filthy lane?" Lancelot asked. "I have never seen it from this spot under moonlight," she replied.

For some reason there suddenly rose before her the terrified visage of Saint Margaretta trampling upon the dragon and killing it whilst holding aloft the Cross — she felt herself to be like the saint and thought sadly, "If I were Titian, I would not have painted Margaretta coming out of those frightful rocks but from this mean alley."

They sat in the gondola that Lancelot had prepared during the day. As they entered the Grand Canal, fabled Venice swam into sight, bathed in argent moonlight, and the vista brought new life to her. She made a rapid gesture with both her hands, like a bird spreading its wings, and threw the ghetto hat into the water.

"But we'll need the hat for our return!" Lancelot expostulated.

"Never mind," she cried spiritedly. "We'll return so late that no one will see us in the ghetto." She concealed from him her intention to return no more. She wanted to surprise Lorenzo, and kept her secret.

At the Rialto landing-stage Lorenzo was awaiting them. "Why have you delayed, Jessica? I have been waiting a long time."

"My father went late to bed."

"What a blessing he doesn't stay up all night," Lorenzo commented. To himself he swore, "If only the Jew would fall asleep forever and be done with it!"

"You seem tired, my Jessica — what ails you?"

"I had a headache the whole day." Lancelot began to show the way to Lorenzo's house. "I want to be alone with you this evening," she said.

"A great privilege!" he exclaimed enthusiastically. "Where shall we go?"

"I have a pretty fancy, Lorenzo — I have all sorts of fine fancies this evening — it is a moonlit night, let us sit beneath the sky."

"How good you are, Jessica!"

"Let us sail to the Lido, to the seashore," she added.

He hugged her to him in a frenzy of love.

"Aren't you ashamed in the open street?" she inquired mischievously.

"Why ashamed? No one is ashamed of love in Venice."

They retraced their steps to the gondola-stage at the Rialto landing. Lancelot summoned a gondolier and after haggling with him for some time they entered the craft.

"To the Lido!" Lorenzo cried. Lancelot took his place by the gondolier as usual. The latter interrogated him as to whether the young couple was rich or married, and when he answered both questions in the negative, the gondolier chuckled and said that loving couples were always rich. He went on to tell Lancelot some spicy stories of couples who repaired of an evening to the Lido and of the debauchery of the rich families of Italy who spent the summer months there. But the trip seemed overlong to Lancelot and he thought anxiously that if they remained out there too long they would not get back home until dawn.

Jessica was happy. The broad waters stretched to the horizon. The moonlight which threw a carpet of shimmering moonbeams upon the sea, the faint echoes of song which reached them from distant gondolas resembling toy craft, the occasional lights flickering from distant islands mantled in a thin mist — all these banished regrets for her father's house, and she marveled at herself for thinking it would be so hard to leave the ghetto and her irascible father and why she had not fled immediately, on the morrow of her first outing from the ghetto. She leaned her head on Lorenzo's shoulder, her small hand placed in his manly one — she placed her fate in his hands.

"You were never so sweet as this evening," Lorenzo murmured, kissing her head.

"It is so wonderful here," she breathed.

"Is it because you are in a gondola or because of me?"

"I find no difference between my Lorenzo and glorious Venice — both of you are one."

Lorenzo lavished upon her transports of love and his voice rippled over her like the moonlight dancing upon the water.

"I have a surprise for you, Lorenzo mine," Jessica whispered. Lorenzo guessed what she was about to say, but put on an expression of feigned astonishment. "I shall nevermore leave you, I am remaining with you." He clasped her to his heart and she clung to him as a child in its mother's arms.

Lancelot's ears were pricked up the whole voyage and when he heard Jessica's last words he breathed a deep sigh of relief. He had finally reached his goal! Now he understood why she had thrown the ghetto hat into the Grand Canal, why she did not care about returning late to the city. . . . The gondolier turned his head back at the moment Jessica fell into Lorenzo's arms. He winked at Lancelot and gloated, "It's what I told you about these little jaunts to the Lido. I saw this beforehand."

"Don't disturb them," Lancelot warned him. "It's the fruit of my efforts for weeks and months."

Lorenzo sang tender ballads and Jessica joined him in a duet. It was as though in their song they had grown wings and fluttered them like the cooing doves in San Marco Square — the golden wings of his voice and the silver wings of hers. . . .

They were wafted to the Lido on the wings of song, and with song wended their path to the sandy shore. Lancelot plodded after them, tired. Now that he had heard from Jessica's own lips that she would never go back, all this seemed superfluous; he wanted to go to bed and regain strength for the morrow. He brooded with anxiety on the morrow. His master would awaken and not discover that his daughter was gone; but when he returned from prayers, what then? If he, Lancelot, said nothing of her absence, then his master would sense that he had a hand in it. It occurred to him that he might entrust the task to Stefano. He had done all the work, let Stefano now do something for the wealth which was to be his.

They reached the seashore. The sands were alive, couples in the hundreds, the thousands, lay stretched upon the ground; here the strumming of a mandolin quavered upon the air, there two voices blended in the harmony of song, and the gurgling tide lapping the sands. Dante, Petrarca, Colonna, Stampa — their odes and lyrics lived intensely in the vivacious singing of the paramours and their beloveds, and their roundelays drifted out over the murmuring sea, over the Adriatic. . . . Lorenzo placed Jessica upon the sand and reclined at her side.

"How beautiful thou art, Adriatic!" Jessica clapped her hands at the expanse of sea across which the moon laid her scepter of diamond-sparkling sheen.

"It is your loveliness, Jessica, that is reflected in the Adriatic." He pointed at the sea. "That is the Doge's, but you are my Adriatic!" He embraced her.

After an ecstatic pause, Jessica murmured dreamily, "The Doge's Adriatic is eternal youth. It will remain glowing with the bloom of youth forever. But your Adriatic, O Lorenzo, will lose her beauty, her face will wrinkle, her hair grow white — will you then love her as much?"

Lorenzo was sober for a moment but then rejoined, "I shall

always see in you the Jessica my eyes lit upon that first time, as I see you at this moment: bathed in youth and moonbeams."

Lancelot sat at some distance from them. When he noticed that Jessica was not using the cloak, he took it and, stretching out on the sand, covered himself. He had completed his task and could now rest tranquilly. He was satisfied with himself; the affair had taken a long time and he had succeeded in concealing it from his master the Jew whose eyes pried into every corner.

He had been particularly afraid of Don Samuel, who was by no means calm about Jessica. Several times, when he had left the house with Jessica, he had feared lest the young Jew be prowling outside — and he was now safe from his eyes too. How fortunate for him that he had resorted to no threats with little Jessica as his conspirators had counseled! He loved her as much as if she had sprung from his own loins, and could not cause her distress or grief. Now she too would reach her haven: she had seen the light of life in a gondola, her first glance had been of the Grand Canal, and now the whole of Venice was open before her, that beautiful Venice which she loved so deeply. Now she would be far from the eyes of her badgering old father and the miserable ghetto, she would not have to don the veil of shame when out in the streets of the city; she would be the wife of a noble, and her great beauty would open even the gates of the Doge's palace. It seemed to Lancelot as though his own cherished daughter, the daughter of a poor man, had been loved by a nobleman who had raised her from a mean dwelling to a mansion.

He then thought of the great fortune that would tinkle into his pocket. He had arranged with Stefano that both should go south, buy some land and become farmers. There were handsome wenches in the South, and although he was no longer a young man he would find himself a poor peasant's daughter, youthful and beautiful; whoever had money in hand could find a wife. But now that the purse of gold was almost in his pocket, he began to be assailed by growing apprehensions. Gold was always gold, but land, bought for gold, was not always worth gold. A farmer worked hard and suddenly a flood or a hailstorm destroyed his toil; and no wonder that most farmers were poverty-stricken. He could buy bread and meat with his gold, but he could not eat land and the walls of his cottage. Stefano could still endure hard work, he was strong, but for himself he was not fit for the back-breaking life of a farmer. He was used to cleaning out rooms and cooking but not to land-work. And Jessica — it was for her sake that he ought not exile himself to the South. He had seen her daily from the day of her birth, heard her voice — he would die of longing for her. Lancelot felt as if something were breaking in his heart at the thought that he might not see Jessica again, and his sharp mind quested for a solution. He stumbled on one. Jessica had told him that if she married Lorenzo she would not remain in Venice — she could not stay so close to her father's abode — she would live with Lorenzo in Rome or Florence. He too, Lancelot, would follow them and go on serving Jessica to his death — and the purse of gold would remain intact.

Meditating thus, Lancelot drowsed off into a deep slumber. His snoring reached Jessica and Lorenzo. The young noble laughed and Jessica, casting a glance at her doubled-up servant with his feet tucked under him, said, "He is tired, the poor man."

"He snores like a pig," Lorenzo remarked.

"The sea air has made him sleepy, he is like a child," she added. "Good Lancelot, he is as faithful as a house-dog."

Lorenzo murmured to her affectionately and caressed her, but it seemed strange to her that he made no mention of the surprise she had sprung upon him. She had the feeling that he was evading talk of the morrow, the first day they would be together in Venice town. When she spoke of Lancelot she found the opportunity to turn the conversation to their marriage. "What will that poor fellow do now in my father's house? It is best he should not go back there. He can remain with us, can he not?"

Her lover was glad she had spoken. He too now found the opportunity of saying what was on his mind. "You are so thoughtful, Jessica, you are so good and wise, and I want you to be happy." He broke off for a moment. Jessica fastened her gaze upon him and saw he was struggling with himself. Her heart dissolved in fear lest he tell her that he could not take a Jewess to wife. She mustered up courage and said tremulously, "Tell me what is in your heart, Lorenzo, without prefaces."

"Dear Jessica, you must go home tonight just this once." She looked at him in astonishment. "Jessica mine, I am deep in debt and I need money to arrange our affairs." She now fully comprehended him. She felt relieved that her fear was groundless but when she meditated a moment upon the direct hint in his words, her face became pale and her breathing labored. When Lorenzo saw that she did not jump up and spurn him, he held both her hands in his and continued, "I am speaking to you as to a good Christian. It is a sacred duty to take from a Jew the money he has accumulated from the Christians. You are his sole heiress, and is it just that he should afterwards give away his money to others and leave you nothing?"

"Do you want to say that I must steal his money?" she asked in a trembling voice.

"If you call this theft, what name can be given to real thieving? He has enough, and in any event he is saving the money for you. It is your money, Jessica."

Jessica gazed at him but said nothing. They were sitting close to the tide and a strong wave curled up and splashed over her feet — but she did not notice. How much better it would be if the sea would suddenly rise and carry her off. She had left the ghetto never to return and now — she must go back and look into her father's face, to sit once more opposite Don Samuel — could she endure it? How could she bear all this? How could she conceal from them what was happening inside her?

"Dear Jessica, are you angry with me?" pleaded Lorenzo, to repair the broken thread of their conversation. She kept quiet a moment and then said, "Had I not loved you I would never have left my father's house — did I lack suitors? But — but why did you not tell me all this before?"

"It is because I loved you, Jessica, because I was afraid until this evening that if I told you this I should lose you, lose all."

"Your fears were justified, Lorenzo, and how can I agree to such an act?" She closed her eyes as though to steel herself to

131

the ordeal of theft. Lorenzo had not heard her last few words and instructed her how to accomplish it.

"Every evening, before he closes the shop, he takes upstairs purses filled with ducats of gold and silver. The gold is in the smaller ones. Take two or three of them, and it will suffice."

She saw the logic of Lorenzo's statement that if her father's money was for herself, his sole heiress, then it was hers; but yet she could not overcome the feeling that it was stealing. Suddenly she sighed deeply and cried, "But I do not wish to go back, Lorenzo. Here, I have two rings with precious stones upon my fingers. Let us sell them and have the money."

"You said once that your father had paid two thousand ducats for them. If you sell them, they will offer half. It is not enough, dear Jessica. I owe three thousand, and —"

"You owe three thousand?" she cut him short.

"My father was ruined and to protect the honor of the dead I signed bonds for the money he left owing, and in addition I have to furnish a house worthy of you, Adriatic mine."

"I would be content with a humble dwelling, Lorenzo mine, if only that —"

Lorenzo checked her by pressing her face to his heart.

"Jessica mine, I have won not only the fairest of damsels in Venice but also a heart which comprehends love." He continued in a serious tone. "I must pay my father's debt, the creditors are insistent, and unless I discharge what is their due, they will seize all the furniture I buy."

"But my father locks his money up in a box built into the wall and keeps the key in his pocket, and at night the key is beneath his pillow."

"I rely upon your cleverness and ingenuity, Jessica."

"But he doesn't always bring many purses from the shop."

"Await the opportunity. My troubles are yours too, Jessica, and you must realize that I have to pay the debt. Believe me the more you take from a Jew, the greater the pious deed."

She now felt that her feet were soaking. "If I must return to the ghetto," her voice shivered, "let us hurry. The route is long." Lorenzo jumped to his feet and extended his hand to help her up. He aroused Lancelot and they went back to the gondola landing-stage. Lancelot rubbed his eyes and dragged after them with flagging knees. He was still savoring a dream he had just had: he stood in a field in which his many cows were grazing and he surveyed their full udders, and then the cows were replaced by young maidens, healthy and buxom farmers' lasses, jostling each other to get near him.

Upon their mounting the gondola he recalled his decision to remain with Jessica and not to return to the ghetto. He wanted to apprise Jessica of it — she would be delighted at the suggestion — but feared lest the gondolier should overhear; and he put it off until they would reach the Rialto and he would remain with Jessica and Lorenzo. Snatches of song echoed here and there, and it surprised him that Lorenzo and Jessica were not singing, but he ascribed their silence to fatigue at this late hour.

Half way across, the gondolier said, "She's a Jewess, isn't she?"

"No," replied Lancelot gruffly.

"Then why did the gentleman tell me to go to the ghetto? You're probably lying, slave of a Jew." Lancelot thought that the man was joking, but when he saw that the gondola was proceeding to the north of the city he shrugged his shoulders. He turned his head and asked, "Where are we going?"

"To the ghetto," Lorenzo answered.

"You lied then," the gondolier rapped. "And why were you afraid? If I had known this earlier, I should not have argued over the price with the gentleman — it is a pious deed."

"It's all a riddle to me," Lancelot muttered. He again turned his head. Both sat in a tight embrace. What had happened? A thousand thoughts thronged his head but he did not guess the truth.

Before they alighted, Lorenzo whispered to Jessica, "Do not tell Lancelot anything about the money you intend taking with you — after all, he is only a menial."

"He never stole a *scudo* in his life," she remarked, and added, "But without Lancelot's help it will be sevenfold more difficult for me."

"It is best that the matter take a little longer; do it without his help," he said, and then overwhelmed her with endearments.

Upon reaching the bridge leading to the ghetto gate, Jessica and Lancelot landed, and Lorenzo went back to Venice in the gondola. After passing the gate, Lorenzo asked, "What happened? I thought the matter was settled."

"I decided to remain a short time longer in my father's house," she returned. Lancelot's knees shook with rage. He dared not admonish his mistress Jessica, but as he could not keep altogether quiet he fumed, "And why did you throw that hat into the water?"

"Never mind, good Lancelot, you will buy me another." She did not look at him.

When Jessica reached home and lay in her bed, the first shafts of the dawn were paling the sky. Yet it seemed to her that it was the evening twilight which would be followed by the night, the gloomy night that would never pass.

Chapter Eleven

JESSICA AWOKE AT NINE O'CLOCK WHILE HER FATHER WAS STILL IN the synagogue. She was deathly tired and when she tried to rise she could not. Her breathing was heavy. She recalled that she had sat for a long time with wet feet upon the beach the night before. "I must have caught cold," she reflected. A short while later she began to cough. Lancelot heard her coughing and came in.

"I am glad you came, Lancelot," she welcomed him.

"You probably slept well, little Signorina Jessica. Your face is flushed."

"I feel feverish, I'm afraid I have the ague," she said. She asked him to bring her the mirror and when she saw her face sighed deeply. "My whole body is on fire — I am ill, Lancelot."

"You are tired. You haven't had enough sleep, Signorina Jessica —"

"No, no, I cannot raise my body. I am ill."

"I can hardly remember your having been ill before."

"I must have caught a chill." A spasm of coughing interrupted her.

"In the summer? How could that happen?" the servant mumbled.

"Come closer," she motioned to him. He took her hand in his as she said, "Swear to me, Lancelot, that you will never in any circumstances tell a soul that I was outside the house last night."

"How could Lancelot do such injury to little Signorina Jessica? I would be doing harm to myself. You must promise *me* not to tell a soul about it."

"You must also be certain that Stefano keeps his mouth closed."

"Upon my head be it," he replied. "In God's name, he fears me like a mouse."

Jessica felt cold and wrapped herself in the blanket, leaving only one hand outside. She held the mirror and examined her burning face with alarm.

"Lie in bed quietly today and you will get up tomorrow. *He* awaits you," Lancelot whispered.

"Perhaps my father will hurry to call a physician and he will ask what I did and where I was — remember I warned you, Lancelot, to say nothing."

"Heaven forbid, little Signorina Jessica," he cried, and then whispered, "Your Lancelot keeps your secret — have you aught to complain of me?"

"You sacrifice yourself for me, good Lancelot." Her voice quavered. She gave him a grateful smile and his face became radiant with joy.

"You will be able to get up by the evening, little Signorina Jessica, and we shall go to the city again. Lancelot your servant won't rest until he brings you safely to your heart's desire." He left the room.

Her head felt like a wheel. But she thought more of the events of the previous night than of her illness. There were both light and shadow in her reflections upon the long meeting with Lorenzo and of their conversation. Lorenzo loved her with all his being, his taste was charming, his manners polished. . . . Yet who had thought that she would still be lying in this place today, who had wondered. . . . She would again have to see her father's face, and Don Samuel. Her eyes were deep in their sockets, her face betrayed something of her inward agitation — it was better that she had fallen ill so that illness could hide her embarrassment. . . .

When she heard her father's steps mounting the stairs, she began to breathe quickly. How could she face him? What could she say? Oh, if she could only get up! When she walked about she could reply more easily to his questions, without meeting his steely, irate eyes. She lifted her head from the pillow by a supreme effort, and sat up in bed; but she at once had to lie back as though a millstone were crushing her.

Shylock no sooner entered the house than he heard Jessica coughing. From the distance he judged her to be in bed. He opened the door of her room, muttered *"Shabbath Shalom — a peaceful Sabbath,"* and when he saw her still lying in bed he said ironically, "Even the children of kings do not lie so late. Your father has come from synagogue —" His eyes fell upon her flushed countenance, he drew closer and scrutinized her, and saw there were tears in her eyes. "What ails you, Jessica?" he asked gently. He felt her head and hand, and his face became grave. "You are feverish, my child, what ails you?"

"Nothing, I have a headache."

"I shall send for the physician."

She tried to summon a smile. "There's no need, Father. The window was open. I must have caught a chill."

"But you always sleep with an open window, and it's mid-July," he said in surprise. His voice changed. "One can suffocate in these wretched alleys even when the windows are open! Confound them, they have the fresh air, wide streets, and parks, and don't catch chills."

"They get colds too." She essayed a smile. He felt her head and hand again, and deep anxiety etched his face. But not to alarm her he said, "It's not bad at all, my child, to have the physician in."

"Let us wait a little," she whispered. She half-closed her eyes and added, "I am very tired, I want to sleep."

Shylock called for Lancelot and asked him to bring a potion, gave it to her to drink, and stroked her ruffled hair. "Sleep now, my child," he said gently. "You will perspire and all will be well." He himself brought another blanket from the next room and covered her. "It is Sabbath today, the street is quiet. You can sleep undisturbed, my child." He again touched her fever-ish forehead and left the room, leaving the door ajar.

From time to time the sound of her labored breathing reached him, arousing painful memories. He had lost three, two sons and a daughter — may God have mercy! Jessica had always been healthy, yet now, when he was about to give her in mar-riage, she had to fall ill — was not Satan's hand in it? Only yesterday morning, when in the city, he had gone to Maestro Jacopo, the goldsmith who in his youth had been an apprentice with Benvenuto Cellini in the workshop of Marcone in Florence, and bargained with him for a silver binding for a thick book, with the family crest inlaid in gold — was the hand of God against him, heaven forbid, for having gone to a gentile only because he was a great craftsman, to prepare the binding for a prayer-book for Jessica on her wedding-day? He tried to dismiss these melancholy thoughts. She was his only daughter and he was the more careful about her. . . . How often had he been feverish, yet gone out of the house — would a man forego his business because of a fever? Jessica was spoiled, an only daughter, she only had a slight chill. On the morrow he would ask Job the scribe to prepare him an amulet with an inscription from the holy writings with the letters "18" (the numerical equivalent in Hebrew for "Life") on top. But his uneasiness grew. He ate sparingly, recited more Psalms than usual, and kept on going into Jessica's room to ask how she felt.

Her weakness was increasing. She could hardly move a limb and she was breathing with difficulty. Her father again gave her a medicine and told her that he would send for a physician, but she held him back and cried, "I am much better. There's no need of a doctor."

"Why should you mind, Jessica?" Shylock was displeased. "Are you worried over the few coins I shall spend?"

"Let us wait, father. I'll fall asleep and all will pass over," she answered. Shylock went out and continued reciting Psalms. A little later, when Lancelot came in, she asked him to bring her father.

"Your reading aloud disturbs me," she said when he entered. "Please close the door and take some rest yourself."

"That means that you're not better. . . . Lancelot, do go and call Mordecai the physician!"

Marshaling the last of her strength, Jessica sat up in bed and protested, "I will not allow him to examine me today."

"But you are ill, my child, and I have no knowledge of the medical science."

Jessica tried to bring a smile to her dry lips. "See, father, I am sitting up, I am much better. Please close the door and go lie down. You always rest on a Sabbath afternoon."

Shylock obeyed her. He went out with Lancelot and shut the door of her room. Jessica closed her eyes but could not sleep. A throbbing noise beat in her head and seemed to surround her in a fog; her heart palpitated so loudly she felt it would burst from her breast — and her thoughts too throbbed and palpitated. Why had she gone last night to Lorenzo? Why had she not jumped up and fled from him when he had suggested carrying out the theft? The water had not then dampened her legs. . . . Her father was a man of hot temper, his ways were inimical to her, but he was her father — how grave his anxiety at her slightest chill. . . . And how deeply he would grieve if he came in one morning and found her bed empty and his daughter fled. . . . Out of her lassitude and weakness, tears came to her eyes and rolled down her cheeks slowly on the pillow, as though they too were weary. She felt better as one drop after another crept between her eyelashes and trickled a wet path down her hot face. With this slight relief she slept.

It was already three o'clock in the afternoon when she woke. The door was ajar and at the slit she saw her father's face, as though he had heard from afar the noiseless opening of her eye-lids. He came over to her bed with gleeful face. "You slept well," he whispered, placing his hand on her brow. "Still hot," he murmured.

"Did I cough?" she asked.

"Very little," he replied.

"I told you I would be better, but I am very weak," she said listlessly, and a wistful smile parted her lips. Shylock went out and returned with Lancelot, who brought a warm beverage.

"Won't you eat something?" Shylock asked.

"I couldn't!" she cried, and her face became distorted, as though the very thought of food sickened her.

"No appetite is a sure sign of illness," Shylock said nervously.

"I shall be much better tomorrow."

"Let's hope so, daughter," he sighed. A moment later — "At the Scuola Cantone there is an *academia* today and Samuel is the principal debater. I shall go and return immediately after the prayers." He took the opportunity of introducing a word of praise for Don Samuel who was remarkable in argument, and reviled the Christians who prevented such dialecticians of high standard, only because they were Jews, from becoming pleaders of law and appearing before the tribunals of justice.

With none seeing, Shylock took his red hat and left the house. Instead of going to the synagogue, he went on foot to the city to bring back the greatest of physicians, Rabbi Kalonymus himself. It was an axiom he had learned from his father that an eminent doctor saved people much anxiety and distress and, in the end, money too.

It was the first time he had covered the long journey on foot. Many of the passers-by jeered at him and even stuck out their sharp tongues at the Jew dressed in his Sabbath raiment, holding his fine Sabbath hat in his hand, and upon his head the conical mark of ignominy. More difficult was the way back to the ghetto walking alongside Rabbi Kalonymus in his black *beretta*. Within himself he exulted now at recollection of the rumor that the distinction in favor of physicians was to be abolished and that they too would have to wear the hat of shame.

"Leone Medico of Venice who was murdered in Moscow

seventy years ago was my cousin," Shylock said, both to begin conversation with Rabbi Kalonymus and to show that his family too had possessed a famous physician who had been invited at the time to the Czar's Court.

"And who was responsible for his murder save himself?" Rabbi Kalonymus rejoined. "The same Czar, Ivan I think his name was, marries a woman from Italy and invites learned men and physicians from her country to his Court, and a foolish Jew is duped into going to those barbarian Slavs — and what happens? The son of that savage Czar dies of his illness, and the Jewish physician is executed publicly."

"And are our barbarians any better?" Shylock argued. This provoked the stern displeasure of Rabbi Kalonymus.

"How can you compare the cultured and courteous people of Italy to these Russians?" he demanded.

Shylock lowered his voice and said, "A similar act of savagery, perhaps worse, occurred thirty years ago in our Modena."

"You mean the incident over Rabbi Mordecai the physician," Rabbi Kalonymus interrupted him. "That matter still needs investigation." It was apparent from his flushed face, however, that he too believed the story about that famous doctor of medicine in Modena, who held a decoration bestowed by Charles V, whom the Christian practitioners in his city had poisoned out of jealousy. Without looking at Shylock, he went on in a moderate tone, "You merchants jump to hasty conclusions — if you don't others will forestall you — but not us doctors. Even after an examination, we do not reach a conclusion lightly."

Shylock argued against the remark and flung at the other a flock of hard facts, but Kalonymus walked with lowered head, deep in meditation, and answered neither one way nor the other. Shylock was convinced that the physician had uneasy premonitions over similar treatment one of these days at the hands of the envious rival Christian medical men of Venice — and he felt some complacency at the thought that Rabbi Kalonymus, to whose son the Signioria had given a scholarship at their academy in Padua, and who wore the head-dress of a free man, was not serene about his future.

When they reached his house, and Shylock opened wide the door to the patient's room, she was affrighted. The old banker remarked that his daughter had not wished him to summon a leech.

"Perhaps she is right," Kalonymus responded, and motioned to Shylock to remain outside.

He spent a long time examining her and asked her to tell him of her doings in the past few days. Jessica at first was confused but then recovered and, with an artificial smile, said, "Why, nothing at all — what can the daughter of a money-changer do? I visited the house of a friend I had not seen for a long time, went to the seamstress, and yesterday took a Hebrew lesson."

"You can speak Hebrew? How excellent! Shall we talk Hebrew?" But Rabbi Kalonymus at once answered his own question. "No, you are tired, my child, and must not exert yourself."

When the medico left her room Shylock bombarded him with questions, asking particularly if there were any possibility of complication. Rabbi Kalonymus repeated to each inquiry that he would return at noon on the morrow and at the moment could say nothing more than that the patient needed complete rest and on no account must be disturbed by any noise in the house. When Shylock pressed him for a more definite answer, he answered testily, "If I needed a loan and you insisted on an extra one per cent of interest, there would be some point in your importunings; but of what advantage is it to press me to reveal knowledge which I do not yet possess?"

Shylock, who was accustomed to retorting in full measure, this time swallowed his gall, for there was none like Kalonymus among the physicians and he required his assistance. "Send your man with me and I shall give him a physic. I will return at noon of tomorrow, but remember above all — rest!" Kalonymus murmured a greeting and left, followed by his own lackey (who had attended him from Venice) and Stefano.

The day wore on. After Shylock had recited the evening prayer, Lancelot lit the lamp. Jessica wished to have the door closed as the light hurt her eyes. "But she cannot lie in the dark," Shylock snapped to Lancelot, and the door was left ajar.

A few minutes later Don Samuel came. Shylock's absence from synagogue the whole afternoon had worried him, fearing that he might be ill.

"Jessica's ill," Shylock blurted out in response to Don Samuel's salutation.

"Since when?"

"From this morning — may God have mercy." He motioned to Don Samuel to speak in a lower voice. Don Samuel sought details of the illness, and Shylock described the physician's call at length.

"Shall we call in another physician?" Don Samuel asked.

"I got Kalonymus here by a trick," Shylock said. When Don Samuel heard a sigh from the next room, he repeated his suggestion of summoning another physician.

"I do not know Rabbi Kalonymus," he said, "but my late father always brought three at once from the outset on the principle of 'three for a cure' [actually an invitation to guests offered a third helping]. You must bring a consultant."

"Rabbi Kalonymus is one of the greatest of physicians, but I have no objection to bringing another five — go you inside and speak to her!" He went into the bedroom and told Jessica that Don Samuel wished to see her.

"Heaven forbid!" she cried. "I cannot see anyone but you." Before Shylock could open his mouth in reply, she added — "The stream of light coming from the other room hurts my eyes. Please go out, Father, and close the door."

Don Samuel's words had aroused grave anxiety in him, and he tried to persuade her to let him call Rabbi Kalonymus again that evening.

"Leave me, Father," she implored.

"Very well, my child," he pacified her, but went on, bending over, "Must you really lie in the dark?"

"I feel much better that way," she whispered. "Leave the door into the passage-way open."

"And if you need anything?" he asked. She said that she required nothing. "But it's impossible, my child, you are ill." He remembered that there was a bell in the house and brought it. "If you want anything, you can ring."

"Thank you, father," Jessica sighed.

"The bell," Shylock recalled, "came to me from my father who had it from his grandfather." To escape further speech she said that she knew the whole story, but he continued in a low voice, "When my grandfather was a peddler buying old clothes he used to ring the bell, as his voice was weak and the gentiles on the top floors couldn't hear him." He accompanied his narrative with objurgations against the Venetians for permitting the Jews to pursue no other livelihood than the *Strazzarie* — dealing in second-hand clothes — and as his indignation rose, so did his voice.

"Forgive me, Father, but speech dins in my ears," she interrupted him.

"You are right, my child," he returned contritely. He tip-toed out and closed the door behind him. "She is ill, my son," he told Don Samuel outside. "She needs a lot of rest." He spoke highly of Rabbi Kalonymus, in whom the Doge — known to be an ailing man — placed his full trust, no less than in Andrea Vesalio of whom the whole country rang with approbation, and remarked that although the physician was really needed only for a serious illness, he believed that anyone with an only daughter, the surviving one of four, must take greater caution. And in the same breath he added that he harbored a grudge against Kalonymus because of the scholarship he had obtained from the Signioria for his son. If a Christian gave, why should a Jew not take? But they gave him the bursary in the very days when the decree ordering the burning of the Talmud had been issued — had Kalonymus any self-respect, he opined, he would have thrown the purse of money back in their faces! The narration led him to revile the hypocritical Venetians who held out a finger to this or that Jew but were oblivious to the spirit of the whole community.

Don Samuel only half-heard his employer's words. From time to time he heard Jessica's labored breathing from the next room, and it perturbed him. "Good Jessica, why do you not allow your

Don Samuel to come in to you?" The question buzzed continually in his mind. She had asked him yesterday to leave her alone, something had troubled her, but she was as good as an angel — "dear Don Samuel," she had addressed him. No, she was not vexed with him; she refused to admit him because she was bashful when in bed before a strange male; and that is why she had refused to have a physician — she was a pure and modest daughter of Israel. . . . She had been so sad the previous day — was this not the first symptom of her illness?

"We curtailed our lesson yesterday, she did not feel well," Don Samuel interrupted Shylock who was retelling the wickedness of the double-dyed villains of Venetians.

"True," Shylock agreed. "When I came home last night she was asleep, she had a headache. It is seldom that she misses being at the table for the Sabbath eve meal. It is the first time in many years it has happened." Yet, to ward off any suspicion Don Samuel might have that she was of poor health, he added quickly, "It's a simple cold. Perhaps she drank cold water when perspiring. She is really sturdy and healthy, and has never been really ill, thank God!"

"Shall I remain here overnight?" Don Samuel asked.

"No, no — how can you help her?" He continued, "If she sleeps tonight she will be better in the morning."

Shylock remembered that he had not yet pronounced the benediction over wine for the conclusion of the Sabbath. A deep sigh escaped him when he began, after the benediction, to intone the hymn *Who Differentiates* and the words, "We have sown and our silver shall multiply as the sand." The Almighty had taken three out of four, and the wife of his youth, and yet his silver in that time had grown threefold and more. Had it been otherwise — had his silver been taken and his seed preserved! But God forbid that he should blaspheme: the Lord had given and the Lord had taken away; only that he should have this girl who had remained to him of all of them. . . .

Both he and Don Samuel were ill at ease and could not continue singing. It was on that awful Sabbath forty years ago and more when the Jews of Venice had been expelled from their beautiful houses and immured among the ruins of the isle of dunghills that he had also sung the close-of-Sabbath hymns; and Don Samuel — though hungry and thirsty in the dark dungeon-holes of Ancona, the eighty imprisoned Marranos had sung in unison, "At the close of the day of rest, give Your people freedom." A voice had cried: "Send Elijah the prophet to Thy unfortunates that agony and suffering may cease"; and another, "I shall rejoice and be gladdened in heart when my foes shall fight my fight." Cell to cell responded, voice with voice merged, and the hymns rose in concerted paean to heaven. . . . Why did they recall those awful days, each his own experience of the near and distant past?

Both murmured rapidly the break-of-Sabbath song, and when Shylock suddenly halted, as though something had stuck in his throat, Don Samuel could not continue. No, Shylock could not continue singing! He wanted to howl the words instead of trilling them, and as the physician had forbidden any noise, he could do naught else than recite them in an undertone as a prayer, and that he could not. . . .

Jessica's tossing back and forth and her sighs showed that she could not drop off to sleep. How much did Don Samuel crave to see her, to stroke her delicate hand for a moment, and to open the door and call out gently "Good night!" — but he dared not. Yet when Shylock escorted him to the corridor, and he saw the door of her room open, he tip-toed forward and whispered, "Good night, Jessica," through the crack.

"You will still find pleasure in her," Shylock breathed in his ear, and in both their hearts, throbbing with both anxiety and gratefulness, the prayer echoed: Good night to Jessica. . . .

Shylock wished to remain alongside his daughter's bed all night but she refused. She said that Lancelot and Stefano could take turns.

"I shall in any event not fall asleep," Shylock pointed out.

"You will sleep tranquilly. Lancelot will give me something to drink."

"But the door must remain open," he cajoled. He kissed her on the forehead and went out. She lay languidly, much weaker than before. Her father had kissed her! She never remembered his having done so before. . . . And the kiss burned as the brand of Cain upon her brow. . . . She was young, at the beginning of her life, the doors to the wide and beautiful world were open to her, and yet how good it would be to sleep, to sleep without waking ever and ever. Yesterday she had broken her bridges behind her, and tonight she was again back on the other side of the bridge, and a wall of feeling which she had not experienced yesterday separated her from the world for which she longed — the filial feelings of a daughter. . . . No, she no longer yearned for the world beyond the ghetto walls, but she could not remain in the ghetto — and the escape? To close her eyes and slumber until world's end. . . .

These thoughts increased her weakness and she lay helpless, her panting becoming more irregular. She was very thirsty and Lancelot gave her a little water from time to time.

Shylock lay on his bed and thought he could not close an eye for anxiety, but no sooner had he stretched out than his snoring broke the stillness of the night.

"Please close the door," Jessica begged Lancelot. "The snoring hammers in my head, and go you to bed too, Lancelot, you are fatigued."

"No, little Signorina Jessica, the master told me not to shut an eye for a moment."

Jessica put her hand out weakly to Lancelot. He knelt at her bedside and Jessica held his hand. She whispered to him, "I am only a little ill — yet he is broken and sick. Was I right to want to fly from him?"

Lancelot was frightened. The whole affair was over! After a short pause, he said; "And only yesterday you believed he did not love you. But your happiness comes before his. He is old, and you are young. Life lies before you, little Signorina Jessica."

It seemed as though a heavy stone had been rolled off her mind. Lancelot, her father's devoted servant, had not wavered in his opinion. "I am so tired, good Lancelot. Go on speaking, your words soothe me; but speak quietly lest my father hear."

Lancelot had little more to say, but he kept on repeating the assurance that she was performing a pious deed and that she must thank God for having sent her the noble, handsome Lorenzo who had scorned the beautiful women he met in the mansions of Venice and had chosen her, daughter of the ghetto. In his limited vocabulary he lauded her courage, the splendor of Venice, and the sweet flavor of freedom, and his simple words dripped as healing balm on her remorseful soul. . . .

"I am afraid, good Lancelot—" She suddenly halted him.

"Lancelot is at your side, little Signorina Jessica. You may confide and trust in him," he encouraged her.

"I am afraid of one thing," she murmured. "I fear that the fever will rise and in my delirium I may speak of Lorenzo, mention his name, that my father will hear."

It had not occurred to him. He promised her fervently that he would not stir from her side at night. She explained that in fever a person might reveal matters concealed during consciousness.

"Rest easy, little Signorina Jessica, the physic which the medical man gave you will banish the fever," he said. But his mind was perturbed. Anxiety rode his countenance and his cunning brain sought an expedient. Soon Jessica slept and he lay on the sofa opposite her bed, racking his brains. Now and then Jessica stirred in a fit of coughing, but slept on. But her slumber was restless and she murmured weakly. Lancelot leapt from his couch and almost shouted out loud. When he approached her bed she awoke. In the dim moonlight his face loomed over her with villainous aspect and for a moment she was alarmed. But she was immediately reassured and asked for a little water.

"I have found a way out, little Signorina Jessica; you need not fear," he whispered in her ear. She recalled what they had spoken and her glance invited his counsel. At that moment the door opened slowly and Shylock entered: in his shirt and underclothes he seemed to have risen from the grave. He approached the bed, touched her face, and shook his head dismally.

"How do you feel, my daughter?" he asked.

"Middling. She slept a little, Signor," Lancelot replied in her stead.

"And who closed the door?"

"Signorina Jessica asked me to. You were snoring."

"I didn't shut an eye," rejoined the old banker indignantly. Lancelot added that she was tired and motioned him to go into the next room. Shylock saw that the man was right and went out.

"She did not sleep at all," Lancelot said in a low voice. "She spoke strange things to me. The fever is very high, Signor." Shylock remarked that in his opinion the fever had diminished somewhat, but Lancelot went on, "She thought I was the Doge and said, 'How nice of you to visit me, Messer Doge.' I told her that I was Lancelot her servant, and she smiled and whispered, 'True, your name is Lorenzo Priuli. My father told me that you have become a convert to Judaism so that you might take me for wife.' Then she held my hand and murmured, 'Come, Lorenzo my beloved, let us go to the Lido and you will marry me and not the Adriatic. The rabbi will perform the ceremony.' Thus she murmured and then stopped. Just now I heard her again repeating the name of the Doge, 'Lorenzo, Lorenzo' — she burns with fever, Signor."

"She sickens with fever, my little girl," Shylock lamented "Mordecai the physician is not as high-and-mighty as Kalonymus. If I had called him, he would have spent the night here." Going back to his bed he ordered Lancelot to leave the door open Lancelot returned to Jessica, gestured that her father was awake and lay on the sofa.

For a long while Shylock remained sleepless. Lancelot's stor meant little to his mind except that it showed that in her de lirium she was babbling all manner of things; but various bitte memories and reflections thronged his brain; and the fact that i this period, between the fast-days of the seventeenth of Tammu and the ninth of Ab, the demon of pestilence was abroad ir creased his apprehensions. Yet the moment he fell asleep l again began snoring, and Lancelot closed the door.

"Everything is all right now, little Signorina Jessica," he kne at her side and whispered. "I told him that you were speakir nonsense and gave him some yarn about the Doge whose nam is Lorenzo." Jessica expressed alarm at her father guessing som thing and to reassure her Lancelot repeated the fabrication, word for word. She held his hand and said, "You are clever, and as good as an angel, Lancelot." The man preened himself at the compliment. "I really feel easier. Please go back to the sofa." Nothing loath Lancelot lay down and fell asleep, but she could no longer rest. The fear of revealing something had left her, but the throbbing of her temples and the noise in her ears annoyed her, and she kept on turning over painfully from side to side.

No sooner was it morning than Shylock instructed Lancelot to go to the city and bring Kalonymus the physician at once. Jessica raised no protest. She even said it might be as well for Lancelot to seek him first at his house in the ghetto but Shylock said, bitterly, "He is allowed to live in the city. He is probably there. It's a pity to waste time — hurry, Lancelot."

"I'll bring him at once, Messer," Lancelot cried and ran out of the house.

But he did not find the physician at his home and one of his two servants went off to fetch him. Meanwhile Lancelot ran from the Rialto, where Kalonymus dwelt, to Lorenzo's lodging which he happened to know. He awoke the young nobleman and told him of Jessica's illness. Lorenzo jumped from his bed. His first impulse was to speed to her house and ascertain how she fared; but he swiftly realized that this was impossible, and paced to and fro in nervous excitement.

"Can she indeed not come out tonight?" he asked.

"God forbid, she is seriously ill," Lancelot rejoined. He had to repeat over and over again the previous day's events. "But she left the ghetto last night never to return — what happened in the meantime?" Lorenzo evaded a reply but at length said, "She had a few things to arrange in the Jew's house and I could not detain her."

"She had nothing to arrange. You are no man, Signor Lorenzo," the servant rebuked him. "If she had not returned so late over the water, nothing would have happened."

"Do not annoy me, slave of the Jew!" Lorenzo scolded. But he thought better of insulting Lancelot, the sole contact between

Jessica and himself, and modulated his tone. "Good Lancelot! Is there really no danger? When will she get better, in your opinion, wise Lancelot?" The man wrinkled his forehead and, after some cogitation, said without answering the question, "Little Signorina Jessica is wonderful. I have taught her from childhood to be cautious, and you must now show your caution. Control yourself. Don't go upstairs, and don't call me. I shall find a way of letting you know how she feels."

Lorenzo stood like a pupil before his teacher and nodded. He tried to extract more from Lancelot about Jessica but Lancelot was in a hurry and ran back to the Rialto, to the physician's house.

Over two hours passed before Lancelot brought the medical man back to the ghetto. Don Samuel had come in the meantime, and he and Shylock leaned over the window-sill of the second room awaiting the physician. Don Samuel was quiet but Shylock seethed. At one moment he cursed Lancelot roundly, saying that he had probably dropped in at some church for prayers; the next he abused the townsfolk who gorged and gourmandized and kept the physicians busy day and night; nor did he spare Kalonymus — raging that Jewish patients meant nothing to him. Yet when he saw the black *beretta* approaching with a lackey and Lancelot bringing up the rear, his respect for the distinguished man was revived, and he said to Don Samuel, "He's the Doge's own doctor. That's no small thing."

Shylock awaited Kalonymus on the staircase and showed him into the house with great unction. "You had no patience to wait until noon," the rabbi fumed. Before Shylock had time to answer he was in Jessica's room, with the door closed behind him.

"He tells the father to keep out as though he were the Doge himself," Shylock grated.

"A doctor needs calm —" Don Samuel began.

"And what am I doing? Beating a drum?" Shylock ranted.

"He must concentrate when he examines a patient."

"You are right, my son."

Kalonymus remained a long while in Jessica's room. He gave her a thorough examination, felt her pulse several times, paid special attention to her eyes which had yellowed slightly, and looked at her tongue. After each examination he addressed her in light vein to reassure her.

"I feel much better now," she said.

"Then my errand is in vain," the old physician smiled.

"Is it a serious illness?" she asked.

"Heaven forfend!" he protested. "It is a child's malady, just a cold." He remembered another question. "Tell me, have you taken a bath in the past two days?" She answered in the negative. He rose, patted her hand fondly, and said, "I'll come back tomorrow to see you but rest calmly, do not speak at all — silence is a golden cure — and in two or three days you will be out and about. That will be excellent, won't it?" Again warning her against exerting any effort he went out, closing the door softly.

Shylock and Don Samuel approached to hear his opinion. Kalonymus called his servant, took the bag from him, and extracted potions from it. Shylock could not contain himself.

"What ails my daughter?" he asked.

"Possibly a slight inflammation of the lungs," the physician returned. He sat at a table and wrote down his instructions. "She's your only daughter, isn't she? And who is this young man?"

"My scribe, my right-hand man in the banking-shop."

"It is not my habit to speak of the illnesses of those who seek my advice when there are strangers," the physician remarked.

Shylock wanted to say that Don Samuel was not entirely a stranger in his household but to avoid argument, and to hear in more detail what was ailing his daughter, he motioned Don Samuel to leave.

"If we assume that it is an inflammation of the lungs, it perplexes me how it occurred," Kalonymus began. "She doesn't work amidst a lot of rubbish and dirt like most of the girls in the ghetto who repair old clothing, she doesn't go about much, she didn't damp herself down by the water —"

"She stays at home, and it's Tammuz now," Shylock interjected.

"Yet it sometimes happens under the most favorable conditions and we don't know the reason — we physicians actually know but little. At all events there is no cause for alarm. Her fever is not high; the inflammation — if there is any — is at one spot. I believe that everything will pass in eight or nine days."

"You have revived me. She is the remaining child of four." Shylock's voice shook, and tears came from his eyes.

"But great care is needed, since every illness, even a cut finger, can be dangerous and cause greater malady. The cure is in your hands — she must lie quietly, not read, not talk, the less effort the better; I must treat her as a patient with lung inflammation, which is a fatiguing illness. Thank God her heart is strong." He handed Shylock the instructions on how to use the potions, ordered no other liquids save the juice of fruit, and reiterated his advice about rest. Before leaving he promised to return the following midday.

"Thank God we have physicians like yourself," said Shylock, escorting him to the door.

"In this illness, of which in fact I am not certain, a physician isn't needed at all," the other asserted. "Rest does its function, and more than that we do not know — the physic I gave her is only to allay her headache."

"You are modest, Rabbi Kalonymus," twinkled Shylock.

"It is a doctor's fortune that if he says he is needed, he is not believed; and when he protests that he is really not needed, no one believes him again — such is human nature."

"Yet I would not forego your visit tomorrow for a fee of a hundred ducats, Rabbi Kalonymus."

"I knew it, and that is why I said I would come tomorrow, although it is unnecessary — the main thing is rest, rest! Nor must the patient be told that I fear lung inflammation. Patients are like children, everything worries them."

Don Samuel was awaiting Shylock with anxious eyes when the banker returned. "She is ill, seriously ill, God have mercy," he divulged. Shylock went in for a moment to Jessica, putting on a cheerful manner, and vowed to her that the illness was a slight one and that all she needed was complete rest. He went out again to Don Samuel who was pacing to and fro with downcast mien. Shylock continued, "She is weak now and her illness makes her nervous. I know that you want to see her but she has no wish to. She is bashful and no male has ever seen her lying in bed — you must suffer patiently for her sake, my son."

"It is a suffering I readily assume," the other declared.

"That is wisely put, my son. When she recovers, with God's help, you can see her as often as you please. And now go in peace, my son, and pray for her health." He added a few words of effusive commendation of Rabbi Kalonymus, but when he remembered that he attended the Venetians too, he exclaimed, "I would never have helped them, confound them. Let them linger in torment!" It was the cue for a stream of vituperation and malediction.

"You must speak quietly," Don Samuel cautioned him, nodding at Jessica's room.

"You are right," Shylock whispered shamefacedly, and fell quiet.

When he was outside on the stairs, Don Samuel smiled wryly to himself: Shylock can curse and revile only at the top of his voice.

It was Sunday, and Don Samuel entered the banking-shop through the back door, occupying himself in sorting out promissory notes which fell due in the next few days. He then went back to Shylock's house and, after the midday meal, came back again. As Jessica's temperature had not fallen, both men were deeply perturbed and conferred anxiously whether or not to call in more doctors. Shylock reproached himself with not having invited three or four more at the outset, and Don Samuel was apprehensive lest Rabbi Kalonymus take umbrage if this were done, pointing out that it was wiser not to forfeit the services of the physician who attended the Doge. To this Shylock rejoined that the yellow visage of the Doge aroused doubt of the proficiency of Kalonymus his physician. After the evening prayer, Tubal came and joined in discussion of the problem of inviting more doctors, and decided in favor of Don Samuel's viewpoint.

The following morning Kalonymus the physician cupped

Jessica of blood. When Lancelot removed the utensil and his eye fell upon the blood, he dissolved into tears. Nor did Stefano fail to pray fervently for the recovery of the patient — he kept on thinking of the money he would lose if Jessica should die.

For a short time Jessica felt better and Shylock was full of praise for the "miracle-working medical man." But with noon her aches and pains returned, and Shylock seethed with harsh thoughts of the "pagan *medico*." He explained the physician's quality to Don Samuel with subtle casuistry. "He pretends to be modest and says he knows nothing so that people might think he knows everything, yet in actual truth he knows nothing."

"He probably knows what he is about, but the illness is a stubborn one," Don Samuel pacified him.

"He may know how to deceive gentiles, but that's about all," rejoined Shylock, who thereupon launched into a tirade against physicians and Christians generally.

While at home Shylock maintained some semblance of moderation, but when in his banking-shop, during the few hours he spent there, he raged against all physicians and compared them with sorcerers and necromancers. He made no effort to conceal his ire even when clients came, and motioned to Don Samuel or Lorenzo to settle these affairs.

Lorenzo found it difficult to conceal his distress, but to avert suspicion from himself, he said one afternoon to a client, in a loud voice that Shylock might hear, "He has an only daughter, the survivor of four — he is a good and honest Jew, the only one among the money-lenders. Pray for him!"

Lorenzo's remark came as balm to Shylock — he had never before heard commendation of himself from a Christian. When the client left he edged up to Lorenzo, put his hand on his shoulder, and said, "I thank you, Lorenzo, for taking a share in my sorrow. You are the only Christian I ever met who has a real heart in his chest." But the thought at once occurred to him that the gentile was uttering a falsehood, and coming near Don Samuel he whispered aside, in Hebrew, "May he be denied."

After the shop was closed, Lancelot stole out of the house and met Lorenzo outside the ghetto-gate. Lorenzo interrogated him as to how Jessica looked, what she said, and how she felt, but Lancelot who was in a hurry to get back answered curtly. Lorenzo urged the servant to arrange for him to see her for a moment the next morning but Lancelot reminded him that the physician had emphatically warned against all excitement and that he must not see her face. Yet Lorenzo could not master his emotions and at ten o'clock the next forenoon, when Shylock had to hurry off to the Rialto on urgent affairs for a short time, Lorenzo escaped from the counting-house and went upstairs. Lancelot met him at the door.

"Have you left your senses, Signor Lorenzo?" he cried aghast, and before the other could respond he pushed him outside and slammed the door in his face.

"Slave of a Jew!" Lorenzo stormed to himself. He was ready to batter the door down and run Lancelot through with his rapier for having dared to manhandle him, a nobleman, yet thinking of Jessica, who must be safeguarded against excitement, he forbore. When Lorenzo left the shop at noon for his dinner, Lancelot came down to tell him of Jessica's condition following the physician's visit, and the young man was grateful. Lancelot rebuked him, as though he had been some scamp, for having dared to come upstairs, but he kept silent.

"Everything is on my neck, yet you want to hinder me and spoil everything with your rashness," Lancelot scolded. "Everything falls to me to do — I must watch over little Signorina Jessica, I must work on those ghetto constables to hold their tongues, and I must keep an eye on Don Samuel —"

"That's the main thing," Lorenzo halted him. "I see the way he sits around morosely in the shop. It is not just sympathy with his employer. He loves her, and the Jew regards him with favor."

"Of course that's the main thing, but everything matters," Lancelot exclaimed. "Signorina Jessica must get better and I have to encourage her lest she lose her spirit. The scoundrelly ghetto guards must hold their mouths lest they reveal anything unwisely. The young Jew — true, it's a tough problem; he doesn't budge from the house. But Lancelot is seeing to it that little

Signorina Jessica shouldn't even glimpse his shadow or hear his voice."

"I put all my trust in you," Lorenzo said tremulously.

"And in the Holy Mother — pray for little Signorina Jessica too, Signor Lorenzo. Another voice in prayer has some virtue. One of them may perhaps reach heaven."

"Perhaps — ?"

"It's all in the lap of God, Signor Lorenzo. If I had a Mohammedan friend, I would ask him to pray too — in time of distress no one knows where the truth lies, may I be preserved from blasphemy, Mother of God!" — And Lancelot ran off.

In the evening, when they went upstairs, Shylock suggested that Don Samuel go to prayers without him and return later to spend the night. Lancelot reiterated that Don Samuel could help nothing, but Shylock paid no attention.

Walking to synagogue, Don Samuel felt moved to tears. Never had he been so grateful to a man as to Shylock at this time for having suggested what he dared not ask. He almost went out of his wits at home during the nights: his ears were alert, his eyes fastened on the door — he feared evil tidings of which he dared not think a moment, yet from which his heart never ceased agitating.

Shylock went in to Jessica, who lay with open eyes.

"Shall I call Kalonymus the physician this evening?"

"As you wish, Father," she whispered. His compassion rose at her weak voice. He could no longer speak or stand there. He left the room softly and left her under Lancelot's care.

Half an hour later Jessica felt as if some buzzing saw had stopped whirring. The noise in her ears subsided and the headache left her. She drew a deep breath without its catching at her throat and opened her eyes.

"I feel easier," she told Lancelot. Even though it was twilight he saw the flash of her eyes and at once recognized the improvement. He ran into the second room to call his master, and Shylock, who lay drowsing on the sofa, was alarmed at the door bursting open. But when he saw Lancelot's beaming face he was reassured and hurried in. She welcomed him with a pleasant smile and murmured, "I am better, Father." His trembling hand passed over her forehead and cheeks and descended to her hand, which he stroked, and he said in a choked voice, "You have been spared, my poor little child." Turning to Lancelot he said, "Send Stefano to bring Kalonymus the physician at once."

"It's unnecessary, Father," she said.

"On the contrary, let the artist be proud of his handiwork." And to Lancelot — "Don't let Stefano tell the old man that she is better — he might not come."

Shylock sat quietly stroking her hand. When Lancelot returned he left hurriedly and went to the last room, into which he closed himself. His whole being cried out for expression of his joy yet he feared he might disturb Jessica. "Blessed be the healer of the sick!" he prayed to himself. "Blessed be the healer of the sick!" He began to sing, "There is none like our God, none like unto our Almighty" but broke off, looked around him as though he stood before a great congregation, hit the table with his fist, and cried in a hoarse voice, "And what now do the gentiles say? A Jew has no need to recognize God by His face; he knows Him by His deeds — what will the gentiles say now?"

Don Samuel was detained at the synagogue by a friend who asked about Jessica's condition. When he left the building he was accosted by Deborah, Jessica's friend, who also sought information about her. She had not come to see the patient for fear both of contagion and of Shylock who had insulted her a short while ago, as he had insulted other friends of his daughter.

"The temperature has fallen, blessed be the healer of the sick!" Shylock greeted the young man as he entered the house.

"Thank God!" Samuel cried, and tears glistened in his eyes.

Shylock took him into the inner room and began lauding Kalonymus the physician who knew all, adding, "You have purchased her, my son, with suffering — may it be a virtuous possession!"

Don Samuel could no longer restrain himself. He fell upon Shylock's neck and wept as bitterly as a lost child finding its mother.

He lifted his head from the banker's shoulder when Lancelot

came in to inform his master that the physician was coming — at sight of Don Samuel in Shylock's arms, Lancelot was dumbfounded and spoke in a quaking voice.

Chapter Twelve

RABBI KALONYMUS VISITED JESSICA ON FRIDAY FOR THE LAST TIME. When she begged the physician to allow her to get up, Shylock remarked that she seemed as impatient to rise as though she had maturing bonds to pay.

"You may get up today, in honor of the Sabbath eve, for half an hour and tomorrow, for the Sabbath, a full hour; and on Sunday you may walk about the house as much as you please," said Rabbi Kalonymus. Yet Shylock was disquieted and asked if it were not best to be over-cautious in such circumstances. "She only had a slight fever although it was somewhat peculiar," the physician remarked. "Had she been a poor man's daughter ("God forbid!" cried Shylock), her father would not have sought a physician's advice in a case of simple fever. At all events, I shall not visit her again, and if all goes well come to see me, my child, at the end of next week."

Going down to his shop Shylock was in an excellent mood and to Don Samuel he spoke disparagingly of Kalonymus the physician who had, he claimed, learned irreverence from the Venetians who were known to be more light-minded than women.

On Sunday morning, when he was alone with Don Samuel in the closed shop, he told him: "Jessica is modest, both modest and innocent, and that is why she did not allow you to come into her room and greet her. But today she said she would eat at the table. Come to the meal and see her, Samuel — or perhaps you would rather not?" He winked roguishly at Don Samuel to whom it occurred that this was the first time Shylock had ever ventured anything in the nature of flippancy.

When they came in, Jessica was already at the table. She wore a pink woollen scarf. There were few traces of illness on her countenance, and the suffering she had undergone imparted a unique charm. Don Samuel pressed her hand fondly and she showed him a returning sign of affection. She had heard from her father how sorrowfully he had reacted to her illness, and when he cried "Blessed be the healer of the sick!" she rejoined, "I am so grateful that you supported my father in his bitter trial, Don Samuel Morro."

The stress she placed on the word "Morro" threw Don Samuel into trepidation and he replied, "I hope that you will soon be able to resume the lessons."

Shylock interposed, "If it had not been for him, God alone knows what would have happened."

He did not refer to her illness but to his business. He had neglected almost everything in the past week, first out of grief and then from joy, and there were several debtors who had not paid up on time. During the meal he grew irate at them and at Christian borrowers generally, and did not spare even Lorenzo.

"He sighed over my distress," he remarked, "but the Christian debtor means more to him than the Jewish lender. They did not discharge their due — what mattered it to him?"

When Shylock mentioned Lorenzo's name, Jessica made some pretext and left the room for a few moments. She felt that either one of them might suspect the cause of the slight blush upon her face. Shylock took the occasion of her absence to admonish Don Samuel. "You seem a little embarrassed. You thought she would greet you with a confession of love. I told you she was obstinate. When she regains her strength, I'll speak to her sharply, my son, and everything will be all right."

"Not sharply," Don Samuel said in a low voice. "Love cannot be whipped by compulsion."

"She loves you but —" Jessica entered at this moment and Shylock jumped to another subject, beginning as if in mid-sentence: "And now I must run to repair what others have spoiled — if a Jewish eye is not upon them, confound their souls, they are ready even to steal the walls of the banking-shop."

Jessica could not help but ask, with a quizzical smile, "Have they stolen the tables at least?"

"If you let them, they would do it with pleasure, as a pious deed," cried Shylock. His temper was rising again but he kept quiet. He had no wish to agitate Jessica for whose very life he had been alarmed only a few days ago. But he nonetheless added, "If you managed my business, I would now be a beggar at the doors."

"Jessica is clever, she would be able to deal with them." Don Samuel smiled. He felt he must defend her.

"It's not true," she said. "Father is right."

"Anyone can deal with them," Shylock answered Don Samuel. "Wipe off their debts and they become easy to deal with." He went on: "These gentiles have the instincts of dogs. When they feel that a Jew is of weak character, they fall upon him as if he were a corpse." He told, as they ate, of several instances of non-payment to Jewish money-lenders, including Tubal. "Tubal could have been three times as rich if he were not so tender-hearted. Listen, Don Samuel, a banker and a tender heart are two different things. And don't think that a good heart and a tender heart are the same thing — they're quite unlike."

"I agree with all you say, Messer," Don Samuel replied. Jessica ate quietly and took no part in a conversation so repugnant to her. From her early youth she had heard these sentiments expressed by her father in a thousand ways and forms, and it was always repulsive to her. She interpreted Don Samuel's acquiescence as flattery of his benefactor, the father of the girl he desired, and was contemptuous of him at that moment. She could not imagine that a young and gentle man like Don Samuel could really have a heart as full of bitterness and acrimony as her hot-tempered, rancorous father. She had forgotten his experiences at Ancona and Pesaro which had rooted in him a deathly hatred of the Christians — and yet he had told her so much of those terrible sufferings.

When she finished eating, Jessica said she was tired and went to her room after a parting greeting, without looking at Don Samuel.

"She is like her late mother," Shylock said. "If I had listened to the advice of my Leah, peace upon her, I should have stripped the shirt off my back and left it in the hands of the Venetians, and even have held my tongue — and yet the heart can burst unless you empty the sorrow and chagrin which gathers in it! Such are women, my son. One must not heed them."

Don Samuel found an excuse to go, and a few minutes later left the house. His legs were heavy under him. He had not seen Jessica for nine long days, days as unendurable to him as his period at Ancona, and he had come with singing heart yet left in downcast spirit. She had uttered a few words of thanks but it had been with the lips. Why had she thanked him for having supported her father and not having shared the anxiety for herself? Why had she laid stress upon the word Morro? Had she loved him in the least she would not have left him with her father at the end of the meal; and when she left, she had not glanced at him. . . . Shylock was right when he told him once that no man found favor in her sight, and even today the old banker had said she was obstinate. If the sufferings he had undergone during her illness, day and night — and she knew of them from her father — had not won her heart to love of him, in what way could he win her? Shylock wished to give her to him; he was ready to admonish her severely, but what availed all this if she had no love for him? He tried to delude himself that her indifference was only the result of her illness, but a demon which danced within him pulled away the veils from truth: she was not indifferent at all, she had displayed her real feelings — she had desired him to see that she loved him not. . . .

But she acted otherwise two days later when her father invited Don Samuel to supper and he remained to study with him and Tubal. Though far from exhibiting any affection for him, she spoke to him, asked him jestingly if it had been pleasant on the Tuesday night to sleep in one room with her snoring father, expressed sorrow at having caused him grief, and bantered that he had feared to lose his assiduous pupil.

"Enough, Jessica, you are speaking like a foolish child!" her father scolded.

"And did you think I was an old woman?" she said with raillery.

"Stop it," her father fumed. "Stop your foolery."

"We must be glad she is merry," Don Samuel remarked. He dared say no more in Shylock's presence.

"I have no taste for that kind of drollery," said the banker.

"And what do you like?" The question beat ceaselessly in her mind. He loved her because she was his daughter, he loved Don Samuel because he wanted him as son-in-law. Whom more could he like? As the period of her illness grew more remote, the old feelings were revived in her: she hated the ghetto, this house. That day, at twilight, Lorenzo had come upstairs to her for a short while, and had hugged her with tears in his eyes. He could only ask "How are you feeling, Jessica?" and when he left something weighed heavily on her heart. The illness had brought her closer to her father who had shown such deep devotion, and again she felt she could not leave him but must leave — and it gnawed at her. When she saw Don Samuel she felt easier. He made a decision harder and she helped him in this: she spoke to him kindly, playfully, jokingly; and her father trampled through the web of her feelings, and she was suddenly jerked into the days preceding her illness.

Don Samuel did not perceive the change in Jessica. She went to her own room as soon as Tubal came. She whispered good-night and sent a pallid smile at Don Samuel before retiring. Lancelot came in before she prepared for bed. He brought tidings that Lorenzo would come to the house the next night; he would have some pretext of business.

"You are good, Lancelot. You support me so I shall not fall under the burden of my fate."

"Be happy, little Signorina Jessica. There is none other in the ghetto for whom a similar fate is promised."

Lancelot's words encouraged her but could not throw off the heavy burden. She had traveled too far and could not return. If she rejected Lorenzo's suit he would reveal everything, and perhaps even invent things which had not transpired between them — and she would be cut off by her father and Don Samuel. . . . Ah! Had it not been for the question of money which Lorenzo had raised she might now have fled — she could no longer endure the mask upon her face. Once more she recalled her illness, her father's sorrowful anxiety, and his groaning resounded in her ears: "My child, Jessica my child, how can your heart drive you to abandon your old father?" And so her mind went in circles.

The following evening Don Samuel came for the usual Talmudical discourse, but before Shylock had returned home. He knew that he had been summoned to a consultation at the rabbi's and took the opportunity to see Jessica alone.

They spoke of trivial matters. Jessica said she was eager to leave the house at night but immediately repented — she had been thinking of a meeting with Lorenzo somewhere in Venice.

"Another few days, Jessica," Don Samuel consoled her, adding, "You will honor me with the first outing, won't you?"

Jessica evaded a reply, saying, "Actually I am confined to the house in the evenings — where can one promenade in the ghetto?"

"One may promenade wherever there is sky overhead, Jessica."

"One might promenade in the sky —" she smiled.

"There's a ghetto too in the sky and a great gate, but there the inferiors are above, while they are in torment below." Jessica smiled deprecatingly. "Do you not believe in a paradise and a purgatory?" She shrugged her shoulders. "Without that belief it would be impossible for us Jews to exist even a day, even an hour."

"There may be paradise above, but purgatory is down here below, on this earth," she said.

"Well said, Jessica." It seemed to him that he heard Shylock's steps coming up the stairs. "And so, Jessica, are you willing to have your first walk with me? Your father will raise no objection."

"I shall have my first walk with Deborah my friend. She is a nice girl, you ought to meet her, Don Samuel. She stopped coming here because of father — I am the only woman in the world who can tolerate his stormy temper," she added with a sad smile.

"He is like a Venetian and carries a mask. But beneath the mask of his anger is a soft and good Jewish heart."

To break off the talk about Shylock, his master, Don Samuel asked about Deborah. He told Jessica that she had awaited him on the past Tuesday when he left the synagogue and asked him about her sick friend.

"Yet she did not come to visit me. Father insulted her like some base creature once when she came to call me to go to Venice. And the truth was that I had suggested that we might take a gondola for a while upon the wide waters."

At this juncture Shylock and Tubal entered.

"Bad news comes from the Papal territories. The old tyrant is raging again," Shylock cried. Tubal supplemented him.

"Take care!" Jessica warned. "The servants are devout Christians."

"Shall I be afraid of my servants? Must I hold my tongue in my own house?" Shylock shouted; and as if to spite her, he raised his voice still higher and heaped calumny and abuse upon the personage in Rome. "He should have crumbled to dust long before he ascended that bloodstained throne. He was old enough to die then!" he cried, and accompanied his words with quotations from the maledictory passages of Leviticus XXVI and Deuteronomy XXVIII.

"Do not shout so loud," Tubal pacified him. "She is right. There is no loyalty in servants."

"She is right," Don Samuel assented. Shylock sent him an angry glance. He desisted when Lancelot came in and served supper. Jessica said, without being asked, that she had already eaten, and escaped from the room.

The study-period lasted an hour and when Don Samuel went home with Tubal, and recalled Jessica's treatment of him compared to that of the first day he had seen her after her illness, he felt as if the bitter memory of that meeting were now mitigated. When she was alone with him, he reflected, she was lovable; and it was her father's rabid temper which vexed her — and for the first time he grew angry with Shylock, his benefactor, who caused her so much aggravation.

Lying down to sleep, Don Samuel now pondered the whole sequence of their conversation. Purgatory was upon earth, she had said — how shrewd she was! If it were possible to walk in the sky — how cleverly said! And why had she told him that he must get to know Deborah her friend? If she had loved him, she would not have said this. And as always he gravitated between despair and hope, and as always he determined that at their next encounter he would tell her clearly that life meant nothing to him without her.

At three o'clock the next afternoon Jessica came down to her father in the banking-shop and told him she was going to Kalonymus the physician who had asked to see her at the end of the week.

"I am going there too," he said. "Wait for me a few moments." He looked at her. "It is hard for you to stay indoors. I don't believe you. I want to hear myself what he says."

Shylock continued to negotiate with a client. Jessica stood upon the threshold and looked outside. She felt that both Lorenzo and Don Samuel were stealing glances at her. She could not restrain herself and turned her face as though to see if her father were ready to leave. She met the glances of both young men. Lorenzo lowered his eyes to the ledger. Then he turned his face to Don Samuel and saw him giving Jessica a restrained smile. Lorenzo dropped his eyes again and smiled to himself. "We shall see who laughs last, vile Jew," he thought. Jessica walked a few paces forward and awaited her father outside.

At the ghetto gate Shylock donned the red hat and Jessica covered her head in the veil. They entered a gondola and were rowed to the Rialto. Shylock sat, sullen and silent. Jessica gazed in front of her and a thrill of joy passed through her at seeing these waters for the first time since she had gone out that night with Lorenzo to the Lido. Were her father not with her, she would have burst into song as the gondola entered the Grand Canal and resplendent Venice unfolded itself before her eyes. The marble walls, the gilded pillars at the gates, the towers, all bathed in sunshine, and the *gonfalons* of St. Mark fluttering over the palaces, were like a display put on in her honor, and the winged lions seemed to be dancing merrily in the breeze in welcome.

Kalonymus was not at home when they reached his house. The servant said he would return shortly. Shylock muttered to himself, "He is amassing wealth like Croesus. It's a much better business than a bank." When he saw that Jessica was smiling at his statement, he added, "This business has a great advantage: he finds them stretched out on their beds of sickness." Jessica signed to him to keep quiet: the doctor's servant was not his own Lancelot. He nodded affirmatively and breathed heavily.

Shylock had no patience to sit quiescently and await Kalonymus. He asked Jessica to accompany him to see one of his debtors near by.

"Go you alone, and I shall await the physician," she said.

"I want to hear what he says too," Shylock insisted. "That wicked fellow owes me three hundred ducats. It is best that we go to him together." On occasion, though rarely, Shylock took Jessica with him to the Rialto. Those with whom he dealt were abashed in the presence of the beautiful girl and refrained from gibing at the "Jewish vampire."

Jessica went with him to a business house near the German warehouses. The owner, a man of about fifty years, approached and bowed. "He has never bowed to me before. May his eyes drop out at sight of the daughter of the Jew," Shylock thought. Before he could speak, the other took out a purse of a hundred ducats and, giving them to Shylock, said, "I know that I was late in payment. I shall bring you the balance in a week."

"You promised thrice and failed to keep the promise. You will need me again. You must know that I am strict in these affairs," Shylock remarked. Before the Christian could reply, he left with Jessica. "Confound the man," he said to himself. "Why should I let him feast his eyes on her?" Aloud he said to his daughter, "I thought the debt lost. It is your doing." His thoughts became distracted. He slowed down and said, "Jessica my child, I am getting old, and the wickedness of these Christians is increasing. I cannot carry the burden much longer, and I say, 'Don Samuel is the man.'"

"Let us hurry. We may miss the physician," she said rapidly. Shylock's blood rushed to his face in anger, but he restrained himself. "He is perfect in every respect, my child," he added.

"This is no time for conversation on such matters," she protested.

"Neither now nor yesterday nor tomorrow," he rapped out. Then he changed his tone and spoke gently again. "I want to see you happy, my child. You must be worthy of your lamented mother's name." He noticed that the words had touched her heart. "She loved you. She gave her soul for you, Jessica."

"Let us speak of this another time, Father."

"This is another time! Tell me, what fault have you found with him?"

"I have found no fault with him at all," she replied, gazing stonily ahead.

"Then there must be some fault with you, that you don't fall on my neck publicly when I want to give you a husband of his sort," Shylock snapped. "It has happened before that girls proud of their beauty, who rejected all suitors, grew to have white hair."

"I've just been ill, Father. Leave me alone," she begged.

"Don't talk nonsense," he cut her short. "If not he, no man will ever find favor in your eyes, and you'll remain an old spinster." He recalled what Lancelot had told him on the first night of her illness when she spoke in her delirium, and added angrily, "There's no Jewish Doge, and even if there were, he would have chosen someone from the family of Jochanan Levy or the house of Abarbanel, and not Jessica daughter of Shelah, grand-daughter of Saul the rag-dealer." (Shylock always claimed that his name came to the family from the original of Saul, his grandfather's name, and the Poles who settled in Venice called him Sheyel and then, in the Polish Jewish dialect, Sheylick.)

They were standing in front of Kalonymus' dwelling. "Leave me alone until after the festivals, Father — let us go in."

"Until after the festivals — three months!" he exclaimed. But suddenly a load fell from his mind, his eyes sparkled gleefully, and in a tender voice he said, "I seek only your good, my child.

There is none better than Don Samuel. I know him from business, from study, and I have always longed for such a man."

"Then say nothing to Don Samuel—"

"I swear by all that's holy to say not a word or half a word to him!" Shylock said with emotion. "If God be willing, we shall speak to you again at Tabernacles—I shall adorn our tabernacle as it has never been adorned before, my child." Jessica tried to summon a smile to her lips but could not. "You are as sad as though you already stood beneath the wedding-canopy."

Kalonymus himself met them as they entered. "I am being awaited elsewhere. It is good that you have returned. What is the matter?"

"May she now go out in the evenings? She finds no rest at home. It's the modern generation," Shylock forestalled Jessica.

Kalonymus felt her pulse, asked her some questions and, patting her on the shoulder, said, "Everything is all right, my daughter! You can take walks, go sailing, dancing, as much as you wish." Shylock bombarded him with questions but he checked him. "If all were like her, there would be no physicians in the world. But now excuse me, I have to hurry to a real patient." Taking them to the door, he added, "You have money, Signor Shylock, and you spend it on a doctor needlessly—I'll confess the truth: when I examined her, I was again certain that she had no trace of inflammation of the lungs. The temperature had no sooner fallen than the illness passed as if it had never been."

"Why do you say I have money—people just exaggerate, always exaggerate," Shylock grumbled. "But I have only one daughter."

On leaving, Jessica expressed the wish to remain a short while longer in the city.

"What will you see here? Come home with me," Shylock said in a fatherly tone.

"I shall be home early—I haven't been in the city for so long a time." Shylock shook his head disapprovingly but raised no protest.

"In another week, God willing, you will resume your Hebrew lesson—there's a great deal to learn out of our books, Jessica."

With a smile on his lips, he whispered, "You may also let him teach you to dance — why not? You must sing and dance. The day of your happiness is near, my daughter."

He turned to go to the gondola landing-stage, she to San Marco Square.

Shylock jumped into the gondola with the agility of a young man, and goaded the gondolier to hurry him to the ghetto — he wanted to bring the tidings to Don Samuel: he would tell him, "Where you failed in telling her, I succeeded — learn from me, my son!" But on sitting in the gondola he remembered having sworn to Jessica, in his great emotion, not to breathe a word to Don Samuel. "Well, whatever happens, I'll hint at it without breaking my vow," he thought. His heart overflowed with joy and he was only sorry that he could not share his happiness with Don Samuel.

Jessica walked on listlessly. Her heart was harried with remorse: Why had she allowed Lorenzo to approach her? Why had she promised her father to answer his question about Don Samuel after the festivals? It was impossible for her to give the reply for which her father was waiting. She consoled herself with the thought that there were still three months ahead, a long time. Yet she had to steal into her father's room, extricate the key to the wall box from beneath his pillow, and take some purses of gold. How could she do it? And if she failed, what would Lorenzo say? No, she was afraid; she could not succeed. Her father would awake, catch her hand, and cry out. A cold perspiration broke out over her as she imagined the scene in the dead of night. The blue sky seemed covered with a gray pall. San Marco Square which she had reached was blurred. Lorenzo and Don Samuel, they were all one to her — she did not care if it were the one or the other, so long as she was rid of this unbearable burden. . . .

She bought grains for a few coins and fed the multitude of pigeons in St. Mark's Square. They picked out of her hand, perched on her shoulder where she placed some grains, and cooed fondly around her. The Basilica of San Marco, the towers of the proud cathedral, the Doge's palace girt with marble pillars —

Jessica no longer saw them. She sat bowed and watched the flocks of jostling birds who brought her love and tranquillity with the beating of their wings, their wheeling about her, their pecking at the palms of her hands.

Chapter Thirteen

AT FIRST DON SAMUEL HAD INTENDED RESUMING HIS LESSONS TO Jessica on the following Tuesday but as it was the day before the fast of the ninth of Ab, Jessica — with her father's acquiescence — thought it better to postpone the occasion until Sunday.

On the Sabbath the Ashkenazic temple was in a tumult. A controversy had broken out over an ordination to the rabbinate conferred by the rabbis of Ferrara upon a learned scholar aged about thirty who had resided in Venice some five years. Both factions were almost at fisticuffs when a woman and two children, one aged ten years and the other a couple of years younger, came to the synagogue; and when the woman picked out one of the older men, David ben Yekutiel, who was among the leading controversialists, she forced her way to him, fell upon his neck, and cried, "We fled for our lives, Father," and burst into tears. The elder boy added, "Our father is trying to sell the furniture and he will come too in a few days."

The quarrelling subsided in the synagogue as by magic, and all thronged round the woman and children. Men who had been in violent argument a short while back asked each other anxiously, "Who is the woman? What does she tell?" Shylock left the synagogue, taking Don Samuel with him.

"What need you to hear, my son? These things are well known," he groaned. Outside he added, "These things are known, my son. According to some, the days of the Messiah have come, the troubles and persecutions are unceasing; and in the opinion of others, the Messiah himself has come."

"Well said, Signor," remarked Don Samuel, walking alongside him.

"The Almighty has sent the persecutors upon us," Shylock

smiled bitterly, "to remind us that we are one people — just as He is the one God. Yet the Ashkenazim are separate and the Sephardim are separate and the Italians are separate, forgetting they are all Jews."

"That plain fact is known only to our tormentors and oppressors," Don Samuel said.

A few minutes later the woman left the synagogue, her father leading the two children by the hand, and many of the congregation followed to hear what had occurred in the wicked kingdom of the Pope. She told brokenly of all that had happened to the Jews of Civitanova where she lived. A few months earlier the citizens of Civitanova had appointed a new administrator of the public property, one Achille Montecchio, who was a notorious Jew-baiter. He had incited the gentiles to expel the Jews from their dwelling-places near the synagogue, and they had been compelled to go outside the city in the vicinity of the dunghills and garbage-dumps, adjoining the bawdy-houses. The Jews had also been forbidden to purchase their food at the market until six o'clock in the evening, and the itinerant vegetable-sellers had been instructed not to go to the Jewish quarter. Achille had also written to Rome calumniating the Jews, wherefore the edict had come to the Duke of La Marca forbidding the Jews to collect their guaranteed debt-bonds unless they undertook solemnly to swear not to export silver or gold from the state, and to bring them to trial if gentile debtors had claims from past years. Six of the leading members of the community had been arrested and sent to Rome to be interrogated by the Inquisition.

After the midday meal had been finished at Shylock's house, heavy footsteps were heard coming up the stairs. Jessica rose and hurried to the door. After each meeting with Lorenzo in Venice she was uneasy and every unfamiliar noise caused her disquiet. She was beset by several anxieties: the police were coming to question her about a theft at the casino; the priests were coming to take her away with the false claim that she had already been baptized; Lorenzo had jilted her and was coming with a friend to reveal all to her father so that he might drive her from the house. A sharp pang of remorse stabbed her heart. Yet when the door opened, the feeling passed.

The visitors were David ben Yekutiel and his daughter Esther who had arrived an hour ago from Civitanova. They had sought Don Samuel at Tubal's house and learned that he was now at Shylock's. Tubal came with them.

"That is Don Samuel Morro." David pointed at him. "Speak to him. She has something to tell you and did not wish to rest from her arduous journey until she had seen you, Signor Samuel."

The woman in a broken voice narrated:

"I swore to the wife and children of Rabbi Benjamin Nehemiah that on reaching Venice safely I would immediately seek you out and bring you their request. Rabbi Benjamin Nehemiah was arrested with five other eminent notables four weeks ago. Many were taken into custody six months ago on the accusation that the Jewish community still owed sixty thousand ducats to the Papal treasury from the fine of a hundred and fifty thousand ducats imposed thirteen years ago. They remained in prison eleven days while they undertook to raise the tremendous sum from the community — and we hoped that they would be released again this time."

"Confound them, sixty thousand ducats!" Shylock exclaimed.

"But we haven't learned this time of what they are accused," went on Esther Cohen. "At the orders of Cardinal Alessandrini, signed and sealed by himself, they were sent five days before the ninth of Ab under an escort of six horsemen to Rome to be tried before their Grand Court."

"God only knows what awaits us from our oppressors here!" Shylock cried. Tubal hushed him and asked him not to interrupt the poor woman's narrative.

"What can I hear that I don't know? — I know the clergy, the notables, their wicked people," declared Shylock.

"The Christians in our city were not so bad until that evil Achille came along and incited them."

"Let anyone try to speak good of the Jews to them — it would be like addressing the trees and stones," Shylock interrupted her again.

"There's no one among them who will take up the cudgels on our behalf," said David ben Yekutiel.

"That is not true, father, there are even now honest people among them," retorted Esther his daughter. "Many of the townsfolk and the judges stood up for the Jews against Achille, and one of them, Federico Topino, an eminent and respected man, even went to the Cardinal in Rome to plead for intercession, but Achille's followers had preceded him with their letters, and nothing availed. And when the Jewish leaders were taken from prison to be sent to Rome, and the guards were about to put fetters on their hands and feet, many of the city's notables gathered and prevented them, and the guards had compassion and took them unfettered."

Jessica had been seething with indignation, and only Esther's last few words about the good Christians assuaged her. But Shylock reviled them too.

"They just pretend to be merciful. There's no virtue in them, damn them!" he cried.

"But you hear what happened, Father," Jessica remonstrated.

"Did she see all this? The Christians must have spread such rumors and the Jews believed them! There's a lot of truth in the saying that he who believes a gentile eats pork!" Shylock raged. Jessica lowered her head and kept silent. She knew it best not to enter into an argument with her father.

"Two were saved," Esther continued. "One was Mose Peperdillo, whose name had been inscribed at the foot of the Cardinal's missive. He was a poor man clad in rags and the constables thought him to be a nobody, and left him in the prison at Civitanova. But he lost heart and went over to their religion, confound him." She narrated in detail the circumstances of his conversion. The night after the others had been sent to Rome, he summoned the chief warder at the prison and told him, "I had a dream. A man or woman came to me and said, 'Take shelter beneath the wings of the Christian faith and you will escape all harm and your transgressions will be atoned.'" On the morrow the warder told the wicked Achille, and the Jew was taken out of prison and baptized; and many Christians sent him presents. "And now," said Esther, "he is called Angelo Silzo and he is in the hands of the Fratri di San Agostino who are teaching him the Christian religion."

"They are exchanging their immortal souls for a few years of earthly life, may they go to perdition!" groaned Tubal.

"It is hard, brothers, to withstand the test. Many are abandoning the true faith," said David ben Yekutiel mournfully. Jessica sent him a look of gratitude. Shylock shook his head but said nothing.

"The other one saved was Abraham Cohen, own brother of the proselyte Giovanni Batista. Abraham Cohen was saved before the others were taken to prison because his brother came to tell him that his name was among the eight, and he fled at night with his wife; some say to Turkey." She sighed and continued, "Giovanni Batista knew of the Cardinal's orders before the arrests, and the Jews of Civitanova now know that his hand was in the plot. He became a convert this year; in the first few days after his baptism he pretended to be a lover of Israel, but he later showed his true character and is now among their principal agitators."

"Here's another one, Giovanni Batista, like the grandson of Rabbi Elias! May the names and memories of both be expunged!" Shylock grated between his teeth. His seamed face was convulsed with rage and the creases on his forehead had become deeper.

"Thy destroyers and demolishers from amidst thyself shall come! The words of the Prophet have come true among us," sighed David ben Yekutiel. Jessica sat pallid and shivering at hearing the simple but piercing words of David ben Yekutiel. Don Samuel saw that her face had changed color and said to her, "It is hard to stand all this. The hair rises at the agony of it — please go out!"

"What can you help if you hear more?" Shylock told her half-lovingly, half-complainingly. Jessica's eyes filled with tears and she retired to her room.

Esther went on with her tale of woe and of more horrible deeds, and then rose to go. At the threshold she remembered she had not delivered the most important message and returned with her father and Tubal.

"I am so downcast with suffering and the hard journey that I forgot to tell you," she cried and burst into tears.

"Calm yourself, my daughter. Your husband Rafael will reach here safely. I'll share my crust with you." Her father's voice trembled, and he went on, as though speaking to himself, "Rafael was the son of rich parents; Rabbi Elias Levita composed an ode in honor of his marriage with my daughter, and now —"

"Don't recall Elias Levita's sin which has made him a hissing and a by-word among the great," Shylock protested. David ben Yekutiel tried to defend the dead grammarian and scholar, but Shylock insisted, "None can shield him. He taught the Zohar and Talmud to the cardinals and bishops, and now his pupils and their pupils are inciting the wild mobs against us. Apart from his books he has left us his two grandsons, blast their memories, who are also among our detractors."

Esther wiped her eyes and turned to Don Samuel. "Rabbi Benjamin Nehemiah was always loud in your praise, read your letters out in synagogue, and regarded you always as a son. You must now help him as if he were your father — thus said his wife, and I swore to bring you his message on reaching Venice."

Don Samuel sat with his head between his hands and, shading his eyes, said in a choking voice, "I am ready to give my life to save his!"

"That is forbidden by the Holy Law," said David ben Yekutiel.

"If they want the soul of the rabbi they won't exchange it for the soul of the pupil," added Tubal.

The naïve words of Tubal and David struck Shylock as being most stupid, but what could he say to men whose grief had turned their minds? His grief was no less than theirs, and although the knife had not been turned in his heart more than usual, it was Don Samuel's sorrow which tore at him pitilessly as though Don Samuel were his own son, blood of his blood and flesh of his flesh.

"The Venice community is renowned for its good deeds, and

you are close to one of the foremost rich men," said Esther without looking at Shylock. "Do what you can, Signor Morro, to save your preceptor and the other good men of the community — every day is precious."

"I shall do it! And this very evening I shall speed a letter to his wife to reassure her!" cried Don Samuel, and Shylock sighed heavily, thinking, What can a Jew do against beasts of prey?

"Was that all you had to say, my daughter?" asked David ben Yekutiel. She pondered a moment and then stood up.

"You live here in peace and calm," she said at the door. "Help those who are in danger."

"We sit here in peace and calm — ? I hope this sort of calm speedily overtakes the Venetians!" Shylock called after her. She left with her father. Tubal made a move to follow them but Shylock deterred him. "We must do something for them, Tubal."

"What can we do?"

"Let us do the impossible!" Don Samuel interrupted.

"We cannot achieve the impossible, Samuel, but we must think of what to do, and it is obvious that the earlier the better," Shylock said.

After thinking awhile Tubal said, "Let us go, this evening, after the benediction over wine, to the rabbi's, and prepare letters to be sped to the rabbis of Rome by the horse-post."

"That's not enough. The rabbis of Rome are there and doing what they can," returned Don Samuel. "And one must be careful of what is written in Paul's lands."

"We must write that we shall contribute whatever sum is placed upon us," Shylock supplemented Tubal without referring to Don Samuel's warning.

"But we must know of what they are impeached, and if a ransom is required at all," Don Samuel pointed out.

"That Asmodeus of the Carafa claps cardinals and counts behind bars. If bribery were of any avail, they would immediately be set free," remarked Tubal.

"It's our misfortune that he won't take bribes," Shylock asserted. "Yet if he is above it, his underlings and retinue are not averse. They chase us because they chase our money, confound them to eternal damnation!"

Shylock and Tubal went on arguing, but Don Samuel sat dejectedly and cast about in his mind for a plan.

"The day is still long. Let us lie down to fulfill the injunction 'Rest upon the Sabbath is a luxury,' and then meet this evening with the heads of the community to see what can be done," urged Tubal; and a few minutes later he left the house.

"Someone must hasten to Rome and arouse the communal heads to do something," Don Samuel said to Shylock. Shylock shrugged his shoulders. "I am ready to go, master."

"Have you taken leave of your wits, Samuel? You are a Marrano and if, God forbid, the Papal Government, let alone Rome, learns of it you are as good as a dead man. The wicked old fanatic throws even Christians into the valley of death if their piety is not sufficient for his liking."

"The rabbi's family depend on me, and I promised to do what I could to save him and the other prisoners! Writing letters is not enough."

"Do not be so downcast, my son. We shall consult this evening at the rabbi's house. Whoever goes, it won't be you, my son."

Don Samuel sat distracted. "The one who has this closest to his heart must go," he said in a low voice.

"I will not let you go, my son. I won't let you jump into the fire!" Shylock cried. "I would be ready to go in your place, but I am old and I am a wrathful man; I might blurt out some imprecation or curse which might land me in prison."

"God forbid!" Don Samuel ejaculated, lifting his head fearfully. Shylock was gratified at Don Samuel's expression of concern for him. How much he desired at this moment to tell him of the conversation with Jessica in the Rialto! He knew well that he had promised Jessica to say nothing, but threw out a hint. "You are dear to me, my son, and I shall spare no money to fulfill your requests — my money is in effect your money. Another month or two — Jessica is obstinate, but she will get used to you. I know my daughter Jessica like my ten fingers."

When Shylock mentioned the name of his daughter a thought

flashed into Don Samuel's mind of which he was at first himself apprehensive.

"Yet for me she is a puzzle," the young man said. Then — "Is she like her father ready for sacrifices on behalf of her persecuted people?"

Shylock did not grasp his full meaning and said, "It is good, my son, that a housewife should not be extravagant. I always esteemed Leah my wife, may she rest tranquilly, for being so economical. But I never deterred her — on the contrary, I fear that Jessica is more than necessarily extravagant by nature, and it is your duty to direct her in appreciating the value of money in all its aspects."

Shylock went on to lecture to Don Samuel on the value of money in commerce, in family life, in its influence upon society, and the like. Don Samuel heard him but vaguely; he was busy with his own thoughts. He again put the question to Shylock, "There are sacrifices other than money — is Jessica capable of them?"

"Suffering and pain are sacrifices, and it's a great axiom, my son, that birth-pangs are the greatest of all pain. A woman accepts all these. Let us be grateful for them — they keep us lest we perish from the earth and they nurture the next generation, in spite of all the devilish plots of our enemies."

Shylock told with enthusiasm of one girl who had given birth at sixteen years of age and another at twelve, and expressed regret that he had only had four children.

Don Samuel was glad that the other had become so prosy and verbose. He had time to ruminate and ponder the matter carefully. There was no doubt that someone had to go to Rome — but who ought it to be? Every Jewish male imperiled his life and could do no good. It was imperative that a woman should travel to Rome — if she were wise and modest, no harm could come to her; and if she were beautiful too, the doors would spring open to her as to no illustrious ambassador. It was enough to recall several of Boccaccio's tales to suspect the impure thoughts of these prelates; yet a daughter of Israel was no Christian woman confessing to them and in any event had no trust in them. Don

Samuel suspected himself of entertaining these fears so that he might not deprive himself of the joy of her presence for several weeks; he chid himself for the thought, and so he came to the full-born conviction that Jessica and none other, male or female, must travel to Rome.

"What of this affair of Rabbi Nehemiah, my teacher and preceptor?" he addressed Shylock.

"But we agreed that we should discuss it tonight."

"Yet permit me to repeat my first question — is Jessica ready like her father to undertake sacrifices for her oppressed race?"

"I do but little," Shylock deprecated.

"But you will be asked on this occasion to do much, both by myself and by our Jessica," continued the other. He emphasized "our Jessica" for the first time to give more force to his demand.

It suddenly became clear to Shylock where Don Samuel's remarks were driving. He was flabbergasted.

"But it's out of the question," he stammered. To give him no time for reflection, Don Samuel continued, "I too was startled when the thought struck me, but after I pondered awhile it was clear that no one save her could help — perhaps my sacrifice is the greatest, my good benefactor, since I shall not see her for many weeks —"

"Do you believe too that I won't feel her absence?" Shylock objected. His face grew more tender and he added, "No, my son. I cannot let her go for so many weeks."

"She need only bring us news," Don Samuel rejoined. "And no man can reach as far as a woman. Jessica is clever, she will bring us a true report." He went on speaking, cajoling, arguing, and the more he spoke, the more convinced Shylock became. When Don Samuel repeated that Jessica was intelligent, the banker smiled and he whispered, as if to himself, "And she is also beautiful."

"I did not dare mention it. No one could refuse her." He wanted to bring up the memories of Queen Esther and Judith but it struck him with loathing that they had submitted to the tyrants; and he cited only the narrative of Jael the wife of Heber the Kenite who, as told in the Book of Judges, went out and killed Sisera. Shylock remembered that because of Jessica, who came with him on that Thursday before her visit to Kalonymus the physician, the Christian client gave them a cordial welcome in admiration of her beauty, and even repaid him a hundred ducats on account of a loan which he had almost written off as lost.

"Why should we go back to the days of the Judges? Even today a beautiful woman strikes them blind!" he said. Don Samuel was now certain of Shylock's consent. He rose, pressed him affectionately, "It is indeed the Sabbath of Consolation today. You have comforted me, my father."

Shylock held Don Samuel's hand. "Let us think this over. Perhaps it is as well that she become accustomed to good deeds, rare deeds; perhaps her grace came to her to assist her unfortunate brethren. But it is a long way, and a woman alone —"

"There is no need to fear for Jessica going that long way alone — she is proud and sagacious," Don Samuel assured him.

"Let us first hear what she has to say," Shylock said. Jessica was asleep but when her father opened the door she awoke. "Jessica, will you come out a moment? I have something to say to you." She rose and a few moments later came into the next room. "Listen, Jessica, it is essential that someone go to Rome to see what can be done for the captives — you will hear the details later. Would you agree to go?" He looked at her with his scrutinizing gaze. Don Samuel did not take his eyes from her as though he were trying to influence her with his stare. Jessica was astounded at the proposal. Yet she swiftly saw the benefit to herself, and with a happy face cried, "To Rome? Of course I will go!"

"I fear you have not weighed the matter carefully enough," said Shylock after a brief pause. "It is a long and weary journey—"

"But the physician said that if everyone were as healthy as I, there would be no need for his profession in the world!" Jessica interrupted. The more she thought it over, the greater was her desire to travel for a while, far from the place where her soul was tormented between fear and sorrow and hesitancies.

"It's good you recalled the physician," Shylock commented

"I'll go to ask his advice immediately. He may be in his house in the ghetto. If not, I'll take a stroll to the Rialto." Don Samuel wished to accompany him to hear how Shylock would put the question to Kalonymus.

"No, you stay here with Jessica," Shylock hinted as he went out.

Don Samuel began to tell Jessica what it was all about, but she smiled and said, "I understand, Don Samuel. I am to ascertain what they are being accused of. I am to penetrate into the palaces of the cardinals and princes and to help the unfortunates — I shall do it to the best of my ability, Don Samuel. I have never been in Rome, nor in Florence for that matter. Father thinks that traveling is a vanity. Has he yet fully consented to my going?"

"Not yet, but I shall not relax until he agrees," Don Samuel declared.

"Then the matter isn't yet settled," said Jessica disappointedly. "You don't know my father." Deep inside himself Don Samuel lamented the fact that she was eager to leave and that she did not mind being far from him, but the desire to assist his preceptor who was in peril banished the feeling of dismay at her indifference to himself.

"Rest assured, he must agree," he declared.

"Must? You show again that you don't really know him," she remarked.

Without answering her, Don Samuel continued, "You must discharge this mission with wisdom. God forbid that you utter anything indiscreet! The sword of the wicked old tyrant hangs over Christians too."

"You know that I am of cautious speech, Don Samuel."

"Far too much," he smiled. He repeated the details, gave her instructions in several respects, and for a long time spoke to her as eloquently as if he were an attorney pleading before a bar of justice. Lancelot came in several times and asked Jessica a number of trivial questions, but Don Samuel did not stop and the more he spoke, the broader his conceptions and the more brilliant his oration.

"You might have been a great pleader," remarked Jessica. Don

Samuel was visibly gratified at the compliment, saying. "Religion, law and forensic debate have interested me since my early youth. Rabbi Shlomo Yehya, peace to his soul, took me into that vineyard."

"To be a pleader at the bar it is necessary also to have a morsel of bitterness and irony, and these you lack, to your good fortune," Jessica added.

"One needs cunning in addition to bitterness and irony," he commented. "But all these come to the surface even in as quiet a man as myself when he is tormented by distress of soul — and the arrest of my teacher and preceptor pierces my soul to those depths."

Both of them kept glancing out of the window, impatiently awaiting Shylock's return. What would happen if he said the doctor had forbidden the long journey? "If he only says that there is no real danger in her journey, she must go," thought Don Samuel. Jessica could not imagine that she might not go now. For some reason she thought that she would be lost unless she went; she must reveal all today or fly from the house without waiting for Lorenzo to take her to him. A cold sweat broke out over her at these thoughts which conjured up terrifying pictures: Don Samuel would not forgive her foolishness; he would refrain from speech, but her father would learn of the matter from Lorenzo and, enraged at her, would turn her from his house; she would flee from the house without seeing Lorenzo — she could not implore him to take her for wife — she would seek refuge in a convent, and the gate would close behind her for ever. . . . She could not take either one path or the other. She must go out alone at night in a gondola and jump into the Adriatic. . . .

Both remained leaning over the window-sill and when they saw Shylock coming, a cry of excitement burst in unison from their throats. Shylock saw them from afar and waved his hand reassuringly sending them a confident smile. They drew back almost simultaneously from the window. In his exultation he put out his arms to embrace her, and she retreated a few paces.

"Forgive me for my stupidity," he said abashedly. "I am so excited at being able to help my preceptor and teacher."

"I understand you, Don Samuel. You have a compassionate heart," Jessica returned.

Shylock entered and stretched himself on the couch.

"Confound them! One merchant cried, 'The Jew comes on his Sabbath to the Rialto, money means more to him than his religion!' And the others burst out into wild laughter, may the shades take them! Two of them also spat at me." A cloud of grief and anger sat upon his creased face.

"And what said Kalonymus the physician?" asked Jessica, although she already knew his reply from the gesture her father had given as he approached from below.

"At first he almost drove me out," Shylock replied. "He said that you only had the slightest of ailments which has no connection at all with inflammation of the lungs. The Devil alone understands him, or whether you can believe him! When he heard what I had to say, he remarked, 'If she was ill at all, her illness is a puzzle to me; now it is all clear — it was heaven-sent and she has recovered completely so that she can perform a great act of mercy — she must go,' that's what he said."

Jessica almost burst into song out of sheer joy; but so that she might not be regarded as frivolous, as though the trip to Rome was the main thing, she concealed her elation.

"He will also send here tomorrow a letter of recommendation to Rabbi Eliahu di Nola, an eminent rabbi in Rome," added Shylock. "Rabbi Eliahu is a distinguished physician and a friend of Kalonymus — that's most important. He will obtain a letter today from one of the Signioria to Navagero, the Venetian Ambassador at the Vatican, and even to Mocenigo there, whom I do not know. Yes, Kalonymus is a wonderful Jew, an orthodox God-fearing Jew."

Don Samuel and Jessica found nothing to say and kept quiet.

"But I've thought it over," Shylock continued, "and I feel it's wrong to send a woman alone among those wolves."

"I was afraid you'd change your mind. Please don't refuse,

Father!" Jessica coaxed him. But she at once broke off so as not to show her confusion.

"If you had children you would understand me, and Samuel would understand me too —"

"I rely entirely on Jessica's sagacity," remarked Don Samuel.

Shylock made no rejoinder but went on, "I dropped in at Tubal's to seek his advice. There was a traveler from the East at his house and we learned the authentic news from him, that a Jew who is a Turkish national is leaving on Monday on the fast post-chaise for Rome. What can I do? It is a sign that it is all heaven-sent. Now go out and tell Lancelot to go into Venice immediately and obtain a place for you too."

Jessica went out to Lancelot. She stood for a moment in the corridor and breathed a deep sigh of relief. When she gave Lancelot the message, he cried out, "Rome?"

"Don't shout!" she scolded him, and continued in a low voice, "Find Lorenzo and tell him to await us tonight at ten o'clock. But don't tell him I'm going to Rome — I will inform him myself." She returned to her father and Lancelot hurried to dress. He was confused, and Stefano more so than he. "Yet it's a good sign that she's going to Rome, especially that she wants to meet Lorenzo this evening," he told Stefano. "But it's a riddle to me that she's going with her father's consent — there's something brewing here."

Shylock gave his daughter the key and told her to take some money out of the wall box for Lancelot. Don Samuel remarked that it was permissible to handle money on the Sabbath for the pious act of redeeming captives. Jessica tarried somewhat at the lock; because of her thoughts at that moment, she dared not turn her face to her father and Don Samuel.

"We shall meet tonight at the rabbi's house to work out our plans, and I'll bring everything in readiness — let them see that Shylock knows what lies ahead, and for the sake of redeeming captives doesn't even shrink from allowing his daughter to take an arduous journey," the banker said. His voice encouraged Jessica. She removed a few gold coins from a small purse, closed the receptacle, and handed the key back to her father. "Count

he ducats carefully," he said to Jessica as she went out to give
hem to Lancelot, "and tell him to bring back a receipt." As
hough to himself he said, "The servant is loyal in every respect but
ot with money — it's a great axiom."

"How can I thank you, master?" Don Samuel's voice trembled.
"Don't thank me. Do not diminish the value of my pious act
y words of thanks," Shylock answered. When Jessica came in
e said to her, "You have a very long journey ahead, my daughter,
nd there is still much that we have to talk over. You must get
eady for the way too. Go now and rest." As she went out, a
eatific smile wreathed his face and he said to Don Samuel,
Naturally she's happy about going to Rome, but the serious ex-
ression on her face shows how deeply concerned she is to assist
hose unfortunates."

"Your blood flows in her veins, master," Don Samuel returned.
"A woman's blood runs like ice, but if you manage to warm
, it burns with a fierce heat," said Shylock gaily. He rose and
aid, "I am tired, my son. I am going to rest and I would advise
ou to do the same, and after the evening prayer we shall go
irectly to the rabbi's house — you will come with me." Don
amuel pressed his hand with great affection and left.

Samuel went straight to David ben Yekutiel's house and told
im and Esther his daughter of Jessica's imminent journey.
sther's woebegone face lit up as though salvation had already
ome to the captives in Rome.

"It's impossible for us to be certain she'll succeed in her mis-
on," Don Samuel said, "but the Venetian Ambassador will open
l doors for her and she'll at least find out of what they are
ccused. She will also carry to the community in Rome a mes-
ge from our own community here urging them to more
eedy action."

"That is a great deal. May God bless her errand!" declared
avid ben Yekutiel, and Esther his daughter wept tears of pure
y.

Returning to his lodging, Don Samuel discussed the matter
ith Tubal.

"She is a somewhat strange girl. She has a great deal of her

father in her, but she is of wondrous beauty," remarked Tub[
"She can subdue dukes and princes." Don Samuel smiled. "Sh
lock seeks a Jewish prince for his daughter's hand," added Tub
"If that were not the cause, I would advise him to take you f
his son-in-law."

"You have a weakness for doing me great honor, Sigr
Tubal, even though I am of bitter heart," Don Samuel answer
wryly. Tubal ruminated a moment and said as if to himse
"Shylock is a philanthropist but he is a hard man. A little m
gentleness and goodness of heart would not harm him."

"If you had an only daughter, Signor Tubal, would you perr
her to undergo so difficult a journey for the sake of charity

"Of course I would."

"I doubt it greatly. Even if you did, what would you say
someone were to chide you the same day that a little more go
ness of heart would not hurt you?"

"He is a hot-tempered man, and he causes himself to be ha
by the Christians, by the very last one of them — and we are
exile, Don Samuel, and Venice is the best of all the dispersion

"It is because he has goodness of heart, because Israel's ago
pains him to the core, that he is so full of wrath!" Don Sam
cried.

The time for afternoon prayer had come and together th
went to the Ashkenazic temple. Between the afternoon a
evening services the heads of the community, who had prayed
the synagogue in the Cantoni quarter or in those farther aw
were assembled by Don Samuel at the rabbi's house and th
brought with them the Turkish Jew who was going to Ror
The morning's controversy over the question of ordination h
been forgotten, or shelved for the time being, and every one g;
his full attention to the salient problem of the captives of Civi
nova. All eyes were turned to Shylock and all lauded him up
his act.

After protracted discussion it was decided that the rabbi sho
prepare, by the morning, a long epistle to the rabbis of Rome
addition to the one to be indited by Rabbi Kalonymus, and to
intendant Yehuda Tagliacozzo; another, who was personally

quainted with the intendant Rabbi Joseph di Lattes, a rich and eminent man, would prepare a letter for him and ask him to give lodging to the emissary and assist her with his counsel so that she need not spend an hour more in Rome than was essential; and if, when she completed her mission there, there would be no Jewish traveler available as her escort, a man would be especially delegated to accompany her home at the expense of the community in Venice. Shylock instructed him to write that she was an only daughter, the surviving one of four; that she had been brought up in luxury and could not therefore be lodged in a mean hostel in the ghetto, and that it was in any event improper that a modest Jewish girl dwell alone in a hostel; and that she should sojourn in Rome no longer than a week at the utmost. The rabbi and other community heads tried in vain to convince him that no set period could be stipulated for the negotiation of so intricate a matter — and he kept the gathering in argument for a long time until he was assured that his request would be communicated as a specific direction by the community.

The congregation waited for the evening prayer with impatience and when the consultation was ended, they hurried through the prayers and dispersed to their homes. Don Samuel wanted to sit awhile with Shylock but the latter said, "I am very tired and so are you, my son. Let us retire early — there's a great deal of work ahead of us."

Entering the house, Shylock found the table spread for the close-of-Sabbath meal. He pronounced the benediction in a voice of mingled joy and sorrow, and then told Jessica, "Let us hasten to eat and retire to rest, my daughter. We must talk over everything tomorrow and prepare you for the journey — you will be carrying many letters of introduction and you will be received with all honor there."

During the meal he told of the conference in the synagogue that evening and warned Jessica against remaining more than a week. The Jews of Rome were an indigent community and kept in degradation, and Rome had not been rebuilt since the days of Titus.

"And if it be necessary to remain another day or two? I don't know when the Ambassador will receive me —"

"Don't ask beforehand. Go directly to him and he will receive you at once. I am certain of it." Before Jessica could say anything, he added, "In Venice they treat us vilely, but elsewhere they try to show how they protect their citizens — and your great-grandfathers lived in Venice."

"But perhaps he or the judge in whose hands the matter rests may be ill?"

"The judge! Do they care for justice?" asked Shylock brusquely. "Before their wicked Haman came to the throne in the Vatican he was said to be at death's door; but he keeps on lingering and is yet alive."

At length the meal was over, and everyone retired.

About an hour afterwards, Jessica and Lancelot left the house. She had donned the mantle and headgear of a male. They hired a gondola and were rowed to the Rialto.

Jessica was in downcast mood. Why was she going to meet Lorenzo? Why had she undertaken to go to Rome and thus bound Don Samuel to her more closely? These questions raised the old doubts, the old uncertainties, the familiar misgivings, as though she were experiencing them for the first time. "Nonetheless it is best that I leave Venice for a while," she thought; "that I shall be away from both of them — who knows but that I may see my way with greater clarity at a distance."

Lorenzo already knew of Jessica's impending journey to Rome. Although Lancelot had sworn him to secrecy, he could not restrain himself and demanded the reason of it the moment Jessica alighted from the gondola. She turned her head to Lancelot and berated him in great vexation.

"I wanted to spare you too much talk, little Signorina Jessica," the man wheedled craftily, and he was relieved at her forgiving smile.

Lorenzo had intended taking Jessica to Antonio's house but she refused. "Let us remain alone, Lorenzo. We shall not be seeing each other for several weeks." He interrogated her as to the reason for the journey. "Take me to some casino, where we can have a room, and I will tell you all."

They entered a near-by casino and Lancelot as usual remained outside with the attendants.

"How happy I am, Jessica, that you are once again alone with me!" Lorenzo began in a voice throbbing with love, and embraced her ardently.

"I am tired. I cannot remain long. I wanted to see you before I left, that is all," she replied.

"But why this sudden journey?"

"Father is sending me to Rome and I am going willingly, Lorenzo."

It occurred to Lorenzo that someone in Rome probably owed Shylock money and, as he himself was afraid of going there, he was sending his daughter. Lorenzo felt certain this was the case, since what other business could the wealthy old Jew have in Rome?

"Shall I come with you?" he asked, kissing her on the forehead.

"You want his money — what will it help if you accompany me?"

"I thought you were going to collect a debt, a fairly large debt, if he is sending you on so long a journey," Lorenzo mumbled.

She divined his meaning. No, not even if she was going to collect money would she fly now with Lorenzo — she wanted to be alone for a while, to think before finally deciding upon her next step. She hesitated to tell Lorenzo the truth; but when he swore to keep the secret, even from the faithful Lancelot, she told him all. She only concealed the fact that one of the prisoners was the former preceptor of Don Samuel and that the young man was involved in the matter.

"You are putting your head into a furnace," Lorenzo warned, and his expression was concerned.

"No matter, Lorenzo," Jessica assured him. "I want to be away from my father a few weeks. It will help me to carry out the deed you want done."

Lorenzo felt that she was right; but when he reflected that he would not see her for days and weeks, he tried to coax her to give up the mission. "You have been very ill, Jessica. He has no pity for you and compels you to take this irksome journey — can't you take a few purses of gold from a father of his sort without having to get away from his house for some time?"

His words ate into her heart like fire. "Why do you not slap his face and leave him, why are you so timid?" she reproached herself. In a suppressed voice she said, "He did not spare himself but went on foot to the physician to make sure that the journey won't be injurious to my health. He always worries over me but the distress of his co-religionists rends his heart."

"Let them become true Christians and live in peace among us. They are a stiff-necked people and even mock at our religion," he rejoined.

It would have been simple for Jessica to prove that the mocking and hatred of the Jews were but a pale reflection of the baleful mockery and hatred of the gentile, but she kept her counsel for fear of arousing any suspicion in him that she had changed her mind. She behaved fondly toward him, was gay and mischievous, yet he remained moody; but when he saw there was no use in trying to dissuade her from the journey, he said, "I have an intimate friend in Rome, a Venetian named Giovanni Solari. I'll give you a note to him. He is an artist and can show you the treasures of art in the Eternal City."

Jessica was overjoyed. She had heard so much of San Pietro, of the Sistine Chapel, and the other edifices; and if she went with a Christian, she would be taken for one too.

About an hour later she rose and said, "I have a great deal to do tomorrow."

"Shall we see each other again tomorrow?"

"It is impossible, my beloved. Even now I am uneasy — my father may have wakened."

"It has never happened in his life!"

"You seem to know all the secrets of our household," she laughed.

They left the casino and Lancelot went after them. All that

had transpired that day, and this short visit particularly, remained a complete conundrum to him; and he feared that the money which Lorenzo had deposited with the sacristan might never reach his pocket.

Lorenzo escorted Jessica back in the gondola to the ghetto gate. He kept begging her to write to him and to return quickly, and she reassured him on both counts. Lancelot too would know the date of her return. Lorenzo promised to let her have the letter to Giovanni Solari through Lancelot.

Outside the ghetto gates, he took her in his arms, careless of the presence of Lancelot and Camillo, the constable.

"Let me go, dear Lorenzo, the constable will gossip about this," she pleaded.

"Jessica, Jessica mine," he cried ardently.

Returning to Venice in the gondola, Lorenzo began to sing — and the echo of his voice palpitated with sadness.

Lorenzo labored under great emotional stress on the Sunday. His whole being craved to go to the ghetto and visit Shylock's house — to see Jessica once more before she left. But he overcame the desire. Yet his lover's heart, and it is the ageless custom of the lover to seek a stratagem, found a way; and when, early on the Monday morning, Jessica and her father came to the post-chaise stage, he stood in the window of a business house opposite, and in the early light of the morning scanned her every movement with rapt intentness. As Jessica fell into her father's arms for the final embrace before her departure, Lorenzo's heart, filled with animosity toward the Jews and passion for the Jewess, seemed to contract inside him and he was moved to tears — he felt that she had parted from him at their last meeting forever.

Chapter Fourteen

JESSICA'S TRAVELING COMPANION, THE TURKISH CITIZEN, HALTED HIS journey upon the eve of Sabbath, but she refused to lose a full day and continued. She was inwardly glad at ridding herself of the companion, who instead of protecting her against others threw himself upon her protection.

She reached Rome upon the Sabbath. Some miles from the city she saw upon the horizon the dome of St. Peter's Cathedral; and as the chaise drew nearer the city the domes and spires upon the Seven Hills came into view. But as the chaise swayed into the streets of Rome a mood of melancholy descended upon her. The narrow winding streets, the jostling crowds — was this Rome, the Eternal City? Could this be the seat of authority for the whole of Christendom? She was accustomed to the broad canals and far horizons of Venice, and her first impression of Rome was disappointing.

Jessica went on foot to the ghetto and the porter who carried her bags strode ahead to show the way. She did not wear the Jewish veil (travelers from the outside were exempt from the obligation upon the first day of their arrival), and the passers-by did not eye her with contempt.

"This is the entrance to the Piazza Judaea," said the porter when they reached the Church of San Angelo. "It stinks and is filthy."

Before her rose the great cross of the Church of San Angelo, inscribed in great letters in Latin and Hebrew: "I have spread out my hands all the day unto a rebellious people" — taken from the second verse of the sixty-fifth chapter of Isaiah. Jessica breathed sobbingly. Thus did the gentiles inscribe the gate to the Jewish habitations! she thought. Ah, could she but remain here, inside the ghetto walls, far from everything which had passed over her! As she went through the gate and into the cavernous, murky alleys, she realized what a spacious paradise was the ghetto in Venice compared to this in Rome. Pallid children, men and women with lined and wrinkled faces, woe etched upon them, gazed at the handsomely attired Jewess who had entered the ghetto upon the Sabbath with a porter carrying her box. She felt shame rising in her, and were it not for fatigue would have told each and every one of the wondering onlookers that she had come on a mission of mercy and that all the rabbis of Venice themselves knew she might have to travel upon the Sabbath and had not enjoined her against it.

"Here is the Piazza Judaea itself," grunted the porter. The

square was bathed in afternoon sunshine but was of meager appearance.

She asked one of the bystanders to show her the house of Jacob di Lattes, and he pointed at a near-by building, the most seemly in the square. On entering the house of di Lattes, followed by the porter with her box, she was received by the housewife with forbidding look and, in embarrassment, she stammered, "I have been sent from Venice upon an errand of mercy." The woman showed her into a large room and offered her a seat.

"You have probably come in connection with the persecution of the Jews — is it there too?" The wife of di Lattes began to bemoan the anguish of Israel in Rome and, in passing, stated that her husband's uncle, who bore the same name, Jacob Bonit di Lattes, was forty years ago physician to the pious Pope Leo X; and she went into a long recital of her own lineage on her father's side, stating that he was a descendant of one of the four eminent families of Jerusalem exiled by Titus to Rome.

"I am very tired," Jessica halted her gently. Her head was swaying backwards and she was almost fainting with weariness.

"Lie on the couch, my daughter," the housewife said solicitously. "You are probably hungry and thirsty."

"I can hardly speak, I have no strength left," Jessica faltered. Signora di Lattes assisted her to the couch. She ran out and returned with a glass of wine and cake. Jessica drank the wine but could not touch the cake.

"And where is your husband, Signora di Lattes?" Jessica asked.

"He is asleep — if it is urgent, I can wake him."

"No, no — I would be unable to speak to him at the moment."

"Tell me briefly what is your errand and your name."

I forgot to tell her who I was out of sheer weariness, Jessica thought with amusement. "I am Jessica of the house of Shylock, the banker of Venice, and I have come in regard to the captives of Civitanova."

"I am Stella di Lattes — it is a great tragedy!" the woman cried, clapping her hands together woefully. "They are held in the Inferno, the Papal prison. No one knows of what they are accused. God alone knows if some great evil won't befall us all."

Jessica took the letters from her pouch and gave Signora di Lattes the one for her husband. "I have two letters here for Rabbi di Nola and one for Signor Tagliacozzo," she said.

The woman went and aroused her husband and while he was still half-bemused with sleep told him in a few words of their visitor. He hurriedly dressed and ran to the synagogue, where the Christian servitor opened the letters. He read the one addressed to himself and hastened to the rabbi. The rabbi's beadle took the letter to the intendant Yehuda Taliacozzo, who soon came to the rabbi's house.

"Israel is not orphaned," the rabbi cried, "if the community of far-off Venice shows such concern for the fate of six souls in Israel." Di Lattes expressed astonishment that the community should have sent a woman as their emissary, and a woman, he added, whom his wife reported as very young. The rabbi sighed with profound melancholy.

"Nonetheless the rabbi speaks of her in high praise, and adds that her father Shylock is the greatest banker in Venice," remarked Taliacozzo.

"He is a banker and philanthropist of renown," supplemented di Lattes.

"He can serve as an example to us all," said the rabbi. "Kalonymus the physician writes me that only a few weeks ago the young woman rose from an illness, and it was her father who suggested that his daughter be the emissary to Rome." The others commended Shylock's generosity. "Kalonymus the physician is a strict and cautious man, and if he writes that she will find favor among the dukes and princes there is substance in what he says. He also writes that she holds a letter for the Venetian Ambassador."

"It is an epistle of great value," commented di Lattes. "If she can enter the presence of an ambassador of an important state like Venice, it is the door to the Court of Cardinal Alessandrini."

"And who will go to the Cardinal? He is the voice and soul of the tyrant," another pointed out.

"She will go. And if it be required, I shall go with her!" the rabbi asserted. "If a father hazards his only daughter, the surviving one of four, I can hazard the few remaining years of my miserable life."

"They live in a free country there. They know nothing of what dangles over our heads," sighed Tagliacozzo.

"We sit here with folded arms out of fear — and yet a far-off community has been spurred into action," groaned the rabbi.

"But we have done all that we could, and we were even told that the Cardinal promised the *bargelo,* the court delegate who brought them from Civitanova, that he would examine their case expeditiously," said di Lattes.

"Put no reliance in the gentiles," warned Rabbi di Nola. "The *bargelo* probably invented it all so as to get a reward."

Meanwhile, news of the arrival of the emissary from Venice had reached the ears of Rabbi Yehuda Ha'Neeman, delegate for all the communities of La Marca, and he too came to the rabbi's house with the delegate Mose ben Lavella (the Italian rendering of the Polish-Jewish name of Leib or Leibele) who happened to be with him at the time. Rabbi Yehuda Ha'Neeman, who had great experience in the craft of diplomatic negotiation, declared: "The people in Venice were clever to have sent a woman, and a young woman at that!"

The rabbi was gratified at hearing this opinion. After some discussion, the gathering agreed to meet again after the Sabbath benediction at the di Lattes home to receive the emissary's report.

When Jessica awoke it was an hour after the benediction. Signora di Lattes entered the room holding a lantern.

"You slept sweetly, Signorina. You were very fatigued. The rabbi and several of the elders await you outside."

"They await me?" said Jessica in surprise at the honor extended her. It was only now she realized the full portentousness of the mission she had undertaken.

"No matter, Signorina. Dress yourself and eat quietly." She went out and sent in her servant-maid with a jug of water for Jessica's ablutions and a repast. Jessica donned the holiday attire she had brought and, having eaten, went to the door and opened it. She was at first distraught at seeing the six men in their Sabbath clothing sitting there, and for a moment stood transfixed on the threshold.

Their faces were turned to the visitor and they rose in unison with the rabbi. A silence pervaded the room. None had expected so comely and stately a creature. The rabbi broke the hush.

"Come closer, daughter, and be seated," he invited, pointing to a chair at his side and, when she sat down, he held her pulse. "I am a physician too," he smiled. "Thank God, you are well. You were wise to rest, daughter." The rabbi's fatherly tone put Jessica at her ease and restored her full composure. She banished from her mind all thought of Lorenzo, which had come fleetingly as though to tease her, and gave her full attention to the matter in hand. The rabbi introduced all those present and she curtsied to each.

"You will have learned from the letters in your hands, gentlemen, the nature of my mission," her voice tinkled in the still room. "Have you any good tidings for me?"

"We have tried our utmost but have achieved naught," sighed Rabbi Yehuda Ha'Neeman.

"Our own lives are in peril here every instant," added di Lattes. "Your people there in Venice, who have lived in the ghetto for decades and have prospered in spite of the gentiles, have no inkling of our position. We were thrown into this place only a few years ago and we are nigh unto the gates of purgatory — we have no future here, daughter."

"And my father believes that Venice is purgatory itself," remarked Jessica with a rueful smile.

One spoke of the intrigues of the Pope whom all knew to be deranged; another of the looting of the ghetto which went on and the outrageous demands of the convert monks who compelled the Jews to hear their harangues even on the Sabbath. A third spoke at length of the portents of the Messiah who, although the mystic calculations of Shlomo Molcho had not been fulfilled, was awaited at every moment; and yet another, possibly to encourage the gathering, recalled how David Hareubeni had appeared at the gates of Rome riding a white horse and had been received with every mark of respect due to kings by Pope Clemente VII in person. Mose ben Lavella narrated the favored position of the Jews in Poland who were the protégés of the landed gentry.

Jessica listened intermittently to their discourse. She was certain now that these Jews had no dealings with the Papal Court, and she planned in her mind how to utilize her own resources. She interrupted the last speaker and, rising, said, "I shall endeavor to do whatever lies in my power."

"I am ready to follow wherever you lead," declared the rabbi.

"And I — and I," the others chorused. Her appearance, attaining almost to majesty, encouraged the gathering to a display of fervor. Jessica's glance traveled over them before she said, "I have no wish to endanger you. I shall go alone tomorrow to the Venetian Ambassador."

"But tomorrow is Sunday and the Ambassador will not receive you," one of them pointed out.

"Then I shall go at once," she returned after brief reflection.

"The ghetto gate is closed, daughter," the rabbi said; and, when Jessica said she would be permitted to pass as she did not wear the veil, he asked whether she intended to conceal her origin.

"I cannot say. Yet would it be wrong to do so even if it were for an act of pious mercy?"

"Everything is allowed for the redemption of captives, daughter."

"Then take me to the gate. I shall pass."

"But how will a woman alone pass through the streets of the city?" asked Signora di Lattes from the corner in which she had sat mute the entire evening.

"I have no fear!" cried Jessica confidently. None dared persuade her to change her mind. She went into the next room and returned with a cloak. "Let us go!" she ordered, and all six left the house with her.

Yet when they reached the square and the darkness of night coiled about them, they lost heart and Rabbi Yehuda Ha'Neeman went to the synagogue to summon the Christian servitor to accompany Jessica with a lighted torch.

"Go wherever the signorina goes and bring her safely back,"

the rabbi instructed the synagogue attendant. Only the rabbi escorted her as far as the gate.

"Open!" cried Jessica. "Open at once!"

The gate was pushed ajar and the guard peered into her face.

"I am a Christian. I had an urgent errand here and was delayed," she said.

"Yes, yes, she is a Christian," the servant supported her. The guard hesitated but she thrust a gold ducat into his hand, and the gate opened.

"I shall return here tonight," she said, and the guard bowed, fingering the gold coin, muttering submissively, "I shall be awake all night. Come when you will, noble lady."

"Rest assured, rabbi, I shall return safely," she told Rabbi di Nola at parting from him. The rabbi said he would await her at the di Lattes home, and his lips moved silently as he pronounced a blessing for the success of her errand.

The servant lit the way before her and led her through the squares and narrow streets until they stood in a spacious piazza. There he asked passers-by to show him the residence of the Venetian Ambassador, and in a few moments they came before a splendid mansion, where lanterns glowed at either side of the portal.

Jessica handed the letter from the noble member of the Council of Ten at Venice to one of the flunkeys and said, "Tell the noble Navagero that the signorina who brought the letter waits below and wishes to see him."

"But he is now entertaining guests."

"It is an imperative matter. Do as I say!" she ordered imperiously. The man went up the stairs and, unable to restrain himself on handing over the missive, said, "She is as beautiful as a princess, Your Excellency."

The Ambassador called to his sister, who lived with him, and said. "She has come."

"Show her into the Purple Chamber," she signed to the flunkey. The Ambassador and his sister read the letter and thereafter His Excellency begged leave of his guests and went to the Purple Chamber.

Jessica sat, confused, on the edge of a velvet sofa. An unknown trepidation filled her, and the strains of music which reached her from the adjoining hall recalled for some reason the same tunes which the mobs had sung at the time the holy books of the Jews of Venice were thrown on the bonfire: she had only been a child at the time but had been deathly afraid. Yet she was inspired to confidence by sight of the Venetian glassware of the workshops at Murano adorning the shelves — every urn, every vase, had the breath of life in it, and seemed to whisper voicelessly to her with the faintest of vibrations in the mysterious language too delicate for ear to catch but which linked man with animal and living being with the inanimate; and united all in a sublime destiny, transient and eternal in one. How peculiar, she pondered, that there should be a gulf between classes of mankind? And yet no such gulf existed between sentient man and brittle glass creation.

When the door opened she rose. The Venetian Ambassador, a man of over fifty yet as agile and elastic of gait as one of forty, hastened forward, took her hand in both of his, and cried, "I had become anxious about you, Signorina. I had expected you this forenoon."

"Expected me, Signor? Had you known of my coming beforehand?"

He motioned gently to her to be seated and himself sat at her side.

"There are those in Venice who concern themselves for you, Signorina, and I see now that you are deserving of it," he murmured.

"Is Lorenzo's hand in this?" she asked herself. Yet she could not believe it. Probably Kalonymus the physician arranged this. "He is a remarkable man," she answered her thought.

The Ambassador asked her how she had fared upon the long journey, if she had seen Michelangelo's "David" when she passed through Florence, and how she had liked the Palazzo del Podesta at Bologna and Padua the home of knowledge, where he, Navagero, had served as mayor — and had she seen the monument to Gattemelata, the work of the great Donatello? More particularly

His Excellency asked as to the appearance of Venice, of which he thought day and night. He also inquired solicitously as to her health and if she had fully recovered. Jessica fastened amazed eyes upon him. The latter question had of a trice removed the barrier between the State Ambassador and herself.

"The Ambassador of the Republic of San Marco knows all that transpires in his country," he smiled.

"Is it so important then, Your Excellency?"

"All is important for an Ambassador, Signorina."

"Is Your Excellency acquainted with the physician Kalonymus?"

"He was physician to my father's household."

"And did the word of my coming reach Your Excellency from him?" she interrogated Navagero. He laughed.

"You are most inquisitive, Signorina. I am disposed to satisfy your natural curiosity and reveal who wrote me, but you must try first to guess."

"Lorenzo!" she thought but had not the audacity to trust his name to her lips.

"Do I know the person?" she asked mischievously. She felt she was sitting with a friend whom she had known for many years.

"I believe so."

"Signor Lorenzo of the house of —"

"No, Signorina — Antonio of the house of Barozzi wrote us."

"Barozzi? — Signor Antonio, agent of the Court!"

"Yes, indeed. Both he and Portia his wife wrote us of your coming."

It was now clear to Jessica that Lorenzo was shielding her from afar; and it seemed as if the barrier had once more risen between her and the other. He had been courteous to her not because she was a native of Venice but out of his Christian piety, and he served as a kind of link in the iron chain which was being forged around her soul. Here, too, she was being denied the spiritual repose for which she thirsted so much, for achieving which she had undertaken the long journey. On the one hand, the quailing Jews who clung to her; on the other, the shadow of Lorenzo who had spread his snare as far as Rome.

The Ambassador gossiped lightly and Jessica answered. She listened as he conversed, but her thoughts were far from this mansion; they were somewhere in Venice, at the casino or in Antonio's house where her happiness was ever alloyed with the terror that her father might learn of her whereabouts.

"I know why you have come," the Ambassador eventually said. "I shall do whatever I can to help you." He emphasized the last word and his intention was clear to Jessica — it was she and not the fate of the incarcerated Jews, who concerned him.

The door opened and the Ambassador's sister entered. "This is the signorina whom we awaited." Donna Camilla Navagero gave Jessica a gracious welcome and invited her into the hall to meet the other guests. "I am so tired from my long journey," Jessica excused herself.

"Then we shall expect you to the midday meal tomorrow," said Donna Camilla. Jessica expressed her gratitude for the honor and, curtseying gracefully, parted from them.

Upon returning to the di Lattes house, Jessica was met in the corridor by Signora Stella, who perceived from the smile on the girl's face that she had already seen the Ambassador. Stella went into the room ahead of her and cried, "Here indeed is a valiant woman!"

Apart from di Lattes the old rabbi and Rabbi Yehuda Ha'Neeman were there. As she entered the rabbi rose, took her hand, and murmured, "May Israel be blest in thee!"

"The Ambassador has promised to assist me. I am to have the midday meal with him tomorrow," said Jessica, still standing. She was moved by the radiance which illumined their faces. The rabbi, noting her emotion, thought it due to chagrin at having to eat with the Ambassador on the morrow.

"Do not grieve, my daughter," he said. "Danger threatens the Jews and the piety of the act you are performing is illimitably greater than the transgression of eating ritually forbidden food."

"I am fatigued," she returned. She wished to escape the eyes of these admiring people. Rabbi di Nola held her pulse. "You are excited, and no wonder! It is best that you go to rest." Jessica murmured a farewell and was shown by Stella di Lattes into the room prepared for her. "I must see another person outside the ghetto tomorrow. Perhaps he too can help," she told Signora di Lattes as the latter was leaving.

"But be careful not to enter a convent," the other woman warned. "They are always waiting for victims."

Jessica for a long time could not fall asleep. Why had Lorenzo not told her that he was writing to the Venetian Ambassador about her intended change of religion? She would have found some excuse to remain in Venice. She had no cause to be vexed with him — he loved her and did all he could as behooved an ardent lover; yet she could not forgive herself for having allowed him to approach her and to have requited his love. Ought she now to write all to her father, to confess the whole truth, and remain in Rome? But her father and Don Samuel would come speeding to her and it would bring calamity upon all three, and possibly too on the Jewish community in Rome who trembled at each fluttering leaf — fanatic Rome was not Venice. Perhaps it was best that she pack her belongings and return at once to Venice? She weighed each thought at length, although she knew none of them was feasible. She must discharge the mission entrusted her, and then return to Venice.

The next morning she went to the house of the artist Giovanni Solari, Lorenzo's friend. He lived near the Tiber. Jessica walked along the river embankment, and the sight of the muddy waters aroused in her a powerful nostalgia for the blue Adriatic, the wide canals of Venice her city. She passed many churches and palaces, but more evident were the ruins and heaps of masonry — Rome compared with Venice appeared to her cold and stern reality against a shimmering, marvelous dream. The ruins and stones and broken statues strewn over the desolate spaces within the city, the remains of ancient Rome, seemed as portents of a true prophecy that the fine palaces now rearing their splendor skyward would one day be heaps of rubble. The waters of Venice were always in motion, always alive, and would be ever so; yet Rome was bursting with pride in lifeless churches and spires which could never endure. Ah, Venice! Gondolas!—Had she imagined the previous Sunday that on reaching Rome she would yearn so passionately for Venice? The solid buildings oppressed her, and she walked slowly, her head lowered, as though she shouldered a heavy burden.

Giovanni Solari, a bachelor of about twenty-five, was at home. He dwelt in a large chamber that served both as living-quarters and studio. Before opening the letter she gave him he said, "You are Signorina Jessica. I am happy to serve you, Signorina."

"Did Lorenzo write you of the purpose of my coming?"

"He sent me a long letter by the fast horse-post." Giovanni placed wine and cakes upon the table and before he filled the glasses he began to speak with enthusiasm of the Eternal City. Jessica sipped a little of the wine, but he poured tumbler after tumbler down his throat, and the more he drank, the more vivacious his manner.

"Shall we go out and see the city?" Jessica asked.

"Why, yes, indeed, Signorina Jessica. Why should I praise it if the Queen of Cities can be seen face to face?"

He took her to St. Peter's Cathedral. St. Peter's Square and the gigantic marble pillars adorning it struck her with a burst of wonderment as though she had emerged from a dark tunnel into a blaze of brilliant sunshine. She stood long in fascinated contemplation of the great dome, the handiwork of Michelangelo, and Giovanni Solari explained the plan and recalled the ridicule to which the master had been subjected because he disdained the traditional form of round dome.

They reached the central bronze door of the cathedral. Giovanni knelt and Jessica, after a momentary hesitation, knelt too. Priests stood in the wide niches or passed before the pulpit. Giovanni prayed briefly at the first niche and immediately returned to Jessica. They walked down the aisle of the giant marble columns, past the niches, and Giovanni gave her a full explanation: there was the lectern from which the Pope delivered his sermons; the bones of holy Peter; the graves of Sixtus IV, Julius II, and Paul III; the ancient tombs of Leo II and Leo III, of Gregory the Great and Innocent VIII; statuary and marble columns; and gold and precious metals as though all the treasures of the world were stored here. It took them an hour and a half to tour St. Peter's, and Jessica felt as exhilarated as though she had been sipping nectar the whole time. She had heard much from the pious Antonio of the sanctity of their churches, yet all he had said was a faint echo compared to the sonorous voice in which the great edifice spoke to her.

They went outside and, turning left, passed into the Vatican grounds. Jessica sat for a few minutes upon a bench, tired and confused.

"You have not yet seen all, Signorina. We shall come again to St. Peter's," Giovanni said. "Did you observe Michelangelo's 'Pieta'? What grace and adoration!"

"The old Florentine has golden hands," Jessica remarked.

"I don't think much of his fresco work," said Giovanni dubiously, "but in sculpture and architecture he has no equal." Reverting to the beauty and glory of St. Peter's, he went on: "They've been building for over a hundred years, and it will take hundreds of years more to complete — it is a sign of the virility of Catholicism, and the stupid Protestants delude themselves into thinking that they can undermine its foundations!"

They entered the Sistine Chapel. Jessica saw the murals by Botticelli and Rosselli, and by craning her neck gazed at the Michelangelo frescoes upon the vaulted ceiling, which fascinated her. The Almighty distinguished between light and darkness, He made brightness and gloom, He made the grass grow and sowed the seed, He ordered His angels to create every living creature that crawled and every winged bird of its kind, He gave life to Man by the touch of His finger — He was God the Omnipotent, no passing fancy of imagination but the Eternal. Noah's Ark and the Flood — this was no legend. Here was Noah and his ark, here the rising waters which covered the lofty mountains. The prophets: Jeremiah, Joel, Zechariah, Isaiah, Jonah; they were flesh and blood, with eyes and legs — it was so vivid, executed with such devotion. The figures seemed to be hovering above as though they came from remoter worlds, forgotten ages, and congregated here to prove beyond all doubt that there was an Almighty God in the skies and these had been His prophets.

Jessica felt giddy and lowered her head, but once again she looked up at the wonderful images. She inspected them a long time and, leaving, turned back more than once to glimpse the ceiling frescoes.

"It is hardly believable that one person created all this," she told Giovanni. He remained silent. "What are the Venetian painters compared with Buonarotti!" she cried.

"He is a great sculptor and architect and even, I grant you, a great poet," Giovanni said. "Yet one cannot help being sceptical of his talent as artist." Jessica did not betray her amusement. "Thus are the minnow when they speak of the whale," she thought. "Even Paolo Caliari Veronese spoke scornfully of Titian when he was painting me."

Giovanni wished to show her the Vatican library. But she pleaded fatigue and said she could absorb no more. He went with her into the garden and they sat upon a marble bench.

"Lorenzo wrote me of the object of your journey," he remarked. "You must visit the library. There is one there who can procure you an audience with Cardinal Alessandrini."

"There is no one like you, Signor Solari!" she cried rapturously. She rose, but he caught her hand and made her be seated.

"We shall not find him today. It is Sunday and he is not at his work," Giovanni reminded her. Gazing in front of him he said, "He too is of Jewish origin. His name is Giovanni Paolo Eustachio, a great scholar. He is a copyist in the Vatican library."

"He too is of Jewish origin." Did Solari believe she had already changed her religion? Neither he nor the Venetian Ambassador had mentioned her Judaism, yet without doubt Antonio and Lorenzo had written them she was still a Jewess. Her heart demanded that she state openly she was a Jewess but she forbore, to avoid discussion.

"Will he wish to help the Jews?" she asked.

"He is a good man," said Giovanni. "It depends on why they are accused."

"That is all I want to know."

"Then he will certainly help you."

Jessica again asked his name and Giovanni repeated it. "He is a son of Rome, and his name in his Jewish life, he once told me, was Elijah di Nola."

Di Nola? It was the name of the rabbi whom she had seen last night! The proselyte must be a kinsman. Doubt turned to certitude, and she experienced a thrill of comfort at the thought that a relative of the rabbi should have changed his faith.

Yet she was careful not to mention the rabbi's name to Giovanni beside her and only asked, "You said you knew his name from his own lips — do you then know him so well?"

"Yes, I painted him. He has a marvelous appearance, nothing like a Jew." He looked at her. "Nor is your face that of a Jewess."

"That is not true," she smiled.

"You know it too, as otherwise you would not walk through the streets of Rome without the ghetto veil. Your features have a Greek beauty."

"Not Egyptian?" she asked whimsically. Then she became serious and added, "You must take me to see him tomorrow."

"As you wish, Signorina. I am at your service. There is none like him for friendliness."

Jessica rose and both left the Vatican quadrangle. When she told him she was invited to the midday meal with the Venetian Ambassador, Giovanni cried: "It is a great honor! Do not be annoyed if I say that the Jews always cry they are persecuted and yet they enter the most exalted houses into which a Christian is not privileged to go."

"It is the whim of fate," she smiled. "Fate is a great jester."

On their way Giovanni informed her that he was vexed with the Ambassador. He once brought him several paintings done in Venice and offered them for sale. The Ambassador kept the canvases for two days and returned them with a lackey without deigning to receive him.

When they reached the Ambassador's residence, Jessica and Solari agreed she would come early the next morning, and she went up the flight of stairs to the portico. She was shown into a small room where Donna Camilla soon joined her. Donna Camilla was most gracious. To her questions, Jessica told of her visit to St. Peter's and the Sistine Chapel, and spoke with deep admiration of Michelangelo's works.

"Signor Antonio wrote us of your errand, and I have invited to luncheon with us one of Cardinal Alessandrini's close friends and confidants, Fra Ruberto. My brother is now preparing the ground for your conversation, and you will be able after the meal to speak with him as much as you wish."

"I thank both of you with all my heart for your kindness," returned Jessica.

The door opened and a servant bowed. Donna Camilla and Jessica went into the dining-room and the Ambassador came shortly afterwards with Fra Ruberto, an old man close to seventy.

During the meal they discussed a variety of subjects, but at its conclusion the hosts discreetly retired, leaving their two guests by themselves. For some moments there was a deep hush.

"Your face is as noble as the Holy Virgin's, Signorina. What a pity you must spend your life in the ghetto," Fra Ruberto began. Jessica was startled. In eloquent tongue the old priest went on to speak of the advent of the Messiah, the Holy Mother, and the great privilege which the Jewish people were given of recanting. She hardly heard him at first, but, as he spoke on, her composure returned and she became more cheerful. She was no longer angry with the old man; on the contrary, his frankness charmed her. "After all," she thought, "I would already have been one of them had not Lorenzo compelled me suddenly to exploit my father." St. Peter's Cathedral symbolized the strength and power of Christianity, and Michelangelo's paintings in the Sistine, its beauty; she had undertaken a mission and she would complete it, and upon returning to Venice would seek an opportunity of obtaining from her father a fraction of his plenty and then become Lorenzo's.

When the priest had finished, Jessica told him concisely of her errand — she knew that the Ambassador had already apprised him of the details — and said: "These Jews of Civitanova are incarcerated in the Inferno without trial or judicial redress, and I must help them —"

"If you were not already on the threshold of the true religion," Fra Ruberto interrupted her, "no ambassador of a Christian state, not even the most powerful kingdom in Italy, would have received you. Why must you engage in the affairs of the Jews? They are a bad lot, my daughter. They all blaspheme the Messiah."

"I promised the Jews of the Venetian ghetto that I would exert myself for the captives, and you cannot conceive, Messer, that I would betray their trust," she answered.

"Yet why must you do all this? The Holy See regards all heretics with suspicion, and justly so, my daughter."

Jessica meditated a moment and said, "I must confess the truth, Father. I have a lover in Venice, a young noble —"

"I know it — and so?"

"Whenever I sit in my father's house I have not the courage to flee from him. I decided to travel from my home and on returning to take the step. It was I who suggested I be sent."

"You were wise, my daughter. I advise you to accept the true faith in the holy city, and you will be able to do this cleverly so that your father will not know beforehand."

Jessica tried to evade a direct reply and said, "I must fulfill my duty and bring them back the good tidings."

"How will they know you stood at the baptismal font?"

Again she meditated a moment and said, "I could not look my father in the eyes, I could not." The priest tapped his fingers on the table but said nothing. "I could not deceive him in any circumstance, I could not."

"You speak like a pious Christian," he remarked. He rose and added, "I shall see His Eminence Cardinal Alessandrini this evening and ask him to grant you an audience."

"I thank you, exalted sir!" she cried with emotion. She accompanied him to the door. "I hope to see Signor Eustachio tomorrow morning —"

"Oh, you wish to see the excellent copyist?" Fra Ruberto interposed. "He is more devout a Christian than a Christian by birth. He is a favorite of the Cardinal. Speak too with him. Two are more capable than one."

Jessica remained alone in the room after the priest had left. A sudden fear possessed her. Had she indeed given expression to what she told the priest? She consoled herself with the thought that she had already told this to Lorenzo a long time ago. No, her statement had not committed her in the least — she was still free to decide as she willed.

Donna Camilla came in. "You have succeeded, Signorina!" she cried with beaming face. Jessica at once comprehended that the old priest had been able in the few minutes he left her alone to tell the lady of their conversation.

"Succeeded? We shall see if he succeeds with Cardinal Alessandrini, and then if I succeed with His Eminence. I promised to remain in Rome but a few days."

"One must stay weeks and months in Rome, not days," Donna Camilla objected. She invited Jessica to stay at the Embassy until her return to Venice. "It is no secret to me that you live in the ghetto — it is not fitting that you dwell in such a filthy quarter."

Jessica accepted the invitation willingly. She could no longer remain among those Jews — their gaze would oppress her, their admiration stifle her.

Toward evening she went with one of the Ambassador's footmen to the di Lattes house in the ghetto. She was happy to find no other at home than the housewife. Jessica went into her room, leaving the servant at the entrance. Signora di Lattes followed her.

"We were worried, Signorina. Has anything — ?"

"I am going to be lodged at the residence of the Venetian Ambassador," Jessica halted her.

"In the Palazzo Venezia!" cried Signora di Lattes in astonishment. That same fortress-castle was deeded as a gift to the Republic of Venice only a year later, yet for many years it had been called Palazzo Venezia by all.

"They have invited me to stay with them," Jessica continued as she packed her clothing, "and I must agree. They can help me."

"I shall call my husband from his prayers."

"Heaven forbid. I must not lose one moment." She summoned

the footman and, when he shouldered her box, she turned to go. "Do not be concerned for me. If I have tidings I shall come to inform you." To evade further questioning she said, "I still know nothing, but I hope I may be able to do something for them."

Signora di Lattes stood bewildered at the threshold as Jessica left.

In the evening she wrote to Lorenzo and her father — how difficult it was for her to write to both at the same hour and day! — and gave the letters to a servant to be taken at dawn on the morrow to the express horse-post. She then spent the evening with the Ambassador and his sister in conversing about Venice. The Ambassador was prudent in his speech but his sister accompanied her talk with hints at Jessica's coming conversion.

At eleven o'clock, before they retired to rest, a servant brought an urgent note. It was from Fra Ruberto. He asked the Ambassador to apprise Jessica that he had spoken with the Cardinal and she must come at nine o'clock the next morning to Giovanni Paolo Eustachio at the Vatican library; he, Fra Ruberto, would await her there.

"You move swiftly, Signorina. You could have been an able ambassadress!" cried Navagero.

"Even men old as Fra Ruberto have discerning eyes!" his sister laughed.

Jessica too was glad — something was urging her to leave Rome. She wanted to conclude her mission at the earliest time and depart from the city.

The night was very long. The old cogitations preoccupied her and new doubts were added; and in the morning, while her host and hostess still slept, she hastened to Giovanni Solari. When she knocked at his door he asked her to wait awhile outside and did not appear again for fifteen minutes.

"I had no idea you would be so early; my room was disordered," he apologized. She told him of her talk with Fra Ruberto, and he exclaimed, "He is an important man."

"He sent to inform me I was to be at Eustachio's at nine of the clock this morning. He too will be there."

"You work wonders, Signorina Jessica!" Solari declared.

He suggested they might walk to the appointment among the ruins of ancient edifices. At a distance of a hundred paces from a lofty, splendid arch, Solari stood stock-still. Through the arch a procession of white-robed clergy passed with their sacred utensils.

"It is the Titus Arch," Solari said.

The Titus Arch! Jessica's heart seemed to stop beating and then throbbed with hammer strokes. Could this be it? Was this the monument to the destruction of her people? — this the spot over which the heroes of Israel were led captive in their chains? She seemed not to see the cross-bearer at the head of the procession of monks — these were her ancestors risen from the tomb, the captives of Israel who were crucified or thrown to the wild beasts in the arena, and they cried aloud for vengeance against those who were their brethren in distress and had now turned into their persecutors . . . Here shuffled the dead, in their thousands and tens of thousands, toe by heel; no guard could halt their ghostly progress. Their faces were turned to the Vatican. And there! Shuffling from the Vatican were their persecutors, clanking their fetters also, and following in the footsteps of the wraithlike dead — marching into limbo.

"The procession has passed," Solari broke in. "Let us approach to see the marvelous reliefs."

No, she could not! Not with a gentile — a man to whom these scenes of her people's agony were only marvelous reliefs. She could not gaze upon the depicting of that anguish of which her Hebrew teachers had told so much in her childhood. She must stand alone before this terrible monument, as by the grave of her mother.

"Not now. We shall be late for the librarian," she said quickly.

Solari spoke at length upon the neglect which existed in Rome where ancient buildings were dismantled of their masonry for new structures. The palace in which the Venetian Ambassador dwelt was constructed of the hewn stone taken from the Colosseum. Jessica ruminated over the reluctance of Jews to pass beneath the Arch of Titus, which they regarded as an evil relic. Had it not been for Titus, the Christians would have denied that

Israel was ever a nation among the nations; the Arch was a monument of valor and a tribute of honor to her people and her race. The thought encouraged her, and brought a feeling of remorse at coming to Rome: a devilish web was being woven around her, and perhaps she had been wrong in concealing from Fra Ruberto her consciousness that she was free to act as she herself willed.

They reached the Vatican fifteen minutes before the hour, and waited upon a bench in an adjoining avenue. Giovanni heaped many compliments upon her, giving her inward amusement, and finally said, "Lorenzo is a lucky fellow. He is rich and will win a Madonna."

The suspicion rose in Jessica's mind that Giovanni had been asked by Lorenzo to spy upon her and ascertain her true feelings toward him.

"Lorenzo is good-hearted," she remarked. "See how he was concerned for my welfare."

"That is but nothing," he muttered. "Even a Cardinal would kneel to you."

"Cardinals are celibate," she smiled. Giovanni winked with his right eye and burst into a guffaw.

"We must be punctual," she said, rising.

Fra Ruberto was already awaiting them in Eustachio's chamber. Jessica was taken aback. She had imagined the librarian as a frail old man, but here stood a young man of delicate features and piercing, burning eyes. He placed a chair for her and when speaking kept his eyes riveted on her. After bestowing many well-turned phrases of commendation upon her sagacity, he said, "I now see that my friend Fra Ruberto was right. It is a great sin that a lily like yourself should decay in the slime of the ghetto. Here you see, Signorina, that I arrived at recognition of the true faith through the writings of the Jews."

He drew out a manuscript of the *Zohar* which he had copied and read from the last page: " 'And the sacred task was concluded upon the ninth day of the month of Nisan in the year five thousand, three hundred and sixteen of the Creation; may the Almighty spare us to witness the advent of the righteous Messiah

— so you see only three years ago I was still a sinner in the Jewish faith; and I embraced the true faith not out of greed for gold, as I had been copying missals for cardinals and princes while still a Jew. And I am grateful for the inner conviction which led me to the true religion at the beginning of my years of wisdom, so that I may serve the true God in this holy edifice."

Jessica recognized in his features a resemblance to Rabbi di Nola. It was obvious he must be a kinsman and the thought was consoling.

Fra Ruberto told of his conversation with Cardinal Alessandrini, and urged Eustachio to use his own good offices.

"I shall go up to him at once," Eustachio declared. "An act of great piety presents itself, a great act indeed, and God forfend that I forfeit the opportunity!" He asked Jessica to wait in the quadrangle; His Eminence might be disposed to receive her this very morning.

Jessica waited outside for hours, with Giovanni murmuring veiled suggestions of love into her ears; and, to set himself up in her eyes, conversing at length on art and his method of work, and bitterly reviling the Florence school, not even sparing the dead Raffaello. As he spoke on, Jessica curbed her impatience and meandered along the avenues of her own thoughts. Another half an hour passed, an hour, and yet the man who was at the right-hand of Asmodeus, as the Jews called Paul, made no hurry to grant an audience to the Jewess, and perhaps had no intention of doing so. If she failed to see him through the medium of these powerful aides, the quest was hopeless and she could no longer remain in Rome. . . . Nor could she go back and face the rabbi and the functionaries at the ghetto, or remain at the Embassy under the wing of a Christian household if the Cardinal refused her. . . . Possibly the Cardinal had no wish to receive her because she was a Jewess; aye, that was it in truth, a Jewess; her bitter fate. Could a man escape his fate, and what sense was there in her efforts to elude her own destiny? The very existence of the Jewish people in a world which tried to extirpate them served as evidence of their true faith, and imposed on each of them the obligation to preserve that faith. It was good to be even a tiny speck

in firm rock over which generation after generation of corrod-
ing waters passed without diminishing it in the least. And again
Lorenzo, Don Samuel. If she left Lorenzo he would reveal all
and if she followed him . . . The mill-pool of her thoughts tired
her and her eyes prickled from too much concentration upon
one spot — the door of the library. Every time it opened she
half-rose from her place; and when it closed she sat again, and
struggled with her doubts.

About two and a half hours later, Eustachio came to the door
and beckoned her to approach. Jessica and Giovanni hurried
to him.

"Only the Signorina," snapped Eustachio. "His Eminence
has agreed to receive you. It has cost great effort. I shall take you
to the door of his study and when you enter, you will kneel and
kiss his hand. Fra Ruberto will be there."

With stumbling feet Jessica approached the residence of the
Cardinal. An attendant wearing the colors of the Duke opened
a wide gate for her, and as he closed it after her she felt a sudden
apprehension, as if a decree had been issued, announcing her
doom. With a trembling heart she thought, "He has brought me
here by trickery."

A young priest walked ahead, through the shadowy corridor
and brought her to the waiting room. It was flooded with light
and from the walls little cherubs faced her, carrying musical
instruments. Their little faces encouraged her somewhat, and
she was able to consider her first words to the Cardinal.

A door opened at her left. A lad wearing a white linen cloak
over a black garment beckoned, and she went into the Cardinal's
study. She walked hesitantly over the white marble floor, and
from a distance saw the Cardinal, wrapped in a yellow silk cloak
sitting in his writing chair. He seemed an old man, strong in
body, his face full and flushed.

When she reached his chair she knelt, and as he lowered his
hand from the arm of the chair she kissed the great stone in his
ring. The eyes of Fra Ruberto were upon the Cardinal, and they
sparkled with glee. The Jewess had knelt opposite the great
cross, and the Cardinal's face revealed a momentary expression

of pleasure. The Cardinal nodded silently to Fra Ruberto; then smoothing Jessica's hair, he said, "Arise and sit, my daughter."

She got up and sat on the edge of a chair standing nearby. Her glance met that of the Cardinal and both looked away, as if neither wanted to reveal his thoughts.

Ruberto spoke briefly, explaining the situation to the Cardinal, and hinting that Jessica need not become involved.

"I have told you, Fra Ruberto, that the guilt is deep," stated the Cardinal, in a voice that sounded ominous to Jessica.

And Fra Ruberto said, "I have known this, your Excellency, but it is not proper to hold them imprisoned without investigation."

Again the sure glance of the Cardinal met the frightened eyes of Jessica, and again he lowered them to his papers. He whispered, as if speaking to himself, "They intended to convert a Christian to their religion — something unheard of"; but now the harshness was gone from his voice.

"An investigation, your Excellency . . ." began Fra Ruberto again.

The Cardinal glanced at him quickly. "With what right," he demanded, "are they being held in the Inferno before an investigation has been ordered?"

"That is what the maiden Jessica protests," Fra Ruberto answered.

The Cardinal again concerned himself with the papers before him. Jessica stared at the wall figures — women with their faces revealed, and angelic children, entirely nude. "Would a rabbi have had the figure of a woman drawn on the walls of his court — even if her body were covered?" she asked herself, and suddenly was frightened as if the Cardinal could hear her thought. But he was still perusing his papers. He had only two left, and Jessica suddenly wondered, in spite of herself, if the delay were intentional, if the Cardinal were prolonging his investigation in order to prolong her visit. But finally he turned to Jessica and announced, "They shall this day be transferred to the prison at Ripetta for questioning."

"Thank you, your Excellency." Her voice trembled. She did

not dare look at his face. She turned to Fra Ruberto instead, and asked quietly if that prison were more comfortable.

A pleasant smile crossed the youth's face, and he assured her, "It is a sanctuary for cardinals and counts."

Jessica gathered her courage and faced the Cardinal with a smile that would have entranced any young man, and requested permission to see the prisoners. "You will be able to do so immediately, my daughter," he said in a low voice.

"Thank you, thank you, your Excellency. I have no words..." Jessica whispered, and this time she did not turn her eyes from his, lest his heart grow stubborn and he change his decision.

The Cardinal at length lifted his green eyes and answered with a sigh, "It is not necessary to have the right words in one's heart, my daughter, but rather the true belief in one's heart."

Jessica stirred as if she had awakened from an evil dream, and stammered, "I have nothing else to request, your Excellency, therefore I shall do well to leave." And so speaking, she kneeled before him, kissed his hand again hurriedly, and permitted the young man in the white cloak to lead her out of the room.

As she followed from the waiting room, the shadows in the corridor seemed more menacing, and suddenly she was afraid again that they had lured her there by trickery. If only she could escape, she planned frantically, she would set out immediately for Venice.

And as she hoped and planned, the wide gate was opened. She could see the blue sky. It was as if she had come up from the depths to the light of the world, and her face shone with happiness and relief.

She hurried to Eustachio, and Giovanni came in with her.

"He said that he would cause them to be transferred from the Inferno to the guard of the Inquisition prison in order to expedite their interrogation —"

"That is a great thing!" Eustachio interrupted her. "The condemned to death are placed in the Inferno, but princes and notables are kept in the Ripetta prison. They are fed as king and given beds in which to sleep."

"His Eminence was angry they had been placed in the Inferno

efore being questioned, and ordered their instant removal. He
so gentle and kind, and instructed that I be permitted to see
em. I shall be with them in another two hours."

"That does not mean they will be acquitted by the Tribunal —
e full rigor of the law is exercised even against the greatest
mong the prelates — but you have done your duty."

"And I shall return on the morrow to Venice!" cried Jessica,
d put out her hand in farewell.

"Go in peace and hasten in the fulfillment of your chief mis-
on," Eustachio answered. Jessica and Giovanni left.

Giovanni was disconsolate. "I thought you would sit for me
a model for a Madonna," he lamented.

"I must return, whatever happens," she insisted. They walked
ward the Embassy. "If I still have time, I would like to see
ichelangelo's 'Moses.' I have heard so much about it."

"I shall await you at five of the clock outside the Embassy,"
promised.

"But do not wait if I cannot go."

"I shall wait until midnight. I must see you again, Signorina
ssica."

She took a hasty leave of him outside the Embassy and went
the marble stairs into the building, where her host and hostess
ere awaiting her for the midday meal.

As they ate, she told them of her meeting with Cardinal
lessandrini, and both congratulated her. Donna Camilla was
ppy she had had some part in bringing a Jewess closer to
hristianity — it had great virtue — while her brother Bernardo,
is Excellency the Ambassador, was principally delighted at the
litical advantage he would derive — The Holy See regarded the
public of San Marco with disfavor owing to the activity of the
otestants, and the assistance which the Republic's Ambassador
uld give in bringing a Jewess into the Christian faith would in-
ire more respect for himself, especially by the deeply sus-
cious Pope himself; and it might eventually lead to the ap-
oval of his own elevation to Cardinal. . . . Jessica said she
uld leave for Venice on the morrow, and they raised no ob-
ction. It was as well, they thought, that she return to her
ristian lover.

"I am sure you are longing for him," Donna Camilla smiled. "I was the same at your age." She looked at the profile of her late husband engraved on a medallion hanging at the end of a long necklet, and her eyes filled with tears.

Before leaving in the afternoon, Jessica handed a manservant the sum required to obtain a seat in the post-chaise which was leaving next morning for Venice, and another flunkey went to show her the way to the Ripetta quarter where the Tribunal of the Inquisition was located.

She waited half an hour before being allowed inside. A few minutes later the six prisoners of Civitanova were brought into the ante-room where she sat. They were all manacled at the wrists. A deadly pallor was on their faces, and a fearful terror in their eyes! For some moments Jessica was completely distraught. The prisoners riveted their eyes on her and were afraid to speak.

Jessica took control of herself and said, "Who of you is Rabbi Benjamin Nehemiah?"

An old man, broken and trembling, came close to her.

"I have been sent by the community in Venice to help you —"

"The Almighty has brought you, Signorina. Who are you?" asked Rabbi Benjamin Nehemiah. All six burst into tears.

"I am the daughter of the banker Shelah of the house of Shylock in Venice."

"Don Samuel is your teacher!" Rabbi Benjamin Nehemiah cried joyfully. "He included poetry about you in every one of his letters to me."

Jessica was momentarily confused. Then she told how Don Samuel had persuaded the community in Venice to perform the act; of her audience with the Cardinal; and of her influence in obtaining their transfer to this prison. The captives grasped her hands and pressed kisses upon them.

"May your soul be blest, my daughter," Rabbi Benjamin said in a shaking voice. "Until an hour ago we were confined in a deep, dark dungeon and were given only a morsel of bread and a cup of water. And this place is like an abode of luxury, and important personages are detained with us — yet what is the offense of which we are accused?"

"The Cardinal found in the charge before him that you were accused with wanting to convert a priest named Ambrosio to Judaism, and that you had made all preparations for his journey to the land of Israel."

A cry of woe burst from the throats of all six men, and as they clapped their hands in anguish their fetters jangled as though they too were protesting against the defamation of innocents. The two guards motioned to them that it was time to return to their cells.

"May the Almighty hear our voice and send us His speedy protection!" cried Rabbi Benjamin, raising his eyes. To the other captives he said, "Praise God that He has brought us out of the pit and for His mercy in securing our acquittal."

"I shall inform the intendants of the Rome community of all that has transpired, and may the Almighty help you," said Jessica, standing up to go. Again they put out their hands and kissed her finger-tips, weeping bitterly, and Rabbi Benjamin Nehemiah said in a strangled voice, "May God treasure you as Rachel and Leah! Take my blessings to Don Samuel my pupil — may God treasure him as Ephraim and Manasseh!"

Jessica was bewildered and grief-stricken as she left. The moist tears of the captives were still on her hands, the fetters still jangled hideously in her ears, and before her eyes swam the agonized faces. "No," she whispered, her lips moving, "it is wrong to abandon such tortured brethren and go over into the fold of the torturers." A prolonged shudder convulsed her body. She had never regretted more than at this moment her entanglement with Lorenzo.

She went straight to the ghetto, and at the rabbi's house found the intendant Yehuda Tagliacozzo. The beadle went to summon Rabbi Yehuda Ha'Neeman and di Lattes. Meanwhile the rabbi besieged her with questions.

"I am very fatigued," she pleaded. "I shall tell all of you what I have accomplished."

Rabbi Yehuda Ha'Neeman and di Lattes came running in alarm, and di Lattes was followed by his wife. Jessica told them, though in more detail, what she had communicated to the captives themselves a short while earlier. Overcome by their emotion, her listeners could not adequately express their gratitude, and Signora di Lattes wept aloud.

The rabbi reckoned the necessary steps he would have to take for the welfare of the people. Jessica heard the echo of the hoarse voice of Rabbi Benjamin Nehemiah: "May the Almighty hear our voice!"

"Is it possible there are two-footed wild beasts?" she thought. "How can God see all this and be silent?" A spirit of rebellion overcame her — this time, a fearless rebellion, one against the God of her ancestors who saw all and kept silent. "And their God, how can one believe He is a God of love if in His name such deeds are done?"

The stubbornness which had guarded her race's survival fled before the rebelliousness of a young heart that sought life in every way — and things were eased for her.

"You are an angel from heaven," said the rabbi in a tear-choked voice. "May the Almighty bless your further efforts until they are freed."

Jessica sprang up, relieved as one who has removed a heavy burden. "I can no longer remain here."

"What?" they cried in unison.

"Please do not ask why. I have done my mission. I cannot stay among you, and I must not remain in the Ambassador's house. I am returning to Venice tomorrow."

"But we were begged to send an escort with you," the rabbi began.

"God forbid!" Jessica cut him short. "You must not waste your money. I shall be able to take care of myself."

"Almighty God!" cried Signora di Lattes. "Remain with us one day longer."

"I cannot."

The rabbi reflected a moment. "If you cannot remain with us, it is best that you leave Rome. You are a virtuous daughter of Israel, you are wise and sagacious above your compeers, and you know what is best for yourself."

His words pierced her heart as though by a rapier thrust. She extended her hand to them all, and Signora di Lattes fell on her neck in weeping as though she were parting from a beloved daughter going overseas. The rabbi pressed her to him and said tremblingly, "Your memory will remain engraved on the tablets of my heart until my last day, my child." Perspiration covered her forehead and her heart beat rapidly as she quickly concealed her inner thoughts.

All wanted to accompany her but she declined, saying it was not wise for them to be seen together. But di Lattes and his wife saw her as far as the ghetto gate.

"When are you leaving Rome?"

"Tomorrow morning, in the ordinary post-chaise, at nine of the clock."

"We shall still see each other," said di Lattes pressing her hand fondly.

Jessica almost cried out "No!" but she remained silent as she went out through the gate.

Di Lattes and his wife stood rooted to the spot, gazing after her until she had disappeared from their sight.

Early the next morning, at half an hour after eight o'clock, Rabbi di Nola, di Lattes and his wife, Tagliacozzo, and a number of other notables, headed by Rabbi Yehuda Ha'Neeman with a box full of his clothing, came to the post-chaise station. The community leaders had decided it was impossible to ignore the request of the Venice elders, and Rabbi Yehuda, who was an experienced traveler, had undertaken to escort her as far as the Papal kingdom frontier and find another companion for the final stage of her journey to Rome.

But Jessica was no longer in Rome — she had left at the break of day, at six o'clock, on the fast post-chaise.

Chapter Fifteen

ON THE FOLLOWING FRIDAY EVENING THE HORSE-POST BROUGHT TWO letters from Rome to Venice, one from Ambassador Navagero to Antonio and the other from Jessica to her father. The Ambassador informed Antonio of all he had done to persuade the lovely

Jewess to accept the mantle of the Catholic religion, emphasizing her promise to Fra Ruberto. "She is now in our hands, and you will rejoice as a pious Christian at the privilege which has fallen to you," he wrote. "If she breaks the promise, inform the Patriarch of Venice at once, and we shall take the necessary measures to compel her fulfillment."

Jessica had posted a letter to her father before leaving Rome. "I am hastening to return," she wrote. "I have succeeded in easing their condition and hastening the investigation, and I have decided to remain here no longer." Shylock and Don Samuel read and re-read the brief note several times. Both were overjoyed to learn she had left Rome on the Tuesday and were certain she would be home that day. But when Jessica had not appeared at sunset, Shylock was grievously disappointed.

"She will surely arrive from Rome on Sunday," Don Samuel told him. "If she rests on the Sabbath it will be on the Monday."

During the eve-of-Sabbath meal, Shylock took the letter out again and read it. Don Samuel, examining it, said, "She must have been in a hurry, her handwriting shows it — and she did not send greetings to me."

"Well, there is very little in it — she found no time to write her father a long letter, as it should be," Shylock grumbled. Don Samuel defended her.

"Jews are afraid to write at length from there and perhaps she was warned not to do so," he said. "She was also probably very tired — she only had three days in Rome."

"That's strange," Shylock ranted. "She was always so eager to go, as though houses grow in the air in other cities — what is there to see on a journey? The same windows and roof-tops. But she almost went out of her mind with desire, and suddenly she decides to return — it's very strange."

"Perhaps she is ill?" The thought darted into Don Samuel's mind, but he did not voice it so as not to worry the old man more. But the thought increased his own yearning for Jessica. He reflected on the wretchedness he would feel on her return. He would crave to embrace and kiss her — but would not dare for fear of her displeasure, for fear of plucking the fruit before it was ripe.

On Sunday, Shylock received a long letter from Rabbi Elijah di Nola. He did not mention the matter of the captives specifically in case the missive were opened by spies, but the letter was full of praise and commendation of Jessica. Each sentence opened with "Happy is he who gave her birth" or "Blessed be he who sired her," and Shylock's joy knew no bounds. Don Samuel read the letter and tears of happiness glistened in his eyes.

"And you thought she was just a pretty doll and nothing more. I told you she was intelligent and possessed of great acumen," Shylock berated Don Samuel.

"I never said she was only pretty," Don Samuel smilingly protested. "The Almighty endowed her with everything."

"She is reserved, as though Israel's distress has no effect upon her, but when the time comes she knows how to wage valiant struggle for Israel — such are the Shylocks!"

Rabbi di Nola had written that in spite of his age, he had come to the post-chaise terminus with the community intendants to bid her Godspeed, but they were too late. "I brought with me an ancient Pentateuch inscribed on parchment, the work of a mastercraftsman, as a gift from the Rome community to her revered father, but we shall send it to you, noble benefactor, at the first opportunity."

"That is Jessica my daughter!" Shylock crowed. "She is my only daughter yet she brings me more honor than seven!"

He could no longer contain himself, and revealed to Don Samuel that he had ordered a silver binding with golden clasps and inlay for a prayer-book for Jessica and a pocket-size liturgy inscribed on parchment for himself as wedding gifts. "You must design a suitable family crest showing the union of the two families," he added. Don Samuel remained speechless with emotion. Was indeed that day approaching which he had always regarded as a remote dream? "A family crest," resumed Shylock, "which will denote strength — how can I explain it? — the strength of the weak."

Don Samuel could say nothing and, fervently clasping Shylock's hand, stammered, "The strength of the weak."

Shylock wanted to hurry to the rabbi to show him the letter, but Don Samuel dissuaded him, saying it was best to await her return. Yet, when by the end of the day she had failed to appear, Shylock lost patience and summoned the community elders to the rabbi's house, taking Don Samuel with him.

"Let the rabbi himself read the letter aloud to us," Shylock cried. As the rabbi read the epistle, he sat and gloated, shooting keen glances from time to time at those listening, who expressed more than envy, and generally reveling in the occasion. "She must start wearing the 'Shaddai' amulet against the evil eye," he thought to himself. He sat at the rabbi's a long while, bringing up the question of the letter time and again so that he might hear a repetition of the praise and approbation of the elders.

On the morrow, the joy of both Shylock and Don Samuel turned to anxiety. Jessica had left Rome upon the Tuesday and had not yet arrived! Shylock sent Lancelot to the town in the morning to ascertain the time of arrival of the chaise from Rome, but Lancelot had no clear information when he returned. The old banker and Don Samuel kept on going outside the shop to see if she were in sight, and the nervous expectancy depressed the young man and irritated the older one. He behaved summarily with those coming to seek small loans; he was curt and ill-tempered with clients who came to repay their debts; and he was tyrannical to his clerks: this one seemed to be asleep, that one was walking about too much, and a third turned over the ledger-pages noisily. But he refrained from snapping at Lorenzo — true, the gentile was his agent and received commission fees, but he was actually the inspector installed by the authorities and had the power to cause him injury.

Lorenzo too was aggravated by Jessica's tardiness but he was still more vexed with Shylock's restlessness. "What has he in common with Jessica, who has decided to spit in his face?" he boiled. He was the more incensed at Don Samuel's obvious nervousness. His resentment grew into a burning anger, and the seat beneath him seemed sprouting with nettles. "I have an ache in my stomach and I am going to lie down," he said, and left.

"He probably overate yesterday," Shylock muttered. To Don Samuel he said in Hebrew, "The Almighty sent him that ache so that he might be removed from my sight. His Christian complacency stabs my heart like a knife — may he lie down and never get up!"

Thus passed the day. When Tubal came in the evening as usual for their study-period, Shylock met him at the door with the shout, "Your head is clear for Talmud and Shulchan Aruch — what do you care? Your children and your children's children are sitting here tranquilly in Venice!"

"God willing, she will get here safely. It's a long journey," Tubal tried to smooth him down.

"Are there not enough girls in the ghetto? They had to send my own daughter! If it's a question of money — Shylock's the man! If it's a question of a mission — Shylock's daughter is chosen! And I, the dolt, give in each time and yield my very blood."

Tubal changed the subject but Shylock kept on reverting to the matter plaguing his mind. After a short while Tubal left, murmuring further assurances to which Shylock retorted crossly.

"They find it enough to prate a few words but I have to do things — to send my only daughter, who has remained out of four, on a long journey, through forests and across rivers, among gentile thieves and brigands, in these miserable dog-days, these *giorni della canicola*. And Shylock the idiot always gives in!"

He was too overwrought to sleep alone — he would not have Lancelot or Stefano anywhere near his room — and Don Samuel remained to spend the night with him.

Both indeed were afraid to remain alone, each with his own thoughts, and they sat up late together. It was the first time Shylock had ever asked Don Samuel to play at lotto with him. The first number Shylock drew out of the box was 90; and as it was the numeral for "Fear," both were alarmed. But Don Samuel drew a 44, symbol for the dinner table and their minds were set at rest. Shylock thought: No harm can befall Jessica and Don Samuel. He drew out a 25, or *Hanukkah,* the Feast of Tabernacles.

"*Hanukkah* is the Festival of Miracles," he muttered. But the thought came swiftly to his mind that he himself needed a miracle.

A cloud settled on his wrinkled countenance. Don Samuel, who too was beset with anxious fears, tried to cheer Shylock and said, "*Hanukkah* is the festival of valor. It is from here the valor will emerge. Prince David Hareubeni has already said there is none in Jerusalem and in Egypt and in all the kingdoms of Ishmael who are like unto the Jews of Italy in worthiness of the struggle and of heroism."

"David Hareubeni had too great an appreciation of the heroism of his fellow-Jews and too little of the wickedness of the gentiles — and that's what defeated him!" Shylock grumbled. "The feast of *Hanukkah* reminds us year after year of the battle of the few against the many — have we ever heeded that reminder? Have we ever rebelled over the centuries against our oppressors, really rebelled, I mean?"

To check Shylock's mounting wrath, Don Samuel secretly extracted another slip from the box and it brought the numeral 22, meaning vehicles. "She is traveling!" he cried.

Shylock hastened to draw a number and was delighted at getting 63, or bride and groom.

They continued playing lotto until after midnight, and although they were still as unsettled in their minds as before, they were both able to fall asleep easily.

Lorenzo failed to turn up at the banking-shop again the next morning. He arranged with Lancelot to let him know personally, or through Stefano, when Jessica arrived home. He went to the post-chaise stage in the morning, but saw Shylock wandering in the vicinity and made off. Shylock waited until ten o'clock fruitlessly and went home with a leaden heart.

Jessica arrived an hour later. The first to see her was Don Samuel, who was standing outside the shop door, and a cry burst from his throat, "Jessica has come!" The clerks were alarmed. Shylock ran out in panic, embraced his daughter frantically and refused to let her go. In her excitement Jessica did not observe Don Samuel standing there and did not greet him.

"Did you come alone?" was Shylock's first question. It was in vain for her to explain she had been offered an escort but declined. "Women are light-minded," he said, "but I asked them expressly to arrange it."

"My anxiety for you expresses itself in but one question: how are you feeling, Jessica?" Don Samuel asked her with a meaningful smile.

The first hour passed with Shylock's pestering of why she had been delayed and a description of his anxious suspense. Don Samuel revealed his own anxiety only with his expressive eyes. Jessica explained she had no luck with horses — they were exchanged for worse ones at each successive stage — and the coachmen were slack. They took it in easy laps of eight hours or less a day. Shylock was dissatisfied with her reply and kept on asking why it was that the post-chaises should have such negligent and drunken riders.

At the midday meal Shylock asked her to tell him of all that happened, what her mission had achieved, how she had managed to reach the judges of the Inquisition, and why she had hastened to leave Rome. Jessica's replies were brief but Shylock interrogated her at length.

"She is tired; she must go to rest early," Don Samuel intervened. Jessica acquiesced, not glancing at him. She was both distraught and sad, but Don Samuel ascribed her dejected mien to fatigue. Shylock gave in and urged her to rest, after which they would go to the rabbi's to hear her report.

"I am no orator," she objected. "I shall tell you, and you —"

"I will bring them here then. It is a matter which affects the whole community," he interrupted spiritedly. Jessica tried to insist but he answered, "Please do not annoy me. Go now to lie down." She went to her room.

Don Samuel went back to the banking-shop and Shylock hurried to the rabbi's house, across the square, to tell of Jessica's safe homecoming. When the rabbi asked what news she brought, he said, "She is tired. Send the beadle to summon the elders to my house after the evening prayer. Jessica my daughter will tell them everything, and we may have to consult on what to do further."

No sooner had Shylock and Don Samuel left than Lancelot went in to Jessica's room.

"I prayed a great deal for your safety, little Signorina Jessica. I went to church every day and knelt to the Holy Mother, in a different church every day," he began.

"Good Lancelot," Jessica murmured. Lancelot's fears were dissipated on hearing these two words. Jessica still trusted in him, she still regarded him as the man who would help her to take the proper path.

"And Lorenzo worried about you — how he worried! He did not come to the banking-shop yesterday and today, little Signorina Jessica." Jessica made no reply. "There is no one like him, little Signorina Jessica. He was more troubled than your father."

"Is he really ill?" she asked.

"Really and truly ill, little Signorina Jessica. I am beginning to love him as much as I love you. Both of you are as one to me." He measured her with his look. "I promised I would let him know immediately of your arrival. The master was at home and I could not leave, and I don't want to send Stefano to him. I want to see him myself when I give him the good tidings, little Signorina Jessica." As he turned to go he said, "What shall I tell him on your behalf?"

"Tell him I have returned safely and will see him soon, but let him not come up to the house. He must be more careful now than previously."

Jessica lay on her bed for a long time with open eyes. The same room, the same house; once again her father, once again Don Samuel and Lorenzo — why had she hurried to return? St. Peter's as the symbol of authority, the Sistine Chapel as the symbol of beauty. Lovely Venice — never had it seemed to her lovelier than in the morning as she came in through its gates after a fortnight's absence; never had she felt as today, in passing the ghetto gate, as though she were being forced into a great prison.

The train of thought evoked an echo in her ears of the clanking fetters of the six captives in the Prison of the Inquisition in Rome. Their cringing figures came before her eyes, but their quivering lips were not pleading or imploring for mercy for themselves — they were expectorating in her face, and crying in concert, "We are being tortured in the dungeons and face death, and yet we cling to the heritage of our fathers; but you lack nothing and want to follow a Christian, as though a Jew were not begging for your love!" And Fra Ruberto and Eustachio and the Cardinal — had she indeed expressly promised, or by her silence consented, to be converted? She had no intention of deluding them nor could she in fact deceive them — their long arm would reach out and seize her. And Lorenzo who had been sick with anxiety for her, who was awaiting her. . . . A morsel of courage, a little more skill, and the key to the iron closet would be in her possession — and she could leave the wretched ghetto behind, the wide and glorious world before her. Her courage and skillfulness had been revealed even to herself when she was in Rome — she would steal close to her father's bed, insert her hand under the pillow, and remove the key; and if he awoke, she would place her second hand upon him and say, "Don't snore so much, I cannot sleep." She had never before entered his room at night for such purpose — she would do so as an experiment and then, a few nights later, again, so as to allay his suspicions: and then. . . .

Her musings drifted into the dream-state of fantasy: Giovanni Solari was painting a Madonna and she sat as his model. Suddenly he said to her, "I love thee, Jessica. Come, let me fly with you to the land of Israel and embrace Judaism." She was floating in a gondola at night, two pouches full of gold ducats in her hands, and when she reached the Rialto — Don Samuel was awaiting her. She stood before the large baptismal font in the chapel, the first on the left, and her godfathers were Eustachio and her father. The aged rabbi of Rome sat in the Vatican clad in Cardinal's robes, received her with courtesy, and held out his hand to be kissed; and when she touched his hands, she was bereft of all power, the earth opened at her feet in an abyss, and she sank, sank. . . .

Several times she started up in alarm but fell asleep again. She awoke in earnest on hearing the voices of people in the adjoining room. It was already night, after the evening prayer, and the elders of the community led by the rabbi of the Ashkenazic

Temple had assembled. David ben Yekutiel and Esther his daughter had also arrived uninvited. The door was ajar — an indication that her father had already been in to ascertain if she were still asleep — and she heard her father apologizing to the rabbi for troubling him to come. "If Rabbi di Nola came to see her off," said the rabbi, "I see no reason why it should be irksome for myself." Don Samuel said, "It was a long journey. She is so tired."

Within half an hour she sat at the table, beside her father, telling those present of her stay in Rome. She added nothing but naturally omitted a number of particulars it was wiser to conceal. The gathering was amazed at her nimble wit. "Incredible! Incredible!" — the words were uttered from time to time; and Shylock preened himself. Don Samuel did not remove his gaze from her. She seemed to have matured so much in years during the brief fortnight! The simplicity of her narrative, spoken without vanity or pride, gave the impression that she was performing her strict duty without heeding or wanting their profuse praise.

"Did you travel on the Sabbath?" someone asked.

"I arrived in Rome on the actual Sabbath, but Rabbi di Nola did not rebuke me," she replied.

"But you had no call to desecrate the Sabbath on your way back," the questioner remarked, as though speaking to himself. It was the father of her friend Deborah. Shylock saw it was envy which tinged his words. Yet, strangely enough, he kept quiet; on the contrary, he gloated in the jealousy of this man whose daughter amounted to nothing. He replied carefully, "The postchaise cannot be expected to stop for her. She was longing for her father and hastened to return."

"Had she left the following Monday she would have arrived here too on the Sabbath. The chaise was delayed on the journey," said Don Samuel.

" 'The salvation of souls defers the Sabbath,' " the rabbi quoted, and halted the fruitless argument.

The others plied Jessica with questions to which she replied. They asked several times if indeed the Ambassador of Venice had invited her to his mansion; someone asked if she ate at his table, but as two other questions were put to her at the same time she was able to evade a reply and turned to the others.

"Did you see Michelangelo's 'Moses'?" Tubal asked.

"I tried hard but had no time to see anything," she answered.

Tubal said he had seen the statue in a church five years earlier when he visited Rome. Before Pope Paul mounted the Holy Throne, many Jews were wont to go to see the "Moses" and to stand entranced for a long time before that noble marble figure. The rabbi said he had heard of the statue, but in his opinion it was not proper to enter Christian houses of worship, even to honor Moses the Lawgiver.

"That stupid old fool of Florence who carved Moses out of the stone is just as bad as the rest of them, and his handiwork is just sheer vanity," Shylock said contemptuously.

"You must not say that, Father!" Jessica reproved. She wanted to be careful not to reveal she had been into any Christian holy place but was unable to contain herself, and added, "I was told to wait in a small house until the Cardinal was ready to receive me, and there I saw Michelangelo's paintings from the Bible — he is sculptor and painter and poet. The Almighty has given him everything in abundance — he is the greatest man in the world!"

"Is he then celestial?" Shylock parried ironically. "The wicked Titus was regarded as divine by the idolators, that foul Aretino was a divinity for the Christians, the *Commedia* is said to be divine, and I suppose Michelangelo is super-celestial!"

A shudder shook Jessica as she heard her father's mocking remarks about Michelangelo regarded so highly in Italy as the apostle of all that was good in the entire Christian world. But Shylock paid no attention to Jessica, whose countenance had grown pale with suppressed indignation, and continued: "Rabbi Moses Isserles, who is yet a lad, is years older than he, forgive the comparison!" Pointing at his own portrait on the wall, he added, "And that artist, Rabbi Moses of Castelazzo, may he rest in peace, was superior to all their artists. He too made miraculous paintings from the Bible, but a Jew has no luck."

The gathering nodded their heads in assent. The Jews of

Venice were hostile to Michelangelo. When he lived some thirty years ago at Isola della Giudecca in Venice as a refugee, a year or so before the first temple — that of the Ashkenazi community — was built in the ghetto, the Jewish elders among whom were Shylock's father approached him with a view to painting murals for the synagogue, offering a handsome remuneration, but he refused. Shylock hinted at the refusal by saying it was probably here in the ghetto that he conceived the idea of painting Bible scenes on the ceiling of that place of which Jessica spoke.

Don Samuel, who was perceptive of Jessica's confusion from the way her face had changed color, remarked that the suggestion was inappropriate as Michelangelo executed the paintings in question fifty years earlier. Shylock listened but smiled disdainfully, as if to say, "How can one believe the Christians!"

The rabbi led the conversation back to the captives in Rome. "As you had been so successful, my daughter," he addressed Jessica, "it would have been wiser to have remained in Rome and watched the further course of the affair."

"I could not stay any longer," she managed to say after some difficulty. Her glance fell on Don Samuel. Her father's derision of the illustrious and revered Michelangelo still had her in a ferment and her heart beat with loud hammer-strokes. The fury within her caused a sudden, terrifying fatigue, and she rose. She felt she must be alone, away from these people and especially her father.

"God only knows if they haven't been thrown back into the dungeons," grieved Esther daughter of Yekutiel, tears in her eyes.

"If anyone is removed from the Inferno, he is not returned. The Inferno is only for those condemned to death," was the assurance by one of those present who had lived some years in Rome.

"May God have mercy!" the rabbi cried. "Now we have naught else to do but await good tidings from Rome — with God's help!"

With these words the rabbi parted from Shylock and Jessica, and the others, rising after him, repeated their encomiums to the daughter and thanked her father before leaving.

Don Samuel lay sleepless on his couch a long while. He was seized by an intensity of pride and love never before experienced. Jessica's casual glance at him as she finished speaking was convincing proof, he felt, that her precipitate homecoming had been for his sake.

Jessica hurried to her room and to bed. Closing her eyes, she envisioned Rome and the Sistine Chapel and before her stood Michelangelo. In her imagination she embraced the venerable artist and humbly whispered, "I am not to blame, maestro, for having sprung from his loins — I am not to blame. . . ."

Chapter Sixteen

JESSICA AND LANCELOT WENT OUT THROUGH THE GHETTO GATE AT half-past ten o'clock on Friday night to meet Lorenzo at the Rialto stage, but she was astonished to find him waiting in a gondola at the ghetto bridge. He jumped out, took her in his arms, and tenderly led her into the boat.

"I have a thousand questions to ask, but they can all be rendered in the one brief question — Are you all right, Jessica?" Lorenzo whispered. His words flustered her — it was the same question, perhaps phrased slightly differently, which Don Samuel had put the moment he saw her on her return from Rome. It suddenly seemed as though both had caught hold of her, Lorenzo and Don Samuel, and she was about to be torn apart. But she rapidly mastered her confusion and replied, "I thank you, Lorenzo, for being patient and not coming up to my father's house."

"Your thanks are not sufficient," Lorenzo said. "I did not come to work on the pretext of being ill. I deluded myself too into thinking I was ill — I did not leave the house, Jessica." How enraptured he was to press her again to his heart, to peer into her face in the dim light, and to hear her voice.

"It is good when a man and woman are parted for some time," Jessica laughed. "Absence strengthens love."

A short while ago she had been in sorrowful mood. The old doubts had troubled her as she sat at the Sabbath table opposite her father and Don Samuel; and now, now she was again in Lorenzo's arms, again the rainbow lights of Venice twinkled at her, the flaunting towers and mansions on both sides of the Canal inspired her with a serene calm and confidence, and the water rippled before her as though an unknown hand had cast into them the last of her gloomy thoughts, her secret hesitations, and they were borne on the water away from her never to return.

"You placed a guard over me in Rome, Lorenzo my darling. Were you afraid I would fly from you?" she asked laughing, in a mixture of pride and joy.

"I had no fear, Jessica mine, yet — the loving heart is always afraid; and I wanted to have your stay there a pleasant one. I wanted you to settle your affair quickly and return. Only now do I know what you are to me, beloved of my soul."

"You settled everything properly, Lorenzo mine. I concluded my errand far quicker than I expected. And when it was settled, Rome sickened me. I saw nothing but heaps of stones and the scattered remains of marble columns, and I hastened to return."

Lorenzo again hugged her ardently and showered her with phrases of ecstatic passion. "If you had remained there another week, another day, my little Jessica, I should have gone raving mad. It was only the company of Antonio and Portia, our true friends, that encouraged me."

Lorenzo made no inquiry as to what she had seen in Rome or her impressions of the Eternal City nor asked about his friend Giovanni — he was burning with an excitement of ardor which left no room for anything save the thrilling emotion that Jessica was at his side.

On landing he told her that Antonio and Portia awaited them; Portia was giving a wine party in honor of her return.

"They are very pious," he added, "and they are happy to assist in a great pious act; you and I know we have decided on this long ago, but if it gives them satisfaction to think they are responsible for it, then let them rejoice." He did not expressly name the cause of their satisfaction, and Jessica did not ask: it was all so understandable and clear to her.

Portia folded Jessica in her arms and kissed her with great

fervor and Antonio took her by the hand, leading her into a chamber in which there were a number of other guests. Antonio's face shone as he introduced her: it seemed to him he was leading her straight to the baptismal font as her sponsor. Jessica perceived from the faces of the guests that they had already been told about her but felt no shyness; she felt herself to be one of them, and even possibly better than they — after all, they had been assembled to do her honor.

They ate and drank heartily, and there was a great deal of merriment during the drinking. Antonio himself was in serious and even solemn mood during the meal. His ship, the first in four months, had been expected to arrive from England ten days earlier but word reached him yesterday that she had gone down on the Goodwin Sands. He was keeping the report a secret but they were already whispering about it on the Rialto — and on Monday he had to pay the Jew the three thousand. Who would lend him the money if it became known that one of his ships had sunk and the others were afloat on their voyages far away? But the sparkling Neapolitan wine drove the thoughts out of his head, and the more of the red nectar he poured down his throat, the more jovial he became.

Between the carnival songs and the ribald *Dialogues* of the divine Aretino, Jessica was asked to tell about Rome, which she did in snatches; and as if to confuse her, the memory of the mean and dirty streets of the ghetto, the Prison of the Inquisition in the Ripetto quarter, and the tortured visages of the captives of Civitanova flickered through her mind. No one asked why she had gone, no one recalled her origin; but only one of them, the drunken Signor Graziano, the merchant who traded with the other side of the Alps, hinted at her Judaism when he asked why she had not brought along to their feast some *formantin,* a Rome ghetto delicacy of which the Christians were enamoured. Portia swiftly interrupted with a question as to the Pope's health; he was lying ill. Jessica shrugged her shoulders. She paid no heed to Signor Graziano as she had never heard of the viand he mentioned.

The party dispersed and sat about in couples or groups of three and four on the sofas and divans in the corners. Lorenzo repaired with Jessica to a shadowed corner and embraced her. She raised no objection. Thus had she always wanted to be, in Loenzo's arms and in a house such as this, away from the ghetto.

"When we marry," she said, "we shall live in Florence."

"I thought you would choose Rome," he replied.

"Rome is severe and leaden-hearted, and I am a daughter of Venice."

"Then let us remain here, near the good Antonio and Portia, Jessica mine."

"Never!" she flashed, thinking of her father. Before her eyes came the faces of the Jewish elders of Rome who admired her so greatly and she added, "Nor in Rome, either."

"Never mind, sweet Jessica, I shall go where you elect. But speed the day. Now that you've been away from me so long I cannot endure it."

"It is more difficult for me, Lorenzo mine, to go back to that house, to see his face, to steal in and out during the night. It is only my love for you, dear Lorenzo, which gives me the courage to bear all this."

"But it is so small a thing, Jessica, to take the key under his pillow and —"

Jessica breathed heavily. "A small thing — no, no," she whispered.

"But, good heavens, Jessica! You are taking what is yours, he has enough."

"I am not concerned with decreasing his property," Jessica halted him, "but he takes care of his money. He has never left the key on the table, he has never forgotten to take it out of his pocket on changing his clothes. He is a sound sleeper, but I am afraid he will awake the moment I approach his bedside. I feel it is easier to remove his night-shirt while he sleeps than take the key under his head."

"What a Jew! — Then I fear, Jessica, that the day will never come."

A tremor went through her as if an unknown hand had thrust them apart. She turned him a smiling face and said reassuringly,

"The day will come. I await it more eagerly than you, Lorenzo mine. You cherish only love in your heart, and I — I have love and also the burden of that house under which I am almost staggering. I think of plans and ruses all day — it is so difficult."

Portia approached and sat on the sofa beside them. A few moments later Antonio motioned to Lorenzo to join him.

"You are intoxicated with love, Lorenzo," Antonio began. "She deserves it — you read what Bernardo Navagero wrote of her."

"I know it without his saying so, there is none like her," cried the other and, after a pause, added, "or like Portia."

Both glanced at Portia and Jessica conversing upon the sofa.

"Are they not the most beautiful of the women here?" Antonio queried.

"They are the most beautiful of the women of Venice and the most clever of all the women in the world!" exclaimed Lorenzo.

Antonio held his arm and they entered an adjoining room to which the broad door was open.

"My dear Lorenzo, I must reveal to you that the ship which left England has sunk," Antonio opened. Lorenzo said he had heard of it that day in the Rialto but gave no credence to the report. "There are many in the Rialto who are happy at my misfortune, but one matter is important: on Monday morning I must repay the Jew his loan. You must try to obtain a loan for me."

"Must you remind me of it? It is I who actually owe this money."

"Do not mention it. You will return it when you have the money."

"Of course I shall have money. She will eventually get it out of him."

"Do not force her too much, my young friend. So long as she is not baptized she remains a Jewess, and she can suddenly change her mind."

"Not she, not Jessica," Lorenzo declared. But his friend's last words seemed to have kindled a flame in his heart. A shudder went through him at the thought of Jessica returning to the ghetto and of his remaining alone. He recalled Lancelot's statement that she would resume her study with Don Samuel on the Sunday — she would once more be alone with the Jew from Capo d'Istria who was spinning his web around her. Lorenzo peeped into the next room and gazed at Jessica from afar, as if to assure himself she was still with him. "Jessica will not change her mind," he grated through his teeth. Antonio thought of Shylock who was liable to turn that blasphemous indignity about the pound of flesh into a serious matter.

"But her father the Jew is capable of changing his mind," Antonio retorted. "You know these usurers — find me a loan." Lorenzo did not fully understand him. He had forgotten about the bond.

"I have been to a number of Jewish money-lenders," he said. "It's a large sum, but I am still trying — we still have two full days."

"But tomorrow is the Sabbath," reminded the other.

Lorenzo laughed. "No Jewish money-lender will ignore a handsome transaction of this kind even on the Sabbath, and a Christian money-lender will even do business with me on a Sunday."

"A Christian?" Antonio wondered.

"Yes, yes. I have good prospects of getting the money at a fairly low interest rate from an old priest. The only deterrent is that he's afraid of it being known he takes interest — but I'll speak to him tomorrow and convince him."

"Then my happiness will be threefold: I shall have done a good deed to a friend as yourself, I shall have performed a pious act in sponsoring another soul beneath the wings of the true faith, and my Sunday calm will not be disturbed."

"Do not worry, my friend. Throw the burden on me. I must admit, and God forbid you spread this, that the Jew conducts his business honestly. I hadn't conceived it possible. Yet he fears me — I superintend the business for the authorities. If you don't repay him on Monday, you can pay him back the week after or next month. If I'm not able to get the loan from the priest tomorrow, I'll arrange the matter some way or another."

"A postponement — that is the proper way!" cried Antonio.

"By next month at least one of my vessels will come, either from Tripoli or from Lisbon."

"The Jew is a wrathful man, with mad whims. You saw that when you spoke with him. But if properly handled, one can get anything out of him; and actually he is timorous."

"That last statement is the most important, Lorenzo."

"True, true!" Lorenzo assented. He thought at the moment of Jessica's timidity at fleecing her father. He recalled Antonio's remark that she was liable to change her mind, and his face clouded over. It seemed he had never loved Jessica so much before, that she was deceiving him, and that she might one day vanish altogether from Venice.

"You have reassured me, friend," Antonio asserted. Holding the other's arm, he continued, "What a pity to spend our time in talking business."

They went into the guest-hall and drank a toast in Vesuvius wine to the two beloved Portias (an omen to the time when Portia would stand sponsor to Jessica who would assume her name). They were approached at the table by the drunken Graziano who upbraided them for drinking alone. He picked up *fiasco* after *fiasco,* held them up to the light to judge of the wine, and mumbled, "That's a white Padua. This is an Aleatico, a women's tipple. . . . And this is empty, the devil take it. It should be thrown at a Jew's head."

Antonio thrust a flask of Tuscan Pomino into his hand.

"This is an excellent brand, my friend," he said, "but you must bespeak yourself a pair of broad shoulders to carry you home." Graziano filled a capacious tumbler and tossed off the wine.

"This is what I have been seeking! In God's name, let us drink together." Antonio drank with him but Lorenzo refused. Since Jessica had been with him at the casino she became nauseated on seeing a tippler, whether a noble or a *magnifico,* and remembering this Lorenzo was always careful not to become intoxicated in her company. Now that he was so head over heels in love with her, he made doubly sure of sobriety. Taking Antonio by one arm, he led him as if casually to where Jessica and Portia were seated.

"Of what are you conversing?" Lorenzo asked.

"You must not be jealous of a woman," Portia bantered. Lorenzo smiled. True, he was jealous that Portia could sit so tranquilly at Jessica's side.

"Signora Portia has discovered that we are the only two women not wearing jewelry, not even rings," Jessica replied to Lorenzo.

"A lovely woman needs no adornment," remarked Antonio. "The Madonna as painted by all the artists is never shown with precious gems." Both ladies turned their eyes on him and he was overjoyed at the reception of his witticism.

"Yet you have two diamond rings, Jessica," Lorenzo recalled.

"I wear them but seldom. I have no hankering for ornaments."

"When the talk turns to hankerings, it is time for us to leave you," Portia smiled, rising and taking her husband's arm. They rejoined their other guests.

"There's none so brilliant as Portia!" Lorenzo declared. "But I can see no other person than yourself, Jessica mine. I cannot even listen to Portia talking." Jessica smiled. "Oh, perdition!" Lorenzo thought. "Why cannot she too say the same things?" His ears echoed Antonio's warning and he envisaged Shylock and Don Samuel for a moment.

A few minutes later Jessica took her hand out of his grasp and said she must return home.

"But it's still early," Lorenzo argued. "Only an hour after midnight."

"It's far too late. I cannot remain any longer."

Lorenzo recaptured her hand and caressed her. Jessica surveyed the guests, and Lorenzo sat dejectedly. He found nothing to say. His hand in hers — perhaps for the last time. He was foolish to let her go from him. Don Samuel had begun of late taking the Sabbath meals at Shylock's table; he could feast his eyes on her all day while he, Lorenzo, had to eat his eyes out in craving. And on Sunday they would resume the lessons. It was not only Jessica who lacked courage; he too, Lorenzo, was craven-hearted for allowing her to remain in her father's house — Antonio did not insist upon the immediate repayment of the debt — he could arrange a postponement with the Jew easily —

and there were Jewish usurers in Florence whom he could serve as an agent.

Jessica stood up. "I must go. The hour is very late." Lorenzo stood with lowered head. "What is it, Lorenzo?"

"Why do you leave me? Please stay here."

"I always want to be with you, Lorenzo mine, but —"

"I envy Lancelot who is always near you. Even when you are away, I am consumed by your fire, Jessica!"

Jessica drew a deep breath. Ah, if Lorenzo only knew how great her torments when she had to return to her father's house! Lorenzo was able only to see the reflection of his own anguish in her sorrowful eyes. Yet she was weary of the constant hazards in leaving her father's house. Don Samuel was a Jew, and her father loved him as a son.

"Do not leave me, Jessica mine," he murmured.

"I never want to leave you but I must. It is you who compel me. I must wait for the opportunity to —"

"My heart is expiring for you, my mind is becoming deranged!" Lorenzo broke in. "Stay with me, light of my eyes! I give up the money — I cannot stand this any longer!"

Jessica was startled. Her heart melted in a twinkling, and she fell into his open arms.

"Huzzah!" shouted the bibulous Graziano. Another guest drew some chords from the strings of his mandolin, and several others clapped their hands. Antonio placed his hand on Portia's shoulder, lifted his eyes to the ceiling, and murmured with joyous reverence, "This is the moment for which we have been waiting, Portia!"

Chapter Seventeen

SHYLOCK AND DON SAMUEL LEFT THE SYNAGOGUE WITH THE RABBI and several other worshippers who lived near the Ashkenazic Temple. Shylock supported the rabbi by the arm and was in high spirits. The Ark of the Law in the temple was adorned for the first time with the heavy curtain which Jessica had embroidered as a commemorative offering for her mother's death-anniversary. The rabbi had delivered a sermon on the redemption of captives and the harbingers of good deeds, mentioning the names of Shylock and his daughter. As he was about to leave his followers the rabbi pointed at Shylock, saying, "Two more like him and his daughter in every city, and the Messiah will have come."

Shylock pressed Don Samuel to himself and said, "It was he who brought me the privilege of this good deed — two sages as he in every city and we have a barrier against all our Christian enemies, may they be expunged."

"May the Almighty bestow upon him a good wife, in the words of our revered sages who said: 'Find a wife, find a treasure,'" the rabbi prayed for Don Samuel.

"He will undoubtedly have that bestowal," Shylock remarked. No one now disputed that Shylock, who was not habitually profuse in his compliments, was intending to marry Don Samuel to his daughter.

When the others had left and they were together, Shylock said, "If Jessica had only heard the rabbi's sermon, she would have had her reward for the great effort she made."

"Yet she is so modest she would have been embarrassed," Don Samuel returned.

"And are you and I braggarts?- Yet nonetheless the words were pleasant to our ears, Samuel."

While still in the corridor Shylock called loudly, *"Bueno Sabbat!"* but was surprised to find, on entering the room, that the table had not even been set for the Sabbath benediction.

"She hasn't yet recovered from the fatiguing journey, poor girl. She is probably still asleep," said Don Samuel. A moment later he added with a smile, "The additional effort of traveling by chaise for two Sabbaths must also require repose for her soul."

"Nicely put!" Shylock applauded. He glanced at the table. "And see how careful that gentile is about our customs. He has not placed the wine on the table."

"He probably knows about our law saying that wine is forbidden if touched by a heathen," Don Samuel chuckled, referring to an old Jewish taboo. "But some communities do not give much heed to it."

"I gave him his instructions twenty-eight years ago. The wine was then locked up, but I trust him now. And Stefano would not get away from Lancelot easily if from heedlessness he did anything that was forbidden."

Shylock took the wine from the closet and both men pronounced the benediction. When Lancelot entered, Shylock asked him about Jessica.

"I haven't seen her. She usually sleeps late on the Sabbath."

"The blockhead wouldn't think of saying she is fatigued by her long journey," Shylock grunted.

"A servant is always slaving," Don Samuel said. "How can he judge the weariness of those who are not servants?"

Something prompted Shylock suddenly to think her illness might have after-effects. Spurred by the impulse he went to the door of her room and peered inside. On nearing Jessica's bed he started back. Stumbling in bewilderment to the door he saw Don Samuel and gave a great cry. Running to hold him up, Don Samuel saw that Jessica's bed was empty.

"Control yourself, father! She probably went out for a moment and we did not hear her."

Shylock drew himself up. "You are foolish, Samuel. Disaster has come upon me!"

He ran to the second door and shouted, "Lancelot! Stefano!" Both servitors came in trembling.

"You — you alarmed me, master," Lancelot stuttered.

Shylock caught hold of them by the scruff of their necks and knocked their heads together. He relinquished his hold of Stefano who bolted from the room. But he held Lancelot, growling, "Go to perdition, son of a dog!"

"What have I done, master?" Lancelot whimpered with difficulty, as Shylock held his throat in a vice.

"Let him go, Signor. He knows nothing," Don Samuel pleaded. Shylock quit his hold of Lancelot.

"You are good and merciful, young Messer." Lancelot's voice shook, and he took Don Samuel's hand to kiss it.

"I'll kill you, son of a dog!" Shylock raved. "Stefano is a blockhead, but you— you slept like a corpse and did not hear her leave."

Lancelot felt relieved. He realized that his master had no inkling of his servant having had a hand in this. He assumed a startled expression.

"She fled last night and you heard nothing!" Shylock said, his anger cooling. Lancelot ran to Jessica's room, stood by her bed as though mourning, and cried in a tearful voice, "Little Signorina Jessica! Our Signorina Jessica!"

Shylock and Don Samuel entered after him.

"Perhaps she has just gone out —" quavered Don Samuel. He could not imagine Jessica's having fled, and the noise Shylock had made seemed to him a dreadful mistake.

Shylock thrust his hand a moment under the blanket and scrutinized the pillow. "The bed is cold," he said. "The pillow is uncrushed. She did not sleep in this bed last night — she waited last night until I fell asleep and then ran away."

Lancelot retreated a few steps from his master.

"Ran away?" A fit of shivering seized Don Samuel.

"I was still cleaning the dishes after the meal," Lancelot ventured. Then, fearing his remark would provoke Shylock to more blows, he began sobbing, "Little Signorina Jessica! Good Jessica of ours! In the name of the wounds of the Savior!"

"To blazes with you and the wounds!" Shylock flared. But even in his extreme fury he sensed he had gone too far in blurting out the curse, and moderated his tone. "You're crying now, but where were you last night? Where were your ears, dunderhead?"

"There's a lot to do of a Friday night and I am no longer a young man," Lancelot whined. "I slumber like a dead man on a Friday night, Messer." He broke into tears again. "I brought up little Signorina Jessica — little Signorina Jessica!"

"Don't bray, donkey! The neighbors will congregate and it will become known. Woe to such disgrace!"

Shylock stood in the center of the room, his fists clenched and his teeth grating. It was only when Don Samuel saw

Shylock standing there petrified yet inwardly seething with fury that the full import of the awful truth dawned on him. He fell prostrate on Jessica's bed and burst into loud sobbing, his lips murmuring her name over and over again without pause.

Lancelot went out of the room and joined Stefano. A few minutes later he returned to pacify his master. "What advantage is there in despairing, Messer? Let us look for her. Stefano and I will search all the churches in the city."

The cold mask dropped from Shylock's face and his expression grew more tender. He gripped Lancelot's hand and beseeched, "Please, Lancelot, go and find her. You love her so much. Go and find her."

"Be assured, Messer! By the Holy Virgin, I shall not rest until I find her." Lancelot dropped his eyes. A spark of hope darted into Shylock's heart. He approached the bed, placed his hand on the shoulder of the recumbent Don Samuel, and said in a fatherly tone, "Rise, my son. What can you do by crying? We must think of what to do while there's time."

Don Samuel obeyed and straightened himself. His pallid, anguished face softened Shylock. He closed his lips tightly and made no further utterance. He went into the second room, Don Samuel after him.

A quarter of an hour later Lancelot came in with food.

"I cannot eat," murmured Don Samuel faintly. Shylock gave a brusque gesture of dismissal.

"I'm sending Stefano at once to San Marco, and I won't go until the master eats," said Lancelot.

"No food shall pass my lips, Lancelot! She is my only daughter, all that has remained alive to me, and now—" His voice caught as though blood were gurgling in his throat. "Let Stefano first ask at all the chaise-stages if she didn't leave for Rome this morning." Lancelot went out. "Rome! Accursed Rome! She made pretense she had seen nothing, as if there were no Rome at all in the world—and you, Shylock, whose eyes did not understand why she grew so angry when you spoke the truth about that old marble-carver of Florence, you did not comprehend that she hurried back to Venice with her mind full of secret plots, may Satan take her!"

"Do not curse her, signor," Don Samuel begged. "If she had any secret designs she would not have returned to us—she will come back, she must come back!"

"Everything is as blurred to my eyes as my head—I must put on glasses again," muttered Shylock to himself. Going to his wall box he took out a pair of spectacles, the precious article for which he had had no need these two years. Now he passed through all the rooms and, without knowing what he did, searched under the beds and couches and in the cupboards, his voice trembling, "My daughter—Jessica my daughter—" Don Samuel had followed him into Jessica's room and when Shylock opened her wardrobe, they saw everything orderly and undisturbed.

"She has not run away," Don Samuel cried. "Whoever flees does not leave anything behind." Shylock inserted his hand into a secret corner and took out a little casket in which, on opening, they found the two rings and the amulet studded with diamonds. Shylock was startled and for moments stood motionless, holding the glasses in his hand. His swollen cheeks seemed to become more distended and the pupils disappeared beneath his eye-lids as if turning to see inside his skull. He lowered his eyes and examined the diamonds. No, it was impossible to believe she had planned to fly, and he had no reason to fear that most shameful ignominy. But in a trice his face grew more overcast than before and he whispered to himself, "Yet she has gone—I am not dreaming—it's a puzzle, a terrible puzzle—perhaps she has been abducted."

"That is impossible," said Don Samuel after some reflection. "You did not hear and the servants heard nothing. It's impossible."

"Everything is possible with them, damnation to them!" Shylock asserted, opening his eyes wide. "She is of matchless beauty. Perhaps some villain who saw her in Rome followed her to Venice and hired bullies and brigands to snatch her away."

"How could it happen? Jessica would have cried for help and struggled with them, and someone would have heard her call."

"They may have gagged her, threatened her with—" Shylock could not continue.

"She has given us plenty of proof of her courage—she would at any event have grappled with them," Don Samuel said confidently.

"Mystery, mystery!" groaned Shylock, walking back and forth in the room.

"Yet it is clear she has not fled. You accused her wrongly, Signor, and even cursed her."

"Do not remind me of the sin of impetuous speech—it just happened, my son!"

When they returned to the dining-room Shylock went casually to the wall box, opened the iron door quickly, and after peering inside closed it again.

"Even the money is in its place—she has not fled," Shylock said with certitude. He approached her portrait, held the frame with his hands, and moaned, "My daughter, my daughter, my only child, where are you? Child of my loins, bird of my heart, where have you vanished?" Don Samuel riveted his gaze upon Jessica's radiant face as if expecting the painted lips to open and give them the solution of the riddle.

Lancelot came in. He took his master by the arm and dragged him to a seat.

"My heart is breaking inside me," he revealed. "We must seek her, perhaps we'll find her—and now, Messer, please eat. The mind is not clear without food."

"Good Lancelot, you have the heart of a Jew," Shylock murmured, sending him a grateful look. When the man left, Shylock said, "He loves us, that one, that servant who has grown up among the Jews, the only Christian whom I can look in the face — see how his face has changed with grief."

"One thing's clear," mumbled Don Samuel waking out of a reverie, "one thing's clear—she has not run away."

"I have no doubt of it at all. Everything is in its place. She is a virtuous daughter of Israel—and what she did for the prisoners of Civitanova is additional proof."

A heavy cloud lay upon both their faces. Either way it was a calamity; but the persistent conviction that she had not fled came as a relief to their gnawing ache and they tasted some of the food set on the table.

Suddenly Don Samuel clutched Shylock's hand and cried, "I believe I have found it!"

"Samuel my son — save me! Samuel my son —"

"She has gone demented, she is moon-struck—perhaps you concealed it from me? I love her whatever her defect—tell me the truth."

Shylock was momentarily taken aback as though he were hesitating, but he speedily answered, "I swear to you in her name, my son, that she has never been ill of that vile disease. If she were, God forbid, stricken with a serious malady, I would never have let her go to Rome." Don Samuel became somewhat doubtful. "Perhaps your knowledge of astrology gave you that peculiar thought," Shylock added with a bitter smile. The ironical remark sent all further doubt from the younger man's mind.

"But it's quite possible she has had a sudden fit—it's the only clue," he declared. "It's laughable to suspect her of running away, and foolishness to believe she was taken out of the house forcibly. She was ill and was made to undertake a superhuman effort—it must have turned her brain and she left her senses."

Shylock placed his trembling hands upon Don Samuel's and affirmed, "You are full of knowledge. The treasures of all wisdom lie open before you. Tell me more precisely what is the nature of this rare disease?" Lancelot came in to remove the plates. "Clear out!" Shylock rapped at him.

"The somnambulist leaves the house in a state of sleep at night. He wanders the streets alone—"

"I know all that!" Shylock interrupted. "But the ghetto gate is closed, and if she came to a Jewish house, they would take her home."

"Neither walls nor water can halt a somnambulist. He can carry any load and walk for hours without getting weary — there's no doubt, she's become a sleep-walker!"

Shylock jumped from his chair and rumbled, "I am going to see Kalonymus the physician."

"I won't remain alone," Don Samuel protested.

"Then come with me, my son. You can question him more shrewdly than I, and you will understand him better." Shylock ordered Lancelot not to leave the house until they returned. "She may come back in the meantime," he told the man.

But Kalonymus was not to be found at his house in the ghetto and they returned home — a lurking hope obsessed them that she might have come back in the few moments of their absence. Disappointed, they took their red hats and began walking to the Rialto. On the way through the ghetto they met several acquaintances, some of whom saluted them and then gazed after them in astonishment; others stopped to ask why they were going into Venice on the Sabbath. Shylock was evasive and stalked by the importuning questioners.

To their joy they found Kalonymus at his Rialto house. He was shocked to see their mournful faces—it was he who had permitted Jessica to take the long journey and he feared she may have fallen ill again.

"Both of you have come—has anything untoward occurred?"

"A great disaster has befallen," Shylock blurted, but he was too overwrought to continue. He motioned to Don Samuel to speak.

Don Samuel missed no particular in his narrative to the physician, but omitted mention of his suppositions.

"What can I say?" Kalonymus sighed. "It is a common failing. Many are turning their backs on Judaism —"

"But not my daughter!" Shylock insisted. He explained how all had been found untouched in its place, even the rings, and it was inconceivable that a runaway should take nothing with her.

"Yet there have been cases," Kalonymus ruminated, "where their folly has gripped one of our people — and if love has anything to do with it, how much more—and spurning money, jewels, clothes, he is drawn to them as a moth to the flame. Take my friend to whom I wrote on that matter, Rabbi Elijah di Nola, the chief rabbi of the community in Rome. His nephew, who bore the same name, a scholar and sage, turned his back on Judaism and is now a librarian at the Vatican and copies our holy books for them, damnation everlasting be his lot! And Salomon Romano, grandson of Rabbi Elias Levita! He returned from the East to save his brother, Eliano who had changed his hide and become a Christ-worshipper, but he was caught in their toils too."

"Speak up, Samuel, why do you remain silent?" Shylock upbraided the young scholar. When Don Samuel heard what Kalonymus had to say, the cramping doubt racked him — was there any credibility in his assumption? He could hardly open his mouth and, with labored breath, managed to mutter diffidently, "Perhaps she was struck by somnambulism."

"She had been plagued for two weeks on the journey, she ran about like a madwoman in Rome day and night, as though I had ordered her to remain only three days. When she returned I hardly recognized her — she had changed so much — and now this catastrophe has come upon me." Shylock groaned. Then, with an excess of confidence — "And now she has become a sleep-walker!"

Kalonymus sat immersed in thought, weighing what he had heard. The unfortunate father's supposition was hardly likely. Conversions occurred every day, and a beautiful girl like Jessica must have attracted someone on the way who misled her, but he had no wish further to harass the two wretched men who anxiously awaited his opinion. He shrugged his shoulders and said, "There's no connection between the minor illness she had and somnambulism, but after all we physicians know but little. The malady might have come to a person whose outward appearance was healthy and sound."

"Yet is it possible for her to be stricken with it?" Shylock asked.

"Of course it's possible, but —"

"Then if it's possible," Shylock broke in, "there's no doubt about it."

He again narrated the full detail of what had happened. He praised Jessica as a virtuous Jewess and a home-loving body like her late mother, and each time he turned to Don Samuel to testify if he were exaggerating. Don Samuel was laconic in his replies and tried hard to conceal his scepticism from Shylock. While Shylock was speaking, he visualized all those hours in which he had taught and conversed with her: she had always been fascinated by Venice, adored their festivals, sung their songs . . . Several times she had derided the odes of the Hebrew poets filled, so she mocked, with "Ohs" and "Woes." Once she had even expressed doubt if there were such places as Paradise and Purgatory. During the last lesson he had given her, on the Friday before her illness, he had said, "When you are not singing you seem so miserable, like a bird in its cage." She had struggled with herself all the time, weeks and months, and he had noticed nothing. It was all so clear, and he had been struck by blindness. . . .

"Save us, Rabbi Kalonymus! Is it possible there is no cure for the disease?"

"If the patient has gone, to whom shall I give the remedy? If she were indeed moon-struck, she would have awakened some hours later, and hurried home."

Shylock's eyes bulged in their sockets — he had not thought of that possibility. His knees became limp and his hands shook as doubt hardened into certainty that she had really fled. Don Samuel to whom it was now all intelligible, thought in spite of his profound bitterness of spirit how best to translate Kalonymus' diagnosis so that Shylock might regain belief in Jessica's somnambulism.

"It may be that while she was in her trance she wandered into a convent, and they will never let a Jewess out of their hands once they grab one."

"That's it! There's no doubt, that's what happened!" Shylock cried, his face lighting up for a moment. But he drooped again, heaved a profound sigh, and said to himself, "Woe to the father who believes a serious illness which has stricken his only daughter to be the sole tribulation!"

The door opened and a manservant came in to say that a patient awaited Kalonymus. The physician was secretly delighted at the interruption of the melancholy conversation. He went over to peep into the next room and, returning, said to Shylock, "It's an urgent case. I must receive the patient at once."

"I beg of you most humbly, Rabbi Kalonymus, to keep all you have heard a secret for the time being," Shylock implored on rising to go. Kalonymus reassured him, "Discreetness is a physician's obligation. We don't know much, but that has been hammered into us." Standing with them at the threshold, he added, "I shall pass by your house to hear what has transpired. I still advise you to try to get information from the ghetto guards — money will open their mouths."

Throughout the long walk back, Shylock expatiated and Don Samuel kept his counsel. Shylock had seized on the possibility of Jessica having entered a convent by error and devised all manner of plans how to get her out. He execrated every Christian passerby, and spoke disparagingly even of Rabbi Kalonymus. "He puts on the conceited air of knowing nothing," he gibed. "He knows as much about this malady as you or I, but it had not even occurred to him that she might be moonstruck."

As they came to the ghetto gate and Shylock wanted to pass through, Don Samuel detained him. "There is still another likelihood," he said. "Let us interrogate the guard." Only Camillo was at the gate.

"Who was on the watch last night?" Shylock asked him.

"Me and another," the constable replied.

"Did no one pass through after nine of the clock to go to town?"

"And what am I guarding for? Do you imagine I'd allow a Jew to get out?"

"You will get a hundred ducats in gold," Don Samuel interjected. "Try to remember: didn't a Jewess leave here last night?"

"God forbid!"

"Come, Samuel. We must not waste a moment!" Shylock tugged at him. Entering the ghetto, he said, "For a hundred ducats a Venetian will sell you his father and mother — there you have another proof that she did not take the open road."

"There are two more gates," Don Samuel pointed out.

"Why do you torment me with vain talk?" Shylock upbraided him. "The gates are distant, and anyone who runs away tries to take the shortest route, not the most roundabout."

"You are right, Signor," Samuel agreed.

When they entered the house, they sat down, almost collapsing from exhaustion. The distress of both father and lover was heightened at the sight of Jessica's portrait on the wall. Both spoke with dismal spirits of their tragedy, which each viewed in his own light.

Lancelot entered and said Tubal had sought them.

"Did you tell him anything?"

"God forbid! 'They've gone out,' I said. He said he had heard you were seen going to the city, and marveled at it."

"Was Stefano in San Marco?" Don Samuel asked.

"He was, he questioned the sexton, and the sexton assured him that no Jewess was baptized there lately," Lancelot responded and went out. Shylock was startled. He jumped up and rapped out, "Shylock's daughter and St. Mark's! Jessica and the Cross! If that's the case, she's in their hands!"

"Calm yourself, Signor," Don Samuel pleaded. "She fell ill and blundered into them. She is wise and intelligent, she will find a way to elude them —" But inside of him there was no faith in what he said. He no longer believed what he was saying. He lowered his head on the table and burst into sobs.

It was the time for afternoon prayer. The twilight which seemed to drift from both their somber hearts grew deeper and more clouded until it pervaded the entire house — and Jessica's portrait was swallowed by the gloom.

After the evening prayer Tubal came straight from synagogue.

"What has happened?" he asked on seeing the two mourners.

"Be seated, Tubal my friend," Shylock whispered. Both he and Don Samuel found it difficult to speak. Tubal thought quickly of several possibilities and all had to do with bankruptcy. Finally Shylock composed himself, rose and said, "Let us go to the rabbi. You will hear there, Tubal, of the tragedy which has overwhelmed me."

"What has happened? You tell me, Samuel," Tubal urged the younger man.

"It is not a disgrace, it is a tragedy," whispered Don Samuel looking at Shylock. "Jessica has gone." Tubal was flabbergasted.

Shylock supplemented Don Samuel. "She contracted a dreadful illness. She became a somnambulist, walked in her sleep — and she has vanished."

"I cannot understand it," Tubal stammered.

"I have no strength to say much," Shylock added. "Let us go to the rabbi's and I'll tell the whole story and you'll understand — this tragedy will send me to the grave!"

They came to the rabbi's house.

"Rabbi, a disaster has happened to me!" cried Shylock on opening the door. He fell into a chair and burst into tears. Don Samuel could not restrain himself and followed suit.

"Disaster?"

"A great disaster," Tubal sighed. "She has gone."

"What do you mean by 'gone'? Speak out clearly!" the rabbi chided Tubal.

"She disappeared from the house during the night," Tubal murmured.

"Not that, Rabbi, not that!" Shylock cried. He rose and shut the open doors, and then told the story at length.

"And what did Kalonymus the physician say?" the rabbi asked.

"He said that somnambulism can strike anyone — she had been ill, rabbi, and then shortly afterwards went on that long journey."

"It is possible? Our sages used to say, 'They who perform good deeds are unharmed,'" the rabbi marveled. Shylock realized that the rabbi inclined to some other theory concerning Jessica's disappearance. The same dreadful thought had occurred to him the same morning, and he urged Don Samuel, "Tell them if we didn't find everything in its place, if she didn't sit with us at table last night as any virtuous daughter of Israel." Before Don Samuel could open his mouth, Shylock hurried to repeat what he had already told once and twice over.

"Nevertheless, Shylock, send your servant to seek her in the convents," the rabbi said finally. "Inquire at other churches as you inquired today at their San Marco Cathedral."

Tubal accompanied Shylock and Don Samuel to the house, spoke to them encouragingly, and went sorrowfully to his home.

The same night the news spread through the entire ghetto that the only daughter of Shylock, dean of money-lenders, had flown, and changed her religion.

Chapter Eighteen

JESSICA WAS BROUGHT TO THE BAPTISMAL FONT ON THE SATURDAY morning. At first, Antonio had intended having her baptized at the San Marco, most splendid of all churches, but Jessica was afraid her father would hazard his life and appear there. She asked to be taken to some place far from the heart of the city, and the baptism took place in the Church of Sts. Giovanni e Paolo, the second in eminence among the houses of worship in Venice — the sepulcher of the Doges.

An ornate gondola awaited her in the Rio del Pestrin, a near-by canal to the left. Immediately after the ceremony, she left with Portia to spend several days on the Lido. All that had been close to her until that morning suddenly receded into the distance of many years, and there only remained the secret fear that she might encounter her father. Antonio appreciated her feeling and it was he who suggested that she go to the Lido until her marriage, which was fixed for two weeks hence. Summer visitors came to the Lido from all parts of Italy, and it was brimming with life and gaiety — there, on the seashore, where no Jewish foot would tread, she would have no time to brood or see any member of her father's household, not even Lancelot. At first she had wanted to take Lancelot with her to Florence, but after her christening she decided never to see him again.

The old monk of St. Jeremiah refused to give Lorenzo the loan of three thousand ducats for Antonio, nor had Antonio any prospect of obtaining so large a loan elsewhere. The report of the foundering of his argosy had circulated quickly, and it was even rumored that another two had gone down. He had no other recourse than to ask Shylock for a short extension.

Lorenzo reassured Antonio and promised him faithfully he would settle the matter with Shylock on Monday, but on Sunday afternoon, after he had met Lancelot and Stefano at the home of the sacristan of St. Jeremiah's and watched the money being paid over to them, he changed his mind and told Antonio: "I fear that the Jew who is mourning for his daughter will be late in coming down to his banking-shop, and I shall not have word with him in time. You must repay him the debt by ten of the clock. I advise you to go to him now, and he may possibly give you an immediate response."

It was distasteful for Antonio. It was difficult for him, a proud noble, to come asking favors of a Jew.

"Won't his servants let you have the money back for a short time?" Antonio asked. The idea seemed to roll a heavy load off his mind.

"I spoke to Lancelot but he refused to listen to me," Lorenzo replied.

"You must promise him thirty per cent," Antonio said. "I would far rather pay forty per cent than ask a favor of the Jew."

"I'll confess: I promised him fifty per cent — after all, it was for a short time — but he declined. He's the slave to a Jew after all!"

"You are right, Lorenzo," Antonio brought out after long cogitation. "The Jew is a cantankerous fellow even in normal conditions, and how much more so now. He will probably insist on the condition which I pledged — it's dangerous to wait until tomorrow."

"Go to him today, and tomorrow, if it be necessary, I will speak with him," Lorenzo said.

"Are you not afraid of him?" Antonio suddenly asked. Lorenzo laughed heartily.

"Of a Jew? Anyway, he doesn't suspect I'm the man. Lancelot told me the old man has got some nonsense in his head of an illness she has contracted, and he is certain she went out at night and blundered into a convent, and now he's sending his servants to scour all the convents." Antonio laughed too and said, as if to himself, "The true God addles their wits, may His Name be blest!"

Antonio deferred the unpleasant visit from hour to hour. He remembered Shylock's digs at him when he came to seek the loan. At dusk, when he was about to leave for the ghetto, he asked Lorenzo to accompany him, but Lorenzo for some reason hesitated to go into Shylock's presence, and to meet Don Samuel face to face. He hid this from Antonio and found some excuse to wriggle out of the invitation. He said that if Shylock gave the refusal to his face, he would have no opportunity of appealing to him later.

"You said he might be late in coming down to his shop tomorrow, and might not appear at all — these wretches go mad when one of them accepts the true faith. How will you speak to him if he refuses me?" Antonio asked.

Lorenzo laughed and replied, "Then I shall go upstairs to him — what else? I'll threaten him properly. I won't spare the villainous usurer!" As he spoke his voice rose. "That filthy Jew has all the luck. His daughter left him and didn't take a *scudo*, not even her own rings — and his money is really Jessica's money, my money!"

Antonio left with Lorenzo's optimistic assurances emboldening him, but on reaching the ghetto gate he lost courage. He had sealed a specific bond that if he failed to return the money at the explicit date, Shylock was entitled to cut a pound of flesh from his body. The Doge administered the law rigidly — what would happen if the Jew rejected his request?

When Lancelot came in and said Signor Antonio was waiting, Shylock cried, "Let him go to perdition!" Lancelot remained; he knew his master. "Take him into the room on the right, and tell him to wait a moment," Shylock added. Lancelot hurried out.

"Perhaps the Christian has brought some word of her?" Don Samuel suggested despondently. He was certain it was not the case, but the thought occurred to him and, having uttered it, he awaited a reply.

"That's the agent to the Court of the Doge to whom I gave the big loan of three thousand ducats ten weeks ago — I cannot look a gentile in the face today, even if he has come to repay me the money!" Shylock said, and sighed dolefully. He had vented his rage and mouthed imprecations so much during the day that he was sapped of all strength and was near nervous exhaustion.

As each hour passed, he began more and more to comprehend the bitter truth. Even the fact that none other than Tubal had come in to see him all day furnished proof of the general disbelief in the story of his daughter being moon-struck. Nonetheless he continued to clutch at this slender straw. He had taken down Jessica's portrait from the wall some time ago and placed it behind the cupboard, and from time to time he cursed her in his heart, but he let no word fall from his lips and in front of Don Samuel even forbore to utter the fear that she might have fled.

He went over to the wall box with dragging feet, rummaged inside and took out the bond, and said to Don Samuel, "Go now please, Samuel, into the second room" (he pointed at Jessica's room) "and I won't be long with him." Don Samuel stood for a moment uncomprehendingly and then went into the corridor. Shylock opened the door of the other room and ushered Antonio inside.

"The time for repayment is at ten of the clock tomorrow morning," Shylock said as they sat down. "It is fine of you to be early. The amount is a large one."

"I come to you shamefacedly," Antonio muttered without looking at Shylock.

The banker was disconcerted. "Do they already know on the Rialto what has befallen me?" he asked heavily.

"What has befallen?" Antonio questioned in his turn, assuming a surprised expression. Shylock sat silently a moment. He was amazed at himself for being able to face a Christian. He smiled dismally and said in a drooping voice, "Why should I tell you, that you might rejoice in my misfortune?"

"God forbid! I don't hate you, Shylock."

"My only daughter has been stolen from me," Shylock muttered. "Someone took her away or she left moon-struck and wandered into a convent. Whatever it was, she left my house two nights ago and has gone."

To divert suspicion, Antonio tried to think of some innocuous inquiry, but his choice was unfortunate. "Perhaps she ran away of her own free will? After all—"

"You are a Christian and we have no common language!" Shylock burst forth. But he quickly changed his tone and coaxed, "Signor Antonio, do you wish to earn three thousand gold ducats easily? Find me my daughter!"

Antonio was flustered. The request challenged his Christian piety, and had he not remembered the loan, he would have spat in the other's face and berated him roundly. He looked straight at Shylock and answered, "If a Jew wants to find protection under the Christian wing, shall a Christian like Antonio deter him? You must understand, Jew, my conscience would not let me do this even for ten thousand."

"Conscience—that's their language!" Shylock leapt from his seat. "These Venetians particularly boast of their conscience. The one they call the greatest of the poets they forbade to leave for Ravenna by sea and caused his death."

"Less of your anger, Shylock," Antonio replied tranquilly. "Your early fathers sold their brother Joseph and threw the Prophet Jeremiah into a pit—why should we bring up the sins of our fathers who have turned to dust these many generations, Shylock?"

The banker paced back and forth with lowered head, his hands clasped behind his back—somehow the last spark of faith in Jessica's inculpability had almost expired within him—and suddenly he came to a halt opposite Antonio. "What is the meaning of your statement that you've come to me shame-facedly?" he inquired.

"My ships are tardy on their voyages. No one has yet arrived."

"I heard them saying on the Rialto on Friday that the largest of your ships was wrecked on the Goodwins. If my Sabbath were not already disturbed by the great calamity, that report would certainly have disturbed it."

Antonio put on a blank expression to hide his embarrassment. "My rivals have been spreading false rumors, because —"

"The main thing is, what's your request?" Shylock broke in.

Antonio hesitated between asking for a month or two weeks but, on seeing Shylock's glowering look, he hurried on, "The date of repayment to be put off for a week is my request, Signor Shylock."

"Since when have I become Signor?" Shylock asked sarcastically. "I am a Jew, or just Shylock, for all the world like some servant; yet today I become Signor, and tomorrow I shall be Messer." Antonio repeated his request. "I gave you the money without interest, and yet you ask for postponement?" Shylock added.

A cold perspiration covered Antonio's face. He was ready to listen to insult, but not to have Shylock send him away empty-handed. If he stood up and left, as befitted a noble of the Barozzi, he put himself in the Jew's hands; if he replied with vituperation, not even Lorenzo's intervention would avail.

Shylock sat down, looking directly into Antonio's eyes, and said, "I had no mind for postponements nor for jests as at the time I gave the loan. I'll give you some plain advice: go to your Christian friends and tell them the Jew Shylock intends cutting off a pound of your flesh. If they hear that, they'll probably lend you the money."

"How can I put you in such a wicked light to other people?"

"It is not wickedness," Shylock denied. "The law forbids Jews to engage in any craft. The law says, these Jews may engage in commerce and these Jews must not. Such-and-such a business which requires diligent hands to develop is open to Jews, but such-and-such a craft which has already been developed needs no Jews. In the name of the law our holy writings were burned. Has any one of you, the Christians, perceived any wickedness in it? The law is the law, like a decree from heaven — tell that to your friends and they'll lend you the money."

"You mock me, Shylock," Antonio said, not daring to call him

"Signor" again for fear of annoying him. "Lorenzo and I ran about for three days without success."

A smile curled on Shylock's gloomy face. "Lorenzo knows I am not disposed to accept postponements. That's why he sought you a loan and dared not speak to me. Tell your Christian friends, Signor Antonio, that they may lend ten thousand, even a hundred thousand, if they take no interest, and if no one finds out, they can also permit themselves to accept interest payment. They refuse? Why? Where is Christian charity? They probably say, 'A Jew has money, go to him' — don't they?"

"You are as shrewd, Shylock, as if you had been present at the conversations." It seemed to Antonio that the compliment had softened the other. "Extend the date of repayment a week; my ships have left the danger zone."

Shylock eyed him piercingly and half-earnestly, half-jestingly, spacing the words and syllables, said slowly, "But you have not yet left the danger zone!"

For an instant Antonio's body shook with an icy shudder, and his noble arrogance left him.

"I know it," he murmured in a low voice. "That is why I came to seek a deferment. One of my ships is bound to arrive within the next three days."

"If that were true and if there were no foundation to all the rumors noised abroad, you would have obtained a loan at interest from a Christian. It is an open secret, Signor Antonio, that Christians lend and borrow at interest."

"Interest to a Christian? You are a pious Jew, Shylock, and you will understand a pious Christian."

"Nothing is forbidden to save a soul," Shylock returned. Antonio sat nonplussed. He refrained from asking Shylock if he were threatening him in grim earnest, as this would beg the unpalatable question. Shylock meditated a moment and thought that now he was in one mess, it was unwise to enter another; but only to annoy the Christian — it would never occur to him to cut off a pound of his flesh — he asked, "If you say one of your ships will arrive in three days, why do you want a postponement for a full week?"

Antonio saw he was disposed to some postponement and answered, "I asked for a week for greater certainty."

Once again Shylock changed his tone and cried, "It's a sign your 'certainty' is not so certain! Every part of the ocean is a danger zone for ships, Signor Antonio, just as every Christian land on the European continent is a danger zone for Jews!"

Antonio was afraid he would risk all if he insisted on a week and replied, "All right, then, make it three days."

Standing up, Shylock declared as if in thought, "I have no head now for business. Come tomorrow at nine of the clock and we shall see."

Antonio stood too and exclaimed, "Thank you, Signor Shylock, I knew you were good-hearted. I was astounded when you gave me the loan without interest."

"And I am ready to forego the three thousand if you can find my daughter, Signor Antonio — think it over, it's a large sum."

As Shylock's anger had been aroused by his original answer to the offer, Antonio sought a way out of the dilemma and, after a moment of thought, said, "I am always preoccupied with business, and that's the work of a spy of the lower classes. I shall be prejudicing my position if I lend a hand to such a proceeding."

The old banker heaved a deep sigh. He understood Antonio's reason and it was evident he could not help him in any way. His head fell forward on his chest and nodded back and forth like a tree-top in the storm.

When about to go, Antonio cajoled the other, "So as not to rob me of my night's rest, tell me clearly, 'Come tomorrow morning and we'll go to the notary to extend the date of payment.'"

"You have come at a bad time, Signor Antonio," Shylock responded. He drew himself erect and added with mounting temper, "I have not tasted food for two days, I did not close an eye last night, and many such nights await me — all for what? For whose sake? For Christians who forced my daughter to become converted! Are you asking a Jew like me to make your night's sleep pleasant?"

"Let it be so then. I shall come tomorrow at nine of the clock,"

Antonio acquiesced. He feared that Shylock's wrath might wreck his whole suit.

"At nine of the clock punctually, Signor Antonio! If you are a quarter of an hour late, you will find my claim lodged with the Doge — remember, I warned you!"

"I shall come before nine," Antonio promised as he left.

No sooner had the door closed than Don Samuel came in with Tubal from the next room. Shylock told Samuel that Antonio had not brought the money but come to ask a postponement. He shook his head and muttered, "Now I must pray not for the redemption of Israel or for my daughter to repent, but for his vessels to arrive safely!"

Walking up and down the room with bent and mournful head, he fetched up standing in front of Tubal. He could not look the other in the face — it was evident to him that Tubal had no doubt of Jessica's flight. Yet something goaded him to arouse a flicker of doubt in his friend's mind, but he could find nothing to say. Once again he paced about with bowed head as if burdened with Tubal's thoughts and of all the ghetto's. He reproached himself for not having kept sufficient guard over her, and Don Samuel, especially Don Samuel: he had told him "She is in your hands" but he had not known how to watch over his possession. He had taught her, but had not divined her conspirings.

His imagination visualized scenes as devilish as gamboling imps: Jessica standing in church and an old priest placing a crucifix around her neck; Jessica sitting and feasting in the company of Christians; a priest instructing her to speak evil against the Jews, like the grandson of Elias Levita; Jessica telling them of her own free will of the Hebrew books in her father's house and disclosing their hiding-place.

Suddenly he stood stock-still, as though the frightening images blocked his path, and taking his head between his hands he gave a rending cry, "God Almighty, you have taken the light of my soul — take my soul too!"

Tubal approached and led him to a chair. "Calm yourself, my friend. She is not the only one, not the only one."

"But she was my only one, she was my only one," he whispered to himself and, grasping Tubal's hand, he implored as one begging for his life, "You know full well, Tubal, that I gave generously for the redemption of captives — why has God done this to me? Why? Why?"

"The works of the Almighty cannot be questioned," returned Tubal sententiously. "Speak of her as the dead."

"No! She is not dead!" exclaimed Don Samuel, startled at Tubal's words.

Shylock sat with downcast head, tears coursing from his eyes, and mourned, "If she were dead, I could light a candle for her soul, but her soul is dead. For whom shall I light a candle? For whom? My daughter, my daughter!"

Tubal sighed deeply and, to mitigate his friend's distress, mentioned a family disgrace of his own. Placing his hand on Shylock's shoulder, he said, "When my uncle went over to them, may his bones rot, my grandfather sat upon the ground and whispered, 'The Lord gave and the Lord took away,' and never let my uncle's name cross his lips again — rend your garment for her, my brother!"

"No, no!" cried Don Samuel. "She will return. It is impossible for her not to return." The cry brought new life to Shylock — there was still one who believed Jessica had not fled of her own will! — and the tiny spark burst into a flame which devoured his whole being. He was electrified. He sprang from his chair as though bitten by a serpent and bellowed, "Your grandfather, Tubal, was a dish-rag, a dull Jew who bowed to the inevitable. I was molded of other material! I shall not tear my clothing for her, I shall not resign myself to fate! Just as they burned the books of the Talmud, I'll burn every holy book in my possession, my prayer-shawl and phylacteries — !"

"Do not blaspheme against the All-High!" Tubal warned him sternly. "The Messiah will come and save all erring souls, my brother!"

"*I* want to save her! I am not going to wait for the Messiah!"

Tubal spoke gently. "You pray every morning, 'I shall await his advent whenever he comes.'"

Don Samuel held Shylock's hands in both of his and spoke in a mellow voice. "From now on we shall await *her* whenever she comes — she will come! If she has been bewitched she will return to her sane mind quickly and come; and if the dogs have caught her, she will escape and return!"

Light flashed in Shylock's anguished eyes and he breathed, "Samuel my son, *you* must never leave me!"

"I shall never leave you, master!"

"Call me father!" — And he fell upon Don Samuel's neck.

"I shall never leave you, Father!"

Tubal's eyes glistened with tears at the sight of the embracing men, the two grieving men who sought solace for their misery in each other's arms.

"Stop it, stop it, Shylock," he implored. "God has given you a son in place of a daughter."

"Not in place of a daughter!" Don Samuel cried. "She will return! It is impossible that she will not return!"

"Would that it be so, would that it be so!" Tubal besought. Then he told Shylock he had really come to summon him to the rabbi's.

"I have no mind for public affairs just now," the other protested.

"I know it," Tubal replied, "but the affairs of the community are pressing, new misfortunes bring forgetfulness of the old. You cannot spurn the rabbi."

"Go, my father, you must continue now with greater vigor," Don Samuel encouraged him. He wanted to remain in solitude for a while, alone with his agony, to rid his heart of the accumulated tears, to recall Jessica's portrait and to cry, to cry for the living-dead who would never return, never, and whom he would nevermore see again.

"You must come too with me, my son," Shylock said. "I shall not do anything, big or small, without you henceforth." Before leaving he called Lancelot and said, "Good Lancelot, if she should return, do not scold her or shower her with questions, nor tell her of my mourning! Hold her and call me from the window — I shall be in the rabbi's house."

"As you say, master," Lancelot returned submissively. When Stefano was certain their master had gone down the stairs, he came in to Lancelot. "And he still hopes she will come back!" he whistled scornfully, and began sniggering.

"Do not laugh, Stefano. I am being stifled here. I thought I would go with Jessica, but Lorenzo was angry because I did not lend him the money, and said she never wants to see my face again."

"Never mind," Stefano soothed him. "We'll go to the south and become farmers. Wait, someone's coming up the stairs. It's Salarino or Camillo. I told them to wait until they saw the Jew going out — I thought he would go to prayers. They oughtn't to get the same share as us. What did they do? They opened the gate and closed the gate."

Salarino's voice came from the corridor. "Where are you, to Hades with you?" Lancelot whispered in an aside to Stefano, "What did they do? They opened the door and closed it, that's all."

"The Jew has gone at last!" Salarino cried as he entered. "We have been cooling our heels for hours and hours, as though we stood guard over the Jew's house." He perceived from their silence that something was amiss. "I must return to my post," he added. "Give me our thousand ducats and I'll be off."

"Of course we'll give you the proper share," Lancelot said.

"Why do you say that? Give it and let me go!"

"Everyone will get his share in accordance with the work he put in," Stefano muttered.

"Don't talk nonsense!" Salarino fumed, grasping the hilt of his sword. "The devil take you, slaves to Jews! What would all your work have availed if I hadn't opened the gate to you at night?"

"And what would it have availed if you had opened the gate if I hadn't brought Jessica to pass under it?" Lancelot countered. "We don't want to take your money but —"

"No 'buts'," Salarino warned.

"You don't speak like a poor constable any longer, but like a man of property," Lancelot sneered.

"Like a Senator!" Stefano chimed in. "And what trouble did he have? He opened the gate and shut the gate." He edged a few paces away from Salarino. "How much do you get for that job a month?"

Salarino kicked him and, imitating his shrill voice, said, "Get out, you fool! You ought to get only one ducat out of the three thousand, and Lancelot ought to share the rest equally, a half to himself and a half to me and Camillo."

Lancelot put his hand on Salarino's shoulder and began winningly, "Please listen, my friend —"

"I am not your friend!" Salarino howled. "I didn't know you before this business began and I won't know you when it's over. You've lived so many years in the Jew's house that your bodies probably stink too."

"What is there to quarrel about?" Lancelot continued. "You know as I do that a Christian's body cannot stink — we were all baptized in holy water."

"We've talked it over," Stefano intervened, "and decided, if there's no alternative, to give you a thousand ducats, but not of gold — silver ducats. We didn't agree to —"

Salarino caught hold of his arms and shook him violently, shouting, "Shut up, slave to a Jew! Give me the thousand ducats at once!"

His face convulsed with the pain in his arms, Stefano writhed in Salarino's iron grip and bellowed, "Leave me alone. Lancelot has the money!"

Salrino turned to Lancelot and grated, "By the wounds of God, if you don't pay over the money you'll die on the spot!" He tried to draw his sword from its sheath, but Lancelot held him with both hands.

"Stefano, save me!" he shouted. "Give me a knife, bring me a spear!"

Stefano retreated a few steps and threatened Salarino from a safe distance, "If you don't clear out of here, this will be your grave."

The constable grappled Lancelot whom he held with his right

hand, and his left hand grabbed Stefano. The three struggled together, cursing each other at the top of their voices.

Shylock and Don Samuel came running in alarm. Before he saw what was happening, and while still outside the house, Shylock shouted with radiant face, "Lancelot, Lancelot! You called and we heard at once."

But they were sobered when they saw the three men. The struggling trio had not heard them enter the room.

"What's all this? And the guard — ?" Don Samuel wondered. Tubal and the rabbi came hurrying after them.

"They probably know we've been looking for her in the churches," Shylock said. He approached the struggling men and, with an incensed glare at the uniformed constable, he cried, "Why are you fighting the synagogue servants?"

They were alarmed and broke their hold. Lancelot and Stefano stared for a moment at their master's face and bolted. Salarino remained standing examining his torn mantle.

" 'Why have you attacked them'?" he grinned mockingly. "You're worried about them, Jew, eh? And it was they who got your daughter out of your house!"

"What!"

"They took her to your inspector Lorenzo — they got three thousand ducats for that fine piece of work."

Shylock and Don Samuel stood thunderstruck, but Tubal came a step closer and asked Salarino, "Where did that spendthrift noble get three thousand ducats?"

"A great merchant, the agent of the Court, helped him."

Shylock was dumbfounded, but then shouted in an inhuman voice, *"Antonio!"*

His voice startled Salarino, who bounded to the door. Don Samuel ran after to halt him, so as to learn more details, but Salarino pushed him away and bolted, shouting as he scurried off, "They're going to run away with the money! My thousand ducats!"

Shylock covered his eyes with his hand and whispered, "It's not possible, yet — it was *I* who was moon-struck."

"And I!" Don Samuel gulped. His voice aroused Shylock from his daze and he cried:

"Did you hear, Samuel? Did you hear? What infamy! Antonio, that foul-hearted man with the pious face! He borrowed the money from me, from *me,* to give it to Lorenzo so as to steal the light of my soul! That is why the evil Lorenzo waived his commission fee! My daughter, my daughter!"

He ran to the cupboard, took Jessica's painting from behind, broke the frame with his foot and ripped the canvas into shreds. "Now I know that *you* did all this to me, you mutinous wench! May your memory be expunged and wiped out from the world without trace or hope of the after-life!" He trampled the shreds of canvas beneath his feet.

Don Samuel trembled with mingled rage and sorrow at the contumely. For a split second he had seen Jessica's smiling face before it was no more. She seemed to have died in that instant before his eyes — and how shameful her death! "How could you have been so misled, Jessica?" a voice spoke inside him — he could not blame her.

The rabbi drew close to Shylock and urged, "Submit to your fate."

Shylock paid no heed and stormed: "There is a God in heaven! One of his ships has sunk, the others are delayed, so that the plot be revealed in time, and I may avenge myself of him — now he'll know what the terms of Ephron mean!" (He referred to the hard bargain driven with Abraham by Ephron as told in the twenty-third chapter of Genesis.)

"The Almighty will avenge you, brother," Tubal murmured.

Shylock faced him erectly and, beating his fist upon his chest, cried, "*I* shall take my own vengeance!"

Don Samuel clenched his fist and said, "Vengeance! Such foul villainy — vengeance!"

A bitter smile wreathed Shylock's lips and he uttered in a vengeful voice, "He signed me a bond that I may cut flesh from his body! Now the jest is done with — I shall do it!"

"God forbid, Shylock!" the rabbi rebuked him. He quoted from Proverbs, 'He that diligently seeketh good procureth favor;

but he that seeketh mischief, it shall come unto him." The rabbi resumed, "Revenge may be in the heart, Shylock, but not in acts, not in deeds."

"It is his due under the law," Don Samuel interposed, "and he is bound to do it."

"You will bring disaster upon the whole community, Shylock," the rabbi warned.

Shylock rolled his eye at the rabbi and raised his voice. "Not all the rabbis of Italy can deter me from my decision! The Doge is a man of law. I shall demand my due — a pound of flesh!"

"Now, listen please, Shylock," the rabbi pleaded.

"To what shall I listen? The words of the Prophets and of our sages? I will listen only to the Divine voice, the voice of the God of Vengeance!"

"Stop that profanity!" Tubal reprimanded his friend.

"You are right, Father." Don Samuel came to Shylock's aid and in a strong voice pulsating with fury, as though another spoke from his throat, he added, "If we had the power, we would order a Christian to be burned for every Jew they have burned; and if the power of vengeance is within our grasp, it is a sin to relinquish that vengeance."

The rabbi and Tubal turned on Don Samuel, declaring he was adding fuel to the fire, but Shylock cut them short. "You are cowards, but Jobs like he and I have no dismay. We fear nothing!"

The rabbi took hold of Shylock and said in a trembling voice, "I forbid you!"

Shylock shook him off and fixed him with smoldering eyes.

"If all the familiars of the Almighty descend from heaven, I shall pay no heed to their decrees. That villain has robbed me of my next generation. He has plunged me into mourning. He shall pay with his flesh and with his heart. I shall cut his wicked heart out of his breast — thus!"

Chapter Nineteen

LANCELOT RAN STRAIGHT TO LORENZO BUT, WHEN HE FOUND HE WAS not at home, realized it would be folly to seek him out. Lorenzo would plague him again for a loan of the money. He asked the landlady to tell Lorenzo that the Jew had discovered everything and that his servant had fled from the house.

He thereupon made haste to leave the vicinity lest he should meet Lorenzo.

But Lorenzo returned home only at two o'clock after midnight when the landlady was asleep, and she gave him Lancelot's message only in the morning, close upon ten o'clock. "Damnation to the Jew!" Lorenzo ground his teeth, and hurried to Antonio.

"Now I face the worst!" Antonio cried.

"What can I do for you, my friend? I am going mad!"

Antonio soothed him. "I am in the hands of the Almighty. I did a charitable deed for my friend and performed a pious act."

"I am going mad! We have no other course than to return his daughter to the Jew."

Antonio was alarmed. "Have you indeed gone mad, Lorenzo? To return the Jew his daughter after her baptism? And this you tell a devout Christian!"

"My life is worth nothing without her, Antonio, but —"

"Even if I have to pay with my earthly life ten times over, I shall never agree to a Christian woman recanting on my behalf!"

Both left for the Lido the same morning. They found Portia and Jessica on the seashore.

"You are both jealous," Portia received them smilingly. "It is a sign of true love."

"This is no time for jesting," Lorenzo said, and he told of what had happened. Jessica did not understand the full import of the matter as she knew nothing of the three thousand ducats and the bribe to the servants, and she plied Lorenzo with questions. Lorenzo and Antonio answered evasively until finally she comprehended.

"You have deceived me!" she cried, turning indignant eyes on Lorenzo.

"He did it for love of you," Antonio said.

"You are to blame for everything, Jessica," Lorenzo defended himself. "I am even now convinced that without Lancelot you would not have —"

"If I am to blame for everything," she stopped him, "I must repair the wrong — I cannot be responsible for bloodshed!" She burst out weeping. Portia, who sat deep in thought, drew Jessica's head to her bosom and stroked her.

"Do not weep," she said soothingly. "The Jew will be afraid to do this."

Jessica lifted her head and declared, "He will do it. He will do it out of grief and despair — I shall return to him!"

"Do you know what you are saying, Jessica?" Antonio rapped out. "Are you thinking of abandoning the true faith and clinging to those who repudiate our Savior?"

"For your sake, Signor Antonio, for the sake of good Portia."

"Not for my sake!" Antonio protested. "I am ready for anything except to give my hand to this grave crime."

"And the clergy will never agree," Lorenzo pointed out.

"It is my fate," Jessica sighed. "I have gone through torment, and now I must undergo the agony of seeing evil come of my act. The thought came to her at that moment that she must return to her father and appease him in order to protect Antonio. Then — then throw herself into the canal.

"Your conscience is clear," Antonio said. "I do not agree with you. On the contrary, if you go on thinking as you do, it will be a sin against the Savior!"

Jessica kept silent a moment. All their coaxing and mollifying assurances could not rid her of the thought that no other course lay before her than to return to her father, and she trembled with fear. In a faint voice she asked, "But the Doge is a Christian — will he agree to a Jew hacking flesh from a Christian's body?"

"I hardly think he will agree," Lorenzo said hesitantly. Actually he thought otherwise but had no desire to perturb Jessica further.

"Everyone knows that observance of the law is the last vestige of the authority retained by the Doge," Antonio said. "The Council of Ten and the Senate have gradually taken over all the power, but for fear of being deprived of administration of the law the Doges maintain it with rigid pedantry generation by generation. They show no mercy, especially our own Doge today, who dreams of having a dynasty of the Priuli, a kind of monarchy — and from the purely legal viewpoint my own case is fairly plain: I signed a bond and I must keep it."

Portia, who had been busily scheming how to foil Shylock's intention, suddenly sprang to her feet and cried, "I have found it! Let the Jew come to law with you, Antonio. But do not take a lawyer — I shall plead for you, my husband!"

"You are the wisest of all women in the world," Lorenzo broke out in delight. He took both her hands and kissed them. Antonio's face lit up and he questioned Portia with a glance what brain-wave had struck her.

"I shall tell you, but not now, and you will then judge if you need a lawyer! The Jew will be taught a lesson!" she declared confidently. Jessica was relieved, but she felt deeply for her father, who had lost all and who would have to suffer insult, and possibly even more.

"When you are with me, I have no fear of Devil or Jew," Antonio told Portia as he embraced her.

"Let us now return to Venice!" Portia demanded. "We have a great deal of work ahead. I must go to Padua, to see the great friend of my father's household, the illustrious student of law, Bellario. We must also find a priest of Jewish extraction who will come to testify to some of their wickedness —"

"It will not be difficult to find one," Antonio chuckled. "There are plenty around."

"We must hurry," Portia continued, "because the Doge can summon the Court tomorrow or the day after — that decrepit, sick old man is always overjoyed to hear a ticklish case, just to show that he still has power." To Jessica she said, "Make up with Lorenzo, you foolish girl! If the men told us all their plottings and plannings they would never win us — a heavy price was paid for you, Jessica, and the debt is yours. You must now discharge it — with love."

The four of them went back to Venice. While still on their way, near the Grand Canal, Graziano came hastening to meet them. He jumped from his gondola into Antonio's and, before he had time to be seated, told breathlessly of the reports on the Rialto that the Jew Shylock had brought suit in the Doge's Court that morning for a pound of Antonio's flesh. When he perceived the expression on Antonio's face, he realized it was no mere rumor.

"Have no fear, friend," Antonio remarked, "the wise Portia will frustrate the Jew's design. I only regret the rejoicing of the merchants at my misfortune."

"Their disappointment will be as great as their rejoicing now," Portia said scornfully.

Many came that day to Antonio's house to ask what had happened. How could he have sealed such a pledge with a Jew? Why had he not told of this while there was time? Many were insincere but there were several who, learning of the danger threatening Lorenzo, collected the money required to redeem Antonio from Shylock. Fifteen of Antonio's friends convened by Graziano raised three thousand ducats, and the next morning Graziano went to Shylock to seek the purchase of the bond. From Shylock's excited words he understood that Shylock must have believed Antonio had lent Lorenzo the money borrowed from him. Graziano told him the actual facts, taking a solemn oath that they were the truth, but Shylock stormed and cried that that did not alter the situation: Antonio had given Lorenzo money to steal from him his daughter, and now Shylock had him in his power. Graziano addressed himself to the banker with blandishment, and even tried threats, but Shylock and Don Samuel returned the same grim answer: the fulfillment of the bond was now the lender's due.

Although according to the law no Jew was required to appear before a court on the Sabbath, the Doge fixed the trial for the twelfth of August, the approaching Saturday, and it served as additional bitter proof to Shylock that the Doge was not impartial toward this litigation. He scoured the city for a lawyer, but none wished to prosecute so savage a claim against a fellow-Christian. He went from the more renowned to the lesser-known attorneys and offered large amounts, but in vain. One lawyer stated, "A brief of this kind is hazardous." When Shylock asked another doctor of laws, "But if this claim were by a Christian against a Jew?" the young man, not deigning to reply, burst out laughing and spat in his face. Shylock went home dejectedly. He must now withdraw the suit and God only knew if the money would be returned.

"Heaven forbid your foregoing the claim!" Don Samuel protested on hearing of Shylock's dilemma. "They will treat you with such scorn and contempt as you have never experienced."

"You are right, my son," returned Shylock despairingly. "I would rather choose death than forego my claim — I must have my revenge of that rascal!"

"It's a simple matter —"

"But that gentile," Shylock interrupted, "will hire one of the greatest lawyers and complicate the simple affair — and I shall have no one to plead for me, no Christian. I have always said Venice was Sodom — not a soul will raise his voice for a Jew."

Don Samuel stood for a moment with lowered head, profound in thought. Finally he grasped Shylock's hand and shook it. "I myself shall be your pleader." A beatific smile spread over the old man's face. No particle of doubt entered his mind that Don Samuel could face the Doge and the great lawyers for all the world as if it were a disputation held in the Saturday afternoon "academy" at the synagogue. His glowing face endowed Don Samuel with added courage, and he continued, "Get me a code of the Republic's laws and I shall study them, and God will be my help! Before her —" he threw a swift glance at the square patch on the wall where Jessica's portrait had once hung — "before her whom I loved I was always feeble and despondent, but when I face tyrants I shall have a clear mind and firm vigor — love turns the heart to water, but hate stirs it to courage!"

From that time onward Shylock no longer wept or mourned the loss of his daughter, nor had he room in his heart for anything save the craving for revenge against Antonio. The rabbi and his friends pleaded with him fruitlessly to abandon the suit; they threatened him with excommunication and ostracism in vain — his heart seemed to have turned to stone, and both their suasions and menaces left him unmoved. The elders of the community banged at his door on the Sabbath morning but he refused to open. The rabbi and others, the leaders and the rank and file, gathered outside the house, and when he left with Don Samuel to go to the Doge's palace, they begged and beseeched the two men to retract, but received no response. The venerable rabbi pursued them, threatening Shylock with the most fearful heavenly punishment for going to law on the Sabbath; Tubal threatened Don Samuel with impeachment to the authorities of being a Marrano refugee, causing him to be sent back to the Papal territory to be crucified and burnt alive — but the two men strode on rapidly and passed through the ghetto gate.

They reached St. Mark's Square at fifteen minutes past eight o'clock. Both averted their eyes from the cathedral (through bribery Shylock had learned Jessica was baptized in the Sts. Giovanni e Paolo church and that her marriage would be solemnized in the San Marco). Shylock mouthed the vilest imprecations upon the Christians and his renegade daughter, but Don Samuel bit his teeth upon his lips and the dreadful thought darted through his mind: he would waylay her on her wedding-day inside the cathedral and plunge a dagger into her heart!

Two of the sentries conducted them through the palace courtyard and up a marble staircase into the hall of justice. Statuary and lofty pillars, tens of chandeliers made with exquisite craft, and gold on every hand — all these gave Shylock a severe jolt. "To perdition with them," he thought. "All the treasures of the earth are piled up among them, and they say the Jews are rich!"

As they entered the hall his feet slipped on the smoothly polished marble floor and he slipped, dragging Don Samuel with him. A chorus of laughter reached their ears from the other end of the hall. Don Samuel was the first to rise and saw Antonio among those who were laughing. On approaching their seats a voice came from among those sitting to their left: "It's a bad sign for you, Jews."

There was a feminine timber to the voice. Don Samuel turned his head and saw a young man, clad in the toga of a doctor of laws, with a scroll in his hand.

"Don't look at them, may calamity overtake them!" Shylock muttered.

The Doge's throne stood on a marble dais fronting the wall opposite them. Over it was a golden canopy, on either side were purple-upholstered seats of which the wooden legs were carved with representations of youthful heads. On the wall at the right was a painting of the Doge Dandolo the Great — the work of Marini Falieri — shown holding a fluttering pennant testifying to the integrity of the three ancestors preceding him, and his eyes directed at an inscription on a purple hanging opposite: *Hic est locus Marini Falieri decapitati pro criminibus* (Here is the place of Marini Falieri beheaded for his crimes). Between the two marble columns behind the Doge's throne was the great mural by Paolo Caliari Veronese of "Venice Crowned in Triumph": Venice, Queen of the Adriatic, seated on a throne borne aloft on clouds, and an angel crowning her with the laurel of victory. At the right was a vaulted niche, having grooves and incisions in the arched top to denote the heavens and rays of the sun, within which stood a statue of Virgin Mary, her head turned to the Doge's platform.

Two pairs of eyes were fastened upon the Virgin from time to time: those of Antonio in reverence, and of Shylock in loathing. Don Samuel could not tear his own gaze from the Veronese creation confronting him — he descried, in the countenance of the woman symbolizing Venice, the features of Jessica. His two hands gripped the arm-rests of his chair as he tried to control the tempest within him, lest he leap upon Antonio to throttle him. Shylock sat sullenly, throwing only a cursory glance now and then at Antonio and his party. When he looked at Don Samuel he had no fear, yet when he saw the priest sitting alongside the young lawyer, the thought crossed his mind, "They are the most dangerous," and he cursed silently.

Court officers with drawn swords came in through a door at the back, and ranged themselves at the steps to the platform. The door opened again and the Doge entered with four Senators, followed by the Doge's clerk. The litigants and their companions rose, and were given permission to be seated only when the Doge and the Senators had sat down and the officers were lined up on either side of the dais.

The clerk placed a portfolio before the Doge, who riffled the papers and then, lifting his eyes, asked Shylock: "You are the Jew Shylock, aren't you? And who is the young Jew?"

"Yes, I am Shelah of the house of Shylock, and this is my pleader," the banker replied, suppressing his emotion.

"As no lawyer would appear for my client, Your Grace agreed to my pleading for him. My name is Samuel Morro," stated Don Samuel quietly.

"Morro," the Doge repeated. Privily he deplored the fact that the Jew should be namesake of the great Lodovico Morro. The monk also remembered the proselyte Joseph Morro, now the valiant Felipe who preached Christianity to the Jews in the towns of the Marches. That same Morro was regarded by the Jews with especial loathing and detestation as he had come the same year, on the very Day of Atonement, to the synagogue at Recanati, south of Ancona, and placed an image in the Ark of the Law. Don Samuel read his thoughts from the monk's face and, without being addressed, said, "I am *Samuel* Morro, and I have no kinsman or relative in the Marches."

"So," remarked the Doge after brief reflection. "You are Samuel Morro and you plead for the plaintiff. Who pleads for the defendant?"

"I do, my lord." The young doctor rose. "My teacher and mentor, Bellario of Padua, has written Your Grace he would send a lawyer in his stead — here is the letter." The gentle voice of the speaker gave him a youthful charm, and when he tendered the scroll to the Doge, the latter eyed him with admiration at the thought that Bellario had chosen him as substitute.

The Doge read the scroll and passed it to the Senators.

"You will find it worth while reading — what our friend the

scholar and head of the *juris basilica,* the ancient temple of justice at Padua, writes of his young disciple," he whispered.

A constable entered, approached the platform, and announced: "Two Jews wait outside, Your Grace, an aged rabbi and another old man. They pray to be admitted."

"They've come here; their consciences plagued them at leaving us to our fate," Shylock murmured in an overjoyed aside to Don Samuel.

To the constable the Doge said, "I have resolved to hold this trial in camera to prevent a mob demonstration."

"My lord!" cried Shylock. "Signor Antonio has one other with him beside the doctor of Padua, and a priest too. I beg you not to discriminate."

"I am Graziano his friend; my father was Antonio's godfather," said the noble at Antonio's left. The Doge consulted in a low voice with the Senators and ordered the constable to admit the Jews. Addressing Shylock he said, "Take heed: I am here to administer the law, and the bond has been written and sealed by Antonio. But you are a wise man —"

"I am not wise, my lord! Had I been wise and clever, I should have seen through it all from beginning to end, especially when Lorenzo waived his commission fee. It is all written in my petition."

The rabbi and Tubal entered, and the Doge motioned to them to be seated behind Shylock and Don Samuel. Tubal sat down but the rabbi remained standing.

"Permit me, Your Grace, to say a few words before you hear the plaint," the rabbi urged. The Doge nodded assent. "Antonio had been an accomplice in taking his daughter away from the plaintiff," the rabbi began, "and then he came to ask for a loan because he had given his money a fortnight before to Lorenzo in order to steal the girl. Truly, this act was a base one, and one can readily understand Shylock's bitterness —"

"Very true!" Shylock interrupted.

"Yes," the rabbi continued, "one may appreciate the reason for his venom, yet all this cannot justify his cleaving flesh from a human being."

"What?" Shylock was astounded. "Have you conspired with the Christian?"

"Even a Jew speaks sense at times," remarked Graziano, and those sitting alongside him laughed. Don Samuel rose and faced the rabbi: "This is a Court of Justice. Can Your Honor give the reasons in law for the statement just made?"

"With Your Grace's permission, I shall explain. Our Law says, 'An eye for an eye,' 'a hand for a hand' — is there greater iniquity than gouging out an eye or sawing off a hand with deliberate intent? Yet our Talmudic sages expressly stated that the intention was of compensation in money."

"From this very spot Venice ordered the sayings of those sages to be destroyed," rejoined Don Samuel. "We are concerned here only with the laws of the Republic of San Marco."

The rabbi turned to the Doge in a pleading voice. "We have come on behalf of our community to lay our petition before Your Grace: do not fulfill the pledge in the bond — it is contrary to the spirit of our Law!"

"If one Shylock has a stony heart, why should the entire community of Israel suffer for his sin?" Tubal supported him.

"My sin?" said Shylock in astonishment. "I am only seeking what is due to me."

"You see, Shylock," the Doge said, "even your fellow-Jews are shocked at your design. The Jews love money, but their soul recoils from blood; and it is a fact that among nearly four hundred murderers sentenced to death since the Republic was founded until this day, there were only two Jews among them. If you lament so deeply your daughter's conversion to Christianity, Shylock, it testifies better than a hundred witnesses that you are a Jew with all your heart and soul. How can you desire to cut the living flesh? And if it is the heart you choose, how can your Jewish heart counsel you to kill a human being?"

"Of course I shall choose the heart!" Shylock cried.

"The Jew is stubborn," said the Doge, "and stubbornness is the mother of ferocity."

"Ferocity? There is no reference in the Law of Israel to a law permitting the slicing of flesh from a borrower's body!" declared Don Samuel. "The basis of that law is in the rites of the pagan idolators. It is expressly provided in the Twelve Tablets of the Romans that lenders may rend the body of a borrower and distribute his dismembered parts among themselves. According to the Gulathing laws of the Nordic tribes, a lender could cut the flesh of a debtor, no matter where, as in the law of Venice. The law is the expression of moral feeling, and it is *your* law, probably the evolution of your moral sense, and no one can argue that a Jew who lives among you, and whose fathers and forefathers for generations have lived among you, is ferocious for demanding that you uphold your own law. Forgive me, Your Grace, for these harsh words, but I must defend my venerable client."

The Doge glared at Don Samuel in anger but his allegiance to the law came uppermost and he replied, "Do your duty, Jew, and I shall listen so long as you keep to the matter in hand." To Shylock he said, "I have occupied this seat for three years, and I have been a member of the Grand Council for twelve years, yet never has a claim such as this been brought before me."

One of the aged Senators remarked that in his day he had been clerk to his cousin, the Doge Andrea Gritti, yet he had not heard even then of such a case.

"That is because the law is severe and men are careful not to run foul of it," Don Samuel asserted. "The law stands even if it is enforced only once in a hundred years."

"It is clear," said the Doge regarding Shylock, "that I cannot deny the law which I have taken the oath to maintain, but I expect you to show mercy and charity. We all await a gentle answer."

Shylock remained silent a moment and Don Samuel whispered to him not to yield. He drew himself upright. "I paid for the pound of flesh in hard round ducats, and Your Grace the Doge, who comes of a banking lineage, must understand the banker's viewpoint."

Shylock's appeal to the Doge as one banker to another provoked an outburst of hearty laughter in the hall, and the sickly-yellow countenance of the Doge mounted a brief smile. But to preserve the decorum of his eminent Court, he assumed a stern demeanor, and again addressed Shylock: "We are awaiting your act of charity and mercy."

"Charity and mercy! The example my friend has brought is but one of a thousand!" Don Samuel intervened. "That which I saw with my own eyes at Ancona — were they acts which merciful men committed? And Pesaro! And the blood libel in Rome! And the arena race of naked Jews, with only a belt around their loins, among the horses and asses until they had run exhausted to their death — before the eyes of the Holy Father! Are the brothers of those who burn human beings alive and torture them with pincers until their breath expires entitled to demand mercy from the brothers in faith of those who are burned and tortured? The Christians have torn and are tearing every vestige of mercy from our hearts, and let it be no wonder to Your Grace to have a Jew before him who finds no mercy in his heart!"

"Forgive me, Your Grace!" cried the rabbi. "This young man was the betrothed of his daughter and he is therefore full of rancor and is of bitter tongue."

"Does not your honor the rabbi know all this?" Don Samuel asked. "It is all written in the books and portfolios of letters which are as well known to you as they are to me."

"I have long said there has been too much laxity in the burnings," the monk commented.

"Father to son has told the story! And children snatched from their mother's arms —" Don Samuel went on. The Doge halted him with the remark that it had no concern with the suit.

"All that he has said is right and true, to my heartfelt sorrow," the rabbi continued, "but we are commanded to show mercy, and our sages have said, 'Even if a sharp sword be placed on the neck of a man, do not refrain from mercy.'"

The monk interposed at this juncture and stated: "I have been sent by the Patriarch to reply should a question of this sort arise. I must respond that the intention in that saying was that no man should refrain from *hoping* for mercy."

It was a shrewd retort. Antonio and his friends shook the

monk's hand, and the rabbi was taken aback at finding a priest who knew the Talmud.

"Your Grace," his voice quavered, "we are commanded to have pity even on animals, and it is written in our law, 'Thou shalt not muzzle the ox when he treadeth out the corn,' and 'That thine ox and thine ass may rest.'"

"The rabbi wishes to arouse the impression that the Jews love the Christians," responded the priest, "and I who was one of them until the thirtieth year of my life, to my shame and ruin, know that is not the case. To understand this case thoroughly it is essential for this point to be properly clarified."

"He is an apostate," Shylock whispered to Don Samuel, and his blood seethed at the thought of his daughter Jessica being the same. Don Samuel's glance rose again to "Venice Crowned in Triumph."

"It has nothing to do with our hearing," the Doge answered the priest.

"But it is important to hear what the priest has to say," the doctor of Padua insisted. "Shylock is not unique. He is a son of his people." The Senators nodded their heads affirmatively, and one pointed out that as the rabbi had not been called by the plaintiff he had no right to join in the argument.

"Your statement is right as regards the defense of the Jew, but not as regards the argument, which in itself has no concern with the affair," the Doge replied to the Senator, and he gestured to the monk to proceed.

"A religious dispute — that which we dreaded has befallen," groaned Tubal, and he execrated Shylock and Don Samuel in his heart.

"According to the Theodosian code," the priest commenced, "it was forbidden for the Jews to celebrate their *Purim*. The reason was that on this day they hang an effigy of Haman and crucify him, an allusion to our Savior, and then they burn him."

The rabbi began perspiring. The old slanders! Before he could think of something to say, Shylock replied, "It is an infamy! Several nobles attended our last *Purim* festival, and what did they see? A play named *Esther* by Gomez Duarte was performed. The nobles were entranced with the performance."

"Have you seen this with your own eyes?" the Doge interrogated the priest.

"These matters are well known," the other returned.

"This is a Court of Justice and no place for hearsay or gossip!" the Doge rebuked him. "If you have anything of value to say, speak on."

"I have much that is of value, and very grave matters, to tell," the monk persisted. He reflected a moment and resumed, "In your prayer called *Amidah* you say three times daily, 'And for proselytes let there be no hope.' "

"That is correct," agreed the rabbi, "but the intention is that anyone who has become converted cannot recant and return to Judaism. We have no wish for their return to our fold." Shylock was infuriated and sent an angry look at the rabbi.

The monk continued. "And in the same prayer it goes on, 'And let all heretics perish as in a moment.' Heretics in this sense means priests."

"That is your interpretation, Signor," the rabbi expostulated. "Had it meant to say so, the term used would have been 'priests,' as it says in the Second Book of Kings, twenty-third chapter, 'And he put down the idolatrous priests.' But in the prayer the reference is to people of two kinds, and those who err and waver between the Jewish and the gentile faiths — they shall perish."

Shylock was aghast. All this, he felt, was directed at himself and his errant daughter.

"You have just said 'gentiles,' " the monk caught up the rabbi's word. "Do you deny you call us *'goyim'* or gentiles?"

"Is there any dishonor in the word?" Don Samuel joined the argument. "It is said in the fourth chapter of Deuteronomy, 'And what nation is there so great, that hath statutes and judgments as righteous as all this law,' and it says in Samuel II, 'And what one nation in the earth is like thy people, even like Israel.' I can quote any number of passages in which the term *'goy'* in Hebrew refers to us as Israel."

The priest went pale with fury. "Let us get back to the outrageous prayer!" he cried. "What about 'Let all thy people's enemies be speedily cut off'? It is clear to whom that curse applies."

"It does not say 'thy people Israel,' but thy people, only. We do not say 'our enemies,'" contended the rabbi. "According to your religion, you are the people of the True God, and so it follows we are merely anathematizing ourselves, and not you."

Disputations of this kind were common in those days (cardinals and bishops invited Jews to such discussions and compelled them to take part), and the Doge saw no injury in the sharp reply. But it was distasteful to listen to such discourse and he addressed the monk, "I think the wrangling has gone far enough."

"No, no," the other protested, and he went on interrogating the rabbi: "Is it not true that you call our holy bread 'unclean bread'"?

"It is true. You keep your bread in your churches in which your dead lie buried, and in the Book of Numbers it is decreed, 'When a man dieth in a tent, all that come into the tent, and all that is in the tent, shall be unclean seven days.'"

When the rabbi and the monk embarked on a debate of grammatical points, Don Samuel intervened and quoted chapter and verse to rout the cleric who, annoyed at the pertinacity of the young man and wishing to trip him, chose a familiar and sure method.

"You seem to be a shrewd young scholar," he said. "I would ask you a simple question: which of the two religions is the best, that of Jesus or your own? Give me a straight answer."

Don Samuel saw the hand of God in the fact that a short while since he had read in a book of a similar argument and there seen a reply to the same poser. He turned to the Doge and remonstrated: "Before I answer his subtle question, I appeal to Your Grace to decide on the reply to the following: A friend of mine left a month ago on a long journey and left two precious stones with his two sons. The brothers have now come to ask me to judge the quality of the stones and the differences in them." The cleric jumped from his place and insisted this had no bearing on the matter but the Doge motioned to him to be seated. "I told them: 'Who knows better than your father? I do not know.' And in response to my words, they berated and cursed me. Were they right in doing so?"

"It was not lawful for them to berate and curse you," said the Doge, looking straight in front of him with some tenseness.

"And now listen, Your Grace," Don Samuel pursued. "Esau and Jacob were brothers and the Almighty gave each a gem, a unique faith, and this priest asks me: 'Which is the better?' Send the priest as an ambassador to Our Father in Heaven, the greatest judge of the precious gems of faith, and bring His answer."

The Doge and Senators could not restrain themselves and laughed.

"He is far too wily," Antonio said in an aside to the doctor of Padua.

"Never fear, love of my soul, he will be hoist on his own petard," the latter reassured him.

"When a priest and a rabbi meet, a polemic is at once joined," observed the Doge. "These wranglings have always lasted for days on end without any advantage in them — it has no bearing on the matter before us. Let us return to the essence of the claim."

Shylock had been looking at that moment at the Doge's *beretta,* sparkling with gems set in the shape of shields of David, and thought with satisfaction, "They knowingly sanctify our own prophets in their paintings and statues, but unknowingly they perpetuate our own symbol — for it is our symbol — in the ruler of their Republic!" Hearing the Doge's last words he murmured confidently, "My claim is clear."

The doctor of Padua rose and started: "It is true the law is on your side, Jew, but mercy is the attribute of every man."

Graziano, who had been deeply impressed with Don Samuel's astute parrying of the monk, was ill at ease. He wanted to settle the matter without further ado and suggested that Shylock take the three thousand ducats.

"I stand upon what is written in the bond," said Shylock.

"Three thousand ducats are worth more than a pound of flesh," expostulated Graziano.

"Not always, and not to everyone," snapped Shylock.

"Yet you will agree, Shylock," the Doge addressed him, "that charity is the attribute of every man."

"Yes, Your Grace, both of my people and yours!" he spoke up, as if starting from slumber. "Money cannot buy mercy from me — I am ready to give charity for charity."

A charitable smile creased the Doge's stony face.

"It is as I thought," he remarked. "You are only pretending to be cruel, but at the proper moment, in a Court of Justice, you will reveal a lenient and clement heart."

"I shall strike out the bond if my daughter is returned to me!" he cried in a ringing voice. A tumult arose among the others in the hall. "Will you pardon her?" he whispered into Don Samuel's ear. The latter dropped his head and, taking a deep breath, gave the unfortunate father a submissive look.

"That is a piece of Jewish impudence!" stormed the priest. "To take a virtuous Christian away from the true faith." Those who sat with him vehemently assented.

"But you must understand," the Doge persuaded Shylock, "that such a thing is impossible."

"I do not understand!"

Graziano offered him six thousand ducats. "You are a Jew," he observed, "and you know the value of gold."

"And you are a Christian who knows the worth of charity," Don Samuel flashed back at him. Tubal and the rabbi urged Shylock to agree but he shook his head and exclaimed, "I shall not agree for a hundred thousand nor all the treasures of Venice. But if you only return my daughter I shall forego the whole!"

"It is out of the question — never has it happened, nor will it happen." The voices came from the opposite side, Antonio's the loudest among them.

Don Samuel addressed the Doge and pleaded in a cajoling voice: "Your Grace, when Nathan came unto David after the affair with Bathsheba, he said: 'There were two men in one city; the one rich, and the other poor. The rich man had exceeding many flocks and herds: but the poor man had nothing, save one little ewe lamb' — I pray of you, my lord, there are hundreds of millions of Christians, yet he has only one daughter, an ewe lamb."

"Ewe lamb!" the priest repeated mockingly.

"She is no longer his daughter!" cried Antonio.

"She is blood of my blood, flesh of my flesh." Shylock's voice trembled. "She has not yet been wed to that seducer and deceiver."

"A pity he did not wed her immediately after her baptism," Graziano said.

"She is a Christian! I was her sponsor, and even if I have to pay with my life, I shall never agree!" shouted Lorenzo.

The Doge called the quarreling adversaries to silence, and again turned to Shylock, "You must realize this is not within the realm of possibility."

"I realize nothing! I realize nothing!" Shylock howled.

"I realize nothing either," Don Samuel declared in agitation. "The Jewish brain has been able to survive generation after generation among tyrants and taskmasters, yet it will never comprehend being asked for charity when its own plea for charity falls on deaf ears!"

"She is of age; she changed her faith of her own volition," the priest interposed. A commotion again arose among the defendant and his companions, and under cover of the noise Don Samuel and Shylock held a whispered consultation.

"He takes one more step toward you," Don Samuel said aloud, "a big step. You say she is of age, and I say that in spite of her years she is but an inexperienced girl who has been led astray. Bring his daughter here, let him speak with her in your presence and if she says 'No, I stand by the New Testament,' then he will surrender!"

"That's out of the question — it's nonsense," shouted the other side, thunderstruck.

"You are afraid of her appearing!" called Don Samuel. "It proves better than a hundred witnesses your uncertainty of her, and that her heart is not entirely with you."

"It has no bearing on our affair! It has naught to do with the claim!" yelled the monk, dancing on tiptoe as if on heated tiles.

The Doge, after whispering with the Senators, breathed heavily and rasped, "His heart is as stone and I am bound only by the law." He turned to Antonio, "What have you to say, Signor Antonio?"

"All my powers lie in the hand of the doctor of Padua."

At this point the rabbi, who had throughout the controversy been sitting glumly, intervened and pleaded, "Please, Your Grace, let the tribunal of our community try this suit — please, Your Grace."

"I agree," declared Antonio.

"I have a strong case, but if Signor Antonio agrees, I raise no objection," the doctor of Padua concurred.

"But I am against it," Shylock cried. "See, I have the law of Venice with me — I disagree."

"It cannot be for two reasons," ruled the Doge. "The first is, Shylock is entitled to be judged before me; and the second, it would serve as precedent of creating an authority within an authority, and there is but one authority alone in the Republic of San Marco — that of the winged lion."

He leaned toward the doctor, saying courteously, "Well, my learned young friend, what have you to say in defense of Signor Antonio?"

"The thing is clear: by the law the flesh is due the Jew, a pound of flesh —"

"True!" Shylock interrupted. "You are right, wise man of Padua."

"Prepare then, Jew, to cut the flesh!" the doctor added. The effeminate voice pierced Shylock's ear like a lance. He composed himself and said, "I am ready."

The rabbi and Tubal were dumbfounded. Don Samuel stood as if ready for battle.

"The law says the flesh is due to you and you shall have it," went on the doctor, "but remember this, Jew: it is the flesh and not the blood which is your forfeit. If you shed one drop of blood, you take what is not yours, and your blood will be the penalty. Hurry, Jew!"

Graziano and the priest clapped their hands. The Doge and

the Senators tried hard not to laugh, but exchanged looks and smiled.

"Not so fast, doctor of Padua," interpolated Don Samuel. "The law says he may cut the flesh, does it not? And if it be impossible to cut the flesh from a living body without spilling blood, then it means it is permitted to do so, since if that be not the case, what basis is there to the law?"

"There is no mention of blood in the bond," the doctor insisted.

"If anyone is convicted to be scourged, he is given the scourge, and none says it is forbidden to lash him because that part of the body will swell or stream blood; if a living body be lashed, it is obvious the injured part runs blood and becomes swollen."

The arguments were all addressed to the stern face of the Doge. Shylock gazed with deep affection upon Don Samuel — were they not in the Doge's palace he would have fallen on him and covered him with kisses. The rabbi and Tubal too looked at Don Samuel with respectful admiration although they were deeply angered with him.

After brief meditation, the Doge said, "If there be such a law, then it must be administered in the spirit and the letter."

The doctor's face grew pale but, arousing himself immediately, he cried, "You have not defeated us, Jew! It is written in the bond that he can cut a pound of flesh. Let it be so! But take care, Shylock, that you cut no less nor more than a just pound of flesh, or the division of the twentieth part of one poor scruple." The words were interrupted by applause. "Now go, Jew! You were offered the money and you refused — now you must take your legal forfeiture of Signor Antonio, and you will be hanged at the gallows if you take one scruple more or one scruple less."

"True, it specifies one pound in the bond," declared the Doge with satisfaction, glancing at the document before him.

Shylock whispered to Don Samuel, "Why are you silent, my son?"

"Leave me a moment. So long as he goes on talking I have time to think."

But Shylock took no comfort in the reply and his heart dissolved with fear.

"And if you do not wish to fulfill the bond and cut Antonio's flesh," persisted the young doctor, "because you cannot judge the weight to a nicety and imperil your own skin, then you must beg the noble Doge to release you of taking your due from Signor Antonio's body — perhaps in his great mercy he will respond."

"Beg that you may have leave to hang yourself, and buy the rope with your own money!" called Graziano derisively. Shylock raised his eyes to Don Samuel, who stood with knitted brows, watching the doctor of Padua. Shylock's heart sank.

"Stay, I have not concluded," smiled the doctor. "We Christians are moved by a different spirit. If you persuade the Doge not to compel you to execute the bond, so that you keep your skin, then we will accede to your request." The Doge nodded, signifying his assent. "But we do so on condition that half your property is forfeit to Signor Antonio against whose very life you have contrived, and the other half goes to the privy coffer of the state."

"Nay, take my life and all!" cried Shylock. "What is my life without the prop which sustains it? No Shylock will knock at the doors bargaining for rags."

"See, Jew, to what extent Christian mercy will go. Signor Antonio will plead for your life if the half you are bound to pay to him is deeded here in Court, under your hand and sealed by law, as a gift to the gentleman who took your daughter. And in recompense for the favor His Grace will show you, Jew, Signor Antonio requires you to become a Christian."

"And I shall be his godfather!" crowed Antonio.

"What?" Shylock cried. "You know very little about a Jew when you lay hands upon his money, and how much less do you know of him when you lay hands upon his faith! I am a descendant of those who gathered in the synagogues and massacred each other to save themselves from conversion. If that is the law, I shall observe it; I may slice a scruple more or a scruple less because as a Jew it is not my habit to cut human flesh. But I shall cleave his flesh, and I too will die — I too!"

"Enough, enough!" Don Samuel stopped him.

Shylock stood for a moment as if he wanted to continue, but desisted. The fingers of his left hand gripped his sash, like a drowning man clutching at a straw, and his right hand was pressed against his heart as though to keep it from springing forth. His half-open eyes, gleaming with reproach and accusation, sought the sky through the ceiling. His face had altered entirely: its expression was a mixture of the gentleness forged in the crucible of affliction and of the obstinacy with which the Creator had endowed him.

"I merely wished to hear to what lengths the doctor of Padua would go in his demands," Don Samuel turned politely to the Doge. Then, confronting the lawyer, he flung his shaft of ironic humour: "True, my aged friend is forbidden to take one ounce more, since it is not due to him, but whence have you it, doctor, that we must not take an ounce less?"

Shylock felt a fresh injection of courage at these words and he awoke out of his confusion. He sat down and threw a glance of animosity at the doctor of Padua.

"It expressly says a pound," remarked one of the Senators glumly. The Doge signed to him not to interfere.

"It expressly says a pound!" cried the doctor, pointing to the copy of the bond in his hand.

"That is essentially refutable," Don Samuel continued blandly, "and I can prove my case simply. If anyone owes me a hundred ducats, I may not demand one ducat more, but I am entitled to take ninety-nine or ninety or fifty ducats, am I not? The plaintiff will not take one ounce more than his due of Antonio's flesh, but for safety's sake he will take far less than he is entitled, be it half a pound, as he wishes — but his due is up to a pound of flesh!"

Once again tumult rose in the court. The Doge consulted with the Senators; the doctor of Padua racked his brain, and his confusion grew every moment.

"I would wish to contradict the example of the loan which the Jew has cited," declared the Doge with suppressed fury, "but I do not see how — perhaps, Doctor, you have the answer? It is necessary that you reply."

"It is written here — one pound," the doctor faltered. The Doge brushed this response aside with a gesture of his hand.

To give the lawyer time to reflect on a reply to Don Samuel's contention, the priest once more embarked on a religious argument, and the Doge permitted him to proceed at length. Yet when the debate had ended and the doctor of Padua failed to ask permission to speak, the Doge prompted him.

"It only states one pound," came the reply through gritted teeth.

The Doge gave a sign and both parties were conducted outside under escort, one to a room at the left and the other to the right. A short while later they were summoned to return to the hall.

For some moments the Doge stood with lowered head, wholly engrossed in thought, and then he began: "For the three years of my tenure no such case has come before me and the judgment I must give alarms me, as though I were suddenly projected into the nethermost part of purgatory. The stubborn Jew insists as the condition of revoking his bond that his daughter be returned — now listen, Antonio: if you, as the defendant, ask for the Jew to have his daughter back, to save your life, I shall forward your petition to the Patriarch and recommend the annulment of the baptism."

"Your Grace is most merciful!" cried Shylock.

"May the Almighty bless you, prince of mercy and truth!" chimed in the rabbi and Tubal.

"But it is impossible!" shrieked the monk. "The Patriarch is bound in matters of religion to the See in Rome!"

"That is my concern," the Doge retorted firmly. "I shall instruct my Ambassador to approach Cardinal Alessandrini, and if he fails, I shall hie myself to Rome, to the Holy Throne, although I am in feeble health and such a strenuous journey may cause my death."

"Your doctors have forbidden you the journey," remarked the one seated at his right. "Even this prolonged sitting —"

"Then you will go in my stead on behalf of the Council of Ten," the Doge halted him. It was his brother Gerolamo.

Turning to the defendant again — "If I have your petition, Antonio, to save your life, then I shall find a way of restoring the convert to her original faith."

"No Christian will request it — none will barter everlasting life for this earthly existence!" cried the priest confidently.

The doctor of Padua clasped Antonio by the hand and whispered in a shaking voice, "Think on the matter, Antonio."

"I am in the hands of the law, Your Grace," said Antonio, lifting his eyes to the statue of Mary. "I am a Christian and I will not tarnish my soul."

"The Church may well be proud of such a stalwart son as you!" declared the priest joyfully, shaking Antonio's hand vigorously.

"Is there anything, young scholar, you wish to say in response to the plaintiff's pleader?" the Doge inquired.

"The trial is finished, Your Grace, and by the law — " Don Samuel began.

"The Doge will not pervert the law," the Doge reprimanded him. "These are not the laws of Mammon. The Jew said he would choose the heart; let the lawyer for the defendant say what is in his mouth and you may also continue."

"One pound means no more or less than a pound," murmured the doctor irresolutely.

The Doge motioned and the officers of the Court drew their swords. The Doge took a deep breath and read from a scroll, syllable by syllable, each word sounding like the beat of a mallet:

"By the law of the Republic of San Marco, let the Jew Shylock receive a pound of flesh from the body of the Christian, Signor Antonio, from whatever part he chooses. The convicted man shall be taken to the prison and the sentence shall be carried out at ten of the clock on Tuesday morning, the twenty-second day of August, in the year one thousand five hundred and fifty-nine."

"Antonio mine! Antonio, my husband!" the doctor of Padua burst into a scream, throwing herself at him. There was no doubt now of the female voice.

"You — a woman?" the priest was astounded.

"His wife!" cried Portia. "Antonio, my love!"

The priest comforted her. "He will be canonized — San Antonio he will be called."

The officers separated husband and wife and surrounded Antonio to take him to the prison. Portia followed him, flanked by the proselyte monk and Graziano.

The rabbi and Tubal fell on their knees before the Doge's dais. "Your Grace!" supplicated the rabbi. "He will be excommunicated, he will be expelled from the community of Israel! Do not stigmatize the whole community for his sake!"

Shylock embraced Don Samuel, vowing: "The Almighty God has blessed my latter end more than the beginning, as He did with Job — for a rebellious daughter He has given me a wise and perspicacious son — my son, my son!"

Chapter Twenty

THE DOGE LORENZO PRIULI DIED IN THE EVENING OF THURSDAY, THE seventeenth of August. A mantle of grief descended on Venice which only two days earlier, on the Tuesday, had been observing the Feast of the Assumption of Virgin Mary. Venice in its holiday appearance seemed like a gaily clad bridegroom to whom the news arrived of his father's death. When Tubal came to the Rialto on Friday afternoon it was as gloomy as the ghetto, and although he assumed a mournful expression, as befitted the occasion, there was no mercy in his heart when he reflected that the Christians were for once grief-stricken.

Throughout the week the rabbi tried to dissuade Shylock from his sinister resolve, alternating between coaxing and threatening, but without result. The rabbi still hoped that when Shylock came to prayers on the Sabbath morning, the congregation would detain him until he promised on oath to forego his wicked design; but Shylock guessed what portended and kept away from the service. Don Samuel remained secluded with him in the house.

Returning from the Doge's funeral on Sunday, the elders went in a body to Shylock's house, and reiterated their importunings, arguing that none could know who would be the next Doge and what interdicts threatened the Jewish community in Venice. If Shylock had only himself to consider it was likely he would have yielded, but Don Samuel incited him against retraction. It all ended with Shylock pushing each one to the door, even the rabbi, and shouting after them never to venture over his threshold again.

An excommunication was pronounced on Shylock the same afternoon. The Ashkenazic synagogue was crammed to overflowing and one of the rabbis chosen by lot read the scroll of expulsion by the light of black candles before the open Ark of the Law. After the blowing of the ram's horn, the congregation dispersed, and the beadles ran out into the streets proclaiming the ban at every corner. Their wailing voices struck fear into old and young alike. The clerks employed by Shylock in his banking-shop left him; the woman who had taken the place of his fugitive Christian servants also quit. Any who saw him from afar made haste to turn aside, and people hurried by his house for fear of his accosting them. Only Don Samuel remained with him, and he too was avoided by the community who regarded him as tarred with the same brush. Both ostracized men cheered each other up, but nonetheless they shivered under the impact of that awful solitude. Fear too had seized the people of the ghetto — an excommunicated pariah was in their midst!

A few minutes before the gates were closed that evening, a bombshell exploded in the ghetto: Pope Paul IV was dead! People stood in the streets and heard from those who had come from Venice of the reports sped by special couriers sent by the Venetian Ambassador in Rome: when the Pope felt he was dying, he ordered that his "grandson," Cardinal Carafa, whom he had banished, be brought back to him, but no sooner had he stepped through the door than the cardinal fell dead. The tyrannical Pope died on Friday but some hours before his death there was rejoicing in the streets of Rome at the premature report and the people flocked to the Inquisition where many princes and notables were imprisoned at Paul's orders, released all who were detained, and set fire to the building. The Pope's statue was smashed to pieces, which young boys rolled into the Tiber. There were innumerable rumors accompanying these reports: street-battles were taking place in Rome between the enemies of the house of Carafa, whose number was legion, and its few supporters, and the latter were being defeated; the corpse of the Pope had been strung up and crucified, to the cheering of the multitude; the corpse had been cremated and the ashes scattered over the Tiber; a Jew had placed a ghetto hat on the dead Pope's head, and the Jew's name was Elijah — probably the Prophet Elijah.

"There is a God in Heaven — he is dead!" The Jews of the ghetto had not known such jubilation for years. "Good luck!" they cried to each other in the synagogue in which only yesterday they had prayed for the repose of the Doge's soul. In the Ashkenazic synagogue, where the candles lit for Shylock's excommunication were still guttering, in all the synagogues and places of worship in private homes, men stood whispering a prayer of thanksgiving composed spontaneously, and the seers told of the advent of the Messiah.

The last of the Jews returning from the city before the gates closed brought with them some of the elation which had gripped Venice, although only that day they had brought the Doge to interment. Who had not hated Paul of the house of Carafa! Relatives and kinsmen of the nobles he had imprisoned on the false charge of heresy, scribes whose books he had prohibited and publishers and booksellers whom he made bankrupt through his Index, tavern-keepers and business men whose livelihood he had taken when the pilgrim traffic from the German lands and England fell away owing to his persecutions of the Protestants — the hand of the living Paul had reached into every walk of life, even to the beggars whom he did not forget and forbade to beg. When he was dead, the suppressed fury broke its bounds and, like a river in flood, submerged the whole of Rome and spread to all the Papal cities, and from them to the independent Republics. A strong guard was placed around the Patriarchal mansion in Venice itself, since this was the home of the Inquisition into which the mob threatened to penetrate and wreak the same revenge as their fellows in Rome to the House of the Inquisition.

The attention of the Jews of the ghetto had now been distracted from Shylock to Paul, and only the more ruffianly, remembering even in their new rejoicing the excommunication which had gratified their baser instincts, crowded outside Shylock's house to warn him, under the ban, not to dare go into the street. They left off only when David ben Yekutiel, father of the woman who fled from Civitanova, drove them away. Even so, when Samuel came out in the evening to learn the cause of the jubilation, some young scamps appeared from nowhere and pelted him with stones. "Get out, excommunicant! Tomorrow you too will be dead!" He hurriedly retraced his footsteps.

They learned of Paul's death only on the morrow from the Christian clerks whose voices trembled as they told with joy of the news from Rome.

"So may all thine enemies perish, Lord!" cried Shylock devoutly. It was perhaps the first time in his life he could not conceal from Christians his gladness at the death of a Christian — and the most eminent of them too, the one who was called God's Vicar on earth. He was not satisfied and repeated the passage in Italian, and the Christians rocked on their heels with delight.

"The Prison of the Inquisition was razed, and the inmates released. Then Rabbi Benjamin Nehemiah and the other prisoners of Civitanova were freed," Don Samuel cried.

"It is very doubtful," Shylock rejoined. "The hatred among themselves by no means affects their hatred of the Jew — they have plenty of room in their hearts for hate." Yet he showed many signs of gentleness for the Christian clerks employed in his shop and at midday he said, "It is a festival for all of us today. You may all have the afternoon off." When they left, and he remembered his own tragedy and what awaited him on the morrow, he muttered — "I hope their children and children's children 'enjoy' the festival feelings in my own heart."

Throughout the afternoon Shylock conducted a mixture of

talk with Don Samuel on the death of Paul the wicked and the ban pronounced upon him by the rabbis of Venice, and he alternated between profound joy and profound sorrow. Suddenly, after a long pause, he cried, "Had those hot-headed rabbis waited a while, and not excommunicated me until the good news arrived, it is possible I would have agreed to their request." Don Samuel was startled. "Perhaps she will flee from her seducer," the old man added in a whisper.

"You are much older than I, Father, and you hate them more than I do, but you understand them less than I — they will not relinquish their prey!" Don Samuel declared. Shylock at the same moment rued his statement, which savored somewhat of remorse.

"You are right, my son! But it hurts me to feel you defend her — she is not a prey in their clutches; she is artful and wicked and cunning, may her memory be blotted out!"

Tears rolled from Don Samuel's eyes but he made no response. No, he thought, the heart of man is not of flesh if it does not burst at hearing words like these about the adored one of his soul.

"You are my son," continued Shylock. "I shall find you a better wife than she!" Don Samuel returned a wan smile of thanks, but the wistfulness of his expression testified that he found no solace in the promise.

Another mood entirely descended on them suddenly in the evening. As they left the shop to go upstairs, the runner of the horse-post thrust a letter into Don Samuel's hand. He recognized the handwriting of his teacher and shouted joyfully as he ran upstairs, "Blest be He who redeems the prisoners!" Shylock ran nimbly behind him as though his youth had been restored.

"Ah! What a long letter, what a 'Maschil,' " cried Don Samuel, referring to the 78th Psalm for Asaph which was unusually long. "Let us hear it and imbibe the potion of health."

The letter covered several pages and Don Samuel read it aloud with great emotion. It had been sent from Rome on the Friday afternoon, the eighteenth day of August.

"To my esteemed pupil the wise Don Samuel, greetings!

. . . And his sickness grew worse until his thighs and loins became bloated, and the blood ran from his bowels, although because he was strong and partook of delicious and healthy food of great nutrition his illness was soothed and his attendants and his household concealed from the Cardinals and the entire people the tidings of his illness until the evening of the fifteenth of Elul (the eighteenth of August); and he fainted at midnight, and they sent for the Cardinal Fiori who was his regent, called in their tongue Camerlengo . . . And he came and saw the Pope in his death's agony, and sent letters to his intimates the Cardinals outside Rome but only told them of it by innuendo. But the truth of it was revealed at daybreak and all rejoiced at the death of the Pope and all had ardently awaited for his death and the blotting out of his name, both the sons of Israel and the peoples of the world, unanimously and with fervent desire. . . ."

Shylock forgot his own torment and the horrible deed he was expected to perpetrate on the morrow. He exulted and execrated, the while Don Samuel read on to himself quietly.

Suddenly there was the sound of slow footsteps of someone mounting the stairs outside. Both were startled.

Jessica? A bully sent by Lorenzo to murder them? Or had Shylock's lifelong friend Tubal been struck with contrition for having supported the rabbi and his party? "If it is a murderer it is best that I open the door quickly and frighten him," the thought raced across Shylock's mind. He pulled open the door with a jerk and shouted "Who comes?"

Before him stood a young man half-beggar, half-lunatic, who gazed at Don Samuel and, with a foolish smile on his haggard face, inquired, "Don't you recognize me, Signor?"

Shylock thought it was some ruffian in disguise and rapped out, "Why the hesitation? Tell me who you are!"

"I see Signor Shylock every day and he does not recognize me — I am only a porter. Upon my life, the rich do not notice the poor." Another foolish smile crossed his face and gazing at Don Samuel he went on, "When the young master came to Signor Shylock's house before the Passover, I carried his belongings — does the signor remember? He gave me two ducats, and Joseph the porter has never forgotten this, on God's life! I shall come here by stealth at night and bring you food, and even cook for you for the morrow and clean the house."

It was only now Shylock gathered what had brought the porter to the house.

"Is not this wretched pauper," Shylock turned to Don Samuel, "more estimable than all the worthies of the community combined? He has a heart inside him!" He thrust his hand into his pocket for a coin.

"No, no, I don't want money. I have a compassionate heart," the other mumbled. "The gentiles took the daughter and the Jews took the food. Joseph cannot see two such noble men without aid or servant."

"There is no one like you, Joseph," asserted Don Samuel. Shylock gave him some money and told him what to buy.

"I shall come every evening," the man said before leaving, "but do not reveal it to a soul — upon my life, if a poor man is excommunicated, he can do nothing else than seek baptism." He shook at his own words and spat on the ground.

"Do not be afraid. You are helping the banker Shylock," the old man assured him. When he had left, he cried: "The heavens have a thought for our welfare! In spite of those who wield the ban, He Who sits above is merciful!" Don Samuel was not listening; he was intent upon reading the letter from his preceptor.

"Read it aloud, don't omit a word," Shylock urged.

"I'll go back to the place where we left off, every line is a treasure," Don Samuel replied. "I must read it again and again, and you too, father, must read it." He went on aloud:

". . . And all the leaders convened together in the courtyard of the Capitoline to consult and take counsel what to do for the prisoners at the Inquisition, because in the prison were immured some men who were charged with idolatry, and also eminent and illustrious men of renown, and for many days none had seen them. . . . And it was finally and firmly agreed, after much discussion among them, all in unison and with no dissent, because it was God's will to revenge the blood of his servants and to have compassion upon us, to destroy the prison, to condemn it to a great fire after having freed the captives who were held there: that this place be utterly blotted out without trace because it was a house of iniquity in which demons had capered and issued false distorted judgments against faith and law, lying and mendacity, the spot from which the evil tyrant had judged. And when they left the Capitoline and raised their eyes, they saw the effigy of Paul IV done in valuable ornamented stone which had been set up to do him honor and glory, than which no other effigy had been created with more craft in this generation. . . . And they set their hand against it and demolished it, and broke the nose from the face and smeared the face with mud and excrement, and smashed the right hand and the fingers of the left hand, and showered it with stones. And they went from there and came to the House of the Inquisition, and they were followed by a multitude of three thousand people, and surrounded the building and besieged it and broke the gates and strode in with violent hands. . . . And then came one of the leading men among them and tried to break the doors to the room in which I was imprisoned but could not do so, and sought here and there and looked through the window and said, Be not afraid, Jew, because I have loved Jews from my youth, and I have come to save you. And he went to find the warden of the prison, and he was old and ill and could not flee, and took from him the keys of the rooms and opened the lock to the door and I came out. And I besought that man to seek and find my brother Jews who were imprisoned in their cells and to set them free, and he answered, Be not afraid, for they have gone out whole. The word has gone forth to ignite a fire and to burn down this whole house, and you must know that none will be left inside; and so fly for your life lest harm or obstacle come to you from the multitude of the people —"

"I cannot understand them!" Shylock interrupted. "They have shown by their action that they have a far greater hatred for him than the Jew — why did those fools not oust him from his seat, at least during the time of the war with the Spaniards?" He approached Don Samuel and said in a low confident voice, "There is a God in heaven! On the one night their evil Pope died there, and the night previously the Doge here, and was taken for burial in the San Zanipolo (Sts. Giovanni e Paolo in the Venetian dialect), in which my hope of descendants was interred. And some time ago their builder of citadels, Sanmicheli, also passed away — this is all no coincidence, my son, these are the days of the Messiah! They will die one by one, together with the rabbis and timorous elders, may they go to oblivion, and you and I will see them in their hangdog shame and laugh: our mouths will be filled with laughter, Samuel!"

He took up the last page and read aloud again the description of the destruction of Paul's monument, and laughed himself into tears where it said the nose of the face was broken off and the face smeared with filth and offal. "What more?" he asked. Don Samuel, heartened by Shylock's delight, declaimed as though addressing an audience:

"And we the six Jews left together and went to the place of the Capitoline, as we were told it had been destroyed and we should see its downfall with our own eyes. . . . And the mob came back to degrade the Pope's effigy, and cut off the head and the left arm and threw the head into the Via Capitolina, and the children sported with it and rolled it through the markets and streets to the district called Pelligrini, and there they lifted and flung it into the river. . . . To fulfill what was written: 'I will utterly blot out the remembrance of Amalek —'"

Shylock walked slowly up and down the room, spacing the words from Deuteronomy to the rhythm of toe and heel, "Remember what Amalek did unto thee," up to the last passage of the twenty-fifth chapter, "thou shalt blot out the remembrance of Amalek from under heaven; thou shalt not forget it." He thought of Antonio and repeated the last words several times, "Thou shalt not forget it!" Only an hour ago his heart had quailed at thought of the morrow, but now that he had reconsidered he awaited it impatiently.

For his part Don Samuel's face clouded over as he came to the part of the letter in which the rabbi extolled the merits and virtues of "the virgin Jessica to the house of Shylock who rescued my soul and the souls of the five other captives." Shylock urged him to continue but he was evasive, and said, "These are reports of his own family. I have finished."

"Who would have imagined I should be given so happy an evening!" Shylock exclaimed. "The Almighty is on our side and not on the side of the rabbi and his cowardly sycophants!" Seeing that Don Samuel put the letter in his pocket, he added, "Give it to me and I shall deposit it in the wall box. It is more valuable than thousands of ducats."

"I shall read it once again," Don Samuel replied, "and then place it in the wall box."

Both were sleepless that night. Shylock envisioned the savage treatment of Paul's statue and the burning of the House of Inquisition with a great wealth of imagined detail; he thought too of Antonio who would beg for his life but whom he would not heed — why should he heed him? That scamp could have saved his hide had he wanted to return Jessica, but refused — let him go to the nethermost parts of Hades, and die like a dog! Don Samuel thought only of Jessica. All the eulogies written about her by his teacher were true — yet what had spurred her to commit this sin which had no expiation or repair? A foolish caprice had seized her, an evil spirit, he reflected, and with this thought he wandered into a train of imagination and visions which brought the blood to his face from excess of shame. He lay flat on his back, put leg alongside leg, closed his eyes and lips, and held his breath — he lay as the dead. Only his heart still pulsated and quivered to the voiceless prayer: Fulfill Thou too, O Lord, the charity of the redemption of the captives — take my soul unto Thee. . . .

After a weary night, during which slumber deserted them and they were prey to the most terrifying figments of half-dreams, both men were delighted at the placid dawn which did not greet them, as they had feared, with grim and lowering aspect, but was gay with the twittering of birds and the cheerful, hearty crowing of cocks. They prayed on rising and left the house before nine o'clock. A light drizzle was falling outside, but the rabbi, Tubal and several others were awaiting them in the open. They wanted to address a last appeal to Shylock, to sway him from his intent, but when he saw them the old banker cried with bitter irony, "Keep away, I am excommunicated!"

The rabbi retreated as did the others. But they followed the two at a distance and pleaded with them to return to their house. Shylock did not turn his head and said to Don Samuel, "Proscription is sometimes a useful thing; had I not been banned, they would have held us back by force."

The couple went out through the ghetto gate, hired a gondola, and set out for the San Marco landing.

"I am not afraid," Shylock kept on saying, unasked. "I am not afraid." Don Samuel remembered Jessica and goaded Shylock on to take his revenge of Antonio. "He has cut off your next generation, my father, he has robbed you of Jessica, the apple of your eye," he prompted.

"Do not remind me of the name of that renegade!" Shylock scolded.

They left the gondola and moved toward the prison near the Doge's palace. With every pace their excitement grew stronger.

"Have you no fear they will take revenge of you?" Don Samuel asked suddenly.

"Why do you ask? May my soul perish with the Philistines!"

"Truly our souls shall perish with the Philistines, but it is best that you undertake this step, father, with the prior knowledge that they are prepared for retribution."

"I know, my son, that we are excommunicated by the Jews, and I know that the friends of that rascal will thirst for our blood, but shall an old man like myself take the step without having thought it over first? I am doing this with deliberation, my son. We are in the hands of the Almighty!"

"Now I am sure of you, my father, that you will have your revenge of him, but — but God forbid that you fail in your target."

"I know, I know!" Shylock cried with a silencing gesture. But he suddenly stood still. "You must return, my son." Don Samuel refused. "I am protected by the law," went on Shylock, "and the Doge's guards will protect me, but you — probably all his friends and kinsmen are gathered around Antonio. Wait for me at the Rialto station."

Don Samuel obeyed. The playing of an organ which reached his ears out of nowhere seemed to throw a net around his feet and he remained stock-still for some moments. For some reason the organ notes brought to mind Emmanuel's words: "What does the art of music say to the Christians? I was stolen away out of the land of the Hebrews." Immediately he transposed the words to thought of Jessica declaring: "What does a daughter of Israel say to the Christians? I was stolen away out of the land of the Hebrews!" He began to shiver in every limb. He expected the earth to open, and again his heart quivered to the voiceless prayer as it had done the night before: Take my soul unto Thee, O Lord! Turning around, he saw Shylock no more.

Shylock parted from Don Samuel and did not turn around. He went right, and in a few minutes stood before the gate of the prison. From a distance, at the bridge leading to the Doge's mansion, he saw several people walking to and fro, and among the women he identified Portia. Perhaps she, the rebellious one, was among them? Involuntarily he turned his head to see, but a corner of the building blocked his view of those walking by the bridge.

One of the sentries escorting Shylock took him to a dungeon and he was shown into its semi-obscurity. There he found two Moorish constables who were both drunk.

"Be stout fellows, good fellows," he urged. "You are the henchmen of the Doge, and not of Signor Antonio!"

"The Doge's name be blessed!" they responded in unison.

"I shall today weigh out ten ducats gold to each of you," Shylock promised.

"Thank you, Signor! There is still a third, who is watching over the criminal," said one, jerking his thumb at a cell on the left.

"He too will be rewarded."

The door opened and a venerable prelate entered. He motioned to the constables to leave and they went out through the door leading to the cell at the left.

"You have probably come to take the confession of the condemned man," Shylock grinned. "I am not the man. I am a Jew."

"I know," the priest replied. "I have come to you. My name is probably not unfamiliar to you — I am Fra Pasquino, the only one who dared oppose the burning of the Talmud."

"Let us assume you did in fact oppose it, Messer, but what did it avail?" Shylock halted him.

The priest unfolded a scroll, and continued: "To me, and to no other, the Cardinal Pighinos sent a copy of a letter he received from Andrea Masio, who is known to you all for his love of your writings."

"What has this to do with the matter before us? One loves our writings, one loves our daughters and one loves our money — and it is all given the name of love — I have a full understanding of Christian love!" Shylock boiled up.

The cleric paid no heed to his words and, holding up the scroll in the dim light, read an impromptu translation from the Latin into Italian as he went along from Masio's screed:

"I have long ago expressed to you my sorrow at the terrible decree passed against the Jewish Talmud, and whenever I think on it I am seized with excessive rage. Upon the complaint of two Venetian booksellers who were jealous of each other and sought monetary gain, and the opinion of two circumcised Christians hired by these same booksellers, you came to a dreadful conclusion, to the everlasting shame of the Apostolic Throne and the detriment of the Christian cause —"
Pasquino glanced at Shylock and saw he was deeply interested in the contents of the letter, and continued:

". . . In this matter you are positively blind, since no one of you has ever read a word in those books. I find it my duty to warn you and the College of Cardinals not to place trust in converted Jews in matters which affect their whilom brethren since there is no greater fanatic or wicked person than —"

"Stop it!" Shylock grated his teeth and thrust his fingers into his ears. He saw before him Jessica his seed. Blood of his blood — these words of contempt by the great humanitarian over the Alps were directed at her. "What sense is there in reading these lines to a Jew?" Shylock fumed. "Two Christians competed with each other. Did one lose or the other? The Talmud lost, the book *The Strong Hand* lost — that is your Christian justice!"

The priest feared that Shylock had recalled the fact, which was widely known, that Masio was in contact with Eustachio the proselyte, just as he had relations with many other copyists (from Portia it was known to Pasquino that Jessica had visited Eustachio at the Vatican), and that it was the cause of Shylock's anger. He found it best no longer to mention the name of Masio. He rapidly rolled up the scroll in his hand and said quietly, "I wished it to be clear to you that before you is a priest who has no hatred of the Jews."

"Even Julius III loved the Jews —"

"True, may his memory be blessed!" the priest interjected. After a pause he added devoutly, "And no more modest man has come to earth! Once the Portuguese Ambassador told him he shared his grief at having to carry the burden of authority for the whole world, and Julius answered, 'You would be surprised and dumbfounded to know how little intellect is needed to rule the world.'"

"Perhaps it is for that reason that the confusion over the books emerged from him," Shylock said ironically.

"I dwell in the Patriarch's household and I know all the particulars of the affair," the priest rejoined. "Believe me, Julius III had no wish of it but the Editor of the Index compelled him. It was Paul III, may he repose in peace, who was then a Cardinal."

"He got his deserts," Shylock mumbled into his beard. The priest bridled with rage at the Jew profaning the memory of a Pope who had died only a few days earlier but controlled himself to avoid frustrating his purpose. Shylock realized he had said something improper, first against Julius and then Paul, and added, "Every Pope has his qualities and faults — but what importance has it here? Listen, Messer, do not think that a Jew is wicked. Signor Antonio brought disgrace upon my head, and much blood have I shed these last ten days, yet — even now I am ready to forego my due if he returns my daughter."

The other shrugged his shoulders and replied, "Portia in my presence yesterday pleaded with the Patriarch to annul the baptism but he rejected the request."

All the fury which Shylock had been suppressing burst its bounds. "And I reject your request," he shouted. "You have not yet made it but I understand where your remarks are leading."

"Antonio is an innocent Christian. Whatever he did was out of his innocence."

"His innocence!" grated Shylock. "The Crusaders whom you revere so much slaughtered whole communities, men, women and babes in arms — in their innocence! Your fellow-clergy in Spain and Portugal and even here at Ancona, sent men and women to the *auto-da-fé* — in their innocence! Under the guise of the sacrament, with the New Testament in their hands, they have shed and are shedding our blood!"

"Let us speak tranquilly, Shylock."

"You may speak tranquilly, you are not slaughtered or persecuted —"

"Savonarola —" the priest's voice trembled and he crossed himself.

"One in an age!" Shylock said mockingly. "It happened in my youth and still today I hear of his burning. But at all events it was not we who burned him, nor we who trample upon you — the wolf can speak tranquilly to the lamb, but not the lamb to the wolf!"

"An innocent lamb," the priest thought to himself as he measured Shylock with his glance. He tried not to smile so as to avoid infuriating further the other who held the life or death of a Christian in his hand. After a brief pause he continued: "During a debate some generations ago between King Alfonso of Spain and the scholar Tomas, the latter told the king: The Jews have righteous laws and ordinances and important customs, like benevolence and justice and mercy —"

"That is hypocrisy!" Shylock interrupted him. "I have no need of Tomas reminding me of these qualities — I know it without your prompting!"

To influence the Jew by using the holy tongue, the priest began in Hebrew, "Thou shalt love thy friend as thyself—"

"Thy friend, not thy enemy!" ejaculated Shylock, pounding his fist upon the wall. "He has done wrong to me, and I shall do wrong to him. He has caused bitterness to me, and I shall cause bitterness to him!"

The priest, after some thought tried again: "Compassion is an attribute of Israel, and if you have no pity, you are no Jew."

"Let it be so! I am no Jew, I am not human at all!" snarled Shylock, pacing back and forth and, in doing so, throwing his hat upon the ground. His glance fell on the crucifix in the monk's girdle and he hurriedly re-donned the hat, continuing with venom, "You have turned me into a beast, a demon, and I shall act as a beast and a demon!"

"But—"

"There is no but!" he shouted, and repeated the words.

The priest persisted but Shylock remained adamant, answering furiously. Losing all restraint he reviled the Christians, more especially the clergy.

"Have pity on him and his young wife!"

"I shall have pity on him—I shall have pity on him—as he pitied me and my young daughter! The Doge offered him his life and he chose death—let him have his death!"

"Shylock," the priest entreated softly, "I heard much good about you yesterday."

"That was once!" the old banker rejoined. 'Now I am no longer the same Shylock, I have nothing left in life except to take what is due to me from the sinful body of Antonio!"

A constable entered and said, "We are ready. We have stripped him."

"Only his mantle and shirt—I am not bound to see his nakedness, only the evil part that is in his chest! Let him don his hose."

With the constable's departure the brother pleaded, "By the Holy Virgin, how can you shed the blood of man? I heard you punished your daughter in her childhood when she pulled the wings from flies in her play—"

"Flies are not Christians!" Shylock almost shrieked. "They bite Christians as well as Jews, humans as well as animals."

"And I was told you never have eaten a fish's head in the past ten years because you once went into the kitchen and saw a fish cut into portions and its mouth still quivering."

Where had the priest heard this detail? Probably she or the servants had been to him! He reflected a moment and his wrath mounted.

"Nor are the fish Christians!" he cried jeeringly. "They have never burned Jews at the stake, they did not steal my daughter."

The constable returned and, approaching Shylock, said, "All is ready in the cell — the cleaver too."

Shylock came to a halt. "Let him confess," he muttered. "Let him confess before I enter."

"He has already confessed," the constable rejoined. "His wife sent him a confessor and he too is in the cell."

Shylock seemed not to have heard. He walked back and forth with clenched fists and encouraged himself, "Do not tremble, Shylock! Have your revenge of him for robbing you of your offspring, and depriving you of descendants evermore!"

"In the name of the Holy Mother! In the name of the wounds of God! Mercy!" the priest beseeched.

Shylock paced back and forth and addressed himself, "Have no remorse, Shylock. Be like Torquemada, like the woman Isabella, like the old Paul, like every pious Christian in the kingdoms of Italy!"

A second constable entered and stood opposite him. Shylock remained stock-still.

"All is prepared," said the guard. "It is a sin to torture a condemned man." He put his hand between Shylock's shoulders and pushed him to the door of the cell at the left where Antonio was.

"Go inside, your reverence," said the constable to the old monk.

"No, no," he replied. "There is a confessor inside — mercy, Shylock, mercy!" He put his face to the wall and closed his ears.

Shylock, with palsied knees, preceded the Moors and spoke to himself in a voice that faltered more and more. "Think of Jessica your daughter and your hand will not tremble —"

On reaching the door of the cell he again paused irresolutely. "Don Samuel, where are you?" he quavered. "Strengthen my heart, hold my failing knees."

Beads of perspiration stood out on his forehead and when he wiped them his glance fell on the wall. The gigantic shadow of his hand, the shadow of his protruding beard, the outlines of his Jewish face terrified him. "You are a Jew! I am a Jew!" his blood cried out from his veins in a thousand voices. And that from which there was no escape crushed him; and his knees trembled.

Then, of a sudden, he grasped both jambs of the door with his shaking hands, bracing himself upright to keep from falling, and groaned between chattering teeth, "Let my soul be damned! I cannot — I cannot do it!"